FULL CIRCLE

Ann Port

ANN PORT

Also by Ann Port
It's All in the Title
The Bernini Quest
A Fair Exchange
The Iznik Enigma

ISBN: 1502960524
ISBN 13: 9781502960528
Library of Congress Control Number: 2014919406
CreateSpace Independent Publishing Platform
North Charleston, South Carolina

ACKNOWLEDGEMENTS

I would like to thank five special women— first readers, editors, and dear friends—who have provided unwavering support. You kept me on my toes and on target. I confess, there were times I wasn't pleased with your suggestions, but in the long run, your superb insight and implacable wisdom transform my sometimes-rough manuscript into the novel it is.

First and foremost to my "editor-in-chief," Jane Williams. How I leaned on you, and what "majestic" finds you made. How I laughed when you said you were keeping a timeline to "keep the dates straight." How glad I am that you did. You kept me accurate and on my toes, and slowed me down when I was moving too fast. You taught me patience—at least in the short term. From you I learned that tearing something down can often make it better.

And thank you Alex Anderson. It's great to have a psychology major on board, both for me when I'm stressed, and especially for the characters in the novel. Your suggestions added depth—making them more complex and believable as they faced challenging and trying times.

To Joan Ellen Lindner, Louise Turner, and Phyllis Bezanson. Thank you for the time and energy you put into the editing process. The "little things" you caught made the book better and more accurate. You pointed out mistakes I had overlooked on the fourth, fifth, and sixth readings of the manuscript.

And finally to my team at Createspace. While working with you on FULL CIRCLE and my previously-published novels, you have been helpful, encouraging, and patient. I cannot thank you enough. You have made the publishing process both easy and enjoyable.

*You know, if you hang around this earth long enough
you really see how things come full circle.*

Patti Davis

*It's amazing how everything comes full circle back to
the way it was always meant to be.*

Author unknown

CHAPTER 1

Doctor Richmond stood at the bedside of the tiny woman resplendent in a pink silk bed jacket with a lace collar and matching lace cuffs. Though ill and frail, sitting upright in her massive hand-carved Louis XIV bed, Veronique Boulet Ellison radiated power and grace. "If you hope to be with us this time next year, Veronique, you're going to have to make some lifestyle changes," Richmond warned.

Veronique fingered her pearl necklace, the last gift from her husband before he died of a sudden heart attack in that very bed ten years before. She removed a lace handkerchief from her sleeve, covered her mouth, coughed, and smiling faintly said, "At my age, Doctor, I'm grateful to wake up every morning. Lately, the idea of joining my dear Robert isn't such an unpleasant notion."

"I'm sure Madeline and Anne have other ideas," Richmond gently argued. "And speaking of your daughter and granddaughter, Veronique. Did you let them know you're ill?"

"Renee left a message for Madeline, but she reached Anne, who's coming by on her way to a meeting at the Met. Did I tell you my granddaughter's a member of the committee charged with selecting the paintings for an Impressionist exhibition opening at the museum in December?"

"You may have mentioned it once, or was it twice?" Richmond said, his eyes twinkling. "You're planning to attend the opening gala?"

"Of course," Veronique answered huffily.

"Then you'll follow my instructions. Let me summarize one more time. You may have *one* glass of wine with dinner. Not every day—once or twice a week. You *must* drink decaffeinated tea and give up imported French butter—"

"That's all?"

"For now. If you watch your diet, and faithfully take your pills, you'll make it to the gala and then some."

The old woman lay back against the down pillows propped up against the walnut backboard. Clearly annoyed, she mustered her strength and said, "If I must, I'll take the pills, but *every* night at dinner with my wine. Sick or not, Doctor, do you *really* think I'm going to give up all life's little pleasures? Last summer Anne and I went for a walk in Central Park. We were resting on a bench before starting back when I saw a burly man wearing a raggedy sleeveless T-shirt. The message on the front expressed what I'm feeling right this moment. In bold, black, one-inch letters it proclaimed, 'Exercise regularly. Eat right. Die anyway.'"

Richmond laughed. "True," he said. "But in your case, Veronique, we're trying to delay the inevitable a while longer. To do that, something has to change."

"What has to change?" Anne Elisabeth de Vries French breezed into the room, walked to the bed, leaned down, and kissed her grandmother on the cheek. "Good morning, Oma," she said cheerfully. "How are you feeling?"

"Better now that you're here, darling. Let me look at you."

As she always did when her grandmother made that request, Anne stepped back and, with arms extended, spun around. Veronique smiled proudly at her stunningly beautiful granddaughter, who wore a designer navy-blue silk pants suit that accentuated her long legs and a light blue silk blouse that showed off her father's blue eyes and her mother's porcelain skin. Her ash-blond hair framed her face, highlighting her high cheek bones and full lips.

Veronique patted the bed. "Come sit beside me, Anne. I need an ally. Doctor Doom and Gloom here says I have to make outlandish changes in my life. Would you believe he expects me to stop enjoying wine with my meals?"

Anne sat down, looked up at the doctor who had cared for her grandmother for almost thirty years and with a hint of bogus sarcasm said, "Certainly you wouldn't make Oma do something that drastic, would you, Doctor Richmond? You must know asking a Frenchwoman to give up her wine is like ordering an American man to forego his hotdog and beer at a baseball game."

"Your grandmother's exaggerating, Anne—no doubt to elicit your sympathy. I told her to *cut back* on the wine. Several glasses a week is okay—"

"But not one with lunch and another with dinner."

"See why I need your help, Anne?" Richmond said.

"Surely you're kidding!" Anne declared. "You don't *really* believe Veronique Ellison will listen to me."

"She will if she plans to be around for your exhibition in December."

"She has to be. She's sitting at my table for the opening gala."

"Really?" Veronique's eyes brightened.

"That's the plan. So will you *please* do as Doctor Richmond says? Will you cut back on the wine?"

"It's not just the wine, Anne. This evil, heartless man expects me to forgo *everything* I enjoy. I can't put butter on my croissant—"

"You mean on your wheat toast!" Richmond interjected.

"See what I mean, Anne? I can't drink my usual afternoon tea because it contains caffeine, and though the doctor here has yet to mention coffee, I'm sure I'll soon have to stop drinking café au lait with my breakfast."

"You will unless the coffee's decaf. So are you going to follow my instructions, or do I have to put you in the hospital to see that—"

"You wouldn't!"

"I would!"

"She'll follow orders," Anne promised. "I have a meeting at the Met, but when we're finished, I'll come back and help Renee purge the house of everything that's unhealthy."

"You mean you and my dearest friend will conspire to make my life miserable."

"If that's what it takes to keep you around, yes. Does Mother know you're not feeling well?"

"I assume so. Renee called the house immediately after she phoned Doctor Richmond. As usual, no one answered, so she left a message. When my shortness of breath eased, I tried again. Preston, her new *butler*, picked up. He said, and I quote, 'Madame is at Yoga and cannot be disturbed. After class she will be attending a charity luncheon and fashion show.'"

"Did you tell Preston to have her call between activities? Better yet, did you try her cell?"

"Why bother? When your mother's otherwise engaged, she turns off the sound."

"I'm sure she'll call as soon as she gets the message," Anne said, pondering the strained and sometimes contentious relationship between her mother and grandmother. "You can tell me about your conversation when I see you later."

"You're coming back?"

"Absolutely, but I'm not staying. You need to rest. My meeting should be over around four. Isn't that your teatime?"

"You mean my *decaffeinated* teatime."

"I actually prefer decaf."

"You're just saying that to make me feel better."

"Why would I lie? Before I leave the museum, I'll stop by the coffee shop and pick up sugar free cookies or scones to go with our tea."

"You can't give a Frenchwoman sugar free pastry," Veronique grumbled. "One bite and I'll think I've already died—and I won't be in heaven. If I had known I'd eventually have to live like this, I would have taken my chances in Paris—"

"Then I wouldn't be here." Anne gently squeezed her grandmother's hand. "I'm sure if you had to choose again, you'd make the same decision. What do you think, Doctor?"

"I think your grandmother needs to start taking her medication as soon as possible." He tore three prescriptions from a pad, walked to the bed, and handed them to Anne.

"Thanks," Anne said. "I'll drop these at the pharmacy on the way to the Met and pick up the pills on the way back to Oma's."

"Good. Before I leave, I'll give Renee a list of foods Veronique needs to avoid, as well as possible side effects to watch for over the next several days. If she has even the mildest reaction to the medication, or if she's not feeling better by tomorrow, call me immediately."

"We will. And don't worry, Doctor, my grandmother will toe the line. Renee, Henri, and Paul will do their part to see that she does, and I'll recruit Laura to search for contraband when she cleans Oma's room."

"You're a cruel woman, Anne," Veronique said crossly. "And you, Doctor, are you happy? You've brainwashed my granddaughter, and now you're pitting my two dearest friends as well as my chef and my maid against me." Sighing in resignation, she muttered, "I don't have the strength to fight, so I *suppose* I'll follow orders."

"I knew Anne would make you behave," Richmond said. "I'll be back tomorrow afternoon. If you need me before then, I'm only a phone call away."

"With all these pills I have to take, I'm sure I'll be fine." Softening, Veronique added, "And thank you, Doctor."

"You're welcome, Veronique. You take care."

Anne stood. "I'll walk you to the door, Doctor Richmond."

"Anne," Veronique said. "If there's time before your meeting, I would like to speak with you."

"For you, Oma, I have all the time in the world. I'll be right back."

⌒○

"That didn't take long," Veronique murmured sleepily as Anne approached the bed. "Did Doctor Death say anything I should know?"

"Only that you need to follow orders, but you said you would, so that's a moot point."

"I guess, but so you know, I uttered the words in a moment of weakness."

Before Anne could respond, Veronique pointed across the room. "Please get my desk chair," she said. "I want you close while we talk."

Anne retrieved the chair and placed it by the bed. She sat down, reached out, and took her grandmother's hand. "Now," she said. "What's on your mind?"

"A great deal," Veronique said pensively. "Perhaps too much. I'm about to begin the most significant conversation I've had in seventy years—perhaps in my entire lifetime. I'm tired, so I may not be able to finish today—"

"In that case, why start? Rest. I doubt one more day will matter."

Veronique shook her head. "No, Anne," she said. "I've procrastinated for decades. I'll start now, and, if you're available, we'll talk again tomorrow over lunch. Will you come back?"

"Of course. But why the sudden urgency? Why didn't we begin this conversation a year ago—or last month?"

"It was never the right time—at least that was my excuse."

"And now it is."

"It has to be. Doctor Richmond's diagnosis is more than a revelation of my physical ailments. It's a long-overdue wakeup call. For the first time since the summer of 1942, I'm facing my mortality. I want and *need* to close the door on a painful period of my life. Until now, I've stubbornly and, I admit, unreasonably refused to discuss what happened to Mother and me during the two years we lived in Nazi-occupied Paris. My perpetual silence had a profound effect on those I love. Unfortunately, I can't go back and make it up to my darling Robert, or to Madeline, or even to Renee and Henri, who for seventy-plus years have put up with me and my moods. But I *can* move on with my life for whatever time I have left. My primary purpose is to tell you about your great-grandmother, Elisabeth Boulet, and what she endured during those last horrible years before she died. Though as you'll soon learn, I *do* have an ulterior motive."

"Of course you do." Despite her increasing apprehension, Anne managed a smile. "So tell me your story."

"Very well." Veronique began tentatively. "Your great-grandmother was a wealthy widow. She inherited her fortune from her parents, who were killed in a train derailment in the French Alps when she was fifteen, and later from her husband's parents, who perished several months after I was born. Before she was thirty, Mother owned two seventeenth century mansions on Île St-Louis, one on Quai de Bourbon where I was raised, and her childhood home on Quai de Bethune. But before I continue, I must digress for just a moment. When you returned to New York after spending a semester studying art history in Paris, you told me you saw Île St-Louis from one of those open-air excursion boats that ferries tourists up and down the Seine."

"A Bateau Mouche. True, though I saw some of the Île, albeit very little, on foot. One Sunday afternoon I took a study break to visit the Deportation Memorial on Île de la Cite—"

"Oh my!" Veronique's jaw tightened as Anne spoke.

"What's the matter, Oma?" Anne asked uneasily. "Should I call Doctor Richmond? He can't be far—"

"No need darling." Veronique sighed deeply. "My reaction had nothing to do with my heart—at least not in a way to cause concern."

"Then what's wrong? Are you disappointed because I didn't spend more time on the Île? I knew you grew up there, but we rarely speak about your childhood. I had no idea—"

"No, Anne. It isn't as though I *asked* you to visit the Île."

"Then what did I say to cause such an intense reaction?"

"Your words triggered painful memories. You'll soon understand why. But first, finish telling me about your experience."

"I was going to say, the day I visited was unusually hot for early May. Truthfully, the heat was what prompted me to cross Pont Saint-Louis in the first place. I wanted ice cream from a shop all my friends were raving about."

"Berthillon?"

"That's it."

"Berthillon was the one place your grandfather went each time he returned to Paris after the Liberation. He always ordered the same thing, an *abricot* and *pistache* ice cream double cornet. I used to tease him because he steadfastly refused to try a different flavor."

"I never asked, but I often wondered why you never went back with him."

"Each time he left, he urged me to go along, but I always said 'ask me next year.' Next year came, and then the next, and then the next. I never went. As time passed, I convinced myself that marrying your grandfather and becoming an American citizen meant I could leave Paris and all it represented behind forever. Down deep, I knew if I returned I would have to face the horrors of the last years I spent in the city I loved and then eventually grew to hate. That I couldn't do."

"And now you can?"

"Rather I must. As I said at the onset of our conversation, I want you to know about Mother and the years—both good and bad—we spent together on Île St-Louis."

"I'll always remember the look on your face when I first asked about Great-Grand'Mere Elisabeth. I must have been ten. I only wanted to know if I was named Anne *Elisabeth* for her. You said yes, and dropped the subject."

"And you never mentioned her again."

"Probably because you looked so miserable when I asked the question. Why didn't you want to talk about your mother, Oma?"

Veronique hesitated. Moments later, her lips pursed and her hands clasped tightly, she murmured, "Because, though decades have passed, the anguish and guilt I felt the night of July 17, 1942, and in the weeks and months to follow still remains acute. I was only eighteen when Mother died at Auschwitz—"

"Auschwitz," Anne blurted out. "I'm sorry! I don't understand! Neither you nor anyone else ever said—"

"Your grandfather, Renee, and Henri were the only ones who knew, and I forbade them from speaking about what happened."

"Does Mother know what you're sharing with me?" Anne asked, perplexed and trying to make sense of what she was hearing for the first time.

"If she does, she never asked me to explain—perhaps because she knew better."

"I still don't understand, Oma. Auschwitz was a Nazi concentration camp in Poland. Poland is a long way from Île St-Louis."

"Geographically, yes, Anne, but not in my mind. My life changed forever in forty-eight unbearable hours."

"How? What happened?"

Anne sat quietly, waiting for her grandmother to continue. A minute passed in silence—then another. Finally, Veronique began again. "You know Renee and I have been best friends since we first met in 1939."

"I do," Anne said, feeling increasingly puzzled. "But what could your friendship with Renee have to do with the worst day of your life?"

"It turns out—everything. On that seemingly normal July afternoon, if you could call life in Nazi-controlled Paris 'normal, Mother told, or rather *ordered*, me to pay a call on Renee at her home in Saint-Germain-des-Prés. At first I thought I was to visit for the rest of the day, probably because Mother was entertaining friends and wanted me out of the way. But she quickly made it clear—I was to stay the night at the Paquet's. I was so excited—"

"I'm sure you were, but clearly your visit wasn't what you'd anticipated—"

"Or ever imagined. Now, whenever I think back to that dreadful day, I feel more than a little foolish. No one came to visit anymore, not even Henri and Renee. So why would Mother be entertaining? As I struggled to come to terms with what happened that evening, I remembered she'd been acting strangely for weeks."

"What do you mean?"

"For one thing, she wouldn't let me leave the Île. She seemed to want, or perhaps *need*, to keep me close."

"Then one afternoon she suddenly let you go."

"In more ways than one," Veronique said pensively.

"Oma—"

"I'm sorry, darling. Yes, she *wanted* me to go. When I asked why, she told me Renee was having second thoughts about her wedding dress and wanted my opinion. Henri and Renee were to be married in Église de Saint-Germain-des-Prés in eight days, so it was a little late for her to be making a wardrobe change. Besides that, I knew she loved her dress—"

"So you suspected your mother had an ulterior motive for sending you off the Île. Did you confront her with your suspicions?"

"Of course not! She was my mother! Asking her to tell me *why* I should follow her instructions would have been both disrespectful and unacceptable."

"Is that the reason you didn't ask?"

"Not really," Veronique whispered introspectively. "Honestly, I didn't care why I was being allowed to leave. I'd been cooped up for weeks. It was a beautiful day, and I was eager to get out and enjoy the warm sunshine. I quickly changed clothes—probably because I was afraid Mother would have second thoughts and keep me home—kissed her goodbye, and rode my bicycle to the continent."

"The continent?"

"That's what residents of Île St-Louis call the city of Paris."

"Did Great-Grand'Mere Elisabeth. . .?"

"Is something wrong?" Veronique asked. "You stopped talking in mid-sentence."

"Because I don't like to change the subject at a crucial point in your story. However, to make our discussion simpler, may I refer to your mother by her first name? Great-Grand'Mere Elisabeth is a mouthful. I mean no disrespect—"

"Of course you don't, darling. It's not like my dear mother can hear what you're saying. And if she could, she'd be so pleased to be having this conversation, I doubt your manner of address would matter."

"Good. So back to what you were saying. Elisabeth had been keeping you at home. Then, out of the blue, she ordered you to go—and even better—to stay overnight with Renee. Were you surprised, or perhaps I should say concerned, by her sudden change of heart?"

"Not at first. With Nazis lurking around every corner, it would have been dangerous for me to return to the Île after dark. It wasn't until I was pedaling across Pont de la Tournelle that I suddenly remembered our phone hadn't worked for months."

"So Renee couldn't have called."

"Right. I *momentarily* thought about turning back, and I mean *momentarily*. But for once I wasn't heeding the little voice that usually pointed me in the right direction—"

"Aka, your conscience."

"Yes, and it wasn't long before I realized that *not* returning home was, and still remains, the worst decision I've made in my long life. However, as Henri and Renee insisted when I told them I was finally ready for this discussion, I was young, excited to get away, and not analyzing the *whys* of my good fortune. I never imagined I was leaving my home for the last time."

"I don't understand. Failing to go back that afternoon was the worst decision you've *ever* made? That's a profound statement."

"Profound and true. This is the first time I've actually said the words, but since July 17. 1942, not a day has passed when I haven't questioned the choice I made. You may not understand the impact of my decision today, but when I finish explaining, you will. By then, I hope you'll have read, or at least skimmed, the information I put in this folder." She held up a file for Anne to see and then placed it back on the bed. "When you've heard everything, if you agree to do what I'm asking, I'll give you something else, something I have never shared with anyone—not even your grandfather."

Veronique reached over to her nightstand, opened the drawer, and pulled out an obviously-old, worn, leather book. "This is the journal I kept during the Occupation." She gently caressed the leather cover. "I haven't opened it since the day I left Paris."

"And now you want to share your most intimate thoughts and feelings with me?"

"I do." She put the book aside. "But first I will put my story in context. Both my mother's and father's parents were wealthy Jews—"

Anne gasped. With that one sentence, everything became clear. She suddenly understood why her grandmother had refused to discuss her past. *I knew Elisabeth was Jewish*, she mulled. *How could I have been so stupid? Why didn't I make the connection, if not in the past, then now when Oma mentioned Auschwitz?* She answered her own question. *Because all my life Oma's been Catholic. I never thought what life was like for her and Elisabeth—Jews in a city occupied by the Jew-hating Nazis.*

Though she wanted to interrupt with a myriad of questions and a profound apology for her lack of compassion, Anne remained silent as Veronique continued. "I told you Mother's parents were killed when she was fifteen. With no relatives to take her in, she remained in her home with the family servants until six years later when she married my father and moved to his mansion on Quai de Bourbon. . ." Veronique's voice dropped.

"What is it, Oma?" Anne asked, alarmed by Veronique's sudden pause. "Do you need a break?"

"I'm fine, darling. Or as fine as I can be under the circumstances. However, since you're unfamiliar with Île St-Louis, I'll interrupt my story yet again, this time to provide a brief but necessary geography lesson. Over the next few days, I'll be referencing various locations on the Île. When I do, I want you to be able to close your eyes and picture the scenes I'm describing. You're always telling me your French is rusty, but I'm sure you know a quai is a wharf used for loading and unloading goods and/or passengers. Île St-Louis is surrounded by four quais. Imagine you just crossed Pont Saint-Louis from the Île de la Cite—"

"Like I did when I craved ice cream from Berthillon."

"That's right. You are now on the far western tip of the Island. Quai d'Orleans is to your right and Quai de Bourbon to your left. Take a few steps forward, and you'll be on rue St-Louis-en lÎle, the main street that runs east/west through the entire Île. Keep walking straight. In half a kilometer you'll come to rue des Deux-Ponts, Two-Bridges Street, that bisects the island in a north/south direction and connects two of the main bridges to the city, Pont Marie to the Right Bank and Pont de la Tournelle to the Left."

"I get the picture."

"Good." Veronique smiled at her granddaughter's intended humor. "If you proceed straight ahead instead of turning onto rue des Deux-Ponts, Quai de Bethune will be on your right and Quai d' Anjou on your left. For our purposes, Quai de Bethune, where Mother lived as a child, and Quai de Bourbon, where I grew up, will be important. Because the Île is small, only one kilometer long and three hundred meters wide, in my day, and perhaps even now, everyone knew everyone else, and neighbors cared about their neighbors. That's something I want you to keep in mind. I often heard Mother say the Île was her 'peaceful oasis of calm in a sea of chaos.' At first I didn't know what she meant, but as I got older, I began to understand. Paris changed over the years, but Île St-Louis seemed frozen in time. Mother spent her whole life in that idyllic world, and though this is mere speculation on my part, I believe—from early childhood—she was intended to marry Samuel, your great-grandfather."

"An arranged marriage? That's rather medieval."

"I agree, but in the early 1900s it wasn't uncommon for wealthy families to orchestrate unions to benefit all parties. When Samuel graduated from the university, he and Mother announced their engagement."

"Do you think Elisabeth loved Samuel, or did their marriage remain one of convenience?"

"I don't really know. Papa died before I was born, so I never saw the two of them interact."

"But she must have told you about him."

"Except in passing, she rarely mentioned him. The only meaningful conversation I recall occurred when I was around eleven. I was looking over her shoulder while she went through a stack of old photographs. She came to a picture of her and Papa the day they were married and held it out for me to take a look. When she started to put it back in the pile, I asked if I could keep it with my things."

"Did she give it to you?"

"She did. That was when I asked her to tell me about Papa."

"And?"

"She said their families had been friends for years. She and Samuel attended the same primary school and went to the same synagogue, though, being a girl, she sat with the women while Samuel sat with the men. I recall her smile when she told me that, early-on, she hated him. Apparently he liked to pull her pigtails and he teased her unmercifully because she was tall and skinny."

"Typical little boy and girl behavior. I assume her feelings changed."

"I guess they did. In great detail, she described their engagement party at the Boulet Mansion and their wedding at the Synagogue rue des Tournelles near Place des Vosges. Finally, she spoke about how emotional it was for her to move from Quai de Bethune to the Boulet mansion on Quai de Bourbon."

"She was describing important *events* in her life. Did she say how she *felt* about Samuel? Did she mention love?"

"Not that I recall. When she spoke about Papa, she seemed sad, which is understandable. He died so young. But there was something else."

"What do you mean?"

"Immediately after she described the wedding, her eyes flashed—she looked angry."

"About the arranged marriage?"

"I don't think so. She was referring to what occurred a month later when, despite her pleas and against the wishes of the family, Papa enlisted in the army. Six weeks before France and Germany signed the armistice ending the war, he returned home, partially blind, and suffering from skin lesions and a debilitating leg injury that never truly healed. Worse, he had a lung disease brought on by a chlorine gas attack launched by German troops trying to overrun the trenches. He was in and out of hospitals for the rest of his life as he dealt with fluid in his lungs, a chronic cough, and recurring bronchitis."

"How long did he live?"

"Almost eight years. He died after a particularly bad bout of pneumonia two weeks before I was born."

"If I were Elisabeth, I'd be angry too. For all but a month of her married life, she was your father's nurse, not his wife. She must have felt cheated."

"Cheated?"

"Yes. Think about it. She was a young woman who, like most brides, dreamed about living the fairy tale. She married the man of her dreams—or not—but she got married and expected to live happily ever after. Suddenly, reality trumped the fantasy. In the prime of her life, she was caring for an ailing husband, and, at age thirty or thereabouts, she was alone—a widow and single mother caring for an infant. She must have been so lonely."

"And perhaps frightened. I was six months old when Papa's parents were killed. They were driving to visit friends in Moustiers-Sainte-Marie when their car plunged off a cliff and tumbled into the gorge below. Because Papa was an only child, Mother inherited the entire estate. She had the option of returning to the house on Quai de Bethune but following her marriage, her servants had found new positions, so she elected to raise me in the Boulet mansion."

"Did she sell the house on Quai de Bethune?"

"I really don't know. I never asked. I wasn't interested, probably because I never lived there. And being a teenager, my mind was on other things."

"Like boys and friends?"

"Never boys." Veronique's eyes again brightened. "Your grandfather was my one and only love. But friends, yes. If Mother was lonely or unhappy, I didn't know. I never stopped to think she wasn't content with her life, probably because I was too caught up in my own. Until early 1938, except for typical childhood crises, I was truly carefree. I wanted for nothing, at least materially. Mother's enormous wealth gave her the freedom to do whatever she liked. She could have traveled the world, but she always seemed content to stay home with me."

"Maybe she wanted to be sure *you* weren't lonely."

"Possibly. Some evenings she'd go out with friends, but never until she tucked me in, and she was always waiting at the table when I came downstairs for breakfast the next morning."

"Did she date?"

"I'm sorry."

"I don't mean did she have a host of boyfriends. I'm asking if there was a man in her life after your father died."

"Absolutely not. Every once in a while she visited Uncle George in Brittany, but—"

"Uncle George? Your mother was an only child. So was Samuel."

"George wasn't really my uncle, though that's what I called him. He and Papa were best friends from primary school through their years at the university. George lived on Quai de Anjou, but he spent his summers with his grandparents on their farm in Brittany. He must have preferred the country life because when his father died in the early 1930s, he sold the house on the Île, moved to Brittany, and became a gentleman-farmer. When I was very young, Mother and I visited several times a year. After I started school, we went less frequently. Eventually we stopped going altogether. When I asked why, she always answered the same way— 'Uncle George will come to town when he can.'"

"Did he?"

"Yes, particularly at the onset of the Occupation when he would bring us food from the farm. Brittany was in the occupied zone, so he was able to travel freely. By that, I mean he didn't have to cross the Line of Demarcation between *zone libre* and *zone occupée*. But as I was saying, Mother was a homebody. That was until late December, 1931. One morning at breakfast she suddenly announced she was taking an extended trip and leaving me home with the servants. Thinking back, her surprising declaration was probably the first time I was ever *truly* upset. Perhaps that's why I remember the conversation so clearly. I pleaded with her to stay home or to take me with her, but my appeals fell on deaf ears. She left on January 4—"

"You recall the specific date?"

"I do because I was afraid she wouldn't make it home for my birthday."

"Was she back by June 4?"

"She returned to Paris in late May."

"Did she talk about where she had been or why she left in the first place?"

"She only said the Great War had kept her from taking a much-anticipated grand tour after she passed the *baccalaureate* exam, and it was 'time to see some of Europe.'"

"But World War I ended in 1918."

"True, but when it came time for her to travel, the countries a young lady of breeding would visit were still recovering and rebuilding. I figure she thought 'better late than never.'" Veronique chuckled. "I guess that phrase would apply to me now. Thinking back, I recall she seemed on edge and irritable for weeks prior to her departure, but when she finally came home, though she was tired, she looked and acted more like herself."

"May I interrupt with a question that's slightly off topic?" Anne asked. "It goes back to something you mentioned earlier."

"Of course you may. This is not a scripted conversation."

"Were you and your mother practicing Jews? I mean did you go to temple and participate in religious observances?"

"We celebrated Hanukkah and Passover, but we certainly weren't orthodox. Perhaps that's why I had no problem converting when I married your grandfather. Mother's closest friends were Jewish, but she also had Catholic friends and acquaintances."

Veronique looked at the clock on her nightstand, and, sighing, said, "I could speak endlessly about Mother and my childhood on Île St-Louis. With any luck, if I take the pills Doctor Richmond prescribed and give up butter, wine, and whatever else is on the list he gave Renee, we'll have years to talk. However, as you predicted earlier, I'm too tired to go on much longer, and I believe you have a meeting to attend. Before I give you the folder and send you on your way, I have a few more things to say."

"Whatever you want," Anne said. "But first, I need to call John—"

"John?"

"The chair of the exhibition committee. If need be, he can start the meeting without me. My cell's on the entry table with my purse. While I'm downstairs, may I make you a cup of tea?"

"You mean a cup of that horrible decaf?"

"No, the *real* thing. Think of it as your last hurrah?"

"In that case, yes, please bring me a cup."

"Your wish is my command."

"Remember that when I ask—"

"Ask me what?"

"Later. Go make your call."

CHAPTER 2

Veronique's eyes were half-closed when Anne returned with the tea. "Are you asleep, Oma," she whispered.

"Not yet, darling," Veronique said woozily. "I was thinking about Mother, though, sadly, the painful memories remain the most vivid."

Anne placed the cup on the nightstand. "Are you sure you want to keep talking?" she asked. "After you've taken the pills, you'll feel better. It might be easier—"

Veronique shook her head. "This conversation will *never* be easy, Anne. But I no longer have the luxury of procrastination. I may not wake up tomorrow morning, and I don't want to die before you've heard everything." She gestured toward the nightstand. "Will you please hand me my tea. The cup looks full, and I don't want to spill."

"If course, but be careful. It's hot."

Veronique took a tiny sip and making a face, mumbled, "I feel like this is my last meal."

"Tea isn't a meal, Oma, and switching to decaf won't kill you. In fact it might help keep you alive. But enough said. What else do you want me to know?"

Still frowning, Veronique took several more sips and put the half-empty cup on the saucer by the bed. "What I'm going to say may seem puzzling at first, but you'll eventually understand. When I began my quest to make sense of what transpired the last few years I lived on Île St-Louis, I learned that, arguably, Adolph Hitler was a frustrated artist."

"Okay," Anne said, startled by the direction the conversation was taking. "What does Hitler's mental state and the fact he was a lousy painter have to do with you?"

"Patience, darling. I'm saying that Hitler's frustration may be one reason he pilfered great works of art from museums and private collectors.

In 1933, when he was named Chancellor of Germany, he began to seize paintings from state-owned collections. His purpose, or so he said, was to create an untainted culture by eliminating what *he* deemed degenerate art and replacing it with pure Germanic works. The definition of the term degenerate was vague, but it eventually came to mean any *objet d'art* *he* felt was unacceptable and indecent. From the beginning, all confiscated works were considered *his* personal property."

Veronique reached for her tea. 'I'm fine," she said when Anne tried to help. "The tea is cooler now." She took a sip and continued. "Beginning in 1934, all confiscated art was stored in massive warehouses both in Germany and in the countries where it was seized. When the purge was over, Hitler declared the museums purified."

"What eventually happened to the stolen art?"

"It was either exchanged for pieces created by German artists, or it was sold. What remained was destroyed in gigantic bonfires. I can only imagine what masterpieces were lost at the hand of that madman and his henchmen, but if I begin this conversation, you'll never get to your meeting, and I won't finish my story. In March 1938, Hitler annexed Austria. He quickly set his sights on art owned by Austrian Jews. That was when mother began to change."

"Change how?"

"She was always easygoing. Then, almost overnight, she became nervous, tense, and, sometimes, fearful. After dinner she'd send me upstairs or outside to play so she and her guests could speak privately."

"That was unusual?"

"Definitely. But despite her efforts to keep me in the dark, I heard that many of Austrian Jews were fleeing the country, and those who stayed behind were being publicly humiliated, physically abused, robbed of their belongings, and, in some cases, murdered."

"If Elisabeth banished you to your room, how could you know what she and her friends discussed?"

"Simple." Veronique smiled sheepishly. "I eavesdropped. I hid around the corner with my ear pressed tightly to the wall and listened."

"Of course you did. I wouldn't expect anything less from my inquisitive grandmother who has to know everything that's going on."

"A grandmother with a granddaughter who's just like her."

"Wow, I left myself open for that one, didn't I? Okay, before your startling confession, you were telling me about the art Hitler stole."

"I was speaking about what occurred in Austria. Tomorrow I'll tell you about the art *Der Führer* plundered from *French* museums, as well as from private collections of prominent *French* Jews. Luckily, though that may be a poor choice of words, some of the Jews who knew they'd soon be targeted, sold or bartered their so-called degenerative art for exit visas or black market goods."

"Did your mother sell art from her collection?"

"She did, though I didn't know until much later when I learned that Renee's father Jules and Henri's father Anton helped her sell two paintings to purchase safe passage out of France for Henri, Renee, and me. Jules and Anton fought for the French Resistance, so they had both the contacts and the resources necessary to arrange our escape. But once again I'm getting ahead of myself on a day when I want to provide a broad overview. Tens of thousands of commandeered French paintings were initially transported to the Galerie Nationale du Jeu de Paume. You studied in Paris, so you're familiar with the museum."

"I am. But what does the Jeu de Paume have to do with your mother's art collection? And for that matter, how did the Nazis justify the theft of personally-owned art?"

"I'll answer your question about the Jeu de Paume in due time. As to how the Nazis could just walk into someone's home and steal his or her art, I asked myself the same question—though, sadly, not until a few years ago when I began to research the topic in earnest. Even though I personally suffered the consequences of their twisted and disgusting beliefs, it was only recently that I truly *understood* the impact of the Party's racial doctrine on Parisian Jews in general and Mother and me in particular. The laws resulting from their sick ideology were what allowed them to justify the confiscation of Jewish art. But in a broader sense, they were an excuse to suppress and intimidate Jews and any other individuals whose views and beliefs conflicted with their own. Though few people knew at the time, including Mother and her friends, the seizing of Jewish property was merely a precursor to the final Nazi goal—the elimination of all Jews from Europe." Veronique breathed in sharply.

"Oma, we should stop—"

"Soon, darling, but before I finish for the day, would you please page Renee and ask her to bring a fresh cup of tea? Be sure to say *no decaf.* I'll live my life on my own terms—at least for a few more hours."

Anne pressed the intercom button on her grandmother's phone. "Renee," she began. "Oma would like a cup of *regular* tea. Would you have Laura—"

"Please bring it yourself," Veronique called out. "Come and sit with us, my friend."

"I'll bring the tea," Renee answered. "But I'm not staying, and neither is Anne. You need to rest."

"I'm leaving soon," Anne said. "When you come up, would you also bring wheat toast for Oma?"

"Make that one of Paul's freshly-baked croissants."

"I heard you, Veronique, but no croissants today or anytime soon. Doctor Richmond gave me a list of forbidden foods—"

"Let me guess. French pastries aren't on the list."

"You're right, so wheat toast it is, and wheat toast it will be from here on out."

"My life is over before I die," Veronique complained as Anne returned to the chair by the bed.

While they waited for Renee to bring the tea, Veronique continued. "So about those horrible laws, and you realize I got my information secondhand—"

"From spying on your mother and her guests."

"Spying is a harsh word, but I suppose that's what I did. One summer evening in 1938, an Austrian friend, a wealthy art dealer from Vienna, came for dinner. When we finished eating, Mother sent me upstairs."

"But you didn't go."

"Of course not. That time I had to strain to hear what they were saying, but at one point during the conversation I heard Mother say she was going to follow his lead. She intended to hide her most valuable paintings and look for buyers for the rest. She was true to her word. During the following months, paintings by well-known artists like Monet, Pissarro, and Corot began to disappear from the walls."

"Elisabeth owned a Monet?"

"Two I believe—perhaps three. There were works by other well-known artists, though, at the moment, I can't recall the painters or the titles of the paintings. When I finally noticed several of her favorites were missing, I asked where they were."

"What did she say?"

"That they were being restored."

"But you didn't believe her."

"Of course not. Remember, I was a super-spy."

Anne was about to comment when Renee Marsolet entered the room and placed a tray on a table between two couches in the sitting area. "You look great," Anne said to the woman who'd been like a second grand-mother. Though not as elegant as Veronique, Renee, too, looked younger than her years. Her silver-gray hair curled attractively around her almost wrinkle-free face, and her blue eyes were bright. Though shorter than Anne, Renee towered over Veronique, who on her tiptoes was only five foot one.

"And you look beautiful, honey," Renee said.

"How's Henri?" Anne asked as Renee handed Veronique her tea.

"He's well. He went to lunch with friends, but he should be home soon."

"If I miss him today, I'll see him tomorrow. Oma asked me to lunch. While we eat, we can devise a plan to make this stubborn woman follow orders."

"You can count on Henri and me."

"I'm doomed," Veronique protested. "Those dearest to me are band-ing together to strip away all of life's little pleasures."

That's right. We're all involved in a vast conspiracy to make you mis-erable. Anne, your grandmother promised to tell you about her mother and what life was like for all of us during the Occupation. I hope she began the conversation."

"She did, though we've just scratched the surface."

"When she finishes her story, if you have questions for Henri or me, please ask." She turned to Veronique. "Enjoy your tea, my friend."

"I'll savor every sip," Veronique grumbled. "No doubt the stuff I'll be drinking tomorrow will invoke ghastly memories of the repulsive ersatz coffee we consumed during the Occupation."

"Nothing could be that bad. So you know, I drink decaf tea and coffee, and I'm none the worse for it." Renee winked at Anne and left the room.

Veronique, took several sips of tea and put the half-empty cup on the nightstand. Suddenly serious, she said, "You studied contemporary European history at Wellesley, Anne, so I'm sure you know Paris fell to the Germans on June 14, 1940. Immediately after the Nazis marched beneath the Arc de Triomphe, my spying days were over. Suddenly, though she never said why, I was again privy to most of Mother's conversations."

"Most?"

"From time to time, she sent me upstairs or told me to go for a walk, though not as often as before. It was then that reality set in. Mother was no longer discussing the state of affairs in Austria and Poland. She was referring to incidents taking place in Paris—in our own backyard. The initial clue that our way of life—and possibly our very lives—could be at risk came in a decree issued in late September 1940. French Jews were ordered to register with the police and carry a card stamped in red with the word JUIF or Juive."

"Did Elisabeth and her friends obey the order?"

"I'm not sure about the others, but Mother and I had no choice—we had to comply."

"I don't understand. Why would you be different from other Parisian Jews?"

"We resided on Île St-Louis, where, as I explained earlier, everyone knew everyone else's business. Our religious persuasion was common knowledge. We couldn't hide."

"Those must have been difficult days for you and Elisabeth."

"They were, but more for Mother than for me. I was still rather carefree, or perhaps a better word would be naïve. Then came the next insult. Mother's Jewish friends who owned their own businesses were forced to display a yellow poster identifying their shops and offices as Jewish-owned. In early October, a new law excluded Jews from government service and from many other professions affecting society in general. It was about then when we first heard the word *Entjudung*, a term the Nazis used to define their ultimate goal, the elimination of Jews and Jewish influence from all areas of public life. Before that, the laws and directives really had more to do with our friends than with us. As I said, I was naïve. I didn't want to see what was evolving, and I didn't think things could get any worse. How wrong I was."

"What happened next?"

"By mid-October, Jews no longer had to worry about hanging yellow signs in their store windows. They were forbidden from owning or operating businesses."

Without warning, Veronique stopped talking and closed her eyes.

"It's time to stop for today," Anne insisted.

"I suppose it is," Veronique said, her voice quivering. "I would prefer to continue, but suddenly I've lost what little energy I was able to muster." She fingered the folder that lay beside her on the bed. "When you come back with my poison, I'll give you this. After you read what's inside, we'll talk about the future and what I'll be asking you to do."

"It's a deal." Anne leaned down and kissed her grandmother on the forehead. "I'll see you later."

At the door, she turned back. Veronique's eyes were shut.

CHAPTER 3

"Damn," Anne said as she neared the Met. *I was in such a hurry to be on time for my meeting that I left Oma's prescriptions on her nightstand.* She looked at her watch. With only ten minutes to spare, there wasn't time to go back, so she removed her cell from her purse, scrolled to Renee's name, and pushed talk. "I can't believe I forgot," she said after quickly explaining her momentary lapse.

"It might be for the best," Renee said. "Henri just came home. Before he changes, he can go to the pharmacy and wait while the prescriptions are filled. The earlier Veronique takes the medication, the sooner she'll feel better."

"After my meeting, I'll stop by the American Wing Café and pick up several different flavors of decaf tea. Oma can try each one and tell us what she likes. It's silly to buy mass quantities of tea she won't drink."

Renee laughed.

"What?"

"Your grandmother has no idea, but she's been drinking decaf coffee and tea for months. She hadn't been sleeping so, unbeknownst to her, I switched."

"This is probably a silly question, but will you fess up now that Doctor Richmond insisted she drink decaf?"

"Are you serious? If Doctor Richmond had spoken to me *before* he broke the news to Veronique, there wouldn't be an issue. Now she'll complain about *any* tea with the word decaf on the label. She may fight, but I believe she'll follow orders. Suddenly she wants to live."

"Does this abrupt turnaround have anything to do with what she plans to tell me tomorrow?"

"It does, and the conversation you're about to have is long overdue. For years, I've been urging her to open up about her past. Until now, she has steadfastly refused."

"I asked her the same question earlier. Why now?"

"Because she's frightened. For the past few months, she hasn't felt well. She was, as she put it, 'a little off,' but I think it's more than that. She's afraid she'll go to bed one night and not wake up the next morning. Until a few weeks ago when she *finally* agreed to share the painful details of her last months in Paris, I worried she was giving up on life and giving in to her illness. Now, though she's still having a hard time, I see newfound resolve in what she says and does. She even had me remove her precious journal from the safe. That book hasn't seen the light of day since we arrived in New York."

"She showed it to me a while ago."

"Did she *give* it to you?"

"Not yet. She plans to read it first."

"I hope she does. Your grandmother's unwillingness to speak about her past has had a profound impact on all aspects of her life and on the lives of those she loved."

"Including you and Henri?"

"To some extent, but more on Robert and Madeline."

"You and Henri lived through the Occupation, and you adjusted. Why couldn't Oma?"

"It was easier for us. We had each other, but, more importantly, we weren't Jews. We didn't have to cope with issues Veronique faced every day. I also think her inability to let go has to do with the fact that she fled Paris the day after her mother's arrest. Suddenly her entire life was turned upside down. Everything she'd ever known was gone, and she had no time to process her grief."

"Oh my God! How could I be so stupid? She said her decision to leave the Île was the worst she's ever made. I acknowledged her confession, but I didn't ask her to elaborate. Now I realize— she was enjoying herself with you in Saint-Germain when the Nazis arrested her mother."

"True, but don't beat yourself up, honey. If your grandmother had been ready to elaborate, she'd have spoken in greater detail. I think she *will* talk, but she'll put off the discussion for as long as possible."

"Thanks for letting me off the hook, but—"

"You didn't do anything wrong, Anne, so please stop feeling guilty. I want you to hear my brilliant psychological analysis as to why your grandmother kept quiet all these years."

"Okay, Doctor R. Analyze away."

"Doctor R. I like that." Renee laughed. "For decades, Veronique has been consumed with guilt. That's why she kept her thoughts, feelings, and memories bottled up inside instead of talking about what happened. The day she left home for the last time, down deep, she knew her mother was in peril, yet she pretended the danger didn't exist and came to see me anyway. She wanted to escape her dark world, if only for a little while."

"She feels guilty because she wasn't there to save her mother?"

"That would have been impossible, and she knows it. No, her guilt is because she lived—"

"And her mother died at Auschwitz."

"Exactly."

"She must realize Elisabeth wanted her to survive. That's why she sent her to see you."

"There's a difference between knowing something cerebrally and knowing emotionally. Am I making sense?"

"You are, Doctor R. You were saying Oma's grief and guilt affected every facet of her life."

"It did, and it still does. Perhaps the most obvious example has been her steadfast refusal to return to Paris following the Liberation. It's as if the city she once loved no longer exists."

"So when she ran away from Paris she wasn't just fleeing the city, she was leaving unbearable pain and sorrow behind."

"Yes and, figuratively, even after she was safely settled in the United States and married to Robert, she kept running."

"By declining to talk about what happened to her and Elisabeth."

"In part, but it goes beyond her inability to communicate her feelings about her mother's death. Until a few weeks ago when she first told Henri and me she planned to share her experiences with you, she wouldn't talk about *anything* that transpired during the Occupation. It's like a two-year gap exists in her life."

"A gap?"

"Between June 22, 1940, when France and Germany signed the armistice through our escape on July 18, 1942. Early-on, Henri and I urged her to confront her fears—to talk about those difficult days. Each time we returned to Paris, we begged her to go with us, but she couldn't bear to be near places that reminded her of Elisabeth, so we finally stopped asking."

"She said Grandfather Robert regularly returned to Paris after the Liberation."

"He went two or three times a year. As a representative of the U.S. government, he was tasked with helping the new French Republic rebuild business and commerce. Every time he planned a trip, he pleaded with Veronique to go along."

"But she never did."

"No. As I said, until recently, any discussion of Paris and the Occupation has been strictly off limits, so can you imagine how astonished I was when *she* broached the subject. At first she wavered about whether to have the conversation she began today or to repress her feelings yet again, but once she made the decision, I glimpsed a side of the woman I met so many years ago. Moments like that have been few and far between, especially since your grandfather died."

"It sounds like she's been depressed. Did you speak with Doctor Richmond? He could have prescribed an anti-depressant."

"A pill to make her feel better? Not on your life. I wanted her to tell you how she was feeling, but every time I suggested you two talk, she begged off, and though I love you, Anne, my loyalty is to Veronique."

"As it should be. But thinking back, I should have seen what was going on without anyone having to tell me. I let my crazy life get in the way of something far more important—Oma."

"You couldn't have known, honey. Your grandmother's a talented actress. When you're around, she's cheery and upbeat, but as soon as you leave, she becomes sad and irritable. It's like she puts on a mask when you come in and takes it off when the door closes behind you."

"When I asked if she'd take a pill for depression, you said 'not on your life.' This morning Doctor Richmond prescribed *three* pills. Will she take them?"

"Yesterday I would have said probably not, but today I believe she will. The wine may be an issue, but I'll figure that one out as we go along."

"I don't envy you."

"Nor should you," Renee chuckled. "Before we hang up, a warning. Don't be surprised if your grandmother suddenly announces she's returning to Île St-Louis. I believe that's her ultimate goal. She won't admit it yet, but over the past weeks she's dropped several hints."

"Maybe she'll say something during lunch tomorrow."

"Possibly, but if she doesn't, don't push. She'll tell you in her own time. Right now she's beginning the fight to get well."

"Thanks, Renee. I'm almost at the museum. I'll be back around four. If Oma's asleep, don't wake her on my account."

"Why don't you call and see if she's up before you come out of your way?"

"Ordinarily I would, but she left something she wants me to read in a folder by the bed. I assume it's more background for whatever it is she wants me to do. And speaking of her upcoming request, can you give me a hint? I gather whatever's on her mind is important."

"I can, and it is, but that's as far as I'll go. This is your grandmother's story to tell and her question to ask. I'm downstairs talking with Paul about the menus for the rest of the week, but as soon as we're finished, I'll put the folder on the entry table. See you soon, honey."

At the entrance to the museum, Anne flashed her pass. "We're about to get started," John said as she entered the Rose Room and, as always, paused to look out over Central Park from the floor-to-ceiling windows that lit the room with a flood of natural light.

"It looks like I'm the last to arrive," she said to the short, slightly-overweight, balding chairman of the committee in charge of selecting the paintings for the December Impressionist exhibition. "I hope I haven't held you up. My grandmother's ill. Before coming here I wanted to speak with her doctor."

John looked up over the reading glasses perched on his nose and pointed to an empty chair at the opposite end of the table. "I hope Madame Ellison feels better soon," he said. "I doubt she'd remember me, though we've met at several charity functions. Please give her my best."

The niceties completed, he looked around at the others gathered at the table and said, "Shall we begin? We have numerous decisions to make before we adjourn for the day."

The sound of rustling papers filled the room as the committee got to work. They quickly agreed to omit Impressionist landscapes from the list—their reasoning, the public's overexposure to works like Monet's *Haystacks* and *The Japanese Bridge at Giverny*. In an equally short amount of time, they decided to include only paintings of well-known Impressionists. At first, all were French, but at Anne's suggestion, they agreed to incorporate paintings by the American Impressionist, Mary Cassatt.

Once they settled on the character and theme of the exhibit, they began the process of selecting the paintings they hoped to borrow from French museums. As the procedure unfolded, Anne's mind often wandered. While she looked at slides of one, then another Impressionist masterpiece, she found herself thinking about her great-grandmother's collection. *Did Elisabeth own a fabulous Degas or a magnificent Renoir? Were there really two or three Monets or perhaps a Pissarro among the paintings in her collection?*

At four, John stacked his papers. "I think we've accomplished a great deal this afternoon," he said. "And far more quickly that I'd anticipated. Next time we meet we'll talk about the paintings we plan to exhibit from the Met collection and those we hope to borrow from the National Gallery, the MFA in Boston, and the Walters in Baltimore. Before we adjourn for the day, let's take a few minutes to look over our preliminary choices and see if anything jumps out that doesn't belong. To put it another way, do all of the paintings we've selected thus far fit into our philosophy for the exhibition?"

While the others did the same, Anne read through her list.

Musée d'Orsay, Paris
    Renoir—*Bal du Joulin de la Galette; Liseuse Vert; Alphonsine Founaise*
    Manet—*Le dejeuner sur l'herbe; Sur la plage*
    Degas—*L'absinthe; Les Repasseuses,*
    Pissarro—*Jeune fille a la baguette*
    Cassatt—*Femme Cousant; Jeune Fille au Jardin*
    Morisot—*Le Berceau; Jeune femme en toilette de bal*

Musée de l'Orangerie, Paris
    Renoir—*Femme nue dans au paysage; Gabrielle et Jean; Jeunes Filles au Piano;Femme a la lettre*

Musée Marmottan Monet, Paris
    Morisot—Julie Manet et son; At the Ball; Reclining Shepherdess.
    Renoir— Portrait de Madame Monet Reading; Portrait de Julie Manet
    Monet—Promenade a Argenteuil; Les Cousines on the Beach at Trouville

With no suggested changes, John adjourned the meeting, scheduling another session for the following Monday at ten.

Feeling slightly apprehensive when she thought about what secrets her grandmother would reveal by then, Anne took the elevator down and walked directly to the exit. *Oh Lord*, she thought just as she reached the door. *Where's my mind these days?* Quickly reversing direction, she went to the American Wing Café and bought several flavors of decaf. *Won't Oma love these*, she mused as she paid the cashier for the tea as well as a package of sugar free cookies.

It was close to five when she rang her grandmother's doorbell. "How's Oma?" she asked as Laura ushered her into the hall.

"I believe she's asleep."

"And Renee?"

"She's waiting in the living room."

Anne walked toward the double French doors leading to the room her grandmother called the 'large parlor.' Renee looked up when she entered the room. "Hi, honey," she said. "How was your meeting?"

"It went well, thanks. But more importantly, how's Oma doing?"

"Better than expected. Shortly after you and I hung up, Henri came home. He immediately went to fill the prescriptions. I don't know what magic you worked, but when I woke your grandmother to administer the first dose, she didn't argue. She took the pills and went back to sleep until two-thirty when she called down to ask for help to the bathroom. I've been back up twice since then, so I assume the diuretic is working. When the other medicines kick in, I'm sure she'll start to feel better."

"I hope so. Tell her I was here and left these scrumptious French cookies from the local patisserie, as well as this delicious tea." She handed the bag to Renee, who looked inside.

"Oh my!"

"What?"

"Teabags."

"Oh Lord," Anne groaned. "I was in a hurry when I bought these, and I didn't stop to think. No doubt Oma will take a sip, make a face, and then imperiously declare as only she can, 'This tea was made with a tea-bag. I can taste the paper.' I'll check in with you later, and unless you call before then, I'll be here at noon tomorrow for part two of Oma's story."

At the living room door, Anne suddenly stopped and looked back. "The folder," she said. "I don't dare leave without it."

"It's on the entry table by the front door."

"Thanks. Next time she wakes up, give Oma a kiss and tell her I love her."

CHAPTER 4

Anne caught a cab to her apartment on Central Park West. She paid the fare, greeted Edward, the doorman, and inserted her key in the elevator slot in the vestibule off the lobby. Glad to be home, she rode up to the apartment where she'd spent three quarters of her life—first as a child growing up, and, after her father died, as an owner when her mother moved permanently to the summer house in the Hamptons.

She unlocked the door, tossed her purse on the entry table, and went to the kitchen to check her emails. One of the messages was from her ex-husband Tom, who wrote, *Hi Annie, Cancelling Monday's lunch— that is unless you'll meet me at the Four Seasons in Old Town Istanbul. Sorry, but business calls. I'll be in touch to reschedule.*

"What's new?" Anne mutterer. *For Tom, life is nothing but work.*

The only other correspondence requiring her immediate attention was from Meg Foster, her closest friend. Anne opened the email and read, *"See you for dinner Monday at seven. No excuses. You hibernate too much. Get out and live a little."*

"Right," Anne whispered. "But I wouldn't trade my quiet life for your crazy schedule any day." She answered Meg, confirming their dinner plans, and then responded to several jokes with smiley-faces before turning off the computer and heading toward her bedroom to change clothes.

On the way, she stopped at her office door and peered in. *Please don't let this be bad news about Oma,* she prayed when she noticed the red light blinking on her answering machine. She held her breath and pushed play. "Thank God," she whispered when she heard her mother's voice.

As she listened to the lengthy message that began with a few questions about Veronique and then became a litany of the goings-on in Madeline's social life, Anne's eyes came to rest on a picture she'd taken of her mother and grandmother standing in front of bed of red tulips and yellow daffodils in the Hamptons the previous March. She picked up the photograph and, continuing to listen, studied her mother's face.

Like Veronique, Madeline Ellison de Vries had aged well. She was in her sixties, but she could easily pass for fifty. She still had her raven-black hair, though now it was thanks to her hairdresser. Her skin was smooth and wrinkle free, but unlike her daughter, who had inherited her father's piercing blue eyes, Madeline's eyes were deep brown. She was thin and fit, spending hours in the gym taking yoga and Pilate's classes, Anne imagined more for the social interaction than for health purposes.

Her musings had kept her from hearing some of what her mother said, so she listened again and then pushed redial. *Oma was right. Mother rarely answers her cell,* she mulled when Madeline's phone went directly to voice mail. She left a short response before going to her bedroom to change.

I really need to do a major shopping run she thought as she took out a leftover chicken breast and a rather limp head of lettuce from the nearly-empty refrigerator. She made a salad, poured a glass of wine, and carried her food and the folder to the living room. More curious than hungry, she put her meal on the table, plopped down on one of the couches, and after several sips of wine, opened the file. As she did, an envelope fell to the floor. Picking it up, she noticed her name written on the front in her grandmother's hand. She opened the sealed flap, removed a single sheet of paper, and read,

My Darling Anne,

When you read this letter, I will have begun to tell my story. I want you to know about the events that shaped my life between June 1940 when the Nazis marched into Paris, and July 1942 when your grandfather, Henri, Renee, and I crossed the Line of Demarcation into Vichy France. As I write, it occurs to me that perhaps a short background lesson is necessary to help you understand. So forgive me while I momentarily digress.

As a result of the armistice signed between France and Germany on June 22, 1940, France was divided into two zones, zone libre, *or Vichy France, that was, for all intents and purposes, a puppet government run by French officials with German oversight, and* zone occupée, *the territory, including Paris, under direct Nazi control. For the most part, Petain, the titular head of* zone libre, *cooperated with the Germans, especially in rounding up Jews and other so-called enemies of the German state. This is important, as these mass round-ups are key to the task I am asking you to undertake.*

Now, back to the matter at hand. The material in this file will provide background information about what I hope you will do for me, and ultimately for you. Some of the articles are outdated, but the information they contain remains relevant. When I began my research, I didn't have access to the internet, so I relied on the library. About two years ago when I finally overcame my computer phobia, I began to investigate in earnest. Just last month I read The Monuments Men. *Those brave soldiers and civilians saved the great masterpieces of Europe from destruction at the hands of the Nazis. I want you to be my Monuments woman. I want you to find and reclaim the art the Nazis took from Mother in one of those mass round-ups.*

"Seriously, Oma?" Anne said, momentarily taken aback. *I thought you wanted to share what you remembered about Elisabeth's art and subsequently learned from your research.* "Who am I kidding?" she whispered. "I knew it was more than that." With increasing trepidation, she read, '*Understand, I am not looking to recover Mother's paintings because they're valuable. They are my heritage—and yours. Read what's in the file, and we'll talk soon.*'

Surprised, yet not surprised, for the next hour, Anne sipped wine and nibbled at her salad while she pored over the articles in the folder, reading some in their entirety and portions of others. About halfway through the stack, she went to her office to scan several articles into the computer, but looking at the numerous pages each contained, she quickly changed her mind. Figuring it would be easier to type a short summary and add notes at the end of each entry, she opened a new Word Document and began to work.

STOLEN ART INITIATIVE: *American museums announced a plan to identify art that might have been stolen by the Nazis during WWII. "Museums will* *be required to disclose the identity and chain of ownership of all works in their collections that changed hands during the Nazi years (1932-1945) and could have been in Europe during that period." Washington Post 01/17/01. Where are the lists? Google Stolen Art Initiative. Speak with museums curators about the results from the directive.*

SERIOUS ABOUT STOLEN ART: *The World Jewish Congress says it will step up its efforts to recover artwork stolen by the Nazis and never returned to rightful owners. "The WJC says it plans to claim thousands of works of art from American museums using lists that were made by the U.S. Army after the Second World War." CBC 07/20/00.* **Check WJC website for recent information. What museums were targeted? What paintings have been recovered in recent years?**

HOLOCAUST RECORDS PROJECT: *In April 1945, deep in the Altaussee salt mines in the small Austrian town of Ebensee, the U.S. Third Army unearthed a huge repository for stolen Nazi art. Among the hidden masterpieces, were Michelangelo's* Madonna of Bruges, *Jan van Eyck's* Ghent Altarpiece, *and two works by Vermeer,* The Astronomer *and* The Art of Painting. *After the initial discovery, the Monuments Men, a group of museum directors, curators, art scholars, educators, artists, architects, and archivists from thirteen nations, faced two huge tasks—first, to locate and remove the pilfered art from the mines or castles, and, second, to transport the pieces to safe storage areas within the U.S. Occupation Zone. Their ultimate purpose—to return each object to its rightful owner. Despite the tireless efforts of these brave men and women, hundreds of confiscated artworks were never recovered. However, the vast volume of documentation left behind by the Nazis and the Allied agencies allows those efforts to continue. Through its microfilming and preservation program,* the Holocaust Records Project *is providing the historical and art communities with greater access to the records that tell the story of artworks and artifacts damaged and looted during World War II.* **Read the Monuments' Men. Google Holocaust Records Project for updates.**

ONLY 55 YEARS LATE: *Germany will publish a list of several thousand works of art seized from museums and individuals across Europe in an effort to* *restore some of it to its rightful owners. Financial Times 04/06/00.* **Check online to see if the list was published. Look for recent update. What works have been restored since the article was published?**

Finished with her summaries, Anne printed two copies of the document, one for her and one for her grandmother. She tucked her copy into her briefcase and put the other by her purse in the entry so she wouldn't forget to take it when she went for lunch. She returned to the kitchen, poured another glass of wine, plopped down on the living room couch, and continued to peruse the material in the folder.

This is interesting. She removed a letter written in Veronique's hand. *Why would Rose Valland merit a handwritten biography?* She read.

Rose Valland was born in 1898, in Saint-Etienne-de-Saint-Goirs, Isere. She earned two fine arts degrees from the Ecole des Beaux-Arts in Lyon and also studied at the Ecole des Beaux-Arts in Paris. Despite her extensive education, in 1932, she took a job at the Jeu de Paume as an unpaid volunteer with the title "charge de mission." She eventually became an assistant and, in 1941, began receiving a salary.

In 1940, the Galerie Nationale du Jeu de Paume became the Nazis' central storage and sorting depot for nearly 22,000 plundered masterpieces seized from Paris museums and Jewish-owned collections pending their distribution to various persons and places in Germany. Because Valland oversaw the daily museum operations, she personally witnessed the Nazi looting machine.

Day after day Rose catalogued the art, keeping track of where and to whom the works were being shipped. She risked her life to provide information about railroad shipments to French resistance units so they wouldn't mistakenly blow up the trains filled with priceless French treasures. The Germans never knew she understood their language, so they spoke freely in her company. As she quietly worked, she listened carefully, using what she learned to create secret lists of the plundered treasures. The Nazis photographed every object in their possession, and after they left for the day, Rose made copies of the negatives.

On four occasions, the Nazis became suspicious of Rose and threw her out, yet each time she found a way to return, acquiring additional information from loyal drivers, guards, and packers and passing vital information on to the French Resistance.

As the war drew to a close, the Nazis were eager to evacuate the museum and ship out their precious cargo. Thanks to Rose, a train bound for Germany carrying French paintings and other objet d'art *never made it out of the city. She reported to the French Resistance, whose sabotage efforts stalled the train until the Allies could liberate Paris. After the war, using Valland's documents, the Allies were able to recover many of Europe's most cherished art treasures.*

The Jeu de Paume is clearly the reason Oma wrote about Rose, Anne mulled as she put letter and the folder aside. She looked at the clock and picked up her phone. *Ten's too late for Oma to be up,* she thought as she scrolled to Renee's number.

"What's up?" Renee answered.

"I hope I didn't wake you—"

"At this early hour? You're talking to a night-owl, remember?"

For the first few minutes Anne talked about the articles in the folder, finishing with, "Oma wants me to help locate her mother's paintings. Did you know—"

"I did. How do you feel about what she's asking?"

"I don't really know. Of course I'll help if I can, but this doesn't sound like a short-term effort, and, truthfully, I have no idea where to start. Can you tell me anything more about what Oma wants me to do?"

"Not really, other than to say she's determined to reclaim what she believes is rightfully hers."

"Suddenly after all these years? Why?"

"I asked her the same thing. I figured she'd eventually open up—though I never dreamed it would take her seventy years. Nonetheless, the suddenness of her decision and her determination to tell you *everything* is baffling. For decades, she's been passive—filled with agonizing sorrow and terrible guilt—"

"And suddenly she's full speed ahead."

"And like the Veronique of long ago."

"Shall I ask her to explain this miraculous transformation?"

"If the opportunity presents itself, though it might not—at least not yet."

"Then I'll just listen to what she has to say. Physically how's she doing?"

"The first thought that comes to mind—she's feisty. During dinner she grumbled about Paul's low fat dishes, that, by the way, were delicious, and she wrinkled her nose every time she took a sip of tea."

"The decaf I bought?"

"She complained it tasted like paper."

"I thought you were going to keep giving her the tea she's been drinking for the past few months."

"I started to, but I changed my mind. She'd either think I was ignoring Doctor Richmond's orders or figure out I've been deceiving her all along."

"You wouldn't want that."

"Not on your life."

"Okay, she figured out the tea bag. How'd she feel about the *I Can't Believe it's not Butter* on her dinner roll?"

"If I quoted her exactly, you would never think of your grandmother in quite the same way."

"It was that bad."

"Imagine the worst, and you'll be half right. We'll see you tomorrow, honey."

"For part two of the conversation. I can't wait. . ."

CHAPTER 5

The TV was still on when Anne woke to the sun pouring through the open curtains. She reluctantly rolled out of bed and trudged to the kitchen. "Thank God I bought this machine," she grumbled as her Keurig brewed an almost-instant cup of coffee.

As usual, Edward had left the *New York Times* and the *Post* outside the door, so over a second cup of strong brew, she scanned the headlines. "Same old! Same old!" she said as she put the papers aside. Figuring she might as well be comfortable for the mysterious conversation to come, she showered and dressed in jeans, a long-sleeved T-shirt, and a vest.

It was a beautiful spring day so with time to spare and still thinking about the conversation her grandmother had started the day before, she walked across the park.

Laura greeted her at the door. "They're waiting for you upstairs," she said.

"How's Oma?"

"She must be feeling better. She's issuing orders—"

"Oh Lord," Anne groaned. "Thanks for the warning." She climbed the stairs to the second floor, knocked on the first door to the right, and, without waiting for a response, entered her grandmother's bedroom.

Henri quickly stood, crossed the room, and enveloped her in a bear hug. "We're glad to see you, honey," he said. "Come! Sit! I've reserved the best seat at the table just for you."

As he pulled out the chair across from Veronique, Anne looked closely at the charming man she loved like a grandfather. Like Veronique and Renee, Henri Marsolet, too, had also aged well. He had a full head of silver-gray hair, and his blue eyes were bright and perpetually smiling, showing off the dimples in both his cheeks. He was tall and fit, she assumed because he worked out every day in the guest room her grandfather converted to a gym several years before he died.

"You're looking much better, Oma." Anne reached across the table and squeezed her grandmother's outstretched hand.

"She is, isn't she," Renee said. "Now if her attitude would improve—"

"My attitude's as good as it can be under the circumstances," Veronique said crossly.

⁓○

Throughout lunch, Veronique grumbled about the fake butter and the absence of wine. More than once Anne stifled a laugh and shot Renee a 'can-you-believe-this?' look.

"I suppose the time has come," Veronique said when Paul had finished clearing the table.

"Are you sure you're ready?" Anne asked, seeing her grandmother's returning color suddenly drain from her face.

"I told you before—I have to be. First, let me say, though Mother was arrested decades ago, in my mind, what happened the afternoon and evening of July 17, 1942, seems like yesterday. When I went back to the Île the next morning—"

"Did I misunderstand? I thought you went to Renee's that afternoon and never returned home."

"That's not completely accurate. I never went back into my house, but Henri and I did go back to Quai de Bourbon—"

"Even knowing what had happened to your mother the night before?"

"That's right," Henri said. "Let me tell you what happened. About eight p.m. on the seventeenth, through his sources, Auguste Lessard, my father's friend and partner in the Resistance, heard that the Nazis were rounding up and arresting Jews on Île St-Louis. Fearing the worst, he sent Bertrand, his ten year old son, to check on Madame Boulet. As Bertrand later reported, he arrived at the spot where Quai de Bourbon curves toward Pont Saint-Louis, peeked around the corner, and saw the Nazis hoisting Madame Boulet into the back of a canvas-covered truck.

Shortly after that truck pulled away, a second arrived. Several soldiers jumped out of the back. For the two hours, they went back and forth from the house to the truck carrying boxes filled with Madame Boulet's personal possessions. When they were finished, Bertrand rushed home to tell his father and mine what he'd seen."

"While he was gone, Auguste and Anton heard the Jews were being transported to the Velodrome d'Hiver," Renee said. "Realizing there was little chance of finding Elisabeth, Anton had to try. He rushed to the skating rink."

"When he couldn't find Elisabeth among the hundreds of Jews being herded into the building, he came to rue Gît. He and Jules told Veronique, Renee, and me what happened."

Her lips quivering and a pained expression on her face, Veronique said. "After the initial shock of hearing Mother had been arrested, I was an emotional wreck. My life was in total disarray. I was still in a daze at one a.m. when Anton came to Renee's room and said that she, Henri, and I were leaving France that afternoon. I was terrified, but for some reason, through the fog of my misery, I knew I had to see my home one last time, and I *had to have* my journal."

"You were overwhelmed with shock and grief following your mother's arrest and frightened because you'd soon be leaving everything you knew behind, yet you remembered your journal?"

"I did, though to this day I don't know how. Anyway, I was determined to go home one last time."

"Henri, you couldn't stop her?"

"Short of locking her up? No! Believe me, Anne, I tried to get your grandmother to listen to reason, but she threatened to go by herself. I took her warning seriously and went along to keep her from doing something foolish—or perhaps I should say even *more* reckless than what we were already doing."

"Will you tell me what happened?"

"Veronique—"

"Yes, Henri. Tell Anne how my irrational demands almost landed *us* at Auschwitz."

"Okay, if you really want your granddaughter to know what a stubborn woman you are."

"Nothing you could say at this point would surprise me." Anne said, smiling at her grandmother's obvious displeasure.

"Okay," he said. "Here goes. On the morning of the eighteenth, Veronique announced that she was going home, and I quote, 'right now, with or without you.' Of course I had to go, but with no time to plan, I was forced to improvise. I knew Pont de la Tournelle was the bridge most German patrols used to travel from the Left Bank to the Île, so we went a little out of our way to cross Pont de Sully. Fortunately, we made it over without incident though, looking back, I have no idea how. The aftermath of the raids had put the Nazi patrols on high alert. There were German soldiers everywhere. Figuring anyone watching the house would be circling the quais, I decided we'd walk along rue St-Louis-en-lÎle."

"There were always more people on the main street, and Henri thought we could blend in with the crowd."

"And we did. When we neared the eastern tip of the island. I left Veronique in a crowd of people who were looking down at the boats passing by on the Seine and joined a group of about ten pedestrians who were walking toward Pont Louis Philippe. When I got to the place where Quai de Bourbon curves toward Pont Saint-Louis, I peeked around the corner and saw a canvas-backed military truck parked with a clear view of Elisabeth's front door. I raced back to where Veronique was waiting and told her it was too dangerous to proceed."

"Let me guess. Oma was determined."

"More like bullheaded. Knowing there was nothing I could do short of dragging her back to rue Gît, which definitely would have aroused suspicion, we doubled back to rue Le Regrattier and, keeping close to the buildings, crept along the quai until we were almost to rue J. Bellay. With every step, I begged Veronique to forget the journal, but—"

"His arguments fell on deaf ears. With or without Henri's help, I was going to see the yellow tape Bertrand said the Nazis draped across my door. And, more importantly, I was going to retrieve my journal."

"When we neared Pont Louis Philippe, I told Veronique not to move until I came back. I think she finally realized it was dangerous to be back on the Île."

"If I didn't know then, I quickly realized the folly of my demand. I glimpsed a Nazi patrol marching toward the western tip of the Île. Then and there I knew we should turn around and return to Sainte-Germain."

"Did you tell Henri you'd leave without your journal?"

"I didn't have a chance. He had just rounded the corner, but not before warning me to stay put." Veronique sighed. "If I had. . . But that's not important now. I entered a narrow alleyway separating the two mansions next door to ours and waited."

"I had no trouble getting inside the house without being seen," Henri continued. "But when I started to climb back out, I saw two French soldiers approaching from the direction of Pont Marie. I quickly ducked back inside and waited—I would say ten minutes—before peeking out again. Fortunately, the men went by without noticing the open window. I hastily climbed out, this time, ironically, praying that Veronique *hadn't* listened to my admonition. My pulse racing and hardly able to breath, I hurried to the spot where we'd separated. But—"

"I wasn't there—"

"I prayed harder, this time that she'd seen the soldiers and returned to rue Gît. My dread intensifying with each step. I made my way along the quai, all the while searching the faces of the crowd walking toward me. I was about halfway past the mansion next door and thinking the worst, when I came to the alleyway. I peered in, hoping Veronique had the wherewithal to duck inside, when suddenly I heard a faint, 'Henri,' coming out of the darkness. I peered in, and there she was, cowering against the side wall. I rushed to where I was, grasped her arm and, if you can shout in a whisper, yelled, 'Let's get the hell out of here.'"

"And you ran."

"Don't I wish! Despite the looming danger, your grandmother stood there—her feet firmly planted on the ground. She *would not leave* until I gave her the *damn* journal."

"Once I had my *precious* journal, I was ready to go."

"What about the tape, Oma?"

"Suddenly, seeing the tape wasn't important. The Nazi parading up and down the quai revealed more than a yellow strip across the door ever could. I wanted to race home, but Henri had a different idea."

"Just as we emerged, I saw a soldier—"

"Henri jerked me back into the darkness. Holding our breaths, we crouched low against the back, praying he wouldn't shine his flashlight into the dark space and see us hiding. As the minutes dragged by, I felt the walls closing in around me. When I couldn't stand the suffocating space any longer, I jumped up and darted toward the opening. Henri grabbed my arm and pulled me down. I had a bruise—"

"I didn't mean to squeeze so hard—"

"I know. I doubt I'd be sitting here telling my story if you hadn't held me back. We continued to huddle against the back wall until he *finally* thought it was safe to look—"

"I ordered Veronique to stay where she was, crept to the opening, and peered out. The quai was clear. I was nervous, but I knew we had to get out of there. I took her hand, and we walked slowly toward rue Le Regrattier. When we turned onto rue St-Louis-en-lÎle and were able to blend in with the crowd, I felt a little better."

"I wanted to cross Pont de la Tournelle," Veronique said. "It was the fastest way off the Île."

"But I said no. I was still afraid the Nazis would be patrolling the heavily-trafficked bridge, so we continued west toward Pont de Sully. We just about there when a caravan of army trucks approached from Quai de Bethune. I gripped Veronique's arm and pulled her into Square Barye."

"Three trucks drove by without hesitating, but the driver of the last truck slowed to a crawl. I was sure he'd stop and the soldier in the passenger seat would jump out to see who we were and what we were doing in the park."

"But that didn't happen."

"Thank God no. But only because Henri thought fast. He pulled me tightly to him and kissed me hard on the lips."

"Hoping the Nazis would think you were just two young lovers enjoying the park."

"That was the idea. Fortunately for us, it worked. The driver stopped for one of the longest minutes of my life and then drove away."

"We crossed Pont de Sully and made it back to rue Gît without further incident. So now you've heard the story of our foolhardy trip to the Île. I still get agitated when I think back to those two terrifying hours. So, for the sake of this old heart, shall we stop talking about that less-than-pleasant experience and get back to what happened during la rafle du Vel d'Hiv?"

"Henri, you know I'll always be grateful—"

"I do, Veronique. Now talk to Anne."

For several minutes they all sat in strained silence, waiting for Veronique to continue her tale. She inhaled deeply, exhaled slowly, cleared her throat, and said, "La rafle du Vel d'Hiv, code name Vent Printanier or Spring Wind, began with a mass roundup of Jews, both in Paris and in the weeks and months ahead, throughout both the occupied and free zones. The Nazi's ultimate objective—to drastically reduce the number of Jews throughout the country. The action commenced at four a.m. on Wednesday, July 16."

Veronique faltered momentarily, and then, as if realizing for the first time, she whispered, "Mother *had to know* we were in grave danger when she sent me to Renee's."

"Veronique hadn't been to Saint-Germain for some time," Renee explained, giving her friend a minute to recover. "Imagine my surprise when I opened the door, and there she was. When she said she'd come to talk about my wedding dress, I was astonished. I had no idea why Madame Boulet suddenly let her leave the Île, but, assuming she had a good reason, I played along. I told Veronique her mother had misunderstood—that the dress wasn't a concern. Rather I needed help with plans for the reception following the ceremony. Remember, it was July 1942, so even the most basic foods were in short supply. We were continually adjusting the menu."

"I accepted her explanation without question. I hadn't seen Jules or Renee's wonderful mother Adele for weeks, and I was thrilled she wanted my advice. Initially, I was to be her maid of honor, but several weeks earlier, fearful of what could happen if the Nazis discovered a Jew in the wedding party, I asked to be excused—"

"That must have been difficult."

"For both of us," said Renee.

"Renee, when Oma arrived, did you wonder if Elisabeth had sent her away to keep her safe—maybe because she knew the Nazis were coming?"

Renee nodded no. "None of us thought Madame Boulet was in danger. She was a wealthy woman, not an ordinary Jew from the Marais. Sadly, we quickly learned that money didn't matter."

"Oma, you believe Elisabeth knew something terrible was about to happen. If that's true, why didn't she go with you to Renee's? Surely she could have sold another painting to pay for *her* safe passage out of the country."

"I have no idea why she stayed home. She knew the Nazis were seizing art from private Jewish collections. Perhaps she thought they'd raid the house, take the paintings and other valuables, and leave her be. Or maybe she figured she'd be causing problems for the Paquets if she asked for help. We'd all heard horrific tales about the dreaded Gestapo. For years I've wondered if my last visit to Renee's put Jules and Adele in danger. The Nazis were quick to arrest any Christian they caught harboring a Jew."

"Are you serious?" Renee said, taken aback. "My father was killed during a raid on a German ammunitions depot a little over a year after we escaped."

"I didn't know—"

"Then why in God's name didn't you ask? I gave you numerous opportunities to share your feelings and concerns—that was until you ordered me not to broach the subject again. The anguish you must have suffered all these years thinking you were in some way responsible for my parents' deaths is one more consequence of your refusal to talk about the Occupation."

"I guess I was afraid to hear the answer if I asked the question," Veronique said, her lips quivering. "I should have—"

"No more shoulds!" Henri said sternly. "From here on out, we're moving ahead, not looking back."

"Renee, with you gone and no one to lean on, your mother must have been distraught when Jules was killed."

"She never knew. She died of breast cancer in December 1942."

"I didn't know, which seems to be my new mantra. Had she been diagnosed before you left Paris?"

"So I later learned. She was always thin, but as the months dragged on and even the most basic foods were hard to come by, she began to lose more and more weight, I naively assumed she was eating less so my father and I would have more."

"Did she go for treatment?"

"I'm not sure. Probably not. Remember, this was Paris during the Occupation. With wounded soldiers being transported to hospitals from the front, a woman with breast cancer would be near the bottom of the treatment list. Besides that, I'm sure she knew I'd refuse to leave if I found out, and she was right."

"What happened to your home after the war?"

"By the time Paris was finally liberated, Henri and I had settled in New York. In 1946, the second time we returned after the Liberation, we sold his home. We kept mine on the outside chance we'd change our minds and want to move back. By 1949, we'd decided to remain here with Veronique, so we sold the house along with all but a few personal items I had shipped here."

"Did you ever regret your decision to remain in the States?"

"From time to time I feel a twinge of nostalgia, but all-in-all, we've been happy here."

"And we do go back," Henri said. "Every few years we visit old friends, and I do mean old. Sadly, over the past decade many have died."

"What about your parents, Henri. You often speak of your father, but rarely of your mother. Was she living when you left Paris?"

"Mother passed in 1933."

"Seven years before the onset of the Occupation."

"That's right. When she was fifteen, she contracted a severe case of scarlet fever that gave rise to rheumatic heart disease. When she and my father married, she was doing well, but shortly after I was born, the disease flared again. She suffered from swollen joints in her knees that made it hard to walk. Her body was often covered with a red rash, and the muscles in her face moved uncontrollably. More often than not, she was short of breath."

"Antibiotics didn't help?"

"Penicillin wasn't discovered until 1928. Five years later it was still hard to come by. Though there were periods when Mother seemed better, I can't recall a time when she was *truly* healthy. During the last two years of her life, she was virtually bedridden."

"And Anton? You said you never saw him after you spoke your final goodbyes and began your journey to the United States."

"That's true. He was killed during an attack on a German supply train in early 1944. Despite extraordinary precautions, the Nazis heard about the plan. As resistance fighters place explosives on the tracks, German troops swarmed out of the trees. Six Frenchmen were killed during the ensuing battle."

"So many deaths at the hands of the Nazis—including Mother's," Veronique said. "Shall we talk about specific events that led to *her* death?"

"Of course, Oma. I apologize for taking us off track, but there's so much I'm hearing for the first time. I'm eager to know everything."

"I know how you feel, darling, though it took me decades to get to where you are now. After the Liberation, Henri spoke with several of his resistance contacts. He learned that Mother's first stop on the way to Auschwitz was the Velodrome d'Hiver, a winter cycling stadium in the Fifteenth Arrondisement. When I *finally* wanted to know exactly what happened, I was taken aback. Not sure I would remember the exact numbers, I wrote them down." She unfolded a small piece of paper and said. "During the two days of la rafle du Vel d'Hiv, 3031 men, 5802 women, and 4051 children were snatched from their homes and transported to the velodrome. They were detained for up to five days with very little food and no medical care before being bused to Drancy."

"What's Drancy?"

"Henri, would you tell Anne about this leg of Mother's journey?"

"Of course, Veronique. And you're doing great."

"Anne, Drancy was the next stop for Jews on the way to their final destination—the Nazi death camps. It was a *sammellager*, an assembly camp."

"Where *is* Drancy?"

"It's midway between the center of the city and Charles de Gaulle airport. When the complex was first built, it was touted as a first-of-its-kind public housing project. After Petain joined with the Nazis to hunt down and arrest French Jews, it became an ideal place to process those taken into custody."

"Why's that?"

"For two reasons. First, it consisted of tower blocks, groups of high-rise buildings constructed with reinforced concrete and steel in the shape of a horseshoe, so it was easy to defend. The blocks were surrounded by barbed wire fences with watchtowers at each corner. Second, it was close to the railway station, making transportation to the death camps less complicated. I did a little research and learned that over 75,000 Jews, including 11,000 children, passed through Drancy during the Occupation. You heard your grandmother say that lack of food and medical care was a problem at the velodrome. The conditions at Drancy were much worse. More than three-thousand internees starved to death while awaiting transport."

"I don't recall seeing a reference to Drancy in *Paris Access*, my bible when I first arrived at the university. I assume the camp was razed after the Liberation? Surely the French government wouldn't want a reminder of the atrocities committed against the Jews."

"Actually, it's still there, at least the part of the complex that was used as the internment camp. The rest of *La Cité de la Muette* was destroyed in 1975. I don't believe in the paranormal, but I often wonder if the ghosts of thousands of Jews roam the grounds at night. I know I wouldn't want to live there. In any case, the remaining buildings are once again apartments for blue collar workers. At the entrance, there's a poignant memorial to the Jews who died there. When Renee and I visited shortly after the monument was dedicated, we took pictures of the sculpture and inside the boxcar museum. We gave them to Veronique."

"I put them aside until about a year ago."

"You never told me—"

"That I looked at them? You would have insisted we talk about Mother, and I wasn't ready to have that conversation. Two weeks ago I looked through the photographs again. I wanted to see more, so I googled Drancy Memorial." She pushed a folder in Anne's direction. "This file contains Henri's pictures and additional photographs I printed from various websites. You look while I talk. If you have a question, stop me."

Anne opened the folder and removed the pictures as Veronique began. "Visitors to the memorial walk up the old tracks to that single boxcar, one that was actually used to transport Jews to the extermination camps. Look closely at the Star of David next to a sign that says the car can hold up to eight horses? It's impossible to believe the Nazis thought this special woman was no better than an animal."

"We spent over an hour looking at the exhibits," Henri said. "There were only ten people in the car with us, but I was claustrophobic. I wanted to leave, but Renee insisted we look at everything so we would be prepared if and when Veronique asked questions."

"Which I never did—"

"Until now."

"Were you able to find out what happened to Great-Grand'Mere Elisabeth after she left Drancy?" Anne asked. "I realize she was transported to Auschwitz, but—"

"I'll answer your question," Henri said. "Fortunately for the families who sought news of their loved ones, the Nazis kept meticulous records. During our first trip back to Paris, I spoke with several resistance fighters who were working for the newly-formed French government. They did a little digging, called in some favors, and learned that Elisabeth left Drancy on July 22." Pausing, he looked at Veronique.

"Go on," she said. "Over the past several months—since I stopped denying what I knew had happened—I've read countless online articles detailing the fate of the Jews."

"There's no easy way to say this, Anne, so I'll be blunt. When Elisabeth arrived at Auschwitz, she was taken from the train and marched directly to the gas chamber."

"Oma, you don't have to listen to this. I can read about Auschwitz online."

"You're wrong, Anne. I want to listen—just not today. I'm sorry darling. I thought I could do this, but it seems I need a little more time. I'll rest and regroup, and we'll begin again tomorrow—that is if you want to hear more."

"Of course I do. And you're right. You should rest. How about ten? Is that too early?"

"Ten is fine, and thank you, darling."

"For what, Oma?"

Veronique sighed deeply. "For more than I could ever say."

CHAPTER 6

Figuring she could put off grocery shopping for one more day, Anne stopped at the deli and bought a pastrami sandwich and a half-pound of pasta salad. Back at her apartment, she put her meal on a plate, set a place at the kitchen island, poured a glass of wine, and went to her bedroom to change clothes.

I might as well get some work done while I eat, she mulled as she stopped in her office, unplugged her laptop, and removed the committee's list of paintings from her briefcase. She sat at the kitchen island and turned on the computer. Thirty minutes later she'd finished her sandwich and circled five paintings she felt required additional scrutiny. For the next hour, one by one, she opened websites, cutting and pasting pertinent information into a Word Document for each, and printing hard copies so she'd be ready to make recommendations to the committee at the next meeting.

It was after eight when she finally tucked the museum list into her briefcase. "Now what," she grumbled, bored and not eager to spend the rest of the evening in front of the TV. *I know. I'll learn what I can about Drancy and Auschwitz before Oma and I get together in the morning.*

Time flew by as she opened site after site and read article after article about Drancy and the Nazi death camps—Auschwitz in particular. Several times, sickened by what she was reading, she thought about quitting, But despite her revulsion, she continued to peruse the ghastly reports.

Two hours later, her eyes tired and her mind filled with horrific images, she turned off the computer and got ready for bed. But when she turned off the light and closed her eyes, she couldn't relax. Images of the pathetic souls who had died at Drancy and Auschwitz played like a horror movie in her mind.

⌒◌

"What a miserable night," Anne groaned as the alarm jarred her awake. She grudgingly got up, plodded to the kitchen, and drank one, then a second cup of coffee. Her head aching, she showered, dressed, and with little time to spare, caught a cab to her grandmother's apartment.

Renee was pouring tea, and Henri was reading the morning paper when she entered the bedroom. "You look tired, darling," Veronique said. "You didn't sleep well?"

"Unfortunately, no. I spent the evening reading online articles about Drancy and Auschwitz. Once I started, thought I tried, I couldn't stop. When I finally went to bed, images of the horrific crimes committed against the Jews kept me awake."

"I know what you mean. I did, but then I didn't want to know what Mother endured during her short stay at Drancy and later at Auschwitz."

"Exactly. I was paradoxically repulsed and drawn-in. There's no reason—"

Veronique motioned to the chair beside hers. "If you're going to say there's no reason to continue, you're wrong, Anne."

"But why—"

"Because it's not enough to read the countless articles about unnamed Jews—individuals I never knew. I can emotionally separate myself from them. But realizing my own mother was forced to suffer a humiliating and excruciating death makes the Holocaust personal. For decades—perhaps to maintain my sanity—I've grouped Mother with all the other Jews who died at Auschwitz. If I'm going to heal, I need to talk specifically about *her* death."

"Then you have our undivided attention," Renee said.

Slowly and deliberately, Veronique began to speak. "Yesterday when I needed to rest and regroup, I had just begun to talk about Auschwitz. I'm haunted by the realization that Mother didn't have to suffer such a gruesome death. That she chose to stay on the Île rather than leave with us is something I'll never understand."

"It was her decision, Veronique. She must have had a good reason for staying behind."

"True, Renee. Perhaps someday I'll figure out what she was thinking. For now, I just want Anne to know what happened the night I was enjoying myself with you and your family on rue Gît. Until this past February, I was afraid to face the horrors Mother suffered at Drancy and then at Auschwitz. Then—though I don't know why—I wanted to know everything. I admit I had two glasses of wine and half of another before I opened the first article, an account written by a former SS Haupsturmfuhrer, a captain, who supervised the unloading of Jews coming to Auschwitz from camps like Drancy. I learned that, collectively, the forty-five boxcars carried 3,700 Jews. I did the math. There were one hundred forty-eight human beings crammed into one car."

"Remember I felt claustrophobic being with just ten other visitors to the museum?" Henri said. "I can't imagine being in that tiny space along with a hundred plus other people."

"Nor can I," said Veronique. "Many Jews were already dead by the time they reached Auschwitz. The rest were quickly separated into two groups—those who could work and those who were too ill and weak to be productive. Mother, a part of the latter group, was immediately marched to the gas chamber. Every detail of what happened to her next is forever fixed in my mind."

"Are you sure it's not best to leave specific details about the past in the past," Anne asked.

"I don't mean to be rude, darling, but please stop asking if I want to continue. I'll talk until, for whatever reason, I can't. Mother's group was led to the showers to be deloused, or so said the Sonderkommando, a member of a special detachment of prisoners tasked with carrying out the exterminations, removing the bodies, and preparing the showers for the next group. These men met the trains and remained with the prisoners until the door of the gas chamber closed, all the while assuring them they'd be fine. Many women weren't deceived. They cried hysterically when the Sonderkommando insisted they undress. Some tried to avoid their fate by revealing the names and addresses of Jews who were still in hiding, but their disclosures didn't help. The Nazis had the information, and the snitches went to the gas chamber anyway. I can't even imagine how Mother must have felt when, standing naked for all to see, she heard the door being bolted behind her."

"I think we've talked enough about Auschwitz," Renee said firmly.

"No, Renee. If I continue to share Mother's story, perhaps I'll stop wondering what she did to deserve such a horrific death. Perhaps I'll stop wondering how Marshall Petain, a French hero, could stand by and watch this horrifying example of man's inhumanity to man. Perhaps I'll stop wondering how a benevolent God could allow such carnage. I've yet to come up with an answer. It makes no sense. . ." Her face red and perspiration on her brow, Veronique coughed into her handkerchief.

"You have to stop," Renee said firmly. "Henri, tell Anne what you learned when you talked with Anton's friends."

"Of course," Henri said. "Anne, the French Resistance rose against the Nazis on August 19, 1944. Five days later, on the twenty-fifth, the Free French Army of Liberation, reinforced by General Patton's U.S. Third Army, came to their aid. The following day General von Choltitz, the commander of the German garrison and the military Governor of Paris, surrendered, and Charles de Gaulle moved back into the war ministry. Paris was free, though the battle for France continued. When Renee and I returned in December 1944, heavy fighting was still occurring in Provence, in the seaports of southwestern France, and throughout the eastern and northeastern parts of the country. These battles and skirmishes were fought until May 7, 1945, when General Jodl signed the unconditional surrender of all Germany Forces."

"Was it safe for you and Renee to return to Paris?"

"Probably not, but we had to know what happened to our fathers and Veronique's mother. Of course the news was bad on all fronts. When we returned to Île St-Louis, most of Elisabeth's neighbors were still living in their homes, though some have since died or moved away. We met and became friendly with Jacqueline Bouffard, nee Cabot, whose family lived next door to the Boulet mansion. Though Jacqueline was only ten, she vividly recalls the night Elisabeth was arrested. She showed us the very window where she watched the events unfold. Veronique?"

"Go on Henri."

"All right. The raid began at seven, so it was still light outside when Jacqueline heard what she initially thought was a big car stop next door. Because gasoline was scarce, there had been few vehicles on the road around the quais, so, naturally, she was curious. She went to the window, peeked out through a small slit in the blackout curtain, and saw a large canvas-covered truck parked in front of Madame Boulet's mansion. She said three soldiers leaped out of the back, while a man dressed in black wearing an armband with a 'funny red design' exited the front seat."

"A Gestapo agent with a swastika on his sleeve," Anne said.

"Right, though at the time Jacqueline only knew the man looked scary and 'very mad.' Two soldiers removed a large pole from the back of the truck and used it to break down Madame Boulet's front door. They and the 'nasty man,' as Jacqueline called him, went inside, while the third soldier stood guard. Ten minutes later the two soldiers who had entered the house came out, dragging Madame Boulet between them. The man in black watched while they hoisted 'the old lady,'—Jacqueline's words—into the back of the truck."

"Did Jacqueline say how Mother seemed?" Veronique asked tentatively.

"Terrified, but that's understandable. She didn't resist. Several minutes after the truck carrying her and, according to Jacqueline, 'lots of other people,' departed, a larger truck drove up. For the next two hours, the soldiers methodically removed paintings, furniture, rugs, silver—anything and everything they thought might be valuable. Jacqueline couldn't see too much through the slit, but she never opened it any wider. She said she was afraid she'd be caught spying and be taken away like Madame Boulet."

"Is Madame Bouffard still alive?" Anne asked. "If so, do you think she'll see me if I go to Paris on Met business?"

"She's very much alive," Veronique said, suddenly brightening. "And I'm *sure* she'll see you. Several weeks ago I wrote to Jacqueline. Just yesterday I received a response, an email from Cecile, Jacqueline's daughter, conveying her mother's message. In 1960, Mother's home was divided into four large, luxury apartments, one per floor. A year ago all of the apartments were renovated, modernized, and put up for sale. I immediately went online and learned that those on the second and third floors of the mansion had been sold. The fourth and fifth-floor residences were still on the market."

"Were? You mean someone bought them between the time you looked and today?"

"They were both purchased by the same person. I bought them for you."

"You did what?"

"I bought the apartments. Your great-grandmother's home is now yours—at least you own half of it. Rent one, or combine the two into one glorious two-storey place. I'm sure you'll be making numerous trips to Paris in the weeks and months ahead, both for the Met and, hopefully, for me. But whatever you decide, you may not sell either place. They will eventually go to your children."

"Aren't you forgetting something, Oma? I don't have children."

"Not now, but someday you will. And stop being so condescending. I never thought you and Tom would have kids. I knew your marriage was doomed before you spoke your vows. Ask Renee and Henri. During the lavish reception your mother threw in the Hamptons, I told them you'd made a mistake. Madeline might have been able to live with an always-absent husband, but I knew you'd eventually grow tired of being married to a man who was off to Zurich, London, or wherever on business and, when he *was* home, entertaining clients four nights a week. Someday you'll meet the right man and have children who will one day inherit their great-great-grandmother's home. I only hope I'm around to meet my first great grandchild. But on to the business at hand. The purchase agreement will require your signature. You have an appointment Monday morning at nine with Catherine Labbe, the attorney I hired to handle the transaction."

"A week from tomorrow?"

"Yes. At my age, I can't waste time. Whether or not you help me locate Mother's art has no bearing on the purchase—though I hope you'll honor a dying lady's last request."

"I'm amazed you'd try such a tactic," Anne said, rolling her eyes. "Don't try to make me feel sorry for you. If you listen to Doctor Richmond, you'll be around for a long time."

"My new diet is doing more to kill me than my heart disease," Veronique muttered. "So will you go, Anne? Can I count on you?"

"If it's important to you, of course. I *may* be able to leave Friday, but I can't promise. When I get back to my apartment, I'll look at my schedule, contact Air France about potential flights, and email John to let him know what I'm planning."

"Good. And one more thing. I know you usually stay at the George V, Four Seasons. This time will you stay on Île St-Louis?"

"You don't want me to move right into the apartment?"

"That would be my preference," Veronique said, ignoring Anne's sarcasm. "But my decorator and her workers won't be finished until Wednesday. Did I mention I'm having your apartment furnished? Not everything I've ordered is an authentic antique, but I'm told the reproductions are excellent."

"I can't believe what I'm hearing."

"Believe it, darling. The Hotel du Jeu de Paume isn't a five-star hotel, but it's a four, and it's near your apartment. When I looked online, I decided the single rooms are too small, so I reserved a suite. When you've made your final plans, you can confirm."

"Okay, I'll stay there, but you haven't explained why—"

"That's where we began our escape," Henri said.

"Oma, is that where you met Grandfather Robert?"

"It is, though in 1942, what is now the hotel were two dilapidated mansions being used for storage. In the 1980s, a French couple converted the warehouses to a hotel. Don't frown, Anne. The entire place was recently renovated. The cellar where I met your grandfather is now the breakfast room."

"So now that I know where I'm staying, would you be a little more specific about what you want me to do once I get to Paris?"

"Simply put, I want you to locate Mother's art collection. As I said in my letter, I'm asking you to be my Monuments Woman. Those paintings are my heritage, and I want to reclaim them before I die."

"Maybe we can make that happen," Anne said, trying to hide her skepticism. "I have a meeting in the morning, but I'll call when we break for lunch. By then I should have a clearer picture of the week ahead, and we can make a definite plan."

"Thank you, darling.

"You're welcome, Oma—at least I think you are."

CHAPTER 7

"How the hell can I be ready to leave for Paris by Friday?" Anne muttered as she entered her apartment. She took a deep breath and answered her own question. "By taking it one step at a time, beginning with plane reservations."

She went to her office and googled flights from New York to Paris. Because there were no first class seats on the Delta/Air France flight on Friday the ninth, she reserved a seat on Flight 8581 departing Kennedy at seven Thursday evening and arriving at Charles de Gaulle at eight thirty-five Friday morning. Though she had no idea how long she'd remain in France, she figured two weeks would be enough time for her initial trip, so she booked a return flight, arriving in New York at twelve forty-five on the afternoon of April 24. Next she sent an email to the Hotel du Jeu de Paume requesting early check in on the ninth and checkout on the fourteenth, the day her apartment would be ready.

Those initial tasks completed, she poured a glass of wine and sat back down at her laptop. She emailed John, explaining she was leaving for Paris on personal business on Thursday the eighth, and, unless he objected, would take an up-close-and-personal look at the paintings on the committee's preliminary list.

Assuming John would accept her offer, she emailed the curators of the Musée d'Orsay, the Musée de l'Orangerie, and the Musée Marmottan Monet, letting them know she would be in Paris for two weeks and hoped to meet with them to discuss the paintings the Met wished to borrow as well as, time permitting, a matter of personal importance. She provided each with her cell number and wrote she'd be in touch once she arrived.

Next she scrolled to her mother's name on her contact list and pushed talk. "Are you all right, Mother?" she asked, when, sounding winded, Madeline answered.

"I am, darling," Madeline panted. "But this isn't a good time. I'm late for dinner. I planned to call earlier, but time got away from me. I wanted to say I'm coming to town to visit your grandmother Tuesday morning. If you're available for lunch—"

"I am."

"The Carlyle at one. I'll see you then, but I really must go."

"Have a good time," Anne said as the line went dead.

"Though she wasn't especially hungry, Anne made a salad and poured another glass of wine. While she ate, she scratched out a list of things to do, both at home and after she arrived in Paris. At the top of the list was a web search for information about art the Nazis commandeered from French Jews. *Where do I begin to search for Elisabeth's paintings?* she wondered. *I don't have time to do what I need to do, let alone. . .*All of a sudden she had an idea. *I'll do a little preliminary research, give Oma a list of potential sites to explore, and let her take over.*

Eager to share her idea, but concerned that a call to the house might wake her grandmother if she'd already gone to bed, she called Renee's cell. "How's Oma doing," she began.

"Pretty well. She ate a good dinner, believe it or not without complaining about the low fat foods. She seems to have a goal that's keeping her going."

"You mean our search for Elisabeth's paintings?"

"That and returning to Paris. Note—she bought *two* apartments in Elisabeth's mansion. Don't be surprised if she knocks on your door someday soon and tells you she's moving in downstairs for an extended visit."

"Email me when she starts ordering furniture for the fourth floor. I need fair warning. I promise to act surprised if and when she shows up. Do you think she feels like chatting?"

"With you, of course. Hang on while I see what she's doing. When I last checked, she was watching a recording of *Castle.*"

Minutes later, Veronique answered. "How are you, darling," she asked.

"Great, but, more importantly, how are you? You sound stronger."

"I am. Talking about Mother was cathartic, and, though I hate to admit it, Doctor Richmond was right, the pills are working."

"In that case, are you up to taking on a project that could help us find Elisabeth's paintings? I'm leaving for Paris Thursday afternoon, and I have Met business to complete before I go, so—"

"I didn't think you could get away until Friday?"

"That was the plan, but there wasn't a first class seat on the Friday afternoon flight, so I decided to go a day early—and no comment that I'm spoiled. Before I go, I'll make a list of websites pertaining to art the Nazis stole from Parisian Jews during the Occupation. When I've done as much as I can, I'll give you the information, and you can continue. How does that sound?"

"Perfect!" Veronique said eagerly. "Don't tell Renee, but I'm bored. I planned to watch old movies on the new flat-screen television Henri's having installed early next week, but helping you find Mother's art will be much more fun."

"And more productive. What you learn could be essential to finding your mother's paintings."

"Oh I hope so. Thank you again, darling."

"For what? You're the one who's helping me."

"For not making me think I'm a worthless old woman."

"The thought never crossed my mind. On another matter, Mother called."

"I know, she called me too. She's coming to see me Tuesday morning. You're meeting her for lunch?"

"As ever. I need to know what you plan to tell her about the apartments and/or our quest to locate your mother's paintings."

"I have no idea. I probably won't decide until she's here. Whatever she says, listen, but don't elaborate."

"Understood. Now go back to *Castle*. We'll talk tomorrow, and I'll be there Wednesday, your assignment in hand. Enjoy your evening."

"Now that we've spoken, I definitely will. Sleep well, darling."

Anne hung up, put her dishes in the dishwasher, made a cup of coffee, sat down at the computer, and googled World War II Provenance Research. "My God!" she exclaimed when the first page popped up on the screen. *There are over nine 963,000 sites dealing with art the Nazis stole from museums and private collections.* She clicked on what appeared to be the most promising website, read the article, and began to cut and paste pertinent paragraphs into a blank Word Document. When she finished, she reread the shorter version, bolding two organizations for her grandmother to investigate.

From the first days the Nazis seized power through the end of the war in Europe, hundreds of thousands of paintings, sculptures, and other works of art were unlawfully and often forcibly taken from Holocaust victims, public and private museums, small art galleries, churches, cathedrals, and educational institutions. After the war, the **Jewish Restitution Successor Organization (JRSO)** *and the* **Jewish Cultural Reconstruction (JCR)** *were created to represent Jewish constituencies and to distribute heirless and unclaimed property. Updated on an ongoing basis, this site will help to restore objects from these holdings to their legal owners.*

This should get Oma going, she mused as she opened website after website, cutting, pasting and making notes while she worked. When she finally finished, she perused the list.

Era Provenance Internet Portal—*Provides a searchable registry of objects in U.S. museum collections created before 1946, and those that changed hands in Continental Europe during the Nazi era (1933-1945).*

Project for the Documentation of Wartime Cultural Losses—*Reports on the Nazi seizure of cultural property in France.*

Holocaust Assets: US State Department—*Makes available links to US government documents relating to looted art.*

Holocaust Era Assets— *Lists current activities regarding holocaust-era assets.*

Presidential Commission on Holocaust Assets in the US—*Presents an historical record of the collection and disposition of the assets of Holocaust victims in the possession or control of the Government of the United States.*

She typed a note.

Oma, the following are links provided by the Museum of Fine Arts in Boston. Each one can be googled. They are websites maintained by organizations and institutions worldwide that are committed to assisting in the search and recovery of works of art looted during World War II.
Art Loss Register
American Association of Museums: Nazi-era provenance
Central Registry of Information on Looted Cultural Property
Commission for Looted Art in Europe
Lost Art Internet Database
Project for the Documentation of Wartime Cultural Losses

She printed two copies, put one aside to take with her to Paris, and placed the other in the folder for her grandmother. It was after midnight when she shut down the computer and, feeling drained, went to bed.

I have to put Oma's project aside and concentrate on the Impressionist exhibition, Anne thought after another restless night. Running late, she quickly showered and dressed in gray slacks, a red wool blazer, and a silk blouse with geometric red and gray designs. "I look rather Picassoish," she said as she glanced in the mirror one last time before calling a cab to take her to the Met.

When she walked into the Rose Room, the other committee members were still milling around. She poured a cup of coffee and, after taking a sweet roll from the tray on a side table, sat down. The last member of the group arrived minutes later, and John called the meeting to order.

By lunchtime they'd settled on paintings they planned to include from the Met's permanent collection. Anne assumed they would break for lunch and work throughout the afternoon, but one of the committee members had an appointment, so they adjourned for the day. Before leaving, she spoke with John, receiving his approval to meet with the Parisian curators on behalf of the Met.

So what now, she pondered as she descended the museum steps. *I'll stop in and see how Oma's doing.* She was heading in the direction of her grandmother's apartment when she suddenly changed her mind. *If she's napping, I don't want to wake her, so I'll call Henri instead. If he's available, he might be able to answer questions I didn't want to waste time asking while we listened to Oma tell her story.*

She scrolled to Henri's cell number on her contact list and pushed talk. "Are you home?" she asked without saying hello.

"I'm heading that way."

"Have you eaten?"

"I had brunch with friends, but if you want to talk, I could have coffee and dessert. There aren't many sweets around the apartment anymore. Suddenly Renee thinks all of us should be eating healthy foods."

"My fault. To atone, I'll treat."

"Sounds good to me. Where shall we meet?"

"How about Caffe Grazie at 26 E 84th Street?"

"Perfect. They make the best cannolis in town. On the way, I'll stop by the apartment and pick up a folder with information I've gathered to date. Hopefully what I've found will help when you get to Paris. I'll see you in about fifteen minutes. If you get there first, go ahead and order lunch."

"And your cannolis?"

"No."

"After that buildup, you aren't having cannolis?"

"Maybe not. I plan to order whatever's highest in calories and since you're treating, the most expensive dessert on the menu."

"I'm sure," Anne chuckled. "See you soon."

Anne arrived at the restaurant first. After studying the menu, she ordered Panini di Parma, a grilled sandwich with prosciutto, mozzarella, tomato and black olive tapenade, and a glass of Pinot Grigio. She had barely taken a sip of wine when Henri arrived. He put the folder on the table, bent down, kissed her on the cheek and, sitting down, said, "This is an unexpected surprise, but a pleasant one."

Before Anne could respond, the waiter arrived. Grinning, Henri ordered Zeppole Rolled in Cinnamon and Brown Sugar and two dipping sauces.

"You *are* indulging," Anne teased. "And all because I'm paying."

"That's right, and you're sworn to secrecy. You can't tell Renee or your grandmother about my sinful extravagance."

"Your secret's safe with me."

"Good. Now what do you want to know? I came prepared."

"I need ideas. Where do I *begin* to look for Elisabeth's art? Last night I emailed the three curators I'll be seeing on behalf of the Met. I'm hoping they can provide direction. I'd also like to meet with someone who knew Rose Valland—that is if anyone's still alive who was privy to what she was doing for the cause. And, hopefully, interview relatives of Jews who've recovered at least a portion of the art the Nazis stole from their families."

"I think I can help, at least with regard to Rose. When we first returned to Paris after the Liberation, Renee and I met with several resistance fighters who fought with our fathers. Most have since died, but over the years we became friendly with their children. About ten years ago at one of our get-togethers, we met Gregoire Drouin—"

"Who is?"

"I'm getting to that. When Gregoire was very young, he worked for Rose at the Jeu de Paume. His job was to help catalogue the art the Nazis seized from museums and private collections." Henri opened the folder and handed Anne a small piece of paper. "I don't know if he's still alive but here's his last-known address. He would be an excellent source."

"Thanks. I'll try to contact him when I get to Paris."

"I have several more people you should speak with, but before I give you their names, I'd like to tell you why I can't be more helpful."

"You're going to explain how the French Resistance operated."

"I am, if that's okay."

"It's one of the reasons I called. So talk to me."

"Okay, but stop me if you have questions. As soon as Germany and France signed the armistice, partisan factions began to crop up, primarily in the occupied zone. The groups functioned as separate units with one common goal, to undermine the hated Nazis. It wasn't until late in the Occupation that they became collectively known as *La Résistance française*—the French Resistance."

"So we're not referring to one large coordinated effort."

"Quite the opposite. Early on in the movement, it was easy for Gestapo and Abwher agents to infiltrate fledgling resistance cells. To keep this from continuing and to be sure one unit did not interfere with the actions of another, the various factions had to find a way to communicate with one another. To that end, they established a complex communication network. Underground newspapers began to publish articles, drawings, and poems to relay encrypted messages about sabotage activities."

Henri waited while the waiter served Anne's meal and his dessert. Grinning, he took several bites and then began again. "There was no general membership list, so resistance fighters relied on these cryptograms for information and instructions. Each man or woman in a unit was identified by a code name. Anton became Andre, meaning man or warrior. Auguste was Dillon, one who's faithful, and Jules chose Alexandre, protector of men."

"Clever."

"It was, but perhaps the wisest precaution was the implementation of a pyramid structure command. That meant a member of one unit never knew anything pertinent about his allies in another group. The various factions would occasionally work together, but, even then, the fighters remained virtually anonymous."

"So if captured they couldn't provide significant information."

"Exactly. One of the tasks assigned to these small groups was to assassinate German officers. Papa told me about one such attack. He served as a decoy while Auguste shot a Nazi colonel at close range. Immediately after the execution, Bertrand took the gun and casually walked away from the scene. You see, no member of the Resistance ever carried his own arms. Whatever was used in the attack was quickly taken to a central stockpile by a courier, often a child—in this instance, Bertrand. Auguste and Anton remained in the area until the authorities arrived. They were both searched, but because neither was carrying a weapon, they were cleared of suspicion."

"Even without a coordinated effort from the top, it sounds like resistance actions were well planned."

"They were, and besides daily overt operations, they established an Underground Railroad. It was originally intended to move downed allied airman back to the front lines, but as the attacks on Jews intensified, they also began to smuggle those who sought passage to Britain, Spain, or elsewhere."

"The Underground Railroad was your means of escape."

"Yes. Thankfully, by July 1942 the system was in place and functioning well. After Elisabeth sold her paintings to purchase our freedom, my father and Auguste Lessard made the initial arrangements for the escape. Once we parted, he and I had no further contact. He didn't know who we'd be meeting after we left Île St-Louis or where we'd be taken."

"Did he know you made it to the States?"

"I'm told he did, though we never spoke after our last goodbye on July 18."

"How difficult for both of you. I can't imagine."

"It was hell for me, and I'm sure for him. Your grandmother and Renee will tell you about our actual escape. I only have a few more things to add to what I've already said."

"Fine, but not before you eat some of your sinful dessert."

"I was concentrating so hard on what I wanted you to know, I nearly forgot. Mmmm," he said after several bites."

"If only Renee could see you now."

"I'm glad she can't, and you promised—"

"I know. Mum's the word. So, finish telling me about the Resistance."

"There's not too much more to say—I mean generally. If you want specifics I could talk for hours. Over the course of the war, brave men, women, and children accomplished sometimes minor but always important victories against the Nazis. They tracked and exposed French collaborators, assassinated a few ranking Nazi officials, and destroyed German trains, convoys, and ships. Men like my father, Auguste, and Jules provided Allied forces with invaluable information, and many paid the ultimate price for their valor. But back to the reason for our meeting. In addition to speaking with Madame Bouffard, I want you to visit Bertrand Lessard."

"Auguste's son."

"Right. Auguste was killed during the final campaign to drive the Nazis from Paris. In 1946, the second time Renee and I returned to Paris after the Liberation, the two of us and Bertrand held a memorial service for our fathers at Église St-Louis en L'Île. While we made plans, Bertrand and I became friends. We've kept in touch over the years, first by letter, and, in the past six months or so, via email. It's surprising how, as we grow older, an eight or nine year age difference becomes insignificant. Bertrand and I wouldn't have been close in 1942, but now we are. Over the years, talking with him about our fathers and their acts of bravery has given me great comfort."

"Have you asked Bertrand if he'll see me?"

"I thought I'd let his grandson make the arrangements. Renee and I met Arnaud Lessard when we flew to Paris for his father Gerard's funeral. Shortly after we returned to New York, Arnaud moved back to the Île from his apartment in the Elysee to help Bertrand complete an extensive renovation project. During the next two years, they turned the mansion into eight apartments—one on the top floor, one on the floor below, and two on each of the first three floors. When the work was finished, Arnaud and his new bride Aimee move onto the fourth-floor, and Bertrand settled upstairs."

"And everyone lived happily ever after."

"Not quite. About six months later, Aimee was promoted. She was, and I believe still is, an investment banker for Credit Suisse. Anyway, she and Arnaud moved to New York. Over the next year, Renee and I met them for dinner, I'd say two or three times. Shortly after our last outing, Arnaud returned to Paris. I didn't hear from him again until six months ago when he sent me an email with Bertrand's new address. Bertrand is mentally sharp, but he requires care Arnaud can't provide. He now lives in a fancy assisted living facility."

"What does Arnaud do for a living?"

"He owns a small company that raises funds for several prominent international charities. Bertrand invested his father's fortune wisely, and Gerard followed in his father's footsteps. Arnaud's inheritance, as well as what he garnered from the sale of the apartments, allows him to dabble in the financial market. He doesn't really work. I mean he doesn't have a nine-to-five job. I guess in that way he reminds me of you."

"Because I don't work? Gee thanks, Henri."

"That's not what I mean. Arnaud's a fine young man who does a lot of good, as you'll soon discover for yourself. Yesterday I sent him an email explaining what's happening and telling him you'll be in Paris for the next couple of weeks. He will introduce you to Bertrand, who may be able to provide additional leads. Unless you have another scheduled appointment, you'll meet Arnaud on Sunday noon at Le Tastevin, a small restaurant on rue Saint-Louis-en-l'Île. I suggested you eat at my favorite place, Brasserie de l'Île Saint Louis, but Arnaud thinks the food is a little heavy for lunch. How would I know a lady wouldn't enjoy pork knuckles and sauerkraut?"

"Even at your age you have a lot to learn," Anne joked. "So tell me. Will Arnaud be wearing a carnation so I can pick him out of the crowd?"

"Better than that. He emailed a couple of recent pictures." Henri removed two photos from his folder and handed them to Anne. "As you see, one is a close up of his face. In the other, he's standing alongside the Seine."

God, what a hunk, Anne mused as she studied a man who was tall and obviously athletic with broad shoulders, muscular arms, and a thick, strong neck. Though immaculately groomed, there was a wild air about him, possibly, she thought, because his light brown, unkempt hair, even in a still photograph, seemed to be blowing in the wind. He had deep green eyes, a sensuous mouth, and an olive complexion, but it was his smile that formed sexy dimples in his cheeks that quickly caught her eye.

"You mentioned Arnaud's wife Aimee—"

"Aimee's out of the picture, no pun intended. She and Arnaud divorced a year ago. She wanted to remain in New York—"

"And he preferred to live in Paris."

"That's what he said, though I'm sure there's more to the story."

Silly Aimee, Anne thought as she put the pictures in her purse.

⌒〇

Though Anne objected, Henri insisted on paying the bill. He walked her to the street and hailed a cab. "Thanks for lunch, the lesson on the Resistance, and the leads," she said as the driver stopped by the curb. "Because of you, I have someplace to start."

"Glad to be of help. I'll look through my papers and speak with Renee and Veronique."

"If you think of anything else, you can tell me Wednesday."

It was after three when Anne entered her apartment. *I wish I didn't have to go out this evening,* she thought as she checked her voicemail.

"Where the hell are you?" Meg began. "Ian has a bug, and Brian can't cancel his meeting. What kind of mother would I be if I left Ian here with his nanny? Call me."

Anne pressed redial. After apologizing for not being available earlier, she spent the next twenty minutes relating Veronique's story. "Considering what you just told me, I'll forgive you for being such a recluse," Meg said.

"Good to know. I have international access on my phone, and, of course, I'll have my computer, so keep in touch.

"You do the same. I wish I were going with you. We'd have a ball. Maybe someday I'll see Paris. Safe travel, my friend."

Anne hung up, went to her room, undressed, and put on sweats. She turned on the news and plopped down on the bed to watch.

CHAPTER 8

"Oh Lord," Anne moaned when she woke her from an unintended nap. She splashed water on her face, went to the kitchen, downed a bottle of water, and took another to her office to check her emails.

She had just sat down when her phone rang. She checked her caller ID and pushed talk. "Hi, Renee," she said tentatively. "How are things on your side of the park?"

"Wonderful, honey. That's why I'm calling. I thought you could use a laugh. Your grandmother just asked me to make a pot of *decaf* tea."

"No!"

"She did, and then she ordered—and I *do* mean ordered—me to bring her computer upstairs and then call the Best Buy Geek Squad to come check it out."

"Did she turn on the computer to see if it's working before scheduling a service call?"

"Of course not, that's what's so amusing. 'The call,' she insisted, 'is purely precautionary. I don't want my computer to crash while I'm doing my research.'"

"She used the word crash?"

"She did. Special Agent Q, I think that's his name, is bringing an external storage drive, so, no matter what happens, she'll still have her documents."

"Actually, that's not a bad idea. I asked her to help me with a little online research while I'm doing the footwork in Paris. Maybe having something meaningful to do has prompted this miraculous transformation."

"I'm sure that's part of it, but I also think sharing her experiences during the Occupation has helped. For the first time, she *knows* what happened to her mother. I mean she already knew, but she had to say the words. Now she can move on. I tell you, Anne, she's a different woman."

"So quickly? Is that possible?"

"Apparently so. Every time she opens up, her revelation prompts her to further admissions and greater understanding."

"Thanks for the good news."

"You're welcome, and by the way, Henri enjoyed your lunch-time visit and, yes, he confessed. I know all about his sinful indulgence."

"I hope you didn't give him too much trouble."

"Of course I did. I'm his wife. It's my job. I promised Paul would bake a few sugar-filled pastries from time to time. I don't want my man cheating on me with a gorgeous woman who lets him indulge in scrumptious sweets."

"Renee—"

"Teasing, honey. Since Henri came home, he's been sending emails and going through his personal papers. He hopes to have several more leads before Wednesday."

"Will you tell him how much I appreciate his help?"

"Seeing Veronique doing well is thanks enough for both of us. I forgot to say that Henri emailed your picture to Arnaud Lessard. Surprise! Surprise! He responded within minutes and can't wait to meet you, but then why wouldn't he want to have lunch with a beautiful single woman?"

"Arnaud and I are meeting to discuss business, Renee. If you mean what I think you do, be clear, I don't need a man to complicate my life—especially one who's on the rebound. I don't do rebounds."

"Not even to have those children who will eventually inherit Elisabeth's home?"

Anne laughed. "Especially for that. I'll call after lunch so you can tell me about Mother's visit. You can be my spy. I doubt I'll hear a truthful account from her or Oma. I also want to know if Special Agent Q got out alive. I don't envy the man."

"Nor do I," said Renee. "Nor do I."

Despite her lengthy nap, Anne slept soundly for eight hours. She got up before the alarm, showered, dressed, and after giving her cleaning lady last minute instructions and paying her in advance for the next two weeks, caught a cab to the Met. An hour later, she left the museum bookstore with two books.

Nazi Plunder: Great Treasure Stories of World War II
The Lost Museum: the Nazi Conspiracy to Steal the World's Greatest Works of Art

This should make for great late-night reading, she thought as she hailed a cab. "Barnes and Noble on Broadway and 82nd," she told the driver.

There she purchased two more books.

An American Heroine in the French Resistance—The Diary and Memoir of Virginia d'Albert-Lake Nazi Paris—The History of an Occupation, 1940-1944

By the time she got back to her apartment, it was after noon. With less than half an hour to get ready, she went upstairs, tossed her packages on the guest room bed, and changed for lunch. At one on the dot, she walked into the larger of the two Carlyle Restaurants, pointed to her mother, who was already sitting in a plush, chintz-covered banquette, and followed the maître d' to the table.

Madeline rose to greet her daughter. "It's good to see you, darling," she gushed. "I wish you'd come to the Hamptons more often."

"Now that the weather's better, I probably will." Anne said, knowing that would never happen. "Have you ordered?"

"Only a Pomegranate Tanqueray Martini. Will you join me?"

"No thanks." Anne settled into the comfortable seat. "You look beautiful, Mother," she said. "Living in the country agrees with you. How was your visit with Oma?"

"Short. She told me she was tired, but I think she wanted to get rid of me. Do you know she has a computer? I saw it on the desk in her room. I gave her my email address and told her I was on Facebook."

"You're on Facebook?"

"I am. Would you friend me?"

"I don't do Facebook, but I'll email you from Paris."

"I'll try to find time to reply, but before we move on to other subjects, back to Mother. She looks better than when I saw her two weeks ago. She's complaining about her new diet, so she can't be that sick."

"She's better, but she still has a ways to go. I'll see her once more before I leave for Paris on Thursday."

"You're going on Met business?"

Oma didn't tell her after all, Anne mulled. "I am," she said. "I'll be negotiating with the curators of several museums for paintings we hope to include in the Christmas Impressionist Exhibition."

"And these negotiations will take two weeks? Mother says that's how long you plan to be away."

"Probably not, but I thought I'd combine business with a little pleasure. Paris is beautiful in April."

"So I'm told. If I'm lucky, maybe someday I'll see for myself."

"You've been to Paris."

"Several times, but never during the spring."

All talk of Veronique and Paris was quickly over. As soon as the waiter left to place their order, Madeline launched into a monologue that lasted throughout the meal. When they finished their last sip of coffee, Anne realized why she didn't meet her mother more often. She had rattled on about her life in the Hamptons, how she was remodeling the four-season garden room, how she had made a grand slam as well as a baby slam during the last bridge tournament at the club, and how she attended a party at the Kinslow mansion. She leaned in conspiratorially when she reported the affair her yoga instructor was having with a married man, a member of the club.

Anne spent much of the lunch tuning her mother out—that was until Madeline dropped a bombshell. "There's a new man in my life," she said excitedly. "His name is Michael Kelly. He's a retired stock broker who lives on the north shore of Long Island. I met him at the club. His wife died—did I mention he's a widower?"

"No, but then you just told me about him."

"As I was saying, his wife died eighteen months ago. It seems he's *finally* ready to rejoin the social scene. He's a hunk, as you young people say. He has a full head of gray hair, no bald spots anywhere, and he's tall and lean. He's an avid tennis player, so, in case we *really* hit it off, I've signed up for tennis lessons with the club pro."

Of course you have, Anne mused. "Have you seen Michael since you were introduced?" she asked.

"When you called Sunday night, we were about to leave for dinner, but I haven't slept with him yet."

"Whoa," Anne said. "That's definitely more than a daughter needs to know about her mother's activities. Feel free to keep those aspects of your relationship private."

"And I thought sex is something you young people talk about all the time."

"I don't know where you got that idea. You're seeing Michael again?"

"He's coming for the weekend. On Saturday, I'm having a small party to introduce him to some of my friends. Sunday evening we're going out alone."

"Maybe you can play tennis Sunday afternoon. How many lessons will you have had by then?"

"I doubt we'll do that," Madeline said, Anne's sarcasm going over her head. "But I'm sure he'll be impressed. I'll show him the indoor courts."

"Why stop there? Give him a tour of the outdoor courts too."

"Anne."

"Sorry, Mother. You know I want you to be happy. Email me and let me know how the weekend went, but be careful. You don't want Michael to think you're too eager. If you believe he's a good catch, there must be dozens of other women pursuing him. You may want to play hard to get."

"I've thought of that. You know, this is fun. It's been years since I've dated."

Me too, Anne reflected. She said, "I'm glad you're enjoying yourself."

Anne waved as Madeline's chauffeur pulled the Mercedes into traffic. *Couldn't Mother have gone out of her way even a few blocks to drop me at home?* Shaking her head, she hailed a cab.

Back in her apartment, she kicked off her shoes, went to her office, and checked her emails. *I guess my hotel's all set,* she thought as she read a message confirming her reservation. Next, she pushed the blinking red button on her answering machine and listened to her grandmother excitedly say, "I'm finally beginning my research. Renee told you about Special Agent Q. When he left he gave me his private number. I'm to call if I have a problem."

Poor Agent Q, Anne thought. *He doesn't know what he's getting into.* Thrilled that her grandmother sounded so much better, she erased the message.

CHAPTER 9

When Anne woke the next morning, the DVR was still asking if she wanted to delete the program she was watching when she fell asleep. She punched yes on the remote and pulled the pillow over her head.

Ten minutes later she got up, put on a robe, went to the kitchen, made a cup of coffee, and popped a piece of wheat bread in the toaster.

"Who woulda thunk?" she whispered as she carried her coffee and toast to the island and sat on one of the stools. *Less than a week ago, all I could think about was what paintings to select for the Christmas exhibition. Before long I'll be drinking my coffee and eating a croissant while I watch the Seine wind its way like a snake through Paris.*

She finished her toast, put the cup in the dishwasher, and with a second cup of coffee in hand, went to her office to type her list of to-dos and people to contact. Fifteen minutes later, with nothing else that required her immediate attention, she showered, dressed, and called her grandmother. "Mind if I come over a little early?" she asked when Veronique answered.

"Come right away," Veronique said, her voice filled with eager anticipation. "I want you to see my storage drive."

"I can't wait," Anne said, stifling a laugh. "I'm leaving shortly. Need anything?"

"I don't think so. Renee sent Paul to the store for groceries. I have no idea what he'll serve for lunch, but I'm sure we won't have éclairs for dessert."

"Are you're disappointed?"

"Not at all. Weren't you listening when Doctor Richmond insisted I cut back on sweets? I think he was surprised when he dropped in earlier this morning. He probably thought he'd be attending my funeral next week. Now, unless I need him sooner, he won't be back until next Monday."

"Good. I'm bringing the list of website. It's a big job—"

"One I can handle. Henri and Renee are joining us for lunch. When you get here, come on up. I've created an office in my bedroom sitting area. In fact I was working when you called. Renee's looking over my shoulder."

"Tell her hello, and I'll see her soon."

⟳

What a difference a few days can make, Anne thought as she entered her grandmother's bedroom. Dressed in slacks, a pink silk blouse, and a dark-rose cashmere cardigan, Veronique sat at the desk with Renee beside her, their heads together in deep conversation. When she looked up, Veronique no longer appeared wan and frail—her eyes were bright. "Come in, darling," she said, smiling. "I'm eager to hear the details of my new assignment."

"Hi, Honey," said Renee. "As you see, we've been busy."

"And you'll soon be busier."

Veronique took the file Anne extended in her direction and thumbed through the papers. "Oh my," she said, sighing deeply.

"Too much?"

"Not for your number one researcher. Look at my storage drive. Agent Q showed me how to create folders and backup my documents. So far I have files for Missing Art, Recovered Art, Göring's Private Collection, and Art stolen from Parisian Jews during the Occupation."

"You're definitely organized."

"I am." Veronique beamed with pride. "Who knows, maybe I can teach you a thing or two."

Before Anne could respond, Veronique turned to Renee, and asked. "If Henri's not too busy, would you ask him to come up? Why wait until after lunch to tell Anne about our escape."

"When I last saw my dear husband, he was doing the *New York Times* crossword puzzle. I'll go down, make a pot of tea, and bring him back with me. He can carry the tray."

After Renee closed the door, Veronique motioned to the couch and said, "Please sit beside me, darling. There's something I want you to see."

When Anne was seated, her grandmother opened a tattered obviously-old envelope, removed a ragged piece of yellow cloth, and with a distant look in her eyes and angst in her voice, handed it to Anne. "This," she said, "was *my* badge of shame. It was my declaration to the world that I was a member of what Hitler and his followers termed a subhuman race. The Nazis compelled all Parisian Jews to prominently display the Star of David on their outer clothing when they left home."

"Did you comply with the order?"

"When I was out with Mother, but not with Renee and Henri. I couldn't put them in jeopardy for associating with a Jew."

A knock on the door kept Anne from commenting. Without waiting for a response, Renee entered, followed closely by Henri, who carried a tray holding a pot of tea and four cups. "Hi, honey," he said to Anne as he crossed the room and placed the tray on the table.

"I gave Anne the Star of David I wore during the Occupation," Veronique announced before Anne could reply to Henri's greeting.

"You kept it?" Renee said, as Anne held up the ragged cloth for all to see.

"I must have put it in pocket my when I left for your house on the seventeenth and found it when I was given a change of clothes in England. For some inexplicable reason, though I was definitely tempted, I didn't throw it away."

"If we're doing show and tell, I also have something to show," Henri said. While Renee poured tea, he sat on the couch, opened the string on a large envelope, and gave Anne a packet of pictures. "I took these during the height of the Occupation. You can see similar photos online, but I thought you might like to see the real thing."

While Henri looked over her shoulder, Anne began to thumb through the stack. "That's a photograph of German soldiers marching on the Champs-Élysées from the Arc d Triomphe," he explained.

"Look at this, Oma." Anne pointed to the horse-drawn carriages in front of the Chamber of Deputies. "I'm struck by the number of bicycles on the street. The German tanks under the Arc d Triomphe are surrounded by bicycles."

"That's how most Parisians got around," Veronique said. "Until things got really bad for the Jews, I rode across Pont de la Tournelle to meet Renee nearly every day."

While she sipped her tea, Anne studied a photograph of two women, one on either side of a heavy-set Nazi officer. "Are these Frenchwomen?" she asked.

"They are," Henri said.

"When you read my journal, you'll learn how Frenchwomen interacted—for wont of a better word—with the Nazi officers," said Veronique. "Their behavior was disgusting."

"You reread your journal?"

"Every word."

"And you're okay?"

"Surprisingly, I'm good. I'm eager to hear your thoughts after you read what I wrote."

"I'll read on the plane and send you an email when I get to the hotel."

Anne continued to look through the pictures—some showing strange-looking bicycles pulling passengers in small cabs; others depicting blood-red Nazi flags hanging from the Louvre and other important buildings. One showed a group of Nazi officers standing beneath the Eiffel Tower. In all the shots there were hordes of horse-drawn carriages that seemed out of place in the modern world of the late 1930s.

"These are amazing photographs," Anne said, handing the stack back to Henri.

Henri shook his head. "You keep them."

"Are you sure you don't mind?"

"I don't need pictures to remember what Paris was like back then." He turned to Veronique and said, "I have another photograph—one you haven't seen. It's of you and Elisabeth walking on the Île de la Cité."

"You really have a snapshot of Mother and me? You never said—"

"Because I didn't think you'd want to remember your mother this way."

Veronique took the picture from Henri and looked closely at the figures. "Oh my. . ." she said, her voice trailing off.

"May I," Anne asked.

Veronique passed the photograph to her granddaughter. Anne looked closely at the women in the square in front of Notre Dame. The older of the two was tall and slim with slightly graying hair. She wore a black skirt that touched her ankles, a matching black jacket, and a black hat. But what quickly caught Anne's eye was the yellow Star of David conspicuously displayed on her breast. "Oh, Oma!" she exclaimed. "How humiliating!"

Veronique remained silent—contemplating. Then she tentatively reached out and took the picture from Anne. While she looked, the others waited, allowing her to come to terms with what she was seeing. Minutes later she sighed and went on wistfully. "I was pretty back then, don't you think?"

"You certainly were, Oma, and you still are. Do you remember the day this picture was taken?"

"Like it was yesterday. It was my birthday. Mother rarely went out, but I talked her into accompanying me to the continent on my special day. Henri and Renee joined us for brunch at the house and then, despite Mother's reluctance, we set off. I recall the day was warm and sunny." Veronique looked at the picture again. "My bag is haute couture, and my suit is too, though I can't recall the designer."

"They're both stunning," Anne said. "You look so much like your mother."

"Thank you, darling. I always thought Mother was a handsome woman."

"Would you like to keep the picture, Veronique?" Henri asked.

"Thank you, my friend. I want Anne to have it."

"I have an idea," Anne said. "I'll scan the picture into the computer and return the original. You can keep it in your safe, or have Henri put it in your safe-deposit box at the bank."

"Maybe I should buy a scanner."

"Actually that's not a bad idea, but why don't you wait till I'm home? We'll shop together."

"I'll try to delay, darling, though, as you know, I'm not a patient person. If I need a scanner before you get back, I'll call Special Agent Q. I'm sure he'll over with the model I need."

"No doubt," Anne said, silently communicating a can-you-believe-this message to Renee.

"Shall I begin the story of our escape while we're waiting to eat?" Henri asked.

"Let's wait," said Veronique. "I don't want to start and have to stop. In the meantime, Anne, tell us about your upcoming exhibition.

Anne had just finished detailing the initial plans for the exhibit when Paul called up to say lunch was waiting in the breakfast room. Henri held Veronique's arm as they took the elevator to the first floor.

During the meal there was no talk of Paris, the Nazis, or art. Unusually quiet, from time to time Veronique fidgeted nervously, crumpling her handkerchief in her lap and sighing deeply. Anne knew her grandmother wasn't thinking about the minestrone soup or the antipasti salad Paul had prepared—she was concentrating on the conversation to come.

"Shall I serve coffee?" Paul asked as Laura cleared the table.

"That would be nice. Thank you," Veronique said. "But upstairs please."

Fifteen minutes later when were settled around the table in Veronique's sitting room, looking apprehensive, she began. "Anne, before you arrived, Renee and I decided to let Henri do most of the talking. We'll add details from time to time." She turned to Henri. "Are you ready, my friend?"

"I am." Henri turned to Anne. "Following your grandmother's lead, I'll begin by providing what I believe is information essential to your understanding. Though there aren't accurate statistics as to the number of downed pilots smuggled out of France during the Occupation, I recently learned that most of the officers who were shot down were escorted across the French border into Spain. That was the preliminary plan in our regard, but, suddenly, the decision was made to take us to England."

"Do you know why the strategy changed?"

"We were never told. In later years, Renee and I came up with three possibilities. First, mileage-wise, the new route was a shorter distance to travel. Second, to insure our safe getaway, Elisabeth may have paid a larger sum of money than the average escapee. And, finally, we were traveling with an American hero who was fighting for the British. The true answer could have been any of those or something entirely different. We'll never know, but at the time, we *did* know to obey orders without question."

"And we were fortunate," Renee said. "We later learned that many escapees were forced to make their way to the border alone. We had at least two guides with us at all times."

"Two guides for three of you?"

"There were seven of us making the escape," Henri explained. "A Jewish family, Levi and Miriam Begin, had purchased counterfeit papers for themselves and their two children."

"Before you continue, I'd like to tell you why I think our destination changed," Renee said. "I've always believed the sudden decision to take us to England rather than to Spain was thanks to your grandfather. He was a highly-decorated airman. His capture would have become instant fodder for Goebbels and the Nazi propaganda machine. I seriously doubt the British government wanted images of his arrest on newsreels around the world."

"I knew Grandfather Robert was a pilot in the Army Air Corps, but I didn't know he flew for the RAF."

"He did," said Veronique. "When I realize how little you knew about my beloved Robert, I feel both guilt and sadness. For all these years, I've refused to hear talk about the war. Because I was so self-absorbed, your grandfather never shared stories about his heroism. You've missed out on so much, Anne. You only knew the man Robert became, not the hero he once was."

"We agreed to move forward," Anne softly scolded. "We can't change what happened in the past, but what you say now will help me understand events that shaped your life and made you the incredible woman I love so much."

"Thank you, darling, but I should—"

"No shoulds," Henri insisted. "We're moving on."

"Henri, you were saying that you and the Begins were taken to Britain," Anne said.

"We escaped occupied France with the Begins, but then we parted ways. I overheard the guides say the family was being taken to Spain."

"Why not to England with you?"

"I don't know, and I'm not sure our guides knew either. If they had, I doubt they would have given us a reason."

"That's what you meant when you told me that partners in one resistance unit were kept in the dark about the activities of the other teams."

"Correct. At each of our stops, we were dropped off by one set of guides and picked up by two new men. The old and new guides never interacted. Beyond exchanging cursory greetings, I never saw them speak, and names were *never* used."

"I would like to tell Anne about the first part of our escape," Veronique said. "We agreed you'd do most of the talking, Henri, but—"

"The floor's all yours, Veronique."

"Thank you, my friend. Anne, when Henri, Renee, and I began our journey, we had no idea who we'd be meeting or where we were going. We only knew we had to be at our first stop at four o'clock. I was distraught. It had been less than twenty four hours since the Nazis arrested Mother."

"Poor Henri was dealing with two hysterical women," Renee said. "I was leaving my mother and father, and I didn't know if I'd see them again."

"I'd say I was both sad and defiant," said Henri. "I loved Renee, but I wanted her to go with Veronique while I stayed behind to fight for the Resistance."

"Anton still refused to let you participate."

"He practically forced me out the door, telling me—as he had so many times before—that it was *vital* I live for the sake of the family. I couldn't understand what he meant. Mother was dead, and Renee was leaving with me. I'm sure he knew he and I would never meet again, but he was unwavering. At the last minute, I broke down, but he never did. Maybe he thought if he showed weakness, I would defy him and stay behind."

"Was Grandfather Robert already at the Hotel du Jeu de Paume when you arrived?"

"He was," Veronique answered. "Though we didn't meet right away. We were escorted to a room where Henri and Renee were given dark clothes. I had on black slacks and a dark gray blouse, so I didn't have to change."

"What happened next?"

"We were moved to a windowless room in the basement."

"Where you first saw Grandfather Robert and instantly fell in love."

"I'm not sure I was in *love*, but I was certainly impressed. Robert was the epitome of a Greek god. He was tall and blond with piercing blue eyes. And that smile. In the days and weeks ahead, he swept me off my feet."

"How incredibly romantic," Anne said, noting her grandmother's joy when she talked about her one great love. "What about the Begins? Were they already at the hotel?"

"They came in a few minutes later with two guides, who then escorted all of us to the Hotel Lambert."

"Then you didn't leave Île St-Louis from the Hotel du Jeu de Paume? I assumed that's why you wanted me to stay there instead of the George V."

"We began the actual escape at the Lambert, a *hôtel particulier* on Quai Anjou near the eastern tip of the Île."

"Another hotel?"

"Not in the way you're thinking. A *hôtel particulier* is a large mansion, not a guest hotel."

"The Lambert was our actual jump-off point," Henri said.

"Oma, it must have been difficult to be back on the Île yet again."

"It was dreadful. At times it was impossible for me to fathom what was happening. So many conflicting emotions raced through my mind. One minute I feared the Nazis would find me and drag me away like they had Mother. The next minute I was furious that an innocent woman was suffering just because she was a Jew. Several times I was overwhelmed with sadness and struggling to find a way to go on. More than once I thought about leaving the Lambert and going home. I didn't care what happened to me. I wanted to be in Mother's house. Even more, I wanted her to come home to me like she had so long ago after her grand tour."

"I can't imagine—"

"No one who hasn't lived through such a dreadful time could, Anne. It's not easy for me to *think* about those days—much less talk about them. Though I remain resolute." She turned to Henri and said anxiously, "I'm afraid I need yet another moment, my friend. Would you go on with the story?"

Henri gave Veronique an understanding nod and said, "When we left the Lambert, we were told we would be going to a safe where we would receive new papers. We couldn't risk crossing the pont in a car, so we walked, which was particularly difficult for the Begins. They were shepherding two children, ages three and five. Levi carried Sarah. I recall that he and Miriam continually admonished her and her older brother Micha to be quiet. The few times we were forced to duck behind a building to avoid a Nazi or French patrol, we all feared that one of the children would scream and reveal our hiding place.

"But that didn't happen—"

"Thankfully no. It was a particularly dark night, so perhaps that helped. Though in some ways, it was a hindrance. There was no moon to light the way—"

"And with the blackout in full effect, the City of Light was both literally and symbolically dark," Veronique said, closing her eyes as if recreating the blackness of the scene.

"Where was the safe house?" Anne asked.

"I have no idea, "Henri answered. "I thought we were in the far reaches of the Marais, but I couldn't be sure. The streets were eerily silent. There were no familiar smells of meals being prepared or people walking on the streets to let us know where we were."

"The stillness in what was once a bustling part of the city was unsettling," Veronique said. "If there were any Jews left in the area, they were probably in hiding."

"I'm sure they were," Henri said. "We had a few close calls—times when we had to round a corner or hide in an alleyway—but we finally arrived at our next destination. We were photographed and issued identity papers complete with rubber stamps and official signatures." He reached into the envelope. "These were mine and Renee's. I thought you'd like to see them."

Anne examined the documents. "They look so authentic," she said, returning the papers to Henri. "How long did you remain at the first house?"

"Long enough to freshen up and have a little something to eat—I would say about thirty minutes. We were then turned over to two different guides and packed into separate cars. I sat up front with the driver. Veronique, Renee, and Robert sat in back. The Begins were traveling in the car behind, though several times when I looked around to see if they were following, they were nowhere to be seen. I assumed they were taking a different route to avoid the Nazi patrols. Two cars traveling in tandem might have aroused suspicion."

"If there were so few private cars out at night, wasn't it dangerous for even one car to be on the road?" Anne asked.

"It was, and not only because of the Nazis. We were driving without benefit of headlights, and, as Veronique pointed out, there was no moon."

"And there was very little light coming from the few streetlights that remained lit," Renee added.

"I was terrified," said Veronique. "Occasionally our driver missed a turn, and we ended up on the sidewalk."

"Every aspect of the escape was perilous," Henri said. "It was ten o'clock, so we had two hours before the curfew would be enforced. Several times the driver had to pull to the side of the road, and we had to duck down as a military truck passed by. We held our collective breaths until we were sure the Nazis weren't stopping to search a seemingly-abandoned car parked on the side of the road."

"I'm sure our driver breathed a sigh of relief once we finally left the city proper," Renee said.

"So did I," said Veronique.

"We finally reached the less-patrolled outskirts of town," Henri continued, "But, though there were fewer cars on the road and less chance a Nazi patrol would be out that far, we kept to the back roads. Eventually we came to an isolated farmhouse. We drove through an open barn door that immediately closed behind us. We had no idea where we were. The second time Renee and I returned to Paris after the Liberation, we rented a car and tried to locate the farm. We wanted to thank the people who had risked their lives to save ours, but after driving for hours, we realized we hadn't been taken directly to our next destination. The guides probably circled back to take a less direct route."

"And we were traveling very slowly," Renee said.

"The Underground had made arrangements with a French driver to take us from the farmhouse to Tours in the Loire Valley between Orléans and the Atlantic coast," Henri said.

"Why Tours?"

"Because the town was near the border between occupied and Vichy France. We left at one a.m. on the nineteenth and arrived at a farm on the outskirts of Tours around two. The farmer who owned the house invited us to gather around a wooden kitchen table."

"Was the farmer a member of the Resistance?"

"We *assumed* he was," Henri answered. "But we *knew* he was risking his life to help us escape. He definitely knew the guards' schedules. After we ate, he told us to get some sleep. We all thought we were staying the night, but at four we were awakened and told we had fifteen minutes to use the toilette because we had to cross the Line of Demarcation before dawn."

"How far was the farm from the line?"

"We don't know," said Renee. "We walked, and walked, and then walked some more. I don't know how the Begins managed, but somehow they did. Despite the arduous crossing, they remained determined to continue, probably because they knew what would happen to their family if they were caught."

"And to me," Veronique added.

"To all of us. In any case, just when I thought I couldn't take another step, we came to a road. I was terrified when I saw German soldiers marching back and forth, back and forth, patrolling the line."

"I doubted any of us had a chance to cross safely," said Veronique. "I was beginning to think we would have to turn around when, suddenly, we saw a momentary flash of light. Almost as one, the guards wheeled around, walked swiftly to the right, and rounded a bend in the road."

"That's strange."

"At the time I thought so," Henri said. "But I later I realized that was part of the plan. Though our suspicions were never officially confirmed, we figured they'd been given money to look the other way. The flash of light was the signal we were in place and ready to cross. We scrambled down an embankment—"

"I was petrified," Veronique said, her hands trembling as she continued. "We were out in the open with nothing to shield us if the Nazis came back. I feared we were caught in a trap—that someone had paid the guards even more money to arrest us once we were vulnerable."

"Thankfully the money from the sale of Elisabeth's paintings, the Begins' contribution, and, we think, a little extra cash from the British government to rescue your grandfather ensured the guards would keep their distance," Henri said. "The guides pointed the way and—"

"They didn't cross with you?"

"No. Their part of the job was over as soon as we left the safety of the trees on the occupied side of the line. The seven of us crossed the road, made our way down another steep embankment, and then up an equally high bank on the other side, where two new guides were waiting. They led us through an open field, and we crossed the Line of Demarcation just as the sun was rising."

"Symbolizing a new beginning," Anne said. "A new day was dawning."

"I guess," said Veronique. "But not for me. As far as I was concerned, Mother was gone. I was leaving everything I'd ever known behind, and I had no idea what the future would bring. I wasn't feeling particularly optimistic."

"I'm sure you weren't, Oma. So what happened next?"

"We hid behind another stand of trees set back maybe fifty meters from the line," Renee said. "We remained there for about ten minutes, though I don't know why. Do you Henri?"

"I didn't ask. I knew I wouldn't get an answer. When the new guides thought it was safe, we followed them to yet another barn where we were given bread, cheese, and blankets before they and the farmer left us there to sleep on the straw. The next morning the Begins began their journey to Spain. Veronique, Renee, Robert, and I spent the rest of the day in the barn. At dusk we heard the sound of propellers. A small RAF transport landed on a cleared strip of land nearby. We were hustled onto the plane and flown to an airstrip on the English coast. When we arrived, we were immediately taken to an empty farmhouse where we spent the night. The next morning a truck transported us to Southampton. We stayed in army barracks until a United States ship arrived a week later. We boarded and sailed to New York."

"And that's how we began our new life. We'll fill in the remaining details another time." Veronique winked at Anne. "Someday I'll tell you about my whirlwind romance with your grandfather several months after we reached the States."

She got up and, waving off Henri's offer to help, walked over to her nightstand and picked up her journal. She returned to the sitting area, sat down, handed Anne the worn book, and said, "This should give you a great deal of insight about our lives during the Occupation. I've put sticky-notes on several entries I believe might help as we search for Mother's paintings."

"Did reading the journal jog your memory?"

"It did, but some of the entries gave rise to additional questions. There are some things I don't understand. I'll do more thinking and share what I wrote with Renee and Henri. Maybe they can help me figure out what I meant."

Anne took the book from her grandmother's outstretched hand. "I'll take good care of this," she promised.

"I know you will, darling. I'm sad to see you leave, but I'm also excited to begin our search for Mother's art."

"I am too. In my wildest dreams I never imagined I'd be living in my great-grandmother's home and searching for her missing art while you work on your computer to help in the endeavor. If we're lucky, maybe you and I will someday hang one or more of her masterpieces here or in Paris."

"I'm going to do everything I can to see that we do," Veronique said, daubing the tears from her eyes. "While you're away, Mr. Google and I will become close friends. I'll begin my research this afternoon. Look for my initial report as soon as you land."

"I'll do that. I'll be back in a few weeks. You'll be so busy you won't miss me. I'll call from the airport, if not before."

"Safe travel," Henri said.

"Thanks. I'll see you all soon."

"Maybe sooner than you think," Renee whispered as she walked Anne to the door.

CHAPTER 10

As soon as she got home, Anne changed into sweats and a T-shirt. She had planned to pack, but Veronique's journal was too tempting. She went to her office, removed a French dictionary from a shelf behind the desk, and picked up a tablet and a pad of sticky-notes. Back in the living room, she carefully removed the journal from her purse. Feeling like she was touching something sacred, she plopped down on the couch, carefully opened the book, and began to read, slowly at first, as she struggled to remember the language she spoke as a child.

Friday, June 14, 1940

Dear Diary,

This is the only time I will begin my entry in this childlike way. I intend to keep a journal, not a diary. A diary is a record of what occurs on a particular day. In this book, I will document my thoughts, observations, and feelings rather than actual events, unless they illustrate the point I wish to make. This morning during the early hours before I got up, the world I know forever changed. Later in life when I look back on what I'm sure will be long dreary months, possibly years, I may not be able to recall how I felt or how the Nazi Occupation personally affected Mother and me. The entries in this journal will help me remember what happened, though I'm not naïve enough to believe it won't also expose experiences and memories I might choose to forget. If I'm lucky and make it through what I imagine will be a painful phase of my life, per-haps I will share this journal with my own daughter or granddaughter at another, better time.

How perceptive you were, Oma. You're fulfilling the prophecy you made in the preface to your journal. Anne moved on to her grandmother's second entry.

Tuesday, June 18, 1940

I sense the future will be challenging for Mother and me. For a long time, we have known the Nazis were coming, but to face the reality that Paris is now a German territory is almost too much for us to bear. As I watched the Germans march down the Champs-Élysées, I saw grown men cry. This afternoon I came back to Île St-Louis, turned on my radio, and listened to General De Gaulle's speech rallying the French people. He begged us to resist the Germans and encouraged us to have hope. I noted his words so I could share them with Mother. "Whatever happens, the flame of French resistance must not die and will not die." I see tears and sorrow all around, but not defiance. Could Parisians already be resigned to their fate? Will they give up our beloved city without a fight?

Wednesday, June 19, 1940

This morning, eighty-four-year-old Marshal Petain responded to De Gaulle's inspiring oration. He told all Frenchmen that he is bestowing on France the "gift of my person." As I walked to Mother's favorite tea shop on rue St-Louis-en-lÎle, I heard people openly expressing their gratitude for Petain's sacrifice. To me he sounds dishonest and arrogant.

Thursday, June 20, 1940

Today the Nazis announced they will not tolerate confrontation. I haven't personally seen an encounter between a German soldier and a Frenchman, but I have heard there are skirmishes occurring throughout Paris. Except for the German tanks, trucks, and soldiers that crowd our streets, Paris seems normal. The schools, restaurants, and theaters are open, and the French police are the ones keeping the peace. As I ride my bike, I get the impression that most Parisians are unconcerned by the Nazi presence.

Saturday, June 22, 1940

What the French are labeling the "ultimate humiliation" occurred today. I turned on my radio and heard that France and Germany signed an armistice agreement in the very same memorial railroad car where the treaty ending the Great War was signed twenty-two years ago. The symbolism was undoubtedly intentional. Under terms of the truce, France was divided into two sections. The northern part of the country, including the city of Paris, is under German military control. Zone Libre, *also known as Vichy France or État français, the French State is to the south—though I think the word "libre" is misleading. I've heard talk that Marshall Petain and Prime Minister Laval are no more than Nazi puppets. But whatever the truth may be, despite these major changes to our nation, I still see little distress on faces of the people on the street. Perhaps they're dazed because Paris was seized so quickly. I can't believe they don't care.*

Monday, June 24, 1940

Did I recently write that Paris looks normal? I was wrong. I hardly recognize the usually bustling city. This morning I rode my bike across Pont de la Tournelle to meet my best friend Renee Paquet at her home on rue Gît-le-Coeur in Saint-Germain As I crossed over to the continent, the sun was shining brightly. I rode along the river until I reached Quai des Grands Augusten and then turned onto rue Gît. Renee was waiting outside the no-name hotel. We left my bike at her house and walked along Boulevard Saint-Germain toward the abbey to reserve the date for her wedding to Henri Marsolet. I wish I could express my excitement in words. Renee invited me to stand up for her at the ceremony that will take place after Henri graduates from the university in June 1942.

As we neared the abbey, we passed Café Fleur and Deux Magot. Strangely, there were few people sitting outside enjoying the lovely weather. At this time of year, the outdoor cafes are usually filled with Parisians engaging in their favorite activity, people watching. We crossed the street and met with the priest. Renee is thrilled. She and Henri will be married on July 25, 1942, at four in the afternoon. Two years seems a lifetime away. When I see Nazi soldiers on every corner, I wonder what we will go through before Renee's special day finally arrives—if it does.

Tuesday, June 25, 1940

The Nazis seem to be fighting for our hearts and minds. There are bill-posters throughout the city. We are told the signs are there to inform and make us enthusiastic. For me, the most shocking examples of propaganda are the gigantic blood-red Nazi flags with the bold black swastikas displayed on all the public buildings and monuments. This morning I spotted a huge banner hanging from the façade of the National Assembly. In bold letters it announced, **DEUTSCHLAND SIEGT AN ALLEN FRONTEN.** *From all I have seen and heard so far, the words are true. Germany* does *seem to be always victorious.*

Anne thought about the six entries she'd read so far. Veronique's words reflected a myriad of emotions—anger, confusion, annoyance, resentment, sorrow, concern, disdain, naïveté. But on June 25, she wasn't frightened about what might happen because she and Elisabeth were Jews. *I'm sure she'll realize very soon.* She continued to read.

Wednesday, June 26, 1940

After breakfast, Mother lingered over her tea. She clearly had something to say, but she seemed reluctant to start the conversation. When she finally did, I began to understand what it means to be a Jew living in Nazi-occupied Paris. She says she recently opened an account in a Swiss bank and transferred all but the money we will need for day-to-day living from her accounts here in Paris. She wouldn't tell me the name of the new bank, but she did mention her account manager's name—I'm sure by accident. Throughout the day, I worried. God forbid, if something happens to her, will I be able to recover the money when France is finally free? Or perhaps I should say if *France is liberated.*

After dinner, arguing I may need the information at some point in the future, I again asked Mother to disclose the name of the bank and provide the account information. She refused, saying she'd hidden the information where the Germans would never find it.

A few minutes later, she sat down at her desk and began to write, I thought she had changed her mind and was doing what I'd asked. Instead, she penned a poem, handed it to me, told me to memorize the words, and then return the paper so she could destroy it herself. Though she would be upset—I'm copying the verse below this entry. I've read the words, but I have no idea what Mother is trying to say. Perhaps someday I'll understand.

I sit in my room; the blackness all around me.
Night's mantle cloaks the Île and my heart.
The fire, my nighttime jewel, blazes; replacing the light of the sun.
The crackling flames warm the bricks of the mantle above
And give my heart hope.
The beauty of man's creation—the faces, the scenes—disappear in
the darkness
And will only return with the dawn of a new day.
There will be a future when the drapes are opened wide
And the lights of Paris return.
But will I be here to feel the joy?

Anne could almost hear her grandmother sighing in resignation as she confessed her next transgression.

I'm breaking Mother's rule again. I'm noting the name Gardiner Vachon, her account manager, in my journal. But I am giving him a code name. His initials are GV, so I'll call him German Victory—though I wish his first name was Franck so I could call him French Victory.

"Gardiner Vachon—German Victory." *Pretty clever, Oma, and you still have your sense of humor. You're also in a state of denial. You realize your mother is frightened, but you can't yet fathom what's to come—or perhaps you* choose *not to see.*

Anne wrote a question on her "Ask Oma" list. *After the Liberation, did you try to locate German Victory or attempt to access your account?*

Of course you didn't, Anne mulled. *Until recently you couldn't talk about, much less come to grips with your past.* In no particular order, she jotted down additional questions.

Was there a brick fireplace in Elisabeth's bedroom? If so, in her poem could she be referring to a hollowed-out area behind the bricks—a place the Germans would never find?

Do you agree the "beauty of man's creation" refers to Elisabeth's paint-ings? She seems to think you'll be able to recover her art if she doesn't survive the Occupation, but how could that be?

Did you ever try to interpret the poem, or did you choose to ignore what your mother wrote because you'd dismissed the seriousness of the situ-ation. Were you pretending the danger wasn't real?

I'm not sure I'll ask the last question, Anne thought as she put the journal on the couch, went to the kitchen, and poured a glass of wine. Fascinated by what she was reading, she returned to the living room, sat back down, took a sip, placed the glass on the table beside her, and opened to where she'd left off.

Friday, June 28, 1940

Today when I got to Renee's, Henri's friend Claude was visiting. Yesterday he and several of his friends stopped for a drink at the Café Flore. The only empty table was next to two German officers who, he believed, must have been drinking for some time because they were carelessly joking about a directive they had recently received from Nazi headquarters at Fontainebleau. Since Claude is majoring in languages at the university, he understands the horrible guttural language we hear everywhere we go. He listened as the officers discussed the rules. Each time they mentioned a new directive, they raised their steins in a toast. Here is how he described the scene: "No swimming in the Seine; clink. No singing or dancing in public; clink. No horse-back riding in the Bois de Boulogne; clink. No purchas-ing pornography; clink. No frequenting French shops to buy collectibles; clink." Though most of the rules are ridiculous, Claude told Henri that one filled him with foreboding. The directive declared there is to be no mingling between them and Jewish women, who the Germans called Judinne. Is this yet another sign that times will soon become even more problematic for Parisian Jews?

Is Oma finally beginning to face reality? Anne wondered. *This is the first time she writes of possible peril ahead. Does she believe what she wrote or does she still trust that she and her mother will escape the Occupation unscathed?* "I guess I'll soon know." She continued to read.

Monday, July 8, 1940

As I pedal around the city, I still see little opposition to Nazi rule. I guess no one listened to General de Gaulle. Perhaps Parisians are afraid, or maybe they believe cooperation will work to their advantage. There is one kind of collaboration I find revolting. I see French women walking around on the arms of German soldiers. When I mentioned this to Renee, she said the soldiers, even though they're our enemies, give single women a chance for romance, and widows a way to support their children. While Renee and I were talking, Henri joined in the conversation. I was surprised to learn that thousands of French women are engaging in what he calls, "horizontal collaboration," with the Nazis. I understood what he meant. I was embarrassed.

I imagine that, despite the Nazi presence, life for Oma was becoming routine, Anne thought as she continued to read.

Friday, July 12, 1940

Bicycles have all but replaced the cars on the strangely-quiet streets. When I pedal through Paris, I am, paradoxically, happy but sad. I ride along empty streets that were once filled with cars and busses. Because I know why our way of life has changed, I'm sad. And then, suddenly, I'm happy because, for bike riders and pedestrians, Paris with so little traffic has never been a more pleasant place.

Early this morning I rode across Pont Saint-Louis to the Place de la Concorde. Near the Egyptian Obelisk I stopped to talk with a friend who says many Parisians are angry. While they struggle to feed their families, German officers are occupying the best hotels—the Meurice, the Majestic, the Lutetia, the Crillon, and the George V. They are enjoying life while Parisians suffer.

Sunday, July 14, 1940

Today is Bastille Day commemorating the storming of the Bastille in 1789. Parisians have celebrated every year since 1880, but now there's little reason to rejoice. The Bastille itself is gone, but, especially today, the symbol of tyranny must cross the minds of all freedom-loving Frenchmen and women as they are forced to view the current emblems of our persecution—the Nazi flags that fly throughout the city. Last year I would have attended a parade and watched fireworks at the end of the festivities. This year I am among the persecuted. Now I know how the citizens of Paris felt two hundred years ago.

It's raining. Mother is visiting friends on Quai de Bethune, and I'm sitting in my room. The forecaster on the radio says the skies will clear this afternoon. When the rain stops, I'll ride my bicycle to Pont de la Concorde. All the while, I'll be thinking about my ancestors who were denied basic liberties that, until a month ago, I took for granted. I'll pedal over paving stones on the streets and sidewalks marking the Bastille's former location. As they go about their business, will other Parisians feel a new-found connection with the freedom fighters of the past?

Monday, July 15, 1940
Yesterday afternoon was a happy, and at the same time, a sad day. There were no firecrackers. No festivals. No military parade on the Champs-Élysées to honor the Republic. But even though we're not celebrating in Paris, the spirit of the revolution is alive. I heard on the radio that the Free French Forces paraded in London. The radio has become our only hope of learning what is going on in the outside world.

Wednesday, July 25, 1940
Two years from today Renee and Henri will be married. They're going to dinner to celebrate. They invited me to go along, but I declined. Mother worries if I am out after dark, and, besides, they should be alone. With each passing day, the question I asked myself after Renee reserved her wedding date still haunts me, though now with even more reason—Will the wedding take place?

Sunday, August 4, 1940
Today I saw two ladies sitting on a bench in the Palais-Royal gardens. They knitted and talked as if nothing is different. In the sidewalk cafes along the Champs-Élysées, well-dressed Parisian women in haute couture still enjoy their coffee and aperitifs. I pedaled along the Seine, stopping twice to watch young boys swimming in the cool water to escape the blistering heat from

the noonday sun. *My overall impression is that Parisians are engaged in* se debrouiller. *We are all coping as best we can.*

Saturday, August 10, 1940

Once again I was wrong. Clearly, Parisians are depressed. Perhaps, like me, they fear life as we knew it is gone forever. The concerns are particularly noticeable in the faces of middle-aged men and women who lived through the Great War and who are once again facing a shortage of food, gasoline, and other essentials.

Friday, August 23, 1940

German Propaganda Minister Goebbels ordered Parisians to present a care-free image. He wants the world to see a city full of contented people. We are to go shopping. To sit in the parks. To walk the streets, all the while looking happy and grateful to be living under Nazi rule.

Thursday, September 5, 1940

This morning as I rode my bike to Saint-Germain, I watched Nazi soldiers loading paintings and furniture from private homes into large canvas-cov-ered trucks. Renee heard the confiscated art is being transported to and stored in the Galerie Nationale du Jeu de Paume. When I told Mother what I'd seen, she wasn't surprised. She reminded me the Nazis seized priceless collections from her Jewish friends in Austria and Poland. Now the same thing is happening in Paris.

Monday, September 9, 1940

Paintings are slowly disappearing from walls throughout our house. Degas' painting of the ballet dancer, one of my favorites, is missing. It's not unusual for Mother to move her art from one location to another, but this time it's different. The paintings are nowhere to be found.

Elisabeth had an incredible collection, Anne pondered, as she wrote "Degas" and "ballet dancer" on her tablet. The next few entries reiter-ated what her grandmother had revealed when she admitted she'd spied on her mother's conversations, so Anne skipped ahead.

Thursday, October 3, 1940

Today was a terrible day for Parisian Jews. We no longer have places to worship. The Nazis demolished six synagogues in various sections of the city. Two people were wounded. A bomb was discovered in a seventh building, but, thankfully, it was defused before it could explode. The synagogue on rue de la Victorie that contains the office of the Grand Rabbi was one of those razed.

Tuesday, October 15, 1940

Everyone is hungry. We must stand in long lines to buy food, and the stores are almost empty of necessities. We wait forever just to get our ration cards each month. But having a card doesn't mean there's food to buy. Yesterday I stood in line for two hours only to reach the front and hear the words, "Go home! There is nothing left." People in the line behind me walked away hungry and dejected. The Nazis are rationing wheat, meat, butter, cheese, fruit, cloth, leather, tobacco, and coal, and only children younger than six are allowed milk.

Tuesday, October 29, 1940

Two weeks ago I wrote generally about the dismal conditions in the city. I said Parisians are hungry. Today I will make my entry more personal. I am hungry. My clothes hang loosely on my body. We cannot buy meat, so Mother and I are making do with potatoes, turnips, and artichokes. Rutabaga is one vegetable that is easy to get. Thought it's not one of my favorites, it fills my stomach. For me, rutabaga symbolizes the misery of rationing.

Monday, November 4, 1940

Yesterday I cut short my ride to sit on a bench in the Bois de Boulogne. The two women sitting next to me were speaking about widespread hunger in the city. I felt sick when I heard them say, in desperation, some Parisians are eating cats and dogs. The image remained in my mind. When I reached the Île de la Cité, I saw a bill poster alerting people to the dangers of eating rats. Rats? What next?

Sunday, November 17, 1940

Uncle George continues to supplement what little food that's left in Mother's pantry. Though every train station in the country is controlled by customs and watched by the Germans, he still manages to bring us fresh vegetables and, sometimes, a little meat. Last Wednesday he and Mother spent the afternoon talking privately, about what I don't know, but whatever they discussed, she seemed troubled. At dinner, Uncle George explained why food is scarce in Paris. He and other farmers throughout France are being forced to send much of what they produce to Germany. Perhaps that's why Mother's distressed. She realizes Uncle George will no longer be able to bring us food.

Wednesday, November 27, 1940

The blackout reflects my dark mood. We are forced to close our shutters and windows after dark. Paris, the City of Light, is a black world.

December 10, 1940

As the holidays approach, Parisians are frustrated. The regulations, the censorship, and the propaganda make life difficult. When the Germans marched into the city, many Parisians escaped to the country. Now they're returning in large numbers. With more people to feed, there's even less food available—if that's possible.

December 23, 1940

There are few Christmas decorations on the Grand Boulevards this year. The season is dark, as are the hearts of the Parisians who have no cause to celebrate. Tomorrow Hanukkah begins. This afternoon I'll ride my bike to rue des Rosiers in the Marais. Perhaps there will be fresh potatoes so Aliza can make potato pancakes. Up to now, I haven't mentioned Mother's servants. Although we can no longer afford to pay them, Aliza our cook, our butler Isaac, and Mother's maid Marthe are still with us. They may remain out of loyalty, or perhaps they have nowhere to go.

December 24, 1940

I found nothing special for Hanukkah, but I wasn't too upset. What did bother me were the posters portraying Jews with long bushy hair, heavy jowls, and hooked noses. More about this later. Mother just called me to Hanukkah dinner.

Tired and emotionally drained, Anne closed the journal. "When I'm on the plane, I'll see how Oma confronts the Jewish issue," she whispered.

She tucked the journal in her briefcase, fixed a light dinner, and responded to several emails while she ate. When she finally went to bed, she couldn't sleep. Vivid Images of Paris during the Occupation kept running through her mind.

CHAPTER 11

Anne had hardly slept when the alarm on her nightstand blared. She dragged herself out of bed, plodded to the kitchen, made a cup of strong coffee, drank it and then another before returning to her bedroom to pack.

An hour later when she finally finished adding to and eliminating clothes from piles on the bed, her large suitcase was bulging. *I'll never get this closed,* she thought as she sat on top and tugged the zippers until they finally met in the middle. *Why can't I ever remember I'm going to a civilized country and can buy anything I've forgotten once I get there?*

She rolled the over-stuffed suitcase to the door and returned to her office to pick up the smaller bag containing the books she had bought at the Met and Barnes & Noble. After checking her briefcase one last time to be sure she'd packed everything necessary to conduct Met business, she placed it and the carry-on beside her large bag.

Her packing completed, she called to check on her grandmother. "You're up," she began.

"I've been working for hours. This is a pleasant surprise, darling. I thought you'd wait and call from the airport. Are you packed?"

"I just zipped the suitcase and, I might add, with great difficulty. What's up with you?"

"A few minutes ago I sent Henri to Barnes & Noble to buy two books they're holding for me at the desk. They're the last I'll purchase. Your modern grandmother just ordered a Kindle Fire. By teatime tomorrow, I'll have downloaded all of the books on my list."

"Really!"

"You seem surprised."

"I suppose I am. Aren't you the one who keeps telling me there's nothing like the smell and feel of a book?"

"I may have made that statement once or twice, but as you often remind me, patience isn't one of my virtues. Very soon I'll enjoy instant gratification. My books will arrive in seconds, not hours, days, or, in some cases, weeks. I called Special Agent Q. He tells me HP makes a LaserJet Pro all-in-one. It's a scanner, printer, copier, and fax. He's bringing one over and setting it up later this morning."

"And how am I supposed to receive your transmissions? You *do* realize there needs to be a machine on the other end to get the fax."

"Of course I know. Do you think you're dealing with a senile old woman? By Wednesday your fax machine will be up and running. I emailed the company that's installing the wireless system in both apartments. They're putting in dedicated lines."

"I'm impressed but not surprised," Anne said. "Is there anything you haven't thought of?"

"I certainly hope not," Veronique said huffily.

"In that case, let's move on to why I called. Last night I read your journal—"

"All of it?"

"Through Hanukkah 1940. I loved reading about how you felt and seeing how your mindset changed between June and the holiday season. In some ways, I was with you on your journey toward understanding. We'll talk about this and more when I get home, but before I hang up, I have a few questions. Are you up to answering?"

"Of course. Ask me anything."

"Great. Do you recall the poem your mother wrote when you asked for the Swiss bank account numbers? You flagged the entry when you reread your journal."

"I remember. Did you decode the message?"

"Hopefully. Was there a brick fireplace in Elisabeth's bedroom?"

"I believe so." Veronique paused momentarily. "Yes," she said. "There definitely was. I remember because I thought it looked plain in comparison to the marble fireplaces in other parts of the house."

"Okay, this is good. Now. Do you know if Elisabeth had any work done in the house after the Nazis occupied Paris—specifically in her bedroom?"

Again Anne waited while Veronique gathered her thoughts. "Come to think of it, yes," she said. "But don't ask me what—"

"Do you know who did the work? A friend? A hired workman?"

"Definitely a friend. Beginning in January 1941, Denis Gaudrieu and his son Edouard began to visit regularly. The Gaudrieus were neighbors who owned a mansion on Quai de Bethune. For as long as I can remember, Denis and his wife Lili were part of Mother's circle of friends."

"Did you ask your mother why Denis was coming by so often?"

"I did. She said he was there to remove and hide her more valuable works of art. Those were the paintings I wrote about—the ones I said were missing."

"I wonder if Elisabeth was referring to more than just the paintings. In her poem, she mentions a blazing fire warming the bricks above the mantle. She calls the blaze her 'nighttime jewel.' Could she be referring to jewelry?"

"I don't know. Maybe. I always assumed the Nazis took Mother's jewel cases when they removed everything else of value from the house."

"What if they were gone before the Nazis arrived? What if Denis hid them in the bedroom above the 'crackling flames?' If not the actual pieces, perhaps Elisabeth left a note explaining where to find the cases after the Liberation. Remember, before she wrote the poem she said she was hiding the bank account numbers in a place the Germans couldn't find—"

"And you think her jewelry's there too?"

"Possibly, but moving on. Did Henri ever attempt to contact Denis Guidreaus or his sons when he returned to Paris after the Liberation?"

"You'll have to ask him, but I doubt it. I imagine he knew Denis, but Giles and Charles were too young to be part of our group, and Edouard, who was closest in age, was so different."

"Different how?"

"He was quiet and shy, and Henri was outgoing and gregarious. Perhaps Bertrand can tell you what happened to the Gaudrieus after the war."

"Which brings me to another question? Were the Gaudrieus Jewish? If so, maybe they were arrested during la rafle du Vel d'Hiv."

"They were Catholic, though, as I said, on the Île a person's religion wasn't important until the Occupation turned our lives upside down. What else do you want to know?"

"You wrote that Elisabeth transferred her money to the Swiss bank in June 1940. By then, had Denis removed the art she would eventually sell to purchase your freedom?"

"I'm not sure of the timeline. All I know is that Mother's collection gradually disappear, but beyond my initial inquiry and her answer that the paintings were being restored. I didn't ask questions. Looking back, I should have urged her to share, but that wasn't something a young woman did, at least not young women I knew. Mother was the boss, and I knew how far I could push. In any case, not long after she wrote the poem, life became increasingly difficult for the Jews. I quickly stopped thinking about the poem and German Victory as we dealt with the realities of life."

"Did you try to contact Monsieur Vachon after the Liberation?"

"When I came here and married your grandfather, I tried to forget that painful period in my life. Had we needed it, I might have made the effort. But with the estate your grandfather inherited from his father, including this apartment and the Hampton house, and with what he garnered from wise investments, we always had more than enough to live comfortably."

"Well we're going to look now. If there *is* a hiding place behind the bricks above the mantle in what was once your mother's bedroom, we'll find it."

"Will I hear from you every day?"

"That's the plan. But remember, I'm on Met business, and then there's the time difference. In the meantime do what Doctor Richmond says and keep getting better."

"I will. Be safe, darling."

"I'll email you when I land. I love you."

⁓◦

At two-thirty, Anne called a cab. Traffic wasn't an issue, and she arrived at the international terminal a little after four. She breezed through check-in and security and went to the first-class lounge. While she waited to board, she checked in with Meg and John. At six-fifteen she went to the gate. Flying first class, she was first to board. As she waited for those with coach tickets to file down the aisle, she decided one glass of champagne wouldn't hurt. "Here's to adventures in Paris." She took a sip.

There was no one in the seat beside her, so when the plane reached flying altitude, she removed her briefcase from beneath the seat in front of her, pulled out the tray in the armrest of the empty seat, and placed her grandmother's journal as well as her tablet and sticky-notes on top. *My own little office,* she thought as the flight attendant came and handed her the dinner menu.

She ordered a filet with roasted potatoes and a glass of Merlot. Though tempted, she didn't read during dinner, but as soon as the hot fudge sundae bowl had been cleared, she went to the lavatory, returned to her seat, covered herself with the blanket and took out her grandmother's journal. She began to read.

Thursday, January 2, 1941

Mother rarely talks about her Jewish heritage. We celebrate Passover and Hanukkah, but we don't keep a Kosher home or observe the Sabbath. Nor do we go to religious services. Until now, when being a Jew means we're enemies of the state, I never gave my beliefs much thought. In my last entry, I spoke about how Jews are being depicted on posters throughout Paris. I was with Mother the other day when we went to visit one of her few remaining Jewish friends in the Marais. When she saw the bill posters, she flinched. I feel sorry for her. Though we don't say the words aloud, we both know there will be difficult times in the weeks and months to come.

Thursday, January 3, 1941

Few Parisians celebrated the beginning of the New Year. It is not a happy time, and we have little reason to be joyful. At three this afternoon, Mother went to visit Denis Gaudrieu and his wife Lili on Quai de Bethune. When she returned, she was pale and shaking. She said a soldier had stopped her on rue des Deux-Ponts and accused her of representing everything evil in the world. When I asked how she responded, she shook her head and whispered, "I said nothing." Could I have shown such restraint? I am shuddering as I wonder if, someday, I may find out.

Sunday, January 6, 1941

Mother remains distraught about the incident with the German soldier. For the first time in her life, she is being defined by her religion. After an unusually quiet dinner, I suggested we pack what would need for a long stay and take the train to Brittany to live with Uncle George until Paris is again free. She had a strange, far-away look in her eyes when I argued that, in these dark times, we should be with those we love, and, though we are not related by blood, Uncle George is our only family.

I was not surprised when she said no, but this time I refused to give up. I argued that here in Paris we are constantly in danger from Nazi patrols on the lookout for Jews. But if we were living on a farm in the country, there would be fewer chance encounters with soldiers. Thinking I was making progress, I continued to make my case. I reminded her that Uncle George is a Christian. If the Nazis think we are related, they might believe we, too, are Christians and leave us alone.

My arguments did nothing to change Mother's mind. I have no idea why—she gave no reason—but, again, she refuses to go. Perhaps she fears that life in the country would be no better than it is here in Paris. Or she maybe she thinks we would be putting Uncle George at risk.

Our conversation ended when she said if I want to leave she will make the necessary arrangements, but she will not go with me. Of course I would never leave her behind.

Monday, January 13, 1941

After dinner, we heard a knock on the door. Since few of our friends visit after dark, I was nervous. I kept out of sight while Isaac went to see who was there. "Monsieur Gaudrieu," I heard him say. When Denis came in, he and Mother went directly to her private parlor and closed the door. They *spoke for about fifteen minute, and then he left. When I asked her why he had come, she said 'to make plans.' She turned and left the room, so I knew that was all she intended to say.*

Anne had just begun to read the entry for February 8 when the overhead lights dimmed. *I should try to sleep*, she thought. Instead, she switched on her reading light and persisted.

Saturday, February 8, 1941
Denis and Edouard continue to visit, though not as often. Last night I watched them wrap one of the few valuable paintings remaining in the house, a colorful Matisse. When they were about to leave, I noticed they had walked to the house. Because the package is large, I thought it would be safer if they transported it across the Île by truck rather than carry it on foot. When I said I was worried that a Nazi soldier might stop him and want to know what he was carrying, Denis said he would rather take his chances with the foot-patrols. With the gasoline shortages and fewer cars on the road, the Nazis are stepping up vehicle searches. I pray he made the right decision.

Saturday, February 15, 1941
I keep writing about Denis, but his visits are all I have to report. Mother and I rarely go out, and no one comes to call. I am lonely, and she is always glum. But it is not my intent to use this entry to complain. Today Denis and Edouard drove over and parked directly in front of the house. When they came inside, Denis was carrying a heavy tool box. Mother immediately ushered them upstairs. I was about to follow when she turned and nodded no, which meant to stay behind.

They had been up there for about twenty minutes when Giles burst into the foyer. Out of breath, he yelled, "The Nazis are coming from the direction of Pont Marie! They will see the truck. Hurry! They are getting close!" Denis must have planned for such an emergency because Edouard rushed down the stairs and out the door, leaving his father behind with Mother and me. I peeked out through a tiny crack on the side of the blackout curtain and saw him jump into the truck and speed toward Quai d'Orleans. For the next ten minutes, we waited. Though no one said a word, I know we were thinking the same thing: What if the Nazis saw Edouard leave. Would they come to the door? Would we all be arrested—us, because we are Jews, and Denis and Edouard because they were with us in the house? When we saw the patrol turn onto Pont Saint-Louis, we were relieved. Denis finally went home, but he left his toolbox. He must have more work to do.

Saturday, February 22, 1941
For the past week, Denis has been strangely absent. This time he came alone. He said Edouard had taken the truck to the continent, though he didn't explain why.

I heard him tell Mother he had come for the last painting she plans to hide—a work—I think by Manet—showing men and women happily picnicking on the grass. As he removed the painting from the wall, I suddenly realized how much our lives have changed over the past twenty months. The walls are so bare. Mother is so unhappy. Life is so difficult. To me, the missing paintings, particularly the one Denis took down today, symbolize a time before the Nazis marched into Paris. Like the people picnicking on the grass, we were once happy and carefree. Now our lives are as empty as the bare walls.

How sad, Anne pondered. *There's no joy in Oma's life. And now the last painting is gone.* Suddenly she was no longer thinking about her grandmother's state of mind. *Was the painting Oma mentioned another adaptation of Manet's Le dejeuner sur l'herbe?* When she studied in Paris, she'd written a paper about the version in the Musée d'Orsay collection, and during one of her trips to London, she'd seen a smaller rendering of the same scene at the Courtauld Gallery. *Like Monet with his Haystacks and depictions of Rouen Cathedral in different lights, did Manet paint the same scene three times? If so, did Elisabeth own another rendering?* "I don't know whether to feel sad for Oma or elated about the possibility of finding the painting," she whispered as she began to read the next entry.

Saturday, March 1, 1941

From here on, I won't write unless I have something specific to say or a unique emotion to report. Nothing has changed. Denis still comes by once or twice a week, not to remove additional paintings, but to work in the house. Renee and Henri have visited several times, but what we discuss isn't worth noting. Though she says very little, I know Renee is worried about Mother and me. Henri still wants to join the resistance movement, but Anton still refuses to let him volunteer. I guess life is normal—whatever normal means.

Thursday April 10, 1941

During the winter, darkness descended early, so the blackout was not an issue. Now spring is here. The chestnut trees along the Seine are in full bloom. The daffodils are peeking through the ground. The sun is shining. The air smells sweet. The evenings are warm and inviting. Paris has come alive, especially at night, but, sadly, the Nazis have issued yet another edict. Jews may not leave their homes after dark. While Parisians celebrate springtime, we remain inside with our windows closed.

Thursday, May 15, 1941

Over the past few weeks I have not put my grim thoughts on paper. Now I must. Life continues to worsen for Parisian Jews—if that is possible. Mother and I cannot travel beyond the city. We cannot correspond with anyone who is not a relative. We cannot go to cafes and restaurants. We cannot attend the theater. We cannot stroll in public gardens. We cannot sit on public benches along the quais. We cannot shop on the Champs Élysées. We cannot own a radio. The last rule, I refuse to obey. I must know how the war is progressing. Even though the news is bad, I will continue to listen. I will keep a radio hidden in my room.

Besides the radio, there are other rules I ignore. I know the consequences of my rebellion, but I cannot live with such ridiculous restrictions. I still meet Renee for lunch, but so I am not putting her at risk, I choose cafés away from public thoroughfares. I still stroll in the Jardin des Tuileries. I still sit on a bench by the Seine in Square Barye. When I am out with Mother, I wear *my badge of shame, but other times, I tuck the infamous yellow square in my pocket or leave it at home.*

Earlier today Mother visited the Siegles. When she came home, she said Marjorie and Aaron have heard that one of our local bistro owners is a Nazi collaborator. I find that hard to believe, but, nevertheless, it may be true. Sadly, no one knows who to trust in Paris these days. That is a sad state of affairs.

Anne thought back to Veronique's first journal entries. In June 1940, when the Nazis marched into Paris, she, like the Parisians she described, was complying with the Nazi proclamations. Now, almost a year later, she was rebelling. She was refusing to be confined to her home or be defined by what she dubbed her "badge of shame." Eager to see how her grandmother's thoughts and actions would evolve over the following year, Anne continued to read.

Tuesday, May 20, 1941
Every day Mother grows more anxious about missing neighbors and friends. While she hopes they have gone to the country to stay with friends or relatives, she knows that can't be true—at least in most instances. It has been months since I last rode my bike to the Marais. Mother will not allow me to go, and arguing with her is futile.

Last week on her day off, Aliza told us she was going to visit a sick friend who lives on rue Vieille du Temple in the heart of the Marais. Mother warned her to be careful. She has heard the Nazis are targeting Jews for nothing more than being on the streets. She said she knew, but she had to go.

When she returned several hours later, she was crying. When she finally settled down, she said the Marais she saw today is not the Marais of her childhood. When I asked her to explain, she said the streets that used to be filled with happy people are eerily empty. Her favorite cafes and delis are boarded up. There are no familiar smells wafting through open windows— no Challah bread baking in large ovens, no matzah-ball soup simmering on stoves, no aromas of pastrami, chicken livers, or corned beef. Though she finds all of these changes upsetting, what bothers her most is the absence of people enjoying the outdoors. There are no bearded men standing on the corners conversing or arguing with their friends. No children play on the streets.

When Mother asked about her sick friend, Aliza began to sob. She said when she reached the house, she saw a yellow tape draped across the door. She didn't knock. There was no reason. Her friend was gone—probably forever.

I wonder why Elisabeth won't leave, Anne mulled as she looked at the date on the next entry. "It's Oma's birthday," she whispered and read.

Friday, June 4, 1941

Today is my birthday. Mother and I went shopping on the Île de la Cité. She rarely goes out, but in honor of my special day, she agreed to go. There wasn't much to buy, but that didn't matter. It was wonderful to be with her—just like the old days. While we were gone, Aliza baked a cake. It isn't my favorite kind, but Mother said she thought celebrating with a German Chocolate cake would be inappropriate under the circumstances. Of course she was joking. Our inability to obtain the ingredients necessary to bake such a rich cake is the true reason I can't have German Chocolate. It was good to see her smiling and happy—if only for a moment.

But back to the problems we have obtaining other than the barest necessities. Every Parisian adult is allowed two hundred grams of butter and five hundred grams of sugar per week. Again, because we're Jews, procuring our allotted ration is often difficult. We are required to stand at the back of the line, and when we get to the front, the butter and sugar is usually gone. Unless they have the money to spend on the Black Market, not even Christians can find luxury items like sweet chocolate, cocoa, and coconut. Henri says a kilo of butter can cost as much as 1000 francs. But despite the obstacles we face, Mother insisted there be a cake. She asked Aliza to do the best she could with what we have on hand.

The result of Aliza's effort was a delicious "Occupation Cake," as she called it. With a few eggs, no butter, and only a small amount of milk, she created a cake using vegetable shortening—which is still easy to procure—as well as what was left of our precious light brown sugar, flour, cinnamon, nutmeg, raisins, and baking powder.

Henri and Renee came by to help me celebrate, so I had all the people I love around me. Renee was so impressed with Aliza's cake that she wants to serve it at her wedding reception, that is if she's able to find the necessary ingredients a year from now. After dessert, Mother gave me a single strand of pearls and matching earrings. I will wear them at Renee and Henri's wedding. It was a lovely day, and I was able to forget what is going on in Paris—if only briefly.

Friday, June 27, 1941
There's really nothing new to report. I could mention how depressed I feel about the continuing humiliations the Jews suffer at the hands of the Nazis. I could write about concerns that have become fears. Mother's troubled eyes. Our missing friends in the Marais. But I would only be repeating myself. Conditions in Paris continue to deteriorate. More people are hungry, and the food lines are longer. Uncle George hasn't visited in over a month.

Thursday July 25, 1941
Henri and Renee will be married a year from today. I don't see them as often as I once did. Last year I wondered whether the wedding would take place. Now, if Renee and Henri are able to marry, will they still want me to be a part in the ceremony? Would Renee dare have a Jew stand up for her? And if she insists, would I dare put her and her family at risk?

Anne put the pen down and lay her head back against the headrest. In her first entry on June 18, 1940, her grandmother had predicted the future would be challenging. She had no idea what her comment foreshadowed. Her subsequent writing reflected that she understood cerebrally, but not emotionally. *Now, a little over a year later, she's living in challenging times, and they're proving to be more difficult than she imagined they could be. Her writing is much darker as she finally accepts the reality of her situation. And she is no longer worried only about herself and her mother. She realizes her friendship with Henri and Renee could put them in jeopardy.*

What next? Anne wondered as she looked at the next entry.

Wednesday, August 20, 1941

Even wealthy families are being forced to sell their belongings. Many use their possessions to barter for food or clothing. Mother said the Siegles are drying their laundry in front of the fireplace—that's when they can find wood to build a fire. Just last week they sent their children to live with Christian friends in southeastern France near Avignon. Mother said Aaron wanted Marjorie to go with them, but she refuses to leave him behind, and he refuses to go.

Thursday, September 11, 1941

Today I met Renee for lunch at a café on the Île de la Cité. I left my yellow badge of shame at home. I wouldn't want a patrolling soldier to arrest her for the crime of consorting with a Jew. Our meal was nothing out of the ordinary, so I'll skip that part of the story, though I should note that Renee is very thin. She has lost thirty pounds since the Nazis entered Paris. She says her mother has lost even more. I'm glad she did didn't buy a wedding dress when she and Henri were first engaged. It would be too big. Who knows how thin she'll be next year if the food shortages persist.

As I walked home, I was shocked to see Parisians cooking their meals on campfires outside the Palais de Justice and Sainte Chapelle. Renee said with the lack of coal and electricity, the same thing is occurring throughout the city. I once asked what else could happen. Each day I realize how naïve I was.

Friday, October 10, 1941

The Nazis have stepped up their attacks against the Jews. Though some have stayed, many of Henri's Jewish friends at the university have voluntarily left school. He said just last week he watched a Nazi soldier drag a classmate, a Jew, from the lecture hall because he'd pinned, not sewn, the yellow Star of David on his jacket. If that isn't bad enough, one of Mother's acquaintances went just outside his door to walk his dog. Because he wasn't wearing his badge, he was arrested and hasn't been seen since. I no longer ride my bike to the Marais. Being in the Jewish part of Paris is too dangerous.

Wednesday, December 17, 1941

Last year I quoted Henri when he said many French women are in horizontal collaboration with the Nazis. That type of cooperation has recently become more obvious. How can these women forget what the German soldiers represent? Perhaps they know, but are having affairs with anyone they think can help them through these difficult times. I can't imagine selling my body to buy food or clothing.

Anne looked ahead to the next entry written on January 2, 1942. "I really should put this away and get some rest," she whispered, but she had to finish. She was reading a mystery. Of course she knew the ending—at least to date— but she had to find out how the main character got there. She read on.

Friday, January 2, 1942

Today Henri and Renee came to visit. Renee said she tried to call to say they were coming, but our phone no longer works. Worried they would be caught consorting with a Jew, I told them to leave. They insisted they weren't concerned. Henri says the resistance movement is growing every day. Two weeks ago, two units joined together to blow up a train carrying supplies to Nazi troops at the front lines, and just yesterday another unit assassinated a high-ranking Nazi official. Henri feels useless. He's thinking about defying his father and joining the freedom fighters. I think the only reason he doesn't is because Renee objects. Maybe there's hope after all, if, as Henri says, the Resistance is providing the Allied forces with valuable information.

Tuesday, February 10, 1942

Henri is worried about his father, and Renee says Adele is terrified when Jules goes out at night. The Gestapo is carrying out bloody reprisals on innocent civilians each time a resistance unit completes a successful operation. These senseless and brutal deaths make Henri angry and even more determined to fight.

Thursday, February 26, 1942

It's so cold. Usually Paris begins to thaw around this time, but this year the raw weather reflects our mood. I worry about Mother. She's very thin and frail. She says she's not hungry, but I know better. What little food we manage to purchase isn't enough. This afternoon Madame Huard, our neighbor who raises rabbits in her courtyard, came to visit. She must have been shocked by Mother's appearance because she left and returned an hour later carrying a package of rabbit meat. Mother tried to refuse her generous offer, but she insisted. Aliza prepared a feast, but none of us ate much. With so little in our stomachs, we were afraid we'd be sick, and, besides, we want to enjoy another meal tomorrow. Who knows when we'll have meat again?

Thursday, March 5, 1942

When I got up this morning and looked outside, two things gave me hope. First, the sun was shining. I went out, stood on the sidewalk, and lifted my face to the sky to soak up the warmth. The second miracle was another package of rabbit meat from Madame Huard. This time she also left potatoes and beets. I wanted to walk over and thank her, but Mother said no. She left the food in the dark of night when there was no one around. She must be afraid to be caught aiding a Jew.

Wednesday, April 1, 1942

Madame Huard must have mentioned our plight to our other neighbors. Several mornings a week when we look outside, there is food by the door. We never know who delivers the packages or what our neighbors are sacrificing so we can survive. But I do know, without their help, Mother would no longer be alive. She looks a little better. Her color is returning, and I think she is gaining weight.

Sunday, April 19, 1942

Today I was sad. I told Renee I cannot participate in her wedding. If it were up to me, I would take a chance, but I must think of her—not just of myself. What if, just as she was saying her vows, a platoon of Nazi soldiers burst through the door, goose-stepped up the aisle, and arrested me because I am a Jew and Renee because she is my friend. Renee is willing to take a chance, but when she thinks about our conversation, I know she will be relieved. I promised to attend the wedding and sit inconspicuously in the back. Under the circumstances, that will have to do.

Monday, May 27, 1942

This morning Henri arrived with news—but what he reported is not good. Through his sources, Anton has learned the Nazis are about to embark on a campaign to rid Paris of all remaining Jews. Henri told us about an Underground Railroad that is assisting Jews and other so-called enemies of the state who wish to flee the country. He said Auguste Lessard could make the necessary arrangements, but if we decide to go, we must prepare to leave immediately. When Henri went home, I told Mother we should listen to Anton. We should leave Paris before it's too late. Still, she stands firm. She will not go!

Sunday, June 2, 1942

Henri graduated today. It should have been a time to celebrate, but there wasn't a ceremony. He received his diploma and left the hall. Adele fixed a nice dinner—at least as nice as a meal can be when there's so little food available. Twenty-three days until the wedding.

Tuesday, June 4, 1942

Today I am spending yet another birthday under Nazi rule. This year the realities of life make it hard to feel festive. Like last year, Henri and Renee came to visit, but they didn't stay long. Renee said she had to get back. Apparently her mother isn't feeling well. That may be, but it is also possible that Adele—fearing her daughter will be discovered consorting with a Jew—told her to spend a few minutes and then come home. If that is true, my feelings aren't hurt. I understand.

This year there was nothing special to eat. Aliza felt terrible that she was unable to find the necessary ingredients to bake another Occupation Cake. I told it didn't matter—that I appreciate her efforts. Mother presented me with a pearl bracelet to match the necklace and earrings she gave me last year. I will wear all three pieces to the wedding.

Thursday, June 18, 1942

At five this evening, Denis, Edouard, and Giles came to the door. As soon as they entered the house, Mother told me to go for a long walk and take Giles with me. I was surprised. These days she rarely leaves me out of her conversations. Unfortunately, I couldn't hide around the corner and listen to what they were saying. She was watching. I had to go.

Giles and I strolled along the Seine until we'd completely circled the Île. *When we got back, Denis and Edouard were gone, so Giles went home. I asked Mother why they'd come. She said "to help." To help with what? I didn't ask. I knew better.*

Friday, June 19, 1942

Today Mother made one of her rare trips out of the house. Last night Madame Huard left rabbit meat and a basket of fresh vegetables on our doorstep. She walked around the corner to leave a thank you note. When she left, I went from floor to floor, room to room. Had this been a year ago, I wouldn't have noticed, but with so few paintings remaining on the walls, I saw that Madame Stumpf and Her Daughter *is missing.*

A Degas, a Manet, a Monet, and now a Corot. How could Oma have been so casual about the art when I asked about the paintings in Elisabeth's collection? Anne continued to read the June 19 entry.

The Work Table *has also disappeared. It always hung above the writing desk in Mother's private parlor. After five months of inactivity, why would she suddenly ask Denis to hide more paintings?*

Anne wrote *Madame Stumpf and her Daughter* and *The Work Table* on her pad. She also jotted down a reminder to have her grandmother google the titles to see if the paintings were recovered after the war, if they were currently on display in a European museum, or if they were still listed as missing.

She looked at the date of the next entry. It was written on July 18, the day after the Nazis dragged Elisabeth from her home. With great trepidation, she read.

July 18, 1942

Last night at ten o'clock, my life changed forever. When Anton and Jules came into Renee's room, words were unnecessary. I knew. The looks on their faces told the story. The Nazis had come. Mother was gone

This morning, despite Henri's protests, I returned home. I knew the Nazis would be on patrol, but I had to have my journal—the record of my thoughts, dreams, and fears over the past two years. Henri went with me—he said to keep me from doing anything stupid. While he entered the house through an open window and climbed the stairs to my room, I waited in an alleyway around the corner. As I huddled in the darkness, I came to a sad realization. I was not having a frightening nightmare. I was not going to wake up in my bed with Mother standing over me saying everything would be fine. I was not going to be "fine" ever again.

We eventually made it back to rue Gît. I didn't ask Henri what he saw inside the house. I don't want to know. I'm not sure I'll ever ask. How can I live with this devastating sorrow and all-consuming guilt?

When she closed the journal, Anne was crying. Her grandmother was true to her word. She wrote nothing about what happened to her mother—nothing about the escape. Emotionally exhausted and with tears falling down her cheeks, she turned off the reading light, lowered the seat to a reclining position, and shut her eyes.

CHAPTER 12

Anne drifted in and out of a restless sleep, finally waking to the aroma of fresh coffee wafting through the cabin. Though several passengers were stirring, there was no one in line for the lavatory, so, carrying her complimentary travel bag, she went to freshen up.

Back in her seat, she decided against a hot breakfast, instead opting for a glass of orange juice, a cup of surprisingly good coffee, and a toasted bagel with cream cheese.

As they prepared to land, she tucked her grandmother's journal in the side-pocket of her briefcase. While they taxied to the gate, she turned on her phone and checked for messages. There were two emails from her grandmother. The first was short. She'd forgotten to mention a driver would be waiting just outside customs. The second message was lengthy. *I'll read this when I can respond from the computer,* she thought as the plane arrived at the gate.

Being one of the first to deplane, she breezed through passport control, picked up her baggage, and, without difficulty, cleared customs. As soon as she entered the terminal, she spied a slender, dark-haired, middle-aged man dressed in a black suit holding a sign with "Madame French" written in large black letters. In precise English, he introduced himself as Gustave Ruel. "But please call me Gus."

"Only if you'll call me Anne."

Gus nodded. "As you wish," he said. "Madame Ellison instructed me to take you to the Hotel du Jeu de Paume on Île St-Louis. I am to say I will be your driver while you are in Paris. Her exact words were, 'No arguments, Anne.'"

"When I was just a toddler, I quickly learned it's futile to argue with my grandmother. In the end she always wins."

"That became clear during the first few minutes of our conversation. If I *had* wanted to refuse her request—"

"You wouldn't have dared."

"Right. She also said, if you give me a 'hard time'—her words—I am to say she has a reason for being resolute. Again, I quote—"

"She made you memorize her message?"

"She did. I am glad I had a pencil and paper nearby so I could take notes. She asked me to repeat the statement back to her."

"That's a little over the top, even for Oma. She must have been making a point."

"Oma?"

"My name for my grandmother."

"But Oma is what German children call their grandmothers. Madame Ellison is French."

"Actually, Oma is both German and Dutch. My father's grandparents were Flemish. In fact, one of his relatives—I believe in the late 1500s—was a Dutch sculptor, Adriaen de Vries. I figure I got my love-of-art gene from him. Anyway, my father called his grandmother de Vries Oma. When I was born, Oma became my name for my grandmother. Which, now that I think about it, is ironic since the Germans caused her so much pain. I'm surprised she never objected. But enough. What does Oma want me to know?"

"I am to say, 'Anne, when I lived in Paris, even the most civilized Parisians became homicidal maniacs on the avenues. I am sure today is no different. You are not to rent a car or rely on those insane taxi drivers. Gus will be your driver! Period!' Madame Ellison knows Paris?"

"She was born and raised on Île St-Louis, but she hasn't been back since 1942."

"When you speak with her, please say that navigating the streets is far more difficult than it was in her day. The maniacs now drive twice as fast, and there are many more cars on the roads."

"I'll be sure to tell her next time we talk."

"Good. Shall we go? I am parked in the limousine lot. It would be easier if you wait with your luggage in front of the terminal."

"Okay, but if you don't mind, before we leave the airport I'd like stop at the ladies' room and then have a quick cup of coffee over at that café. I didn't get much sleep during the flight. I had a cup of coffee on the plane, but without another caffeine jolt, I'm not sure I'll be able to stay awake during the drive to the Île. Will you join me? We can continue our conversation."

"I will get the coffee and find a table while you are freshening up."

"Excellent. Make mine black and *very* strong. I'll be right back."

⌒〇

Ten minutes later, Anne took her first sip of coffee. "Most of the time I'd be wrinkling my nose and telling you to bring lots of cream," she said.

"But not this time?"

"Definitely not. This is perfect. So, Gus, tell me. What other little secrets did my grandmother reveal?"

"She said you studied art history here in Paris during your senior year in college. When I drive, I point out famous sites to my clients, but since you are already familiar with the city—"

"I'd like to hear your spiel. While I was here I was more or less a full-time student. Any noteworthy sites I managed to see were in my spare time, and I didn't have much of that. Over the years, I've come back for my 'museum fix'—usually after visiting another European city for pleasure or on Met business."

"Madame Ellison says you are here to borrow Impressionist paintings for an upcoming Metropolitan Museum exhibition. I hope you also came for pleasure. One cannot come to Paris simply to work."

"I'm afraid I won't have much free time."

"How unfortunate. It is April in Paris. One should experience the joys of spring."

"So I've heard." Smiling, Anne sang, "April in Paris/Chestnuts in blossom/holiday tables under the trees."

"I never knew the charm of spring/never met it face to face. I never knew my heart could sing/never missed a warm embrace."

"You have a great tenor voice," Anne said, as several people at nearby tables clapped and smiled approvingly.

"And you are an excellent alto. Shall we, as they say, take our show on the road?"

"Perhaps we should. That song is of my favorites."

"Speaking of favorites, though I am quoting a line from a novel, not from a song. In *The Tropic of Cancer*, Henri Miller wrote, 'When spring comes to Paris the humblest mortal alive must feel that he dwells in paradise.' I believe Miller's words perfectly describe Paris in the springtime."

"I agree, and since we're sharing, I recently read another of Miller's remarks about Paris. He said, 'To know Paris is to know a great deal.' I confess, when I studied here, I didn't take time to enjoy the delights of the city."

"Then during this visit you must *make* time."

"I promise to try. For now, that's the best I can do."

What a personable man, Anne thought as she stood at the curb waiting for Gus to bring the car from the limousine lot. "Great ride," she said when he pulled up in a silver Mercedes sedan. He put her large bag and carry-on in the trunk and reached for her briefcase. "I'll keep this with me. I want to let Oma know I arrived safely and am in good hands."

"I hope you feel the same way when we cross Pont Marie onto Île St-Louis. There is not much to see during the first half of the trip, so, while you work, I will quietly strive to live up to your grandmother's expectations."

Anne settled into the comfortable seat and opened the lengthier of the two messages from her grandmother, who reported she had been surfing the web, but hadn't been able to find information about the Gaudrieu family. The remainder of the email dealt with her ongoing efforts to research art with questionable provenances and paintings that had been returned to private collectors.

Anne wrote back, complimenting her grandmother for her work and thanking her for hiring Gus. The cursory greetings finished, she got to the point.

Oma, when I read your journal, I was mesmerized—which wasn't good. I couldn't put the book down, so I didn't sleep. Thank you for sharing your life with me. Your words made me feel like I was with you as you suffered through the challenges of the Nazi Occupation. We have a lot to talk about when I get back to New York. In the meantime, would you try to answer several questions? Fax your response, send me an email, or wait until we talk on the phone—whatever's best for you. I assume Agent Q has your all-in-one up and running. Though you can't see my face, I'm smiling. The questions are in no particular order.

1. *You mentioned Madame Huard, the woman who brought rabbit meat to your door. Do you remember her address or if she had children? If so, perhaps they're still living in the house and can provide pertinent information.*

2. *You said* Madame Stumpf and Her Daughter *and* The Work Table *were the last paintings Denis removed from the house. I believe those were the works Elisabeth sold to purchase your freedom. Now that you've reread your journal and had time to reflect, can you remember any other paintings in her collection?*

3. *You kept mentioning the Nazi patrols that kept Denis from driving his truck to your house. The Germans had to be watching the ponts too, which makes me wonder how he was able to transport Elisabeth's art to the continent—that is, if he did. Maybe by river, but that, too, would be a dangerous undertaking. This leads me to believe he may have hidden the paintings somewhere on Île St-Louis. Please think. Do you have any idea where they could be—a place your mother may have mentioned in passing?*

4. *You wrote about Elisabeth's servants. How about Aliza? Though you didn't say, I gather she lived in the mansion. Did she have family? If so, any idea where they lived? Do you recall if the servants were around when you left for Renee's the afternoon of July 17? Could Elisabeth have urged them to leave to keep them safe?*

5. *Aaron and Marjorie Siegle, your Jewish neighbors, sent their children to Avignon to live with Christian friends. They stayed behind, so I assume, like Elisabeth, they, too, were arrested during la rafle du Vel d'Hiv. Where did the Siegles live? Perhaps their children returned to the Île after the Liberation. If they're still around, I'd like to speak with them.*

6. *I was particularly moved by your references to June 4, 1941, and June 4, 1942. So much happened between your two birthdays. You mentioned the pearl necklace, earrings, and bracelet—gifts from your mother. I've never seen you wear them, nor did you reference them when you and Henri related the story of your return to the Ile to get your journal. By chance were you wearing them when you went to visit Renee on the afternoon of July 17?*

Now that I've read your journal, I'm eager to see Paris though your eyes. I realize nothing is as it was during the war, but I'll be visiting the places that were once important to you. We're nearing the city so I'm going to logoff and enjoy the sights and sounds of Paris in the spring. I'll write or call after I take a nap. I'm exhausted. Something kept me from sleeping. What could that have been? Oh right! Now I remember.

Anne turned off the computer and tucked it into her briefcase. "I'm through responding to my grandmother's email," she said. "What have I missed?"

"Not much," Gus said. "The traffic is light. Perhaps Parisians are skipping work to enjoy the lovely weather."

"Speaking of the weather, would you mind if I open the window? I vividly recall the fragrant aromas of Paris in the spring."

"Of course if you would like, though I am afraid diesel fumes will be all you smell for the next few minutes. The air quality will improve when we get to Île St-Louis, but then you know that."

"I can only assume. I confess—this is my first *real* visit to the Île. I only caught a glimpse of the quais from a Bateau Mouche late one afternoon when I finally broke down, bought a ticket, and took a boat-ride along the Seine. Several weeks later I returned for ice cream at Berthillon, but I didn't have time to explore. After reading my grandmother's journal, I want to know everything about the Île. When she and I initially spoke about my upcoming trip to Paris, she briefly described the geographical layout."

"Then I will omit the geography lesson and begin by saying that Île St-Louis is one of my favorite places in Paris. Each time I cross one of the ponts that connects the island to the Right or Left Bank, I feel I am entering a small French village in the middle of a bustling city. The neighborhoods remain much like they were centuries ago.

"Henri Marsolet and his then fiancée, Renee Paquet, fled Paris with my grandmother in July 1942. Henri began our discussion about the Occupation with a short history lesson. If you know anything about the history of the Île, would you do the same?"

"Certainly, as long as you realize I am not an authority."

"Duly noted."

"All right then. Île St-Louis is one of two natural islands in the middle of the Seine. It was named after Louis IX, Saint Louis, who ruled France from 1226 until his death in 1270. Nearly every day the king would cross over from the Île de la Cité to read or pray away from the court. During the reigns of his son Phillip III, and, later, his grandson Phillip IV, the Île was chiefly used for jousting tournaments and royal celebrations. It was also a place for lovers looking for somewhere to be alone."

"To revel in the pleasures of Paris and each other."

"Ah, you *do* understand." Gus smiled in the rearview mirror and continued. "For centuries the Île was nothing but swampy pasture-land, but in 1630 it was divided by a man-made canal. The western end, Île aux Vaches, was used for cattle-grazing, fishing, stacking wood, and washing clothes. The eastern island, Île Notre-Dame, belonged to the cathedral. Until the seventeenth century the entire island was left uninhabited. Then Christophe Marie, sometimes referred to as Paris' first real estate mogul, had the idea of filling it with elegant homes. In 1614, Louis XIII and Marie de Medici endorsed his plan. Marie hired Louis Le Vau, the architect of Versailles, to build luxurious mansions and *hôtels particuliers* for aristocrats and wealthy families along the quais."

"We covered La Vau in a week-long architecture class during my semester in Paris." "Good. Remember his name because he is very important to the history of the Île. As the mansions were being constructed, the inner part of the island was quickly inhabited by merchants and artisans who built more modest houses. Centuries later, many of the nobles moved away, and the Île became home to working-class families. During the 1840s, it was a popular bohemian hangout."

"I assume by bohemians you mean artists and writers who rejected bourgeois values and lived nontraditional lives—not natives of Bohemia."

"You are teasing," Gus said.

"You're right, so tell me about the Île's bohemians."

"They were writers and artists. Their leader was the French poet, essayist, and art critic, Charles Baudelaire. He rented an upstairs room of the Hotel de Lauzun, then known as the Hotel Pimodan, at number seventeen Quai d'Orleans. There, he and his bohemian friends, the writers Victor Hugo, Alexandre Dumas of *The Three Musketeers* fame, and Honore de Balzac, as well as the painters Delacroix and Daumier, founded the Hashish-Eater's Club or the *Club Des Hashichins.* The group held monthly séances devoted to the exploration of drug-induced experiences. Ironically, Baudelaire was not truly a devotee of Hashish. In fact he died of syphilis, not from indulgence. But his book, *Artificial Paradises,* is literature's most poetic description of the hashish experience."

"I remember reading several lengthy passages about the effects of smoking hashish in Dumas' novel, *The Count of Monte Cristo.* I'm surprised the Île has so much history. Tell me more, or perhaps I should say, keep dishing the dirt."

Gus laughed. "I thought my English was adequate, but that is one phrase I have not heard."

"And one you'll probably hear quite often in the days to come. What else do you know about the Île?"

"Not too much, I am afraid. From 1950 to 1980, a period Parisians call the Thirty Glorious Years, it regained its initial splendor, and now, unless your family has owned property on the island for generations, you would have to be Bill Gates, Mark Zuckerberg, or an Arab sheik to buy a luxury apartment along any of the quais."

Or my grandmother, Anne thought, only imagining how much money Veronique had paid for the two apartments in her family mansion.

"Most of the mansions once owned by a single family have been divided into apartments; in rare instances one per floor," Gus was saying. "Those were the luxury apartments I was talking about—the ones no average person could afford. Most buildings contain three or more units per floor. Many current owners rent their apartments to tourists for, in some cases, several thousand euros a week. You will soon see what I mean, but we have a little time before we get to Pont Marie. Would you like to hear about a few other famous residents of the Île in years past?"

"You're dishing the dirt?"

"I guess, though I am combining history with the gossip you seem interested in hearing. At number thirty-seven Quai d'Anjou, William Bird established the Three Mountains Press. With his editor, Ezra Pound, he published novels by, among others, Ernest Hemingway and John Dos Passos."

"I've read most of Hemingway's books, and Dos Passos' *The USA Trilogy—*"

"But you may not know that Dos Passos wrote his first major novel, *Three Soldiers,* at number thirty-seven. Expatriate literary agent William Aspenwall Bradley lived at number five rue St-Louis-en-l'Île He represented Thornton Wilder and Katherine Anne Porter. He also made the deal to publish the autobiography of Alice B. Toklas—"

"By Gertrude Stein. How do you know all of this, Gus?"

"I majored in literature and minored in French history at the university. I am not a full-time chauffeur. I drive to support my habit. I am a writer. Driving tourists affords me a flexible schedule."

"Are you published?"

"So far two books, one about Paris prior to, during, and after the Occupation, and the other a more comprehensive study of the effects of the Occupation on Parisian Jews."

"Did Oma know about your books when she hired you?"

"She said my knowledge of the Occupation was one reason she selected me. She thought I could help you, though she said little beyond that you are here to choose paintings for your exhibition and looking for art the Nazis took from your great-grandmother's mansion during la rafle du Vel d'Hiv. She told me you would explain in greater detail."

"Did she also say she recently purchased the fourth and fifth-floor apartments in the aforementioned mansion? You brought up the high cost of purchasing property on the Île. Now I'm wondering what she had to spend to buy back part of her family home."

Gus shook his head. Glancing in the rearview mirror, he said, "I doubt I could count that high."

CHAPTER 13

"Now that we're on the Île, would you like to take a drive along the quais on our way to your hotel, or should I take the more direct route?" Gus asked as they crossed Pont Marie.

"Definitely take the long way around, and please point out my great-grandmother Elisabeth's home—number forty-five Quai de Bourbon."

"My pleasure. We are now turning right onto Quai de Bourbon. As you see, the road circling the quais is one way. Number forty-five is just ahead, directly at the island's prow-shaped western tip where the road curves toward Pont Saint-Louis. Had we crossed the bridge and gone straight, we would have been on rue des Deux-Ponts, the street that bisects the island and ends at Pont de la Tournelle, one of two bridges to the Left Bank."

"In her journal, my grandmother mentioned crossing Pont de la Tournelle to visit her best friend Renee Paquet at her home on rue Gît-le-Coeur in Saint-Germain-des-Prés. She went frequently until the Occupation made leaving the Île too dangerous for a Jew."

"I live near rue Gît on rue Gregoire-de-Tours. When your time permits, I will drive by Madame Renee's house, but now, I shall point out a few of the Île's most famous mansions. To your left is number one Quai de Bourbon. The ground floor was once a cabaret. At one point—though I do not recall the year— the *prévôt*, the chief magistrate of the Châtelet, lived upstairs."

"The Châtelet?"

"Was a fort originally built to protect the northern approach to Île de la Cité. From the Middle-Ages to the onset of the Revolution, it was where common-law justice was dispensed. Interestingly, most Parisians dreaded imprisonment in the Châtelet more than they feared incarceration in the Bastille."

"Yet the Bastille became the symbol of French tyranny, not the Châtelet."

"That is because the rich and famous—the nobles, kings and queens—were incarcerated in the Bastille. Few ordinary citizens knew or had contact with anyone who had served a sentence in the infamous prison. However, many were acquainted with or had heard about those who had suffered in the dark damp cells of the Châtelet."

Gus inched forward and slowed. "This is number three," he said. "What do you notice about the house that is different from what you saw at number one?"

"There's less ornamentation."

"That is because this is not the original façade. Years ago an antique dealer detached the front. It is now on display at your own Metropolitan Museum. Have you seen it?"

"I'm sorry to say, I haven't. When I'm at the museum, unless I'm not working on a special exhibition or a new display, I spend my leisure time in the Impressionist wing, apparently at the expense of expanding my horizons."

"You mean you wear blinders when it comes to other artistic genres."

"I suppose you could make that argument."

"I, too, appreciate Impressionism. In fact, Monet is my favorite artist. Have you visited Giverny?"

"Would you believe four times? If someone were to say I'll give you Monet's home and gardens at Giverny or all of Versailles—"

"You would choose Giverny."

"Without missing a beat."

"I believe I would too" Gus slowed in front of number seventeen. "And speaking of artists, Émile Henri Bernard once lived in this house."

"Did I say I also like the Post Impressionists?"

"Then you are familiar with Bernard."

"I am, and I like his work."

"Do you also like sculpture?"

"I appreciate sculpture. Why do you ask?"

"Because between 1899 and 1913, Camille Claudel, the sculptor Rodin's protégé and lover, lived here at number nineteen. Her most famous works are on display in the Musée Rodin."

"I took a week-long class at the Rodin. It's a fabulous museum."

"It is one of my favorites, and there is much dirt to dish about Camille and Rodin. However, unless you want to be arrested and incarcerated in the Châtelet for blocking traffic, we must move on."

"I bought *Paris Access* before I came to the university. I don't believe the Châtelet was among the top tourist attractions."

Gus laughed. "That is because it was destroyed after the Revolution, but I am sure you knew that." He pulled over to let a particularly impatient driver squeeze by, paused in front of number forty-three and said, "I have always been partial to this next house. As you see, the building is no longer a single-family home. I am told it was renovated and reconfigured fifteen years ago. Though the family of the original owner still occupies the first two floors, each of the remaining levels was divided into two or three good-size apartments. The original mansion had a lovely private courtyard."

"I wonder if this was where Madame Huard lived."

"I am sorry—"

Madame Huard was my great-grandmother's neighbor. During the Occupation, she raised rabbits in her courtyard. Because of stringent restrictions the Nazis imposed on Parisian Jews, it was difficult for Elisabeth and Veronique to purchase food. Madame Huard and our other neighbors provided what little they could spare. Several times a week, Oma would wake up, look outside, and find rabbit meat or a bundle of home-grown vegetables on the steps."

"How kind of Madame Huard—and at great peril."

"To her and other neighbors who also helped."

Gus rounded the corner, stopped, and said, "This is number forty-five. Had I known this was where Madame Ellison was raised, I would have done my research prior to your arrival. I do know the house is called Maison du Centaure because of the two bas-reliefs in the medallions showing Hercules killing the Centaur."

Anne opened the window and peered out at the mansion where her grandmother had spent her childhood. "I see them," she said.

"Francois Le Vau, Louis's brother, built the home for his family in 1659, but I am afraid I know little else about your great-grandmother's home. That may be good. There is a line of cars forming behind us, and we must move on. If you would like to know more, there is a bookstore on rue St-Louis-en-l'Île. It has many books about the island, its history, and the mansions."

"I'll be sure to take a look. Where to next?"

"Quai de Bethune via Quai d'Orleans. I was going to pause along the way, but there is too much traffic. Quai d'Orleans is my least favorite of the four quais, though it has many fine *hôtels particuliers*. Number six, where expatriate Poles used to meet in the nineteenth century, is now the Musée Adam Mickiewicz. It was named after the Romantic émigré poet who amassed the largest collection of Polish writing, art, and memorabilia outside of Poland. The collection includes Chopin's death mask. You might want to come back to take a look."

"I'll try, or at least I'll walk by and take a look at the façade." She looked behind at the building as Gus drove past. "Is there always this much traffic?"

"It depends on the time of day. We are driving during what you would call our morning rush hour. If we are lucky, some of the drivers will turn toward Pont de la Tournelle and there will be less congestion when we reach Quai de Bethune."

"The quai where Great-Grand'Mere Elisabeth spent her childhood."

"So Madame Ellison said. Quai de Bethune was once called quai des Balcons because of the many overhanging balconies that adorn the buildings. Louis La Vau built numbers twenty-eight, thirty, and thirty-three for his father. Your grandmother said the man Madame Boulet asked to hide her art during the Occupation lived at number thirty."

"That would be Denis Gaudrieu. Part of my reason for being is Paris is to try and find out where he hid the paintings and where they are now."

"When Madame Ellison mentioned Monsieur Gaudrieu, I investigated and learned there is a subterranean passageway leading from number thirty to the banks of the Seine."

"You're thinking Denis moved the paintings from Quai de Bourbon to his home on Quai de Bethune, through the passage to the river, and then to the Left Bank by boat."

"It would make sense. Or perhaps he stored them down there until after the Liberation."

"I doubt it. They would have been too easily noticed, and I'm sure Denis knew the dampness from the river would damage the canvases. However, for argument's sake, let's say he left them there, even for a while. Where did they end up? I wonder if the Guidreaus still own the mansion."

"They may own part of it, perhaps a floor or two, but I believe it is now an apartment building. I will see what I can find out."

"Why don't you wait. On Sunday, I'm having lunch with Arnaud Lessard. During the Occupation, Arnaud's great-grandfather, Auguste, and Denis Gaudrieu were friends, and next week I'll be speaking with Bertrand Lessard, Arnaud's grandfather. Until recently, when he moved to an assisted living facility, Bertrand spent his entire life on Île St-Louis. I imagine he knows or knows of the Gaudrieus. Though he was only ten when the Nazis occupied Paris, Bertrand played significant a role in their defeat."

"When I wrote my books, I spoke with many men who, as boys, fought the Nazis. I would be glad to share my notes and, your schedule permitting, set up meetings."

"Excellent," Anne said, again marveling at her grandmother's luck in finding Gus.

"We are now on Quai d'Anjou," Gus was saying. "And over there at number one is the Hotel Lambert. During the Occupation it was a station on the Underground Railroad."

"And the second stop for my grandmother and grandfather as they fled Paris. Grandfather Robert was a decorated American fighter pilot."

"How interesting. I am sure he told exciting stories—"

"Any talk of war or Paris during the Occupation was painful for my grandmother to hear. Respecting her wishes, he never spoke about his feats of bravery, at least to me."

"That must make you sad."

"It does. I loved my grandfather, but I've recently come to realize I never knew him—at least the man he was before I was born. But what about you? Did your grandfather's stories about the Occupation inspire you to write?"

"In some ways. But I would rather leave it at that?"

"Sure," Anne said, wondering at Gus's strong negative reaction.

"We will soon be at the Hotel du Jeu de Paume," Gus continued. "It is a nice hotel, perhaps the best on the island. I hope I am not being rude, but you seem more the George V type."

"You're not rude, and you're very perceptive. My grandmother met my grandfather at the Hotel du Jeu de Paume. I guess she's a hopeless romantic."

"She is a Parisian."

Gus turned onto rue Poulletier, and then quickly onto rue St-Louis-en-l'Île. He gestured to the left and said, "That is Église St-Louis-en l'Île, the last site I will point out during our short tour. The church was built between 1664 and 1726 according to plans drawn by Louis Le Vau. The Baroque façade is nothing special, but the Rococo interior is beautiful."

"My grandmother wrote that she often met friends in front of the church after Mass let out on Sundays. Renee and Henri Marsolet, and Bertrand Lessard held a memorial service for their fathers here after the Liberation. I'll try to attend Mass before I leave. I'm a fallen Catholic, but I'm still a Catholic."

"Whether you go to Mass or not, I hope you will take time to take a look inside the church."

"I promise to *make* time," Anne said. But as they approached the hotel and she thought about all the things on her to-do list, she wondered if she'd have to break this and other promises.

CHAPTER 14

For several minutes Anne was lost in thought. When she finally returned to the moment, Gus was in mid-sentence. All she heard was, "And in the 1600s, the hotel was a clubhouse for nobles of the court of Louis XIII, many of whom were fanatical about the game of jeu de paume."

She had no idea what else Gus had said before, so she commented on what she last heard. "I know," she said. "I mean, I read about the hotel online."

"Very good," said Gus as he stopped in front of a rather non-descript façade, got out, opened Anne's door, and removed her bags from the trunk. She picked up her briefcase and followed him through a glass plant-lined entry to the main door.

A short, pleasantly-plump, gray-haired woman smiled as Anne approached the desk on the side of a chic lobby that, despite its contemporary air, maintained an old-world feel. Stone walls and beamed ceilings enhanced the open floors above an elevator constructed beside a wrought-iron spiral staircase. Behind them, a brightly-painted Provencal-yellow wall made the already-well-lit room look even brighter. In front of the desk, a group of comfortable leather chairs faced a wall-mounted large-screen television. Beside the TV were shelves lined with old books, making the room look paradoxically old and yet new.

"Ah, Madame French, bonjour," the woman said in English with a heavy British accent. "I am Corinne Grenet Bennett, the owner of the Hotel du Jeu de Paume. Please call me Corinne."

"Bonjour, Corinne." Anne gestured toward Gus. "Meet Gustave Ruel, my driver while I'm in Paris."

"Nice to meet you, Gus," Corinne said.

"And you, Madame. Are you British?"

"I am French. I grew up on Rue Garanciere near the Jardin du Luxembourg. In the early 1980s, my family bought the two mansions that now make up this hotel. At the time, the buildings were being used as warehouses. After eight years of rebuilding and reconfiguring, they opened the hotel. I worked the desk until 1991, when I met and married a Brit. William and I settled in London, but when Mother died in 2005, we moved back to run the hotel."

"The lobby is lovely," Anne said, as she looked out at a furnished courtyard teeming with red roses in window boxes and trees growing in large pots.

"Thank you. Just last year William and I finished a three-year renovation project."

"How nice," Anne said, quickly realizing that Corinne was a talker, and, unless she wanted to listen to a lengthy spiel, she should avoid asking questions. "You'll have to tell me more about the hotel some other time. You have my reservation?"

"Your suite is ready. An hour ago Madame Ellison called to say you had landed at Charles de Gaulle. She tracked your flight and wanted to be sure I was prepared for your arrival. Would you like to go downstairs to the breakfast room before I take you to your suite? I just made a fresh pot of coffee."

"I'll pass on the coffee, but I'll take a glass of juice or a bottle of water."

"Of course. We have both."

Anne turned to Gus. "It looks like I'm in good hands," she said. "Thanks for the tour of the Île."

"At Madame Ellison's request, for the next two weeks, you are my only client." Gus handed Anne his card. "Please call whenever you need the car. It is a short drive to the Île from Saint-Germain."

"I hate that you'll be sitting around waiting to hear from me."

"I will not be wasting time."

"Of course—you'll be writing." Anne removed her card from her purse and gave it to Gus. "Here's my cell number. If you're able to set up meetings, I'll adjust my schedule accordingly."

Gus put the card in his pocket and reached for Anne's bags. "Leave them," Corinne said, shooing him away. "William will take them up. He just walked up the street to buy a newspaper. He'll be right back."

"Then I will see you soon, Anne. It is nice to meet you, Madame Bennett."

"I'll be in touch," Anne said. "And thanks again."

As Gus left the lobby, Corinne stepped from behind the desk. "If you will follow me, Anne, we will go downstairs for your glass of juice."

She led Anne through an attractive lounge-bar decorated with two brown sofas and two red chairs set around a glass-topped coffee table in front of a stone fireplace. They took the stairs to the lower level and entered a warm inviting breakfast area with an open view to the level above.

"I've never been here before," Anne said. "But this room already holds a special place in my heart." She stopped at the base of the stairs, looked around, and continued. "During the Occupation, my grand-mother met her future husband, my great-grandfather, in this very spot. It's where they began their journey to England and eventually to the United States."

"The basement was a station on the Underground Railroad. Over the years, many individuals who began their trek to freedom from our hotel have come back—all with interesting tales to tell. I hope your grandmother will one day return to the Île and tell her story."

"Perhaps she will," Anne said. "If you don't mind, Corinne, I have a question—mere curiosity on my part. When my grandmother said she wanted me to stay at the Jeu de Paume, I was confused—"

"You thought she was referring to the Galerie Nationale du Jeu de Paume."

"For a moment, yes."

"Like our famous museum where members of the Court of Napoleon III played the 'game of the palm,' our hotel once contained jeu de paume courts. When my parents were trying to decide what to call the hotel—"

"Jeu de Paume fit."

"It did. Are you familiar with our early version of tennis?"

"Not really, but—"

"Then let me explain," Corinne said before Anne could say she wasn't interested in hearing about the sport—at least for the moment. "Jeu de paume was a game created by French monks in the eleventh century. The players initially used the palms of their bare hands to volley cloth bags full of hair and cork back and forth. Eventually the bags gave way to balls, and wooden rackets replaced palms."

Anne opened her mouth to respond, but before she could get out a word, Corinne inhaled deeply, exhaled, and quickly proceeded. "Though it is a more complicated game, jeu de paume is similar to modern tennis. Did you know the word tennis comes from *tenez* which means 'here it comes' or "let's play?' Those were phrases jeu de paume players shouted before they served the ball. And the term 'love' comes from *l'oeuf*, the French word for egg, as its oval shape represented zero."

"I play a little tennis," Anne said when Corinne briefly suspended her lecture to take a breath. "I've always wondered why the word love was used instead of zero or nothing."

"Well now you know," Corinne said, smiling.

"Yes I do," Anne replied, wondering if she'd ever get to her room, and again reminding herself never to ask Corinne a question that might precipitate a lengthy answer.

Corinne motioned toward a table. "Would you like to sit down?" she asked. "We can continue our conversation while you drink your juice."

Anne nodded no. "Thanks," she said. "Maybe some other time. Suddenly I'm feeling the full effects of jet lag. I'll take the glass to my room—"

"How about a slice of ham and a fresh-baked croissant? I put the food away fifteen minutes ago, but I will take it out and prepare a plate."

"No need, but thank you. I ate on the plane and had coffee at the airport. I plan to drink my juice, unpack, and then lie down."

"Then I will show you to your room. I imagine William has delivered your bags by now, so we will take the elevator directly to the fourth floor."

Minutes later the elevator door opened into a bright open hallway overlooking the lobby below. Corinne opened the nearest of three doors and stood aside to let Anne enter first.

"I'm already impressed," Anne said as she stepped onto the highly-polished wood floor and looked around the two-storey suite that was simply yet tastefully decorated. Downstairs was a sitting room furnished with a white love seat, a matching overstuffed chair, and two wing backed chairs arranged around a glass-topped coffee table holding a vase filled with yellow tulips. Beneath a railed loft overlooking the first floor, a small alcove contained a table, two chairs, and a small refrigerator.

"The stairs are through there." Corinne pointed toward the alcove. "And the bedroom and bath, as well as the small sitting room you can see from here, are upstairs."

"The suite is lovely."

"I am glad you approve. Madame Ellison said you are moving into an apartment in the mansion where she was raised."

"I am," Anne said, ushering the proprietor to the door. "Thank you for such a warm welcome."

"You are most welcome. William and I are delighted to have you with us. Enjoy your nap. If you need anything, call the front desk."

"I will," Anne said, and she closed the door.

Anne slept the sleep of the dead. When she rolled over and looked at the clock, it was almost four. She dragged herself out of bed and went to the bathroom to splash water on her face. Still groggy, she toyed with the idea of taking a walk to clear her head, but realizing she had already lost over five hours, she carried her computer downstairs to the small table underneath the loft overhang and plugged in a converter.

"Let's see," she said as she brought the curators' addresses to the screen. "What's the most logical approach?" Figuring her lengthiest appointment would be at Musée d'Orsay, she wrote to Claire Malet, the museum's associate curator, asking if they could meet at nine a.m. on Tuesday, April 13.

The meeting will probably take two to three hours, she mulled. Not wanting to interfere with his luncheon plans, she emailed Maurice Roberge, the curator of the Musée de l'Orangerie, requesting an appointment for two.

As she clicked send, she wondered when to schedule the Marmottan. Her first thought was four-thirty. *But that's really too late begin a session that could run for several* hours. She decided Wednesday *morning would be* better and emailed Jeannine Simoneau, the curator, asking if they could get together at nine. *My move will have to wait until Wednesday afternoon,* she thought as she sent the message.

With the preliminary museum business completed, she showered, dressed in gray slacks and a black cashmere sweater, and took the elevator to the lobby.

"Did you have a good nap?" Corinne asked when Anne stopped at the desk to turn in her key.

"I did. I slept through lunch so, as you might imagine, I'm hungry—"

"May I suggest a local restaurant—"

"How about a shop where I can pick up a little something? I prefer to eat in my room."

"Certainly." Corrine pulled out a map of the Île from behind the counter and pointed to an X. "We're here at number fifty-four," she said. "Once out of the hotel, turn right onto rue St-Louis-en-l'Île, Calixte is at number sixty-four. The shop has an excellent selection of wines and terrines as well as breads, croissants, finger foods, and fabulous pastries." She chuckled. "One look at me and you know how much I enjoy their sweets. If you want cheese, walk a little further to number seventy-six. You will smell this store before you see it. But wherever you stop, I am sure you will find the shopping to your liking. It is a beautiful afternoon, so enjoy springtime in Paris as you make your selections."

"Gus made the same comment. I guess a walk on the Île is the thing to do, so I'm on my way."

Anne exited the hotel and walked over ancient cobblestones by a mix of chic galleries, funky shops, bookstores, and delicatessens, pausing in front of several before continuing on to Calixte. "Oh my," she whispered, as she stepped inside. *I could eat one of everything in here.*

The clerk behind the counter greeted her with a friendly smile. "Bonjour, Madam," he said. "Puis-je vous aider?"

"Bonjour, Monsieur. Je voudrais du pain," Anne said in her best French. "Est-ce que vous parlez anglais? Je suis americaine."

"I do."

"Great because je ne parle pas francais much beyond what I've already spoken."

The clerk laughed. "You are looking for bread."

"I'm glad that's what I asked for. Yes, a baguette please."

"What else?"

"I have no idea. Everything looks fabulous. I'll wander around and come back when I've decided."

"Very good," the clerk said before turning to help another customer.

The mushroom quiche looked appetizing, but with no means of reheating, Anne chose a small fish terrine. She bought a baguette and a bottle of Pinot Gris. *Oh why not,* she thought as she picked a mille feuille for dessert.

The same hospitable clerk bagged her groceries and wished her a good evening. Back outside, she considered a trip to the fromagier to buy cheese for her bread, but she quickly changed her mind. *This will be plenty,* she thought as she turned toward the hotel.

"Back so soon?" Corinne asked as Anne asked for her key.

"I'm afraid I'm a lost cause. I skipped the walk, and you were right— Calixte is fabulous. Thank you for the suggestion. I'm sure I'll be asking for other recommendations in the days ahead."

She said goodnight, crossed the lobby, and rode the elevator to the fourth floor. Once in her room, she located a corkscrew in the drawer by the refrigerator, opened the wine, poured a glass, and took a sip. The terrine and bread were filling, so she put the mille feuille in the refrigerator for later, topped off her wine glass, opened her computer, and read the longer of two messages from her grandmother.

Hi darling. I know you're jet lagged, so I won't call. I'm tired too. I stayed up late last night. I'm answering your questions as best I can. Madame Huard, her husband, and their three small children lived just around the corner—I believe at number forty-three, but I'm not sure. She was friendly with Jacqueline Chabot Bouffard's mother Elsie. When you meet with Jacqueline, she should be able to tell you if the Huard family still owns the house.

You asked if I remember other paintings in Mother's collection. After much thought, I recall she owned a Self-Portrait by Fantin-Latour. I also remember a painting of a pianist and checker players, I believe by Matisse, and a work entitled Place du Carrousel, Paris *by Camille Pissarro.*

"What other incredible paintings did the Denis Gaudrieu remove from the house?" Anne wondered aloud as numerous thoughts raced through her mind: *Was Denis truly trustworthy? Could he have removed the paintings, sold two to purchase the forged documents, and kept the rest after the Nazis arrested Elisabeth? Did he ever attempt to locate Oma after the Liberation?* With so many questions and little hope of finding answers, she continued to read her grandmother's response.

Henri says there was never a pre-arranged meeting between Denis and Jules. Denis suddenly showed up at Renee's house with two paintings and oral instructions from Elisabeth. He says that neither he nor Renee knew she was selling her art until the morning of July 18 when Jules told them the money from the sale had purchased safe passage out of France for them and for me. Frankly, I'm not optimistic that we'll find information. You recall Mother warned me never to write anything down. Of course, I didn't listen.

"I'm glad you didn't, Oma," Anne whispered as she read,

Regarding Mother's servants: Aliza was Jewish. Most of her family lived in the heart of the Pletzi, the major center of Jewish Paris that you call the Marais. I believe their home was just off rue des Rosier. I have no idea what happened to her. If she was in the house when Mother was taken, she, too, would have been arrested. Perhaps, as you suggested, Mother sent her away like she did me.

Nor do I know what happened to the Siegles. Yes, they sent their children to the country, so it's possible they, meaning the kids, survived and returned to the Île after the war. If Aaron and Marjorie were home, I'm sure the Nazis seized them too. Maybe Bertrand can tell you more.

You asked about the pearls—my birthday gifts from Mother in 1941 and 1942. In the pain and confusion following Mother's arrest, I didn't think to ask Henri to bring my jewelry box along with my journal when we returned to the Île on the morning of the eighteenth. The turmoil of resettling kept me from thinking about them until the following year when Henri and Renee finally married. I'm sure you can imagine how sad I was when I realized the Nazis took my precious gifts when they made off with Mother's valuables.

How sad, Anne thought. Though she wasn't in the mood to respond, she knew her grandmother would expect a reply. She wrote,

Dear Oma, Gus is great, as is the hotel. Would you believe I don't miss the George V? Shortly after I arrived, I went down to the breakfast room for a glass of juice. I have no idea what the place looked like when you first met Grandfather Robert, but since it was in the basement of a vacant rundown mansion, I assume it wasn't very appealing. It is now.

Gus showed me number thirty Quai de Bethune. Do you know there's a subterranean passageway that leads from the house to the Seine? Maybe Denis took Elisabeth's paintings home and, when the 'coast was clear,' transported them to the continent by boat. Where they went after that is the mystery. Surely someone left a clue—the problem is where.

Several questions came to mind as I read your response to my email. When was Elisabeth's mansion converted to apartments? I assume the house was returned to you after the war. When did you sell? Who handled the transaction?

Gus also pointed out number forty-five Quai de Bourbon. The mansion where you spent your childhood is beautiful. I can't wait to see the inside. I intend to a look around as soon as I've signed the papers.

I'll talk with you tomorrow. Thanks for answering my questions. Everything you wrote adds another piece to the puzzle.

One more thing. I'm so sorry the Nazis made off with your pearls. I can only imagine how you felt then and how you feel now.

Anne turned off the computer, went upstairs, and got ready for bed. Snuggling under the warm duvet, she thought about the innumerable changes that had taken place in her life in just one week and what she might discover in the weeks ahead.

CHAPTER 15

Still suffering from jet lag and wishing she could sleep all day, Anne pushed back the covers, stumbled to the bathroom, took a shower, and dressed in jeans and a blue knit top. *Now all I need is a cup of coffee*, she thought as she waited for the elevator.

The breakfast room was crowded, but there was an empty table by the wall. She picked up an *International Herald Tribune* from the table by the door and poured a cup of coffee and a glass of orange juice. Using them to claim her spot, she went to the buffet, put several slices of ham and a piece of cheese on her plate, filled a small bowl with fresh berries, and, though she told herself she shouldn't, picked up a croissant from the pastry tray. *Why not*, she mused, *I'm in Paris*.

While she ate, she visited with a young American couple spending their honeymoon in Paris. *It must be nice to be young and in love,* she mused as the newlyweds left for a day of adventure.

Back in her room, she opened the laptop and checked her email. Veronique had yet to respond, but there were messages from each of the three curators. "I can't believe they're all available," she said. *And at the times requested times.* She emailed each, confirming the appointments, and then sent John a copy of her schedule, promising to get back to him on Wednesday evening—hopefully with good news.

When she looked at the clock, it was only ten. *I have a free day,* she mulled. *Maybe I'll explore Île St-Louis.* Suddenly, she had a better idea. *I'll spend today seeing Oma's Paris.* She removed Gus's card from her purse, punched in the number, and pushed talk.

Forty-five minutes later, Gus pulled up to the front of the hotel. "I hope you hadn't planned to spend the entire day writing," Anne said as she slid into the back seat.

"I told you I was on standby until I heard from you. You said you want to see places your grandmother wrote about in her journal. Where would you like to go?"

"In no particular order, I want to cross the Pont de la Tournelle and then drive along the quais where my grandmother used to ride her bike. I want to see Renee's house on rue Gît-le-Coeur and visit the Abbey of Saint-Germain-des-Prés. I want to drive through Place de la Bastille and Place de la Concorde, and, of course, I have to see the Marais. That's all, at least for now. I may add a few more sites along the way."

"Then we will begin on the Left Bank."

The sun shimmered on the water as they crossed Pont de la Tournelle. At Quai St-Michel, they passed two young women riding bicycles. Anne shifted and looked out the back window. Engaged in conversation, the twenty-somethings were cheerful and full of life as they threw back their heads to take advantage of the warm spring sun and sweet fresh air off the river. She closed her eyes and pictured Veronique pedaling to meet Renee so many years before. *Despite the horrors of the Occupation, was she feeling carefree and happy? Was she able to ignore what was happening all around her and think only of a wedding?*

"The street's so narrow," Anne said when Gus made a right onto rue Gît "This isn't how I pictured Renee's neighborhood."

"What did you expect?"

"I really don't know. When I hear the word mansion, I think of the houses along Quai de Bourbon."

"In Paris, any four-storey home belonging to one family would be termed a mansion. Rue Gît is narrow because it dates from the thirteenth century when it was called rue de Gilles-le-Queux, which, roughly translated means Guy the Cook. Over the centuries the name morphed into Gît-le-Coeur."

"How did that happen?"

"You want me to dish the dirt."

"That goes without saying."

"Very well then. The story goes that in the seventeenth century, Henri IV, the first Bourbon King of France, kept a mistress in a mansion on the street. One day he and his entourage were riding by her home and suddenly he called out, '*Ici gît mon coeur*,' or 'here lies my heart.' And that is how the street came to be known as rue Gît."

"True story or not, you provided an excellent tidbit of ancient gossip."

Anne pushed the button, lowered the window, and peered out at the rows of plain four-storey buildings lining rue Gît, many overhanging the street on the ground floor and then sloping steeply back on the three higher levels. "My grandmother wrote that she met Renee in front of the No-Name Hotel," she said. "That's a strange name for a hotel."

"You would think so, but the hotel wasn't really the no-name. That is just what everyone called it."

"I don't understand. In her journal Oma specifically references the name of the hotel—the No-Name."

"But she was literally writing about a hotel with no name. Unlike other hotels, the no-name was never named—thus the no-name hotel."

"Despite one of the strangest sentences I've ever heard in English or French, I get it," Anne said, laughing.

"I am glad. In American slang, the no-name would be called a dump. Officially it was a class-thirteen establishment, meaning it was required by law to meet only minimum health and safety standards. To give you an idea how bad it was, the rooms had windows facing the interior stairwell so there was very little light. Hot water was only available on Thursdays, Fridays, and Saturdays, and the only bathtub was on the ground floor. Guests had to reserve their bath-time in advance and were forced to pay an extra fee for hot water. In the guestrooms, curtains and bed-spreads were washed every spring, though the linens were changed once a month."

"How horrible. Who would stay in such a place?"

"Primarily artists and writers who paid with paintings. Madame Rachou, the owner, did not think the art would generate money, so she destroyed many of the paintings and gave others away. But let me back up for a moment. Her affection for artists began when she was twelve. At that time she was working in a country inn, a short walk from Monet's studio at Giverny. After a morning painting scenes of haystacks or the Japanese Bridge, Monet would stroll down to the inn to have lunch with his old friend Camille Pissarro."

"Don't tell me Madame Rachou gave away or tossed a Monet or a Pissarro!"

"I don't know about Monet——."

"Pissarro?"

"Pissarro!"

"Amazing. I wonder how many potential masterpieces were lost because Madame Rachou thought they were worthless."

"I imagine enough to make the recipients very rich if they were smart enough to keep them. If you have heard enough about the no-name and Madame Rachou, shall we dodge the homicidal maniacs yet again?"

"Absolutely, if you think you're up to the challenge."

"I am always ready for battle."

Gus inched his way into the traffic and drove slowly up the street. Despite the blare of horns behind him, he came to a standstill in front of number fifteen and, glancing in the rearview mirror, said, "To your left is Madame Renee's former home."

Anne peered out at the house where Veronique had spent her last night in Paris. "It doesn't look like much from the outside," she said. "But Oma says the inside was lovely."

"I'm sure it was, but we cannot tie up traffic any longer. At least you will be able to tell Madame Renee you drove by her house."

"I'm sure she'll be pleased. Where to next?"

"Église de Saint-Germain-des-Prés."

"Perfect. If you're hungry after I've taken a quick look around, we'll have an early lunch across the street at Deux Magot—my treat."

"Thank you. I would like that. As we drive, shall I tell you about history and architecture of the abbey?"

"I hope you aren't offended, but not this time. The only reason I want to visit Église de Saint-Germain is to stand at the back of the nave and think about the day in June when my grandmother and Renee came to the abbey to reserve a date for Renee's wedding. Oma had yet to realize the full impact of the Occupation on their lives, but as she pedaled back to the Île, she seemed to sense the challenges they would all face before July 25, 1945, the day the ceremony was to take place. In her journal entry for the day, she wondered whether the wedding would happen."

"Did it?"

"Not in Paris. Early on, Oma was going to stand up for Renee, but as the date grew closer and the Jewish situation grew increasingly dire, she backed out. She didn't want her friend to be branded a Jew-lover."

"It must have been a difficult decision for your grandmother to make."

"It definitely was. Henri and Renee finally married in New York on July 25, 1943, exactly a year from the day their wedding was to take place. Veronique and Robert, who was then her fiancé, stood up for them, and Renee and Henri returned the favor the following year."

"And, as the fairy tales always end, 'they lived happily ever after.'"

"They were happy couples, though the horrors of the Occupation drastically impacted my grandmother's life with Grandfather Robert."

"I am not sure any Parisian who lived during that terrible time ever truly recovered. And being a Jew, your grandmother's experience was worse than most."

"I'm sure it was," Anne reflected as she thought about what she already knew and what she might soon learn about her grandmother's ordeal.

"This is our lucky day," Gus said, interrupting her thoughts. "It is usually impossible to find a parking place near the abbey, but a car is pulling out just ahead." He sped up before another driver could claim the space and expertly parallel parked.

"I know you do not wish to hear about the church or its history," he said as he opened Anne's door. "But I would be remiss if I did not tell you that Église Saint-Germain is a very special place. I am not speaking about the building. The abbey is the heart of the neighborhood. Without it, this area Parisians love would not exist."

"Next time you can tell me about the church," Anne said. "But be ready to dish the dirt."

"I am not sure there is dirt to dish. We are talking about an abbey—a house of worship."

"There must be something—"

Gus grinned. "If there is, I will find it."

Thinking of her grandmother and Renee, Anne said little else as she and Gus walked toward the abbey entrance. She waited while he pulled open the heavy door leading to the nave. Stepping inside, she paused and closed her eyes, trying to picture the ceremony that would have taken place if there'd been no Occupation. In her mind's-eye, she visualized a young Veronique dressed in a lovely gown proceeding Renee up the aisle to meet her handsome groom. "Gus," she said. "Would you mind if I wander around on my own?"

"Not at all. I am sure you have a lot to think about. I will cross the street and wait for a terrace-table at Deux Magot."

After Gus left the building, Anne turned and proceeded slowly up the center aisle, all the while wondering what Renee would have been thinking as she approached the altar, and how her grandmother would have felt sitting in the back of the church instead of being part of the wedding party. *I imagine she'd have been paradoxically sad, but happy* she reasoned as she neared the front of the church and stepped into a row of chairs set up for both congregants and visitors. She knelt and said a prayer for Veronique, Renee, and Henri, and then another for Elisabeth and her friends who lost their lives during the Occupation.

I'll have to ask Renee if she and Henri came back here during one of their trips to Paris, she thought as she rose and walked toward the spot where they would have spoken their vows. Sighing deeply, she bowed her head, left the altar, turned, and began to wander up and down the side aisles, pausing to admire the stained-glass windows in the Chapel Sainte-Genevieve, and then at the tomb of the philosopher and mathematician René Descartes.

Twenty minutes later and back at the entrance, she turned for one last look at the altar. Still feeling nostalgic about what might have been and sad about the horrible events that had derailed Renee and Henri's wedding plans, she left the church and crossed the square to Deux Magot.

As she approached, Gus stood and waved her to a table "Another lucky break," he said. "Just as I arrived a couple was leaving. Will this do?"

"It's perfect. I love that we're eating where the great literary figures came to talk and share ideas."

"Though I am not an American, I feel the same way when I am here." He seated Anne, sat, and said, "My favorite Deux Magot story is about James Joyce, who came to the café to drink his favorite white wine with everybody except Hemingway?"

"Why not with Hemingway?"

"Because Joyce said 'Hemingway wasn't everybody.'"

"Is that true?"

"I am not sure." Gus chuckled. "But that is how Hemingway told the story."

When the waiter, dressed in a traditional white floor-length apron and a stiffly-starched, black vest came to the table, Anne ordered a salad with chicken and curry dressing, and Gus selected the salmon quiche and a salad of lettuce and tomatoes.

"Saint-Germain was essentially spared during the Occupation," he said as the waiter left to place the order. "Would you like to know why?"

"Absolutely. In her journal Oma wrote that Deux Magot and Le Flore were strangely empty when she and Renee came to the abbey to reserve the date for the wedding. I assumed the Parisians stayed away to avoid the Nazis."

"Quite the opposite. Your grandmother and Madame Renee must have walked by before the lunch crowd arrived. In truth, the Nazi soldiers rarely frequented the cafés of Saint-Germain. Some historians believe the area's intellectual and literary reputation made them feel uncomfortable, but whatever the reason, this was a plus for Parisians who lived here or came to the area to enjoy life in the outdoor cafés."

"I'll be sure to tell them what you told me. I'm sure they'll be surprised."

"Tell me about Madame Ellison," Gus said. "She sounds like a special lady."

"She is. And she's one of my favorite subjects, so stop me if gush. I know I will."

CHAPTER 16

"Do you think your grandmother will ever return to Paris?" Gus asked as they walked back to the car after lunch.

"Last Wednesday I would have said no, but now I'm not so sure. She never ceases to amaze me, and she *did* buy two apartments. There might be a message in that, but only time will tell. So where to next."

"The Place de la Bastille, though I would be surprised if your grandmother went there regularly. There is not much to see."

"She only mentioned the square one time. That was Bastille Day, July 14, 1940, a day that, for her, was especially symbolic. She was upset the Nazis had banned the usual celebratory festivities and, adding to her misery, it was pouring rain. To pass the time, she wrote in her journal. When the sun finally came out later that afternoon, she got on her bike and rode to where the Bastille once stood. As she pedaled, she thought about the men and women who had given their lives in the fight for freedom and equality in 1789. Mentally, she drew a parallel between them and the Parisians of 1940, who, as far as she could tell, were complacent about the Nazi presence in their city."

"Did she understand what was happening?"

"Not yet. It wasn't until early April 1941 that she personally experienced the effects of the anti-Jew edicts. In 1940, when she mentioned the Bastille, Paris had been under Nazi control for a little over a month."

"She was experiencing a disconnect of sorts."

"Apparently so."

"I hate to change the subject, but we are five minutes away from the Place de la Bastille. With your permission, I would like to say something about the *Colonne de Juillet* in the center of the square. We can return to what your grandmother wrote about Bastille Day when we move on to our next destination."

"There's nothing more to say on the subject, so tell me about the *Colonne de Juillet*."

"It was built to commemorate the *Trois Glorieuses*, Three Glorious Days of July 27, 28, and 29, 1830. This was when the people rose to replace Charles X with Louis Philippe. If you are interested, you can read about the Revolution online. For now, instead of speaking about history, I will address your passion—art. I want to know if you truly wore blinders during the months you studied in Paris. I assume you took a class at the Louvre?"

"Every Monday, Wednesday, and Friday morning for four weeks."

"Did you study Eugene Delacroix's *Liberty Leading the People?*"

"For over thirty minutes, I took notes while my professor droned on."

"Do you remember what he said?"

"Is this a test?"

"In a way, yes. I want to know if you were paying attention to the lecture or dreaming about Monet's *Nymphéas* at the Musée de l'Orangerie."

Anne laughed. "Apparently the former because if I close my eyes, I can picture Liberty holding the flag of the Revolution in one hand and a bayonetted-musket in the other as she leads the people forward over the bodies of fallen comrades."

"Did your professor tell you what revolution Delacroix portrayed in the painting?"

"If he did, I was, as you suggested, dreaming about the *Nymphéas*. I assume the Revolution of 1789."

"It is the Revolution of 1830. What else do you remember?"

"Liberty is Marianne, the Goddess of Liberty—"

"And the national emblem of France. She is a goddess, but she is also a powerful woman of the people."

"She symbolizes the triumph of the Republic. And the freedom fighters she leads represent all social classes. If I remember correctly, the young man wearing a top hat symbolizes the upper class, while the boy holding pistols epitomizes the middle class, the bourgeoisie. My professor theorized that he was the inspiration for Gavroche in Victor Hugo's *Les Misérables*. I also remember he said all the figures in the painting have something in common—their eyes reflect fierceness and determination. When the lecture was over and I had the opportunity to look more closely, I understood what he meant."

"I am both impressed and surprised by how much you retained."

"Maybe Delacroix, our infamous friend from the *Club Des Hashichins*, made an impression on me after all. If I have time, I'll go back to the Louvre and take another look at *Liberty*--if not this trip, then next time I'm in Paris."

"I hope you will *make* time. Would you like to get out and take a closer look at the *Colonne de Juillet?*"

"I would rather see other places my grandmother mentioned in her journal."

"In that case, our next stop is the Marais. You said your grandmother rode her bike to rue des Rosier. Did you spend much time in Marais during your semester in Paris?"

"I enrolled in a three-week Tuesday/Thursday class at the Musée Picasso. And before you comment, no, I don't think Picasso was an Impressionist. I'm not a Picasso aficionado, but I learned to appreciate his work. As for the Marias, I don't need to stop. I just want to open the window and breathe in the scent of rue des Rosiers."

"I am afraid the present-day aroma will not be that of the sweet-smelling roses that gave the street its name. We are nearing the Marais, so take a deep breath and tell me what you smell."

Anne breathed deeply. "Definitely pastrami and freshly baked bread."

"And chicken livers and fresh matzo coming from the kosher delis."

"That too, though I prefer the former."

"Truthfully, so do I. Over there is *Église St-Gervais-et-St-Protais, one of the oldest churches in Paris. You will be able to see the building from your new apartment.* Number seventeen in the square behind the church houses the Museum of the Unknown Jewish Martyr. Inside, an eternal light burns for the Parisian Jews who were tortured and killed by the Nazis during the Occupation. Shall we park and take a look?"

"My initial inclination is to say we're here, so why not stop, but since my great-grandmother is among those being memorialized, I would like to spend an appropriate amount of time looking around so I can tell Oma what I saw."

"Then you have another decision to make. On the way to Place de la Concorde, shall we brave the maniacs on rue de Rivoli or along the quais?"

"Which do you prefer?"

"Either is equally daunting."

"Then let's take the scenic route along the quais. As we drive, tell me about the—"

Before Anne could finish, her phone rang. "Excuse me, Gus." She took a deep breath and, her heart pounding, pushed talk. As soon as she heard Renee's voice, she exhaled, knowing there was nothing wrong at home. "Renee," she said, "How's Oma?"

"Great, honey. That's why I called. It sounds like you're in a car. Where are you?"

"Gus, my fantastic driver, is heading from the Marais toward Place de la Concorde. A little while ago we drove by your house on rue Gît."

"What did you think?"

"It looked like a great place to live. When I get home, I want to hear your stories about the happy times you and Oma had there. And speaking of Oma, if she's doing well, you must have an ulterior motive for calling?

"I do. Last night Henri and I were trying to think of people you could contact to help with your search. We decided to look through some old papers. When I opened the Bible Papa put in my satchel just before we left Paris, a letter fell to the floor."

"You didn't know the Bible was in the box?'

"I did. When we arrived in New York, I put it with other mementos and placed it at the back of a storage closet."

"And you didn't think about it again."

"No, and I don't know why—maybe because the box was out of sight, or perhaps I realized what was inside would be painful to see. Anyway, last night Henri reminded me it was there. For now, I'll only read pertinent parts of the letter. If you're interested, you can read the rest another time. Henri, Veronique, and I think we've figured out what Papa was trying to say. We want to know if you agree."

"Excuse me for a minute, Renee," Anne said. "Gus, will you find a place to park? I'd like to hear what Renee's father wrote without distractions."

"Right away."

"I'm back, Renee. While Gus parks, I want you to know we just finished lunch at Les Deux Magot. I thought about the time you and Veronique walked by—"

"The day we went to Église Saint-Germain to reserve a date for my wedding. I'm sure the café wasn't empty today. Ah, April in Paris."

"Why does everyone say that?"

"Because springtime in Paris is magical. *Joie de vivre* finally replaces the winter blahs. I once heard a great simile: 'Paris in April is like a mad symphony of blossoms.' Even today when I close my eyes, I can picture the cherry and apple blossoms, the daffodils blowing in the gentle breeze, and the pale green shoots emerging on bare branches. I know you're busy, but I hope you'll take time to enjoy the glorious sights and smells of Paris in the spring."

"You make it sound like the city is worthy of all those legendary songs."

"It is, honey. It truly is. Stop for a moment, look around, and you'll know what I'm talking about. Let me put it another way. Take a short respite from your work. Soak up the sun and warmth on a café terrace. Wander through the Tuileries. Find romance."

"Except for the romance part, I'll heed your advice. Gus just parked, so tell me about Jules' letter."

"Would you like for me to leave you alone?" Gus mouthed.

Anne nodded no as Renee said, "The first part of the letter is personal. Papa writes that he loves me and will miss me during the weeks and months ahead. He prays we'll meet again after the Nazis are driven from Paris, though reading between the lines I know he doesn't hold out much hope for a reunion. He goes on to say that Mother is terminally ill. Though she knows she will never see me again, it's her fervent wish that I leave Paris. He must have assumed I'd open the letter when it was too late for me to return home. He was lucky. As I said when I first told you about Mother's illness, If I'd found his message before we flew to England. I would have rushed back to be with her until she died and then stayed on to take care of him. I confess, I was crying by the time I finished reading this first part of the message."

"Why wouldn't you be? I'm teary just listening to you talk about Jules and Adele. What about the next part of the letter? Is it equally moving?"

"Quite the opposite. It's strange, confusing, and nothing like what I would expect Papa to write. He rambles. Of course it's possible he wrote cryptically because he was afraid Veronique, Henri, and I would be captured by the Nazis and the letter would be discovered. I'll read what he wrote, and you tell me what you think. The letter is dated July 18, 1942. He begins, 'A *new day will dawn. Someday soon, God willing, the sun will shine brightly on you and on the Paris we love.*'"

"Those were nearly the exact words Elisabeth used in a poem she gave Oma."

"That's what Veronique said."

"Did she share the poem with you and Henri?"

"Not yet, but she says she will."

"I think you'll come to the same conclusion. Go on with Jules' letter. Sorry for interrupting."

"Interrupt whenever you want. Let's see. He continues,

I wish your mother and I could be with you when you marry your great love. Henri is an excellent man. When you finally return to Paris, go back to your secret meeting place on the roof. Sit on the old metal electrical box where you spent so many leisure hours together, but be careful not to open the lid. You could be shocked by what's inside. Perhaps you will move back to the house on rue Gît when the Nazis are finally driven from the city—as I know they will be. When you go through the foyer and onto the street to celebrate that glorious day, be careful not to trip. There is a loose tile on the floor. It is hard to see, but it is there. I have been meaning to have it fixed, but as you know, I have been busy.

"That seems like an insignificant thing to write under the circumstance," Anne said.

"It does, and the letter continues to be disjointed and rambling. Listen to this.

If you are looking for someone to repair the tile, contact a man named Didier Duplessis. He is now a minor bureaucrat in the Vichy government, but before the war, he and his son Leon were handymen—though I do not know if they repaired tiles. They recently came into a large sum of money. With their new-found wealth, they purchased a house on rue de Fleurus in Montparnasse. Didier is the best, but he cannot help, have Henri use any means available to make him give you a name of someone who can. Didier was recommended by Elisabeth's friend Madame Stumph. He works at her house so often that he maintains a permanent work table in the basement.

"So now we know Didier Duplessis bought Elisabeth's paintings of *Madame Stumpf* and *The Work Table*," Anne said, "And I think we can assume he bought the Degas and the Fantin-Latour Thanks to Jules, we know where he lived—the street if not the number. Hold on a minute. I'll see if Gus knows anything about rue de Fleurus. He's already nodding yes, so I'll debrief him after we hang up."

"We also know Didier had a son," Renee said. "But we don't know if Leon survived the war or if the family still owns the house."

"True, but at least we have a lead we didn't have before. What else does Jules say?"

"If I'd read the letter back in July 1942, I wouldn't have given the next part a second thought, but before I continue, there is something you should know. Henri and I *did* meet on the roof of the house to talk and plan our wedding, and we often sat on a metal box, but it was always padlocked, so I don't know what, if anything, was inside. Nor do I know if the box is still there. When the mansion was modernized after the war, it was rewired, so the old box was likely removed."

"After he talked about the box, Jules mentioned a loose tile on the foyer floor. Was the entry renovated when the mansion was modernized?"

"It hadn't been the last time we were there, but that was five years ago. However, I noticed the original floor had recently been re-grouted."

"If the tiles are tightly attached, it may be difficult to figure out which one Jules was referencing. Any idea how many tiles we're talking about?"

"I would say about a hundred."

"So to locate a specific tile could mean tearing up the entire floor."

"Henri says we'll deal with that issue if there's a need."

"Did Jules say anything else you think might help?"

"Possibly. In the next line he writes, '*As you approach the front door look up at the light and count your blessings, for there are many.*'"

"Was there a skylight in the foyer?"

"No. That's the mystery."

"Was there any kind of light?"

"A crystal chandelier—"

"That's it. Jules is telling you the tile in question is below the chandelier."

"Okay, you deciphered that part of the letter, but what about this next line? It makes no sense. Papa says, '*Several weeks ago Adele's dear friend, Denis Gaudrieu, dropped by to visit.*'"

"Why's that strange?"

"Because Denis and *Elisabeth* were dear friends, but unless they were introduced when he brought Elisabeth's paintings to the house, I doubt he and Mother ever met. And speaking of introductions and dear friends, there's something I've been meaning to tell you. It's not pertinent to our current conversation, but it may be significant, and if I don't mention it now while I'm thinking about it, I may forget to say something later. Anton and Elisabeth were friends before Henri and I met Veronique. In fact the two of them introduced us."

"Really? I assumed—honestly I don't know what I assumed. When did the three of you meet?"

"In the spring of 1939. Henri and I had been dating for several months when Anton suddenly announced there was someone he wanted us to know. Fifteen minutes later, we piled into his truck and drove to the Île. As teenagers say today, your grandmother and I became instant bffs."

"I love it," Anne said, laughing. "Any idea how Elisabeth and *Anton* met? She lived on Île St-Louis and his house was on the continent. They were hardly next door neighbors who might casually run into each other walking along rue St-Louis-en-l'Île."

"Neither Henri nor I ever asked. I guess we didn't think it was important. Maybe Auguste Lessard introduced them. He and Anton were partners during the Resistance."

"But you said you and Oma met in the spring of 1939. That was over a year before the onset of the Occupation. There wasn't a Resistance—"

"I hadn't thought of that. If I had to speculate, I would say they met through a mutual school friend, but, again, that would only be a guess, and I'm sure you'd argue their schools were in different neighborhoods, so we're back to square one."

"Do you know *why* Anton wanted you to meet Veronique?"

"Not really, though at one point he offhandedly said he thought we had a lot in common. I can't imagine he had a mysterious motive. Anne dear, why is this important?"

"It probably isn't, so go on with Jules' letter."

"All right. He continues, *'Imagine how surprised I was when Denis showed up at our door with two large packages. He told us they were precious gifts from a friend for a friend, who would be giving them to a sick friend.'"*

"Denis brought them to Jules to give to Anton. I love that your father used the word sick. Didier was despicable."

"He was. And listen to this. *'Tomorrow my friend will do what Elisabeth asks.'* If we're right, that means Anton will deliver the paintings to Didier. In the following lines, Papa gets sentimental. He tries to make it sound like he's referring to packages, but I know that's not what he means. He says,

I am sad to be parting with these precious gifts. I would like to keep them and hold them close for as long as I live, but I must let them go. Like my friend who will shortly arrive to start the packages on their journey, I have a job to do. Parting with them is part of the sacrifice.

"We believe the precious gifts are Henri and me," Renee said.

"I concur. And the job Jules references is his work in the Resistance."

"Then we're all on the same page. I'm giving the phone to Henri. He has something to say."

There was a momentary pause before Henri came on the line. "Hi, Anne," he boomed.

"Hi, Henri. Is Renee okay?"

"She'll be fine once we get there—"

"Get where?"

"Just before we called, Renee and I booked a flight that lands at Orly early Friday morning."

"Seriously?"

"Seriously! Without a proper introduction and a damn good reason, Thomas Bisson, the man who owns Renee's house, won't let you dig up the entry hall or snoop around on roof. And besides that, Jules' letter makes me want to see what—if anything—is hidden beneath the tiles. I wonder if my father left a message for me—there or perhaps somewhere else. He knew Renee and I would eventually marry and come back to Paris to follow the clues Jules left in his letter, though I doubt he could have imagined it would take us all these years. Anyhow, three heads are better than one. We booked a suite at your hotel."

"Stay with me at the apartment. I'm moving in Wednesday afternoon."

"Hold on a minute. Your grandmother's reaching for the phone. If I don't hand it to her immediately, she may become violent."

"Four heads are better than one," Veronique said. "Renee and Henri can move into my apartment."

"Your apartment?"

"Well, it's yours, but since I bought it for you, I'm sure you won't mind if I use it for a few weeks. I'm already shopping for furniture."

"You're coming to Paris?"

"On the same flight with Renee and Henri. I made my reservation about the same time they made theirs. I just hadn't told them."

"You're kidding. Oma, you've been ill. Can you manage a transatlantic flight? Why not wait—"

"I can, Anne. I must. I'm *finally* ready to face the last of my demons. I wish I'd returned to Paris years ago, but using a cliché—'Better late than never.'"

"If you're sure."

"I am."

"Then I'm thrilled you're coming. Is there anything you want me to do before you arrive?"

"As a matter of fact, there is. The contractors and their men will be there at one o'clock Monday afternoon. They assure me they'll be able to make the changes I've requested by Wednesday at three. I hope so, because the cleaning crew is scheduled to arrive at four."

"So what's my task?"

"Thursday morning at eight I want you to open up for the men delivering the furniture. My decorator has a conflict and can't be there until nine. When she arrives, she'll remain until the furniture is properly placed, the paintings and draperies are hung, and the maids have finished making the beds and doing whatever else is necessary for us to get settled. Would you also ask Madame Bennett to cancel Henri and Renee's reservations? Henri is nodding no, but I'll win this battle. I've already lined up a mason. I assume I'll be tired on Friday, so he's coming Saturday morning."

"A mason?"

"To open up the bricks over the mantle in Mother's bedroom. . . That is if the brick fireplace is still there."

"With everything you've been doing for my apartment and now yours, how did you manage to hire a mason? I hadn't even started to look for someone—"

"You're working, and I have time on my hands."

"I can't imagine you've had a spare minute."

"Maybe not, but I may not be around for many more years, so I need to move quickly. An hour ago I emailed my answers to your last questions. We'll talk again tomorrow after you've met Arnaud. I love you, darling."

"I love you too, Oma, and I can't wait to see you. Gus is showing me *your* Paris. Now you can join us and share your personal stories."

"Count on it," Veronique said, her voice filled with excitement.

Anne pushed the red button and put the phone in her purse. "You heard?" she said.

"I did. I will see what I can find out about Didier Duplessis. If he was corrupt and purchased paintings in exchange for false papers, one of my contacts might know of him. It is also possible that someone who still lives on the street will remember him."

"Thank you. Speaking for my grandmother, we appreciate your help."

"I imagine you would like to skip the rest of the tour and return to your hotel.

"You're right. No more sightseeing today. Suddenly, I have a great deal to do."

CHAPTER 17

"I heard you say your grandmother is ill," Gus said as they pulled into traffic. "If she is coming to Paris, she must be feeling better."

"She is, or rather she *was* ill. With Oma, it's hard to know. One minute she was languishing in bed looking pale and wan. Then, literally overnight, she turned into the Oma I used to know. She's bossy, demanding, opinionated, and I say this with love, often overbearing. Ten years ago when Grandfather Robert died, she withdrew, and I mean that literally and figuratively."

"She misses him."

"Yes, but it's more than that. With his death, she suddenly had time to reflect on her own life, including the last years she spent in Paris. For sixty years, she has adamantly refused to talk about the Occupation and how life under Nazi rule affected her and her mother. To show you how determined she was to avoid a painful subject, until a few days ago, I had no idea my great-grandmother died at Auschwitz. Can you imagine? Ironically, when her congestive heart failure flared, Oma came to life. All of a sudden she's raring to go. There's no stopping her, evidenced by her upcoming trip to Paris. She finally opened up and shared her story. Now she's ready to face the last of what she calls her 'demons'—she's coming home."

"I am eager to meet your energetic grandmother."

"You may regret your words. But enough about Oma. Tell me about rue de Fleurus."

"Very well, though I know more about one famous house on the street than the street itself. The residents of rue de Fleurus can claim one of the best-known addresses in Paris. From 1903 to 1938, Gertrude Stein lived at number twenty-seven, first with her brother Leo and later with her muse and lover, Alice B. Toklas. Every Saturday evening, artists, writers, and critics would gather at her salon to talk, argue, and learn from one another. Everybody who was anybody attended, including Hemingway, Ezra Pound, F. Scott Fitzgerald, Sinclair Lewis, and Picasso."

"I read about Stein's salon in Hemingway's *A Moveable* Feast, and I know about her fabulous collection of oils and watercolors by Cezanne and early works by Picasso and Matisse. I'll *definitely* make time to see her home."

"Unfortunately, that will not be possible. The salon is closed to the public. However, if you are truly interested, you could peek in through the window at the rear of the garden."

"If I come back to see Didier's house, perhaps I will. And speaking of Didier, I imagine he bought his house with the money he made from the sale of Elisabeth's paintings and those of other Jews desperate to escape Paris."

"I doubt he could afford such a house on his salary alone, so I would say yes. I will begin to research this afternoon."

"Thanks for an enjoyable and informative day," Anne said as Gus pulled up to the front of the hotel. "I learned you're not only a driver, you're a writer, art critic, historian, tour guide, super sleuth, and great dirt-disher."

"Thank you—I think," Gus said, smiling. "Call if you need the car, or if I can answer any other questions that come to mind."

Anne entered the lobby, picked up her key from the young man behind the desk, and took the elevator to the fourth floor. As soon as she entered the room, she kicked off her shoes, poured a glass of wine, and turned on the computer. *Oma must have written this before Renee called,* she thought. She read.

Hi darling, I'll try to answer the questions you posed in your last email. Robert, with Henri's help, sold the Quai de Bourbon mansion several years after the Liberation. I don't know when Mother sold the house on Quai de Bethune. . .But just a minute. Renee came in with exciting news. After all

these years, she opened her family Bible and discovered a letter from Jules.
I want to hear what he wrote. More later.

With no reason to respond, Anne opened a message from her mother. Like most of their verbal conversations, Madeline's email mentioned bridge, her tennis lessons, and her blossoming romance with Michael. Almost as an afterthought, she asked Anne how she was doing.

"Nothing changes," Anne whispered. She replied to her mother's email with *Doing fine. Working hard. More later.* She clicked send.

For the next hour, she reviewed her notes for the upcoming meetings with the curators, making lists of specific questions she wanted to ask them and coming up with answers to possible questions they might ask her. *I'll work on this again Tuesday afternoon,* she mulled as she put the Met folder aside.

Still full from lunch, she went to the refrigerator and removed the mille feuille she'd bought at Calixte. *Not a great combination,* she thought as she took out the bottle of wine. *Oh well, I've had stranger dinners before.*

With her 'meal' and a glass of wine in hand, she returned to the computer, opened another blank document, and typed a summary of what she'd already learned from discussions with her grandmother, Henri, and Renee. *There's not much to say,* she mused. *But at least it's a start, and it's all I can do for now.*

With nothing more to accomplish, she put the papers aside, went upstairs, and changed into her nightgown. Tired but not sleepy, she turned on the television to watch the BBC World News and turned out the light.

The television was still on when Anne turned over and looked at the clock. "My God," she said as she threw back the covers back and headed to the bathroom. *I was going to get up early, have breakfast, and then take a walk around the Île. I can't believe it's 10:45.* "I'll be lucky if I have time to grab a quick cup of coffee before I have to dress to meet Arnaud." She took a quick shower, dried her hair, put on sweats and sneakers, and took the elevator to the basement.

"You slept late," Corinne said as Anne entered the room. "I just made a fresh pot of coffee. I put the food away thirty minutes ago, but I will be happy to take it out—."

"There's no need," Anne said. "I have a luncheon date in less than an hour. My grandmother tells me everyone who lives on the Île knows everyone else's business. Keeping that in mind, do you know or know of Arnaud Lessard?"

Corinne put her fingers to her lips, kissed them, and flipped the kiss into the air. "Ah Arnaud!" she said breathlessly. "What woman on the island doesn't know the handsomest man in Paris? When Arnaud married Aimee, black flags flew from all the streetlamps, and when Aimee decided to remain in New York and Arnaud came home, all of the unmarried women celebrated."

"Seriously?"

"I may have exaggerated a bit," Corinne said, laughing. "Yes, I know Arnaud, and I knew his father, Gerard. He was a fine man, as is Arnaud's grandfather, Bertrand."

"I look forward to lunch, though I can't imagine how any man could live up to the buildup you just gave Arnaud. I'd like to stay and chat, but if I'm going to be on time to meet a truly perfect man, I'd better hurry."

Anne filled her cup, and thinking a little exercise might help her wake up, took the stairs to the fourth floor. She sipped her coffee while she selected a pair of gray wool slacks, a red silk blouse and a pair of red heels. "Not good for walking on cobblestones," she said. "But it makes my legs look good." *I can't believe I said that*, she mused. She put on a strand of pearls, a twenty-first birthday gift from her grandmother, looked in the mirror, twirled around, and said, "I think Oma would approve."

With ten minutes to spare, she sent her grandmother a short email.

Oma, I'm on my way to meet Arnaud. I overslept and I'm running late, thus the short note. After we talked yesterday, it occurred to me that I have no idea where to go to sign the papers tomorrow morning. Please let me know.

At eleven forty-five, she left the hotel lobby. When she entered Le Tastevin ten minutes later, Arnaud rose from a table near the back of the restaurant and walked to the front to greet her. "Henri sent pictures, Madame French," he said, "But they don't do you justice."

Exactly what I was thinking about you, Anne mused. "Thank you," she answered, hoping she wasn't blushing. "And please call me Anne."

"Anne it is."

Arnaud escorted her to the table and pulled out a chair for her to sit. "Henri said you're in Paris on behalf of the Metropolitan Museum," he said when she was situated.

"Did he also tell you I'm here for personal reasons?"

"He did, though he was light on the specifics. He said you'd fill in the blanks and tell me what I can do to help."

A middle-aged woman approached the table, interrupting the conversation. "Bonjour, Arnaud," she said. "Bonjour, Madame."

"May I present Madame Anne French," Arnaud said. "Anne, this is Madame Pardee. She and her son own Le Tastevin, my favorite restaurant on Île St-Louis."

"Bonjour, Madame," Anne said, smiling.

"Enchante," said Madame Pardee, who, the initial greeting completed, quickly turned back to Arnaud.

While Arnaud and Madame Pardee chatted, Anne studied her handsome luncheon companion. Though he had the chiseled face of a man, in some ways he looked like a boy. His hair, like in the picture Henri brought to Caffe Grazie, looked to be blowing in a windless room. When he smiled, his eyes smiled too, and the deep dimples in both his cheeks became even more noticeable. His open-collared shirt was just tight enough to show his broad chest and well-toned, muscular arms without making her think he was flaunting his sexy physique. *Corrine was right,* she thought. *The man is perfect.* She quickly injected a caveat—*at least physically.*

Her discourse completed, Madame Pardee motioned to a waiter. "Jacques will take care of you," she said. "Enjoy your meal."

"Exactly what is a tastevin?" Anne asked as Madame Pardee moved on to greet her guests at the next table.

"It's a small, shallow, often-silver cup once used by wine-tasters and fine-wine producers. Today you might see one hanging from a chain around the neck of a sommelier as a nod to tradition."

"I've seen them, though I had no idea what they were. Now I know."

"Ici est le menu," Jacques said, interrupting the conversation.

"Merci," said Anne.

"Shall we order wine so the sommelier can make use of his tastevin?" Arnaud asked.

"Not if you expect me to carry on a rational conversation. I intended to get up early, have breakfast, and take a walk before lunch. However, my body-clock had other ideas. I didn't wake up until almost eleven. A cup of coffee is all I've had since dinner last evening."

"Perhaps we should be having breakfast instead of lunch."

"I'm not a breakfast person, so lunch is good." Anne looked around the charming dining room with its wood-beam ceiling and lace curtains. "The restaurant is delightful."

"Henri suggested we meet at La Brasserie de l'Île St-Louis, but I thought you might find sausage, sauerkraut, and pork knuckles a little too heavy at noon."

Anne wrinkled her nose. "Or at night, but the brasserie sounds like Henri's kind of place."

"You and Henri are good friends?"

"I'm as close to him and Renee as I am to my grandmother. I'm sure you knew they escaped Paris together in July 1942."

"I did. Henri said Madame Ellison hasn't returned to Paris since they fled?"

"That's right—that is until now. I just learned that she, Henri, and Renee will be here early Friday morning. But why don't I start at the beginning and tell you the whole story?"

"An excellent idea. Shall we order first so we're not interrupted?"

"You mean so I don't keel over from hunger and embarrass you in front of Madame Pardee?"

Arnaud laughed. "You discovered my true motive. Can you imagine the gossip your fainting spell would cause? I'm sure phones are already ringing throughout the Île, and you're still sitting upright in your chair."

"If they are, it's my fault. I told Madame Bennett I was meeting you for lunch."

"Then I'm sure Madame Richelieu knows. After she and Madame Bennett finished their conversation, one of them called Madame La Durantaye. The time it took her to call Madame Simonds could be counted in seconds— and on, and on, and on."

"I'm so sorry."

"It's not a problem. If you hadn't told Corinne, Madame Nolet would have begun the conversation." Arnaud gestured to his right. "She's sitting two tables over, and she's paying more attention to us than to her companion, Madame Turmel. It would be fascinating to watch them compete to see who can spread the word that Arnaud Lessard is having lunch with the beautiful, rich, American woman who purchased two apartments in her family mansion on Quai de Bourbon."

"They know that?"

"Does Madame Bennett know?"

"She does. My grandmother mentioned it when she made my hotel reservation."

"I rest my case."

"This is small town life at its best—or perhaps I should say at its worst."

"True, but despite the gossips, I love living here. I'm sure Henri told you I chose to move back rather than remain in New York."

"You never regretted your decision?"

"Definitely not. This is my home. I enjoy visiting the States, but I'm always glad to come back to the Île. I imagine you feel that way about New York."

"Actually, I never gave it much thought. I think I live in New York because I've always lived there, not because I love the hustle and bustle of city life, though the cultural offerings are a definite plus. When I was growing up, I spent summers at my grandparent's estate in the Hamptons. Five years ago when my grandmother decided to live exclusively in the city, she gave the house to my mother, who then gave her apartment to me, or rather she sold it to me for a measly sum. I don't go to the Hamptons very often. I can't bear the social scene."

"Then you're a worker and not a player."

"If you mean do I have a *real* job, I don't. I work for the Met, but that's because I love art and I love the museum. They don't pay me for what I do, though they cover my expenses. I also volunteer for several charities. I guess I'm trying to say I don't have a nine-to-five job."

Jacques arrived at the table, causing a pause in the conversation. "What would you recommend?" Anne asked Arnaud.

"The langoustine salad is excellent, as is the Coquille St Jacques."

"I'll have the salad," Anne said.

"Make it two," said Arnaud. "And an order of mussels." He turned to Anne. "I don't know what they put in the broth, but it's delicious. You're sure you don't want a glass of wine?"

"I am, but I'll have a bottle of sparkling water, or as I learned during my first trip to Europe, water with gas."

"A bottle for the table and a bottle of 2003 Les Baux de Provence, Domaine Terres Blanches," Arnaud said.

Jacques quickly brought the water, the wine, and Arnaud's mussels. "Here is a plate for you, Madame," he said. "Perhaps Monsieur Lessard will let you taste the mussels, a house specialty."

"Since you already brought a plate, it appears I have no choice," Arnaud said, feigning irritation. He put two mussels on Anne's plate. "Take a taste," he said. "But don't like them too much. I don't share."

Anne ate one, and then the second. "Oh my!" she exclaimed. "It's a good thing I'm not begging for more. You'd be forced to display your chivalrous side."

"You're assuming I have one. Most of the time you'd be right, but when it comes to these mussels—"

"No problem, I won't put you to the test. Eat your delicious mussels while I tell you why I'm in Paris. Maybe if I concentrate *really hard* on what I'm saying, I won't pass out from starvation."

"Anne—"

"I'm joking. I'll start at the beginning."

Though they were interrupted, first when Jacques brought their food, and later when he came to clear the empty plates and offer dessert and coffee, Anne spent the next hour telling Arnaud about Elisabeth and

Veronique, their experiences during the Occupation, and Veronique's journal. During the conversation, she answered his questions and further explained why she was in Paris.

"It seems you face a daunting task," he said when she finished summarizing Jules' letter.

"You're right, and I don't know where to start. Gus Ruel, my driver, gave me a few ideas as well as a list of people who may have pertinent information."

"Henri said you want to talk with Grandpapa."

"If he's up to it, absolutely."

"Mentally he's as sharp as he was during the Occupation, though physically he has leg issues. He doesn't get around like he once did. That's why he moved to an assisted living facility. Now he complains all the time."

"He doesn't like living there?"

"That's the problem, he loves the place. He insists *I* was the one who forced him to stay on Quai de Bethune when he could have been having fun at 'the home,' as he calls it. When would you like to visit?"

"If he's available, Thursday morning. Tomorrow at nine I'm signing the purchase agreements for both apartments. As soon as I get the keys, I'll do a quick walk-through. I can't wait to see the miracle my grandmother performed from the other side of the pond. For weeks she's been buying antiques and furniture for my apartment."

"What about the fourth floor?"

"Until yesterday, the plan was to leave it bare of decoration. When Oma initially told me about her purchase, she gave me several options. I could rent out one or both places, combine them into one large two-storey home, or leave the fourth floor as is and stay on the fifth when I come to Paris either for the Met or for personal reasons. The only thing I can't do is sell either apartment. They're to go to my children."

"Henri said you're divorced, but he didn't mention children."

"That's because there aren't any. My grandmother believes that someday I'll meet the right man and fall in love—the kind of love she felt for my grandfather. I'll marry my prince charming and we'll have kids. Those perfectly-behaved offspring will inherit their great, great-great-grandmother's home."

"What if you don't live her fairy tale?"

"That isn't an option she's willing to consider. I knew nothing about the apartment until a week ago. Oma suffers from the early stages of congestive heart failure. Shortly after she was diagnosed, I stopped in to check on her. When I left several hours later, I owned two apartments on Île St-Louis. Per her orders, I immediately booked a flight to Paris to meet with the attorney who's handling the sale, and instead of staying at the George V, my preferred hotel, I'm here on Île St-Louis at the Hotel du Jeu de Paume. Why? Because that's where she met my grandfather."

"She's a romantic."

"As Gus put it, 'she's Parisian.' While I'm here, she's in New York on her computer, busily working with '*the best,*'—she says—decorator in Paris. In the process, she's making every up-scale art and antique dealer blissful. She and her more-than-willing ally exchange pictures and make fabulous, and I'm sure exorbitantly expensive, selections in order to create a modern apartment that looks like the childhood home she remembers."

"You just said your grandmother is ill."

"She is. Or she was—I don't know. She hasn't mentioned her health in days, so perhaps the medications Doctor Richmond prescribed are working. To say the least, she's highly motivated, and as we know, attitude is important. Henri says she's like an orchestra leader conducting from afar. She directs the decorator, the first violinist, who then makes sure everyone else in the ensemble is in tune—the shopkeepers, gallery owners, painters, construction crews, furniture movers, and whomever else she needs to complete the task. And now she's doing the same thing on the fourth floor."

"What a great story. I would love to see what she and her elated—but harried—decorator have done with your apartment."

"If you're serious, I'll call when I'm finished with the attorney. Meet me at the mansion, and I'll give you a tour."

"When the tour is over, may I take you to lunch to celebrate your move to my small town?"

"Sure, as long as we stay local. I have a lot to do before Tuesday morning when I stop enjoying myself and get to work. I have a nine o'clock appointment at the Musée d'Orsay. During the afternoon I'm meeting with the curator of l'Orangerie, and Wednesday morning I'll be at the Musée Marmottan. If everything goes well, I'll move into the apartment Wednesday afternoon. If not, who knows? I'll play it by ear."

"For someone who doesn't work, you're a busy woman. Whenever you move, I would be glad to help. After I finish the hard labor, will you come to place for dinner?

"Thanks but—"

"You're thinking too much togetherness. My intentions are honorable. I'm cooking for my sister Sophie. Her husband Lionel is in Washington D.C. on business until Thursday morning. They met on a flight from Paris to Palo Alto."

"Sophie went to Stanford?"

"For four years. I think the two of you will get along famously, but, more importantly, she may have ideas to help in your search."

"Then I accept. I'd like to hear what Sophie has to say."

"Good. While we eat we can firm up plans to see Grandpapa. I'll call him later today and explain why we're coming. Knowing in advance of our visit will give him an opportunity to think of old friends who may be able to provide relevant information."

"Excellent. My grandmother is arranging for me to meet with Jacqueline Chabot Bouffard, I hope sometime Thursday afternoon. When she was a just a child, Jacqueline watched the Nazis arrest Great-Grand'Mere Elisabeth. I'm eager to hear her account of what happened. Up to now, the only thing Oma knows about the actual arrest is what she learned from Anton the night of the raid and what Henri told her just last week."

"I'm acquainted with Madame Bouffard. Her widowed daughter Cecile, who lives with her mother in the mansion, was one of my father's friends."

"Does Madame Bouffard speak English? If not, I could probably understand what she's saying, but responding correctly would be another matter."

"I would be glad to act as your translator. Even if her English is better than I recall, she might talk more freely if I'm around."

"I accept—that is if you're sure I'm not keeping you from whatever you need to do."

"Absolutely not. Is there anyone else you want to meet?"

"Do you know the Guidreaus? For several months prior to la rafle du Vel d'Hiv, while his two younger sons Charles and Giles kept watch, Denis Guidreau and his eldest son Edouard, at Elisabeth's request, removed the valuable paintings from the house."

"I know Giles, though not well. He still lives at number thirty, though now in an apartment on the first floor. I believe Denis died in the early 1960s. Edouard passed two years ago."

"Gus says number thirty has an underground passageway that leads from the house to the banks of the Seine. I'm wondering if Denis moved the paintings through there and then to the Left Bank by boat. Henri said the Nazis randomly stopped and searched cars and trucks crossing the ponts, so it would have been risky to transport the art by land."

"I'll try to arrange a meeting with Giles, though I doubt he knows much that will help in your search. According to Grandpapa, little information was shared during the Occupation, even among family members."

"Henri said the same thing, but wouldn't it be amazing if we walked into Giles's apartment and there were Elisabeth's paintings hanging on his walls?"

"That won't happen. If someone on the Île owned *one* valuable painting, everyone would know. During your great-grandmother's day, it wasn't unusual for wealthy families to display fabulous art, but with the inflation in art prices, not anymore."

"I wonder if Denis sold the art when my grandmother didn't come back after the Liberation."

"I doubt it. The family is well-off, but if Denis sold the paintings, they would be—

using a term I saw in an old gangster movie when Aimee and I lived in New York—'rolling in dough.'"

"Maybe they have money but choose to live modestly. The proceeds from the sale of Elisabeth's paintings could be sitting in a Swiss bank account."

"Why would they leave their fortune in the bank after the war? Like your grandmother, I'm sure they withdrew at least some of the money."

"That's the point. Oma never touched her mother's money. She doesn't even know which bank it's in, let alone how to access the account. That's why we're hoping to find a message in what will soon be my apartment."

"I doubt anything hidden in 1942 will still be there. When the mansion was converted to apartments, it underwent extensive renovations, and the entire building was modernized about two years ago."

"I know, but I don't believe the workers discovered Elisabeth's hiding place."

"Why not?"

"I'm getting to that, but let me finish the story. My grandmother worried that something might happen to the Swiss account manager who handled Elisabeth's money, a man named Gardiner Vachon—codename, German Victory."

"The banker had a codename? I realize Swiss bank accounts are sacrosanct, but even in wartime, that seems bizarre."

"It definitely is," Anne said, laughing. "Oma gave Monsieur Vachon a nickname to help her remember his real name. Then, thinking it would be better if two people knew how to access the account, she asked her mother to let her copy the account numbers in her journal."

"Did Madame Boulet provide the information?"

"No. Instead, she sat down at her desk and penned a cryptic poem. At the time my grandmother couldn't decipher the veiled message— though I'm not sure she really tried. Anyway, I believe I've solved the mystery. If I'm right, Denis Gaudrieu removed a brick or bricks from above the mantle over the fireplace in Elisabeth's bedroom, thereby providing a place to hide pertinent information."

"You think Madame Boulet realized what the future would bring and planned accordingly."

"I do, but if Oma knew, she didn't openly acknowledge how difficult life was and could become for Parisian Jews under Nazi rule—at least at that point."

"Did Madame Boulet keep important information from Veronique by design?"

"At first, though after the Nazis began to issue edicts against Parisian Jews, she started to share. Still, Veronique couldn't imagine what was happening to their friends in Austria and Poland could happen to them—that was until July 17, 1942."

"When everything became painfully clear."

"That's a good way to put it. The next day she ran, and she kept on running until a week or so ago when she finally shared her story with me. Now she's determined to reclaim her heritage. Step one is to see if Elisabeth left a message about the paintings and the bank account behind the bricks. There's also a question of missing jewels. They may be hidden in the same place, or Elisabeth could have left a second note saying where to look for them."

"Perhaps they're in a safe-deposit box in the Swiss bank?"

"Anything's possible. Right now I'm feeling overwhelmed with what I do know, let alone what I don't. At least we have a plan that takes us through Saturday. Depending on what we discover, Oma will decide how she wants to proceed. She mentioned two other families, the Huards and the Siegles. Madame Huard raised rabbits in her courtyard and supplied Elisabeth and Veronique with meat when they were unable to get even the basic rations."

"And the Siegles?"

"All I know is times were so hard, they were drying their clothes in front of the fire. And they sent their children to the country in early July, though they stayed behind."

"Perhaps Grandpapa can fill in the blanks in their regard, though if they were Jewish—"

"They were likely arrested during la rafle du Vel d'Hiv."

"Right."

"Did I mention that Oma already hired a mason to take apart the fireplace? He's coming Saturday morning."

"She *is* eager to get started."

"You have no idea."

"Tell me more about Madame Boulet's poem."

"I don't recall the exact words, but she says the flames warming the bricks give her hope. She also references the beauty of man's creation—the faces and the scenes that have disappeared in the darkness."

"The darkness of the Occupation."

"Probably. I believe the beauty of man's creation is a reference to her art collection."

"And perhaps to the jewels. Pieces of jewelry are also created by men. What else?"

"I'm afraid not much. She says all will be bright when the lights of Paris are again turned back on, which must mean once the blackout is lifted. She ends with a question about whether she will be alive to feel the joy of that moment. We'll know if I've correctly interpreted the meaning of the poem by noon on Saturday—at least I hope we will."

Anne folded her napkin and put it on the table. "This has been lovely," she said, "but I've told you all I know, at least for now."

"May I walk you to the hotel?"

"What? And light up every phone on the island?"

"No doubt the landlines and cell phones alike will be ringing the minute we leave the restaurant, so we might as well give the ladies something to talk about." Taking Anne's hand, he said, "Shall we go?"

CHAPTER 18

"Corinne must have heard you were walking me back," Anne said as she and Arnaud entered the hotel lobby. "Look behind the desk. She's on the phone, and from the look on her face, she's not confirming a reservation."

"She's probably talking with Madam Pardee."

"Or Madame Nolet, the woman sitting at the table to our right."

"Or possibly Madame Turmel, depending on who got home first."

"Maybe one of them had a cell phone and called a friend on the way."

"Shall we give the gossips more to report?" Without waiting for Anne to respond, Arnaud leaned down and kissed her on the cheek. Looking up, he chuckled and said, "I considered giving you a real French kiss, but I didn't want to ruin your reputation. Be glad I showed at least a little restraint."

"Thank you so much. I'd hate to be labeled a loose woman before I even take up residence on the Île. And thank you for a lovely lunch."

"My pleasure. You'll call after you finish with the attorney in the morning?"

"I will if you give me your number."

"That might help. Shall we ask Madame Bennett for a piece of paper? I'll write my number while she looks on."

"That should start the phones ringing."

"By the time you come down for breakfast we'll be engaged."

"And moving in together while maintaining a second home in New York."

"The wedding will take place in Église Saint-Louis-en-l'Île next weekend."

"Which is why my grandmother, Henri, and Renee are coming to Paris."

"It makes sense to me," Arnaud said, laughing. "So let's talk to Corinne and wait to see if you and I are engaged by morning."

Clearly flustered when Arnaud asked, Corinne reached into the drawer behind the desk and removed a pad of paper and a pen. Handing both to him, she said, "How's Bertrand?"

"He's well," Arnaud said. "I'm taking Anne to meet him Thursday morning. I'd hoped he could join her, Sophie, and me for dinner Wednesday evening at my place, but apparently he has other plans."

"Really," said Corinne, not masking her surprise. "How is Sophie? I haven't heard too much about her lately. Does she miss Île St-Louis?"

"I don't see how she could. She visits several times a week."

Arnaud gave the paper to Anne, moved so Corinne couldn't see his face, winked, and said, "As soon as you sign the documents tomorrow, call me. I'll meet you at your apartment."

"I'll do that," Anne said. "My appointment's at nine. The papers are supposed to be ready for my signature, so expect to hear from me around ten."

"Think we gave the ladies something to talk about?" Arnaud whispered as he walked Anne to the elevator.

Anne looked back at the desk and whispered back. "I doubt Corinne is talking to a prospective guest."

"Not from the grin on her face. I'll see you in the morning."

When the elevator arrived on the fourth floor, instead of entering her room, Anne walked to the edge of the hall and peered down over the rail. Corinne, her face animated and gesturing excitedly, was still talking.

Shaking her head, Anne inserted her keycard, entered the suite, tossed her purse on the couch, went upstairs, and changed out of her dressy clothes. Back in the alcove, she turned on her computer and opened an email from Veronique. Without as much as a "Dear Anne," her grandmother began,

I don't have much time to write. I must finish ordering odds and ends for my apartment, and I still have packing to do. Who knows how long I'll be

in Paris. It may take some time to find Mother's art. I certainly don't want to be forced to shop in any of those monstrous department stores I used to order linens and cookware. I have no connections with current designers, at least not yet, so I'm making appointments with my old favorites, Dior and Nina Ricci. At the same time, I'm continuing my research. And speaking of research, yesterday I received an email from Jacqueline Chabot Bouffard— though her daughter wrote the message. She will receive you Thursday afternoon at one.

Catherine Labbe's office is at 42 Bis Boulevard Richard Lenoir. Once the papers are signed, she will give you the keys to your apartments. Be sure to ask for several spares. I'm eager to know what you think of your new home. I'll be up early if you want to call. With everything I have to accomplish, I can't be lying around in bed all day. Let me know how you like Arnaud. Henri says he's a delightful man. Perhaps he'll be the father of my great grandchildren. I'll speak with you soon.

Anne clicked reply and wrote.

Hi Oma, Thanks for the notary's address. Arnaud is great, but don't start planning the wedding. He's going to help with our search for your mother's paintings. If all goes well, he'll take me to see Bertrand Thursday morning. After he, meaning Arnaud, helps me move into the apartment Wednesday (because I didn't want to ask Gus to drive over here simply to transport my luggage from the hotel), I'm having dinner at his apartment. His sister Sophie will join us. Arnaud thinks she may remember something he's forgotten. Edouard Gaudrieu died a few years ago, but Giles is still alive. More later.

Anne sent the message, googled MapQuest Driving Directions, and looked up the distance from the hotel to Catherine Labbe's office. *It's not far*, she thought as she scrolled to Gus's number. *I can certainly walk and save him the trip.*

"I need to be at 42 Bis Boulevard Richard Lenoir by nine," she said after a cursory greeting. "Madame Labbe's office is between Place de la Bastille and Place de la Republique. It's within easy walking distance, so you won't have to battle rush hour traffic between Saint-Germain and the Île."

"You could definitely walk," Gus said. "But at that time of day, it would be better and safer to drive. I will meet you out front of the apartment at eight-thirty."

"Whatever you say. I won't argue with the expert. I'll see you in the morning."

Anne hung up, opened her laptop, and started to plan for her meetings. Two hours later, her mind racing and her eyes burning, she had prepared over forty separate Word Documents. On each page she copied a picture of the painting from the internet and typed a few words about the subject matter and how the work would be a fit for the exhibition. Next, examining the paintings for common themes, she created three working titles: *Special Times, Everyday Life,* and *Enjoying the Outdoors.* For the next hour, she dragged and dropped the documents under the appropriate headings.

Her initial work completed, she went upstairs and splashed water on her face. Feeling slightly more alert, she went back down, poured the last of the wine from her Friday night dinner, and wrote a cover letter to John, explaining that she was attaching her initial ideas for grouping the paintings.

As I look at the groupings, I'm thinking we should put all the paintings featuring children into a separate category. If you and the committee agree, let me know. If you want to include men, there are three on my reject list. Of course we would have to add additional paintings of males if that's your decision. Personally, I would prefer to concentrate on women and children, but then I'm not the boss—though from time to time I may sound like I am. What I've suggested is definitely a different approach. Realizing it's short notice, if at all possible, would you email me with feedback from the committee before eight my time Tuesday morning. I would like to take our tentative design, whatever it may be, when I meet with the curators. Of course I'll explain that what I'm suggesting isn't etched in stone, but it would be better if we can give them an idea of what our initial plans entail. I look forward to hearing from you and, of course, I'll keep you updated. Warm regards, Anne

It was a little after eight when she finally finished planning for her meetings. Though it was dinnertime, she really wasn't hungry, so she went upstairs, put on her pajamas, and removed Veronique's journal from the briefcase. *Maybe I missed clues when I read this for the first time*, she thought as she set the alarm and climbed under the covers.

The light was still on and the journal lay beside her when Anne woke with a start. She rolled over and looked at the clock. It was six forty-five, fifteen minutes before the alarm was set to blare. *I don't think I read more than three pages*, she thought as picked up the journal and put it on the table.

She showered and dressed in a gray tailored suit and a red silk blouse. With time to spare, she stopped in the breakfast room for a cup of coffee, a slice of ham, and another 'forbidden' croissant. At eight twenty-five, she waved to Corinne and went outside to wait for Gus.

"You're right on time," Anne said. "That must mean the maniacs weren't too aggressive this morning."

"Not in Saint-Germain, but I am sure those on the Right Bank will be ruthless. That is where the crazies get serious."

As it happened, the traffic wasn't too bad, and Gus stopped in front of Catherine Labbe's building at eight forty-five. "There's no place to park, so don't get out," Anne said.

"Do you have my cell number with you?"

"I do. It's programmed into my phone."

"Good. When you are finished, call. I will pick you up right here. I may be a few blocks away, so it could take a few minutes for me to arrive. Good luck with your meeting."

"Thanks. If my grandmother's right—and she usually is—signing the papers shouldn't take long."

As Anne entered the third-floor office, a tall woman with black hair pulled severely away from her face and arranged in a bun rose to greet her. "Madame French, it is nice to meet you," she said in English. "I am Catherine Labbe. I will be acting on your behalf as we close the sale."

"It's nice to meet you Ms. Labbe," Anne said.

"Fortunately, there are no issues involved with the sale of the properties," Catherine continued, omitting the small-talk. "I have spoken with the attorney for the buyer. We have agreed to the terms of the contract, so unless you feel it is necessary, he will not join us for the meeting."

"If you're comfortable with that, then so am I."

"Madame Ellison and I have spoken on the telephone several times over the past few weeks. Per her request, I faxed the papers to her attorney. All of us have communicated by email."

"Then what's the purpose of our meeting?"

Catherine motioned to a chair opposite her desk and said, "Please sit down, and I will explain."

Anne made herself comfortable, and Catherine began again. "I am a notaire. That means I am a solicitor and notary whose function is to formalize procedures, usually on behalf of private clients. This includes buying and selling property. You are here to sign a *promesse de vente*, a legally binding agreement saying the seller *must* sell the property to the buyer. The buyer usually has eleven days to change his or her mind, though in this case I have prepared a waiver so the sale will be final as soon as you sign. My responsibility is to be sure the purchase is handled according to law."

"I'm sure everything's in order or my grandmother wouldn't have sent me here. So shall we begin?"

For the next thirty-minutes, Anne signed and dated page after page—all in French. "I hope I'm not signing my life away," she said as she wrote her name on the last dotted line. "I have no idea what any of these papers say."

"I assure you, Madame French, your grandmother scrutinized every one of them, as did her attorney—an expert in international real estate law who reads and speaks French. She told me, if you ask, I am to *order* you 'to relax and sign.'"

Anne chuckled. "I can almost hear her say the words and see the look on her face."

Catherine stood up and handed Anne a keycard she said would open the lobby door, keycards for the two apartments, and an envelope. "These are spare keys," she said.

"I imagine at my grandmother's request. She said to ask for additional keys. Now I don't have to confess I forgot."

"Your building is quite secure. There is a closed circuit security system on the street and in the lobby. Both are monitored at all times, as are the elevator and the hallways. When you insert your card, a signal is sent to the security office. The person on duty will keep track of your progress until you are safely inside your apartment."

"Am I cleared to enter today?" Anne asked. "I would hate for the police to arrive and drag me to some dark dank prison like the Bastille or, worse, the Châtelet."

"The security company has your picture."

"Courtesy of my grandmother no doubt."

"Yes, and you should probably know that both the Bastille and the Châtelet were razed years ago."

"I've heard that more than once over the past few days, but I had to be sure. I figured my attorney would know."

Smiling, Catherine handed Anne one of her cards and said, "Congratulations. If you have questions or encounter problems, please call."

"Thank you. I will. I appreciate your efforts on our behalf. It couldn't have been easy dealing with my grandmother. She's a lovely woman, but when she sets her mind to something, she can be a bulldog."

"She knew what she wanted, but she was always kind, and, unlike some of my other clients, she heeded my advice. I enjoyed working with her."

Anne shook Catherine's extended hand, thanked her again, and left the office. While she waited for the elevator to creep slowly down, she phoned Gus. As she stood by the curb, she opened the folder of papers she'd just signed and flipped through the stack. "Oh my God," she whispered when she reached the Settlement Statement. *Oma paid 16,430,790 euros for two apartments that will be vacant most of the year.*

Stunned, she returned the papers to the folder, removed Arnaud's card from her purse, and punched in the number. When he didn't answer, she left a message saying she'd be at the apartment within fifteen minutes. "My cell number is 212-555-9358," she said. "The building has a sophisticated security system, so if I'm already inside, call and I'll come downstairs and let you in. I'd hate to have to bail you out of jail because the police think you're breaking in to steal everything I own, or, worse, to inflict bodily harm. Though now that I think about it, you probably know all the officers on the Île. If I don't see you outside, I'll wait to hear from you."

"All finished?" Gus asked as Anne opened the door and slid into the backseat.

"I am, and when you said someone would have to be Bill Gates to afford a property on Quai de Bourbon, you weren't far off base."

"Once you see your new apartment, I am sure you will think the view is worth every euro your grandmother spent."

"I doubt it. Oma was never practical, but this time. . .Well, enough said."

Arnaud was standing out front when, ten minutes later, they reached number forty-five. "I got your message and jogged over right away," he said, breathing hard. "I was on my landline with a client when you called. Welcome home. How does it feel to own two floors of your great-grandmother's mansion?"

"A bit overwhelming. This time last week my life was what I would term normal. Now it's anything but—though the possibilities are exciting."

"I found a parking place around the corner," Gus said, joining Anne and Arnaud in front of the house.

"Arnaud Lessard, this is Gustave Ruel, aka Gus, the best driver, historian, art critic, super-sleuth, and dirt-disher in Paris. Gus, meet Arnaud Lessard," *the handsomest man I've ever seen.*

"It's nice to meet you Gus," Arnaud said, shaking hands. "Hopefully Anne will use one or two positive adjectives next time she introduces me to a friend."

"Oh Lord," Anne said. "My introduction was insulting, wasn't it? Shall I try again?"

"No need. My ego remains intact."

"Anne, will you need the car later today?" Gus asked.

"Not until tomorrow morning, but please come up and see the apartments before you go."

"I am not intruding?"

"Not at all. I plan to take a quick look around, have lunch with Arnaud, and then spend the rest of the day back at the hotel making final adjustments to my presentations."

When they got to the lobby entrance, Anne removed the keycard from the envelope and inserted it into the slot beside glass doors that opened into an elegant marble-lined foyer. "Now we need to find a hidden elevator," she said. "I hope it's not *too* concealed because, unlike my building in New York, there's no one sitting behind a desk waiting to tell us where to look."

Arnaud pointed to a narrow hall on the side of the room. "I'll check over there," he said. He rounded the corner, and quickly came back. "I found the elevator. There isn't a button to push, but there's a slot by the door. I imagine the key to your apartment will take us to the fifth floor."

When the door of the slow-moving elevator finally opened, they stepped out into a wide, sunny corridor. Anne inserted the key into a slot beside the first of two doors. When the green light flashed, she turned the knob and led the men through a large marble-floored entry into an enormous living room. "My God!" she declared, catching her breath. "My grandmother *did* work a miracle, and she evidently spared no expense in doing so. Even with the help of a decorator, borrowing and expanding on Henri's seemingly appropriate metaphor, how could she orchestrate all this from afar in only two weeks?"

"When your grandmother sets her mind to something, she obviously moves quickly," Arnaud said as he looked around the room. "Remind me never to get in her way."

"I won't have to remind you. She leaves no room for interpretation. I can't believe this place. I don't know why Oma wants me to wait until Wednesday to move in. At first glance, how could one improve on perfection?"

"Maybe the decorator did her magic more quickly than your grandmother anticipated. The apartment looks ready—at least this room does. Considering, will you wait two more days?"

"Though I'm sorely tempted, I'll be un-Anne-like this one time and stick to the original plan. I have to put my personal preferences aside and complete my Met business."

"Then it's settled."

"It is. When I falter and tell you I've changed my mind, remind me why I'm waiting."

"Shall we take a look at the rest of the apartment?" Gus asked.

"In a minute. First I want to see the views of Paris from that window."

Anne crossed the room, looked out, and turned back to the men. "Come see," she said. "Gus, you were right when you said that once I saw the view from the fifth floor, I'd think the mindboggling amount of money Oma paid for the apartments would be worth every euro."

While Arnaud and Gus admired the panoramas below, Anne turned back and closely examined the room. Beige wall coverings complemented floor-length blue drapes pulled back to allow light to come flooding in through the floor to ceiling windows. The couches and chairs were covered in cream, accented with the same rich blue in various floral patterns and solids. On the walls were fabulous eighteenth and nineteenth century landscapes, and scattered around on tables and on the mantle above the marble fireplace were incredible antique bowls, china bone-dishes, and Dresden figurines. She walked to a closed French door to the right of the entry and looked back at Arnaud. "I wonder where this leads."

"My guess to the dining room, but there's only one way to find out." He walked over and pushed open the doors into a room that, like the living room, was flooded with light from large windows. Below a crystal chandelier was a highly-polished oblong mahogany table surrounded by eight chairs. A matching sideboard sat against the wall beside a door obviously leading into the kitchen, and on the opposite wall a large breakfront contained exquisite pieces of china.

"There is a marble fireplace in here," Gus said.

"Let's hope there's a brick one in the master bedroom. If not, our search for Elisabeth's art and her jewels has suddenly become more difficult."

"Shall we see?" Arnaud asked.

"Sure, but before we do, let's take a look at the kitchen, though I don't know if I truly want to see what kind of stove Oma ordered, or if I'm procrastinating for fear the bedroom fireplace will be marble."

"This is not like other French kitchens I have seen," Gus said, as he pushed open a louvered door. "It is very large."

While Anne opened drawers and cabinets, Arnaud walked to the breakfast area that contained a round oak table and four chairs. "Come see the view," he said. "It's truly spectacular."

She walked to the window and peered out over the Île, the Marais, and Place des Vosges. "Eating here will be tough to stomach," she said, laughing.

Gus joined them and pointed toward the Marais. "There is *Église St-Gervais-et-St-Protais*," he said. "I thought you would be able to see the church from your apartment."

While the men continued to identify the landmarks in the distance, Anne returned to the center of the room and removed a shiny All-Clad skillet from the rack above the island. "Too bad metal pans won't work in the microwave," she joked. "These won't get much use."

She put the pot back on the rack and opened the refrigerator. "There's no food, but there's a bottle of champagne and a card from Oma. It says, *My darling granddaughter, Welcome to your great-grandmother's home. May you love Île St-Louis as much as she once did.*"

Smiling, she put the note on the island and pointed across the room. "That must be the second entrance we saw in the hallway."

"Then the door on the opposite side of the room likely leads to the bedrooms." Gus walked over, opened the door, and looked out. "I was right. If we turn left, we will be heading back to the living room."

"Then we should turn right," Arnaud said.

"As soon as we see what's through there." Anne opened the door opposite the kitchen. "It's a powder room. The Limoges soap dish adds a nice touch, don't you think? It picks up the colors in the towels. I marvel at my grandmother's ability to pull this place together from a computer in New York."

She opened the next door and stepped into her office. Immediately crossing the room, she pulled aside the burgundy-velvet drapes covering the windows, pushed the French doors outward, and stepped outside. "Come look at this," she said. "I can see the Right Bank, the Île de la Cité, and Montmartre in the distance. I could stand here forever, though I suppose it's time to face reality. Come on, let's see if the fireplace in the master bedroom is brick."

"Shall we prolong the anticipation a few minutes longer?" Arnaud opened the door across the hall. "This must be your guest room," he said. "Come take a look."

Anne entered a pleasant room with a queen-size bed covered by a blue velvet spread hanging down over a beige satin dust-ruffle. Between two antique chairs covered in blue and beige, was a marble top table that held an exquisite Tiffany lamp. Beige draperies pulled back with blue ties hung on either side of a double French door. "Nice job, Oma," she whispered.

"There's only one more door in the hallway," Gus said. "It must lead to the master bedroom."

"I'm sure it does, but I'm afraid to open it."

"Because you're worried the fireplace won't be brick?" Arnaud said.

"I think I'm more concerned that, if it isn't, I'll have to break the bad news to Oma." However, waiting won't change a thing, so here goes."

She slowly pushed open door, took a deep breath, and peeked inside. Turning back and exhaling deeply, she announced, "The fireplace is brick, and the bricks look old."

Arnaud followed Anne into the room, walked directly to the hearth, and looked closely. "I would say these are the originals," he said.

"The bedroom is quite impressive," said Gus.

"It's not impressive, it's amazing. I need a minute to take it all in."

Against the wall across from the windows, a king-size bed was covered in a pale-green velvet duvet adorned with dark-green leaves. The color of the leaves perfectly matched the pull-backs on either side of ornamental draperies framing the French doors. Between the windows

Veronique had created a sitting area consisting of lady and gentlemen chairs, one on either side of a leather-covered drum-table holding a magnificent crystal table-lamp. A chest of drawers in the same wood as the headboard had been placed on the wall beside the window providing a view of the Right Bank. On every wall were exquisite seventeenth and eighteenth century paintings, mostly landscapes that reflected the colors of the décor. Antique oriental rugs in greens and beiges interspersed with splashes of pink, burgundy, and brown covered the center of the magnificent parquet floor.

Gus opened a door leading into a bathroom. "The marble vanity has double sinks," he said. "And there is a separate shower. In Paris, this is also rare."

"Forget the shower. Look at my tub. It could hold three people, and it has a Jacuzzi."

Arnaud opened a door opposite the vanity. "Here's the toilette."

Anne laughed. "Thank God Oma didn't forget one of those."

What do you think is through that third door?" Gus asked.

"Probably a closet. Maybe it's filled with designer clothes. *That* I wouldn't mind." Anne opened the door and shrugged. "No clothes, but lots of room. So, unless I missed something, this officially ends the tour. Before we go, I want to take a few pictures. When I get back to the hotel, I'll attach them to an email and send them to Oma. I want her to see the miracle she, her decorator, and the army of workmen who invaded the space have created."

For the next fifteen minutes Anne went from room to room, taking shots of each from every angle. When she finished with the inside, she opened the French doors and stepped out onto the balconies to take pictures of the vistas below.

"Let's take a look at the fourth-floor apartment," she said as she switched off the lights and locked the door behind them.

"I don't see a button to take us down one level," Gus said. "For added security, the elevator may not move from floor to floor."

"There must be a way. After I get settled, I'll figure out the secret code or whatever it is that makes the elevator do what I want."

Back in the lobby, Anne inserted the keycard for the fourth floor in the slot. Minutes later they entered Veronique's living room. "I can't believe this was what my apartment looked like a week or two ago," she said. "I wonder what this place will look like Friday morning when Oma arrives."

"It will probably be similar to yours," Gus said.

"Likely a little grander. Shall we look around?"

For the next fifteen minutes they went from room to room. "Except for an additional guest room, the two floor plans are similar," Anne said.

"The kitchen is different," said Arnaud. "Your grandmother doesn't have a desk."

"That's not the only difference. Oma has a top-of-the-line Imperial stove. I have a state-of the-art microwave."

"Madame Ellison does not have a microwave," Gus said.

"Nor would she. That's the point."

⁓

"Will you join us for lunch?" Anne asked Gus fifteen minutes later while they waited for the elevator to take them down to the lobby.

Gus nodded no. "Thank you," he said. "But I must decline. Realizing Thursday will be a very busy day, I have made it even busier. I have arranged for you to meet with Isaac Thibault and Isabelle Doyan at three. I would have scheduled the appointment for early next week when your grandmother can join you, but Isaac will be visiting friends in Nice and will not be available for some time."

"Thursday afternoon works for me—that is if you think Isaac and Isabelle know anything that might help us locate Elisabeth's art. I don't mean to downplay the appointments, Gus, but I don't have much time. I need to see people who have relevant information."

"The meeting will not be a waste of time. Both Isaac and Isabelle's families had extraordinary art collections—"

"That, I assume, were seized by the Nazis during la rafle du Vel d'Hiv."

"The first night of the raid. Over the years, they have recovered many paintings the Nazis stole. I am sure they will offer ideas to help with your search."

"I hope so. But regardless, you and Arnaud have given me hope that we'll find some, if not all, of Elisabeth's paintings."

"And after the fireplace is dismantled on Saturday, you may find clues about where Denis Guidreau hid the paintings he removed from the house," Arnaud said.

"And perhaps learn about missing jewels and a Swiss bank account," Anne added as the elevator door opened into the lobby.

"You're sure you won't join us for lunch?" Arnaud asked Gus when they reached the street.

"Though I would like to accept, it is not possible." Gus turned to Anne. "I am meeting with a man who was acquainted with Didier Duplessis."

"Who's Didier Duplessis?" Arnaud asked.

"I'll tell you about him over lunch. Gus, how did you locate someone who knew Didier?"

"Through several men I interviewed when I wrote my books. One was a minor official in the Vichy Government. The others are children of French bureaucrats."

"You're the best."

"No praise yet," Gus said shyly. "Enjoy your lunch. Arnaud, it is a pleasure to meet you. I imagine we will see a good deal of each other in the weeks ahead."

"That's something you can count on," Arnaud said, grinning at Anne.

CHAPTER 19

"Since you're on a tight schedule, I thought we would eat nearby," Arnaud said. "How about La Chaumiere en L'Île? The restaurant shouldn't be too crowded."

"Bad food?"

"Excellent cuisine and a lovely view. The restaurant sits on the tip of the Île overlooking Notre Dame. It caters to a summer crowd more than to the locals." L'été, les touristes représentent logiquement l'essentiel de la clientèle.

They strolled along Quai de Bourbon. Just past Pont Saint-Louis Sa terrasse fait face à l'Ile de la Cité et Notre-Dame.they came to a place that looked more like a cottage than a restaurant. A friendly hostess seated them at a table on the terrace overlooking the cathedral.

"Gus seems like a good guy," Arnaud said while Anne studied the menu. "How did your grandmother find him?"

"Simple. She googled Parisian limousine services and saw his web-page. I'm sure she checked his references before making a decision. She doesn't trust anyone without thoroughly investigating."

There was a pause in the conversation while the waiter arrived to take their order. "Is that really all you want?" Arnaud asked when Anne chose the foie gras appetizer and a bowl of onion soup.

"For starters, but I'm already eying the desserts."

"Dessert is *always* a must. How about a glass of wine?"

"Thanks, but no thanks. After lunch I'm going back to the hotel, and I'm not emerging until tomorrow morning."

"You're skipping dinner? You can't survive on hors d'ouevres and a bowl of soup."

"On the way back, I'll stop at Calixte and pick up something to snack on in case I get hungry."

"How about trying a different place—perhaps L'Epicerie? I'm sure you've heard of the Île's most famous store."

"You forget. I just got to Paris. Unless I missed something, a shop on Île St-Louis hasn't been front page news in the *New York Times*."

"It was front page news here in Paris. Maybe it didn't get top billing in the U.S., but it must have been covered on page two."

"You're serious."

"I am. L'Epicerie became an instant sensation when then-President Bill Clinton stopped in during one of his trips to Paris. The owner, Madame Monleix-Wallig, gushed on and on that the world's most powerful man had been unable to resist her delicacies."

Anne laughed. "Sorry," she said. "The mental image I conjured up with that statement wasn't appropriate, nor was it what you meant."

Arnaud thought for a moment and then, like a light going on in his head, he grinned. "I meant the delicacies Madame Monleix-Wallig sells."

"Of course you did. And, yes, I'll try L'Epicerie. What delicacies did you say Madame Monleix-Wallig offers?"

"I'll answer your question and ignore your inferences. Madame Monleix-Wallig specializes in gourmet delicacies like jellies, preserves, spices, flavored mustards, coffees, and best of all— chocolates."

"Then I'll stop at Calixte and pick up ham, cheese, and a loaf of bread to go with my L'Epicerie mustard."

"You'll have plenty of food, but you'll be eating alone."

"True, but I'll ready for my meetings with the curators. And speaking of meetings, are we seeing your grandfather Thursday morning?"

"We are, but let's forget meetings, food, art, and the Nazis, at least for now. I want to hear about Anne French the woman, not Anne French the art expert or Anne French the super sleuth who's searching for her great-grandmother's art."

"I'll be glad to tell you about her, that is if you'll tell her about Arnaud Lessard."

Arnaud laughed. "I think I understand what you said, and it's a deal."

Throughout the meal, Anne talked about her life in New York, her marriage to Tom, and her mother's crazy society world. Once or twice she began to talk about Veronique and her experiences during the

Occupation, but each time Arnaud shook his head, and she went back to talking about herself. She finally finished and, smiling, said, "So now that I've totally monopolized the conversation, it's your turn."

"There's really not much to tell."

"Come on, before I began my spiel—"

"All right, I *did* agree. You know I grew up on Quai de Bethune. Mother died when I was fifteen, so my father and grandfather raised me in a man's world. At the Sorbonne I majored in philosophy and sociology and minored in English."

"So that's why you speak English so well—almost like a native speaker."

"That and because the year I lived in New York, at Aimee's request, I spoke only English, so she could learn to better communicate with her clients. Now I'm back in Paris, but I'm around a sister who attended college in the States and married an American businessman who also prefers to speak English."

"And now you're stuck with me, an American who once spoke French—"

"And who probably understands more than she lets on."

"No comment. So, moving on. You earned your undergraduate degree—"

"And then attended the International School of Management here in Paris."

"And after graduation you began a career in international finance."

"I did, though not really to make money—more for the challenge. I have ten clients. That's all I need or want. I met Aimee in one of my finance classes in graduate school, and we fell in love. She was raised on her family estate in the Loire Valley, so you can imagine how excited she was to be in Paris."

"Country girl loves big city life."

"That's it. We were happy until she took a job with Credit Suisse. It didn't take long for me to realize her clients would always be her first priority. I probably should have broken our engagement then and there, but I convinced myself she was only excited about her new job—that I was equally important—so I did nothing."

"Because you were in love."

"Not really. My lack of action likely had more to do with my ego. I couldn't admit I'd failed in the relationship. Several months after Papa died, Aimee accepted a position in Credit Suisse's New York office. I joined her after I settled the estate, but despite the different location, nothing changed. If anything, our marriage deteriorated. Once she got to Madison Avenue, all Aimee could think about was making money for her clients and, at the same time, advancing her career. We both tried to make our marriage work, but our goals and aspirations were different, and we drifted further apart."

"So you returned to your fourth-floor apartment here on Île St-Louis."

"I did, and when Grandpapa decided to live in the 'home,' I moved upstairs and sold my place."

"I hope my next question isn't too personal. Are you still upset—"

"You mean am I pining away because I'm still in love with Aimee? Definitely not. My feelings gradually changed. By the time I moved to New York, most of the love I felt when we started dating was gone. I think I filed for divorce because I was afraid what few feelings I still had for her would turn to dislike or even hatred if we stayed together. As terrific as Aimee is, when she's unhappy, she's nasty. Our life together was nearly unbearable toward the end."

"Did you make clean break, or do you still stay in touch?"

"We talk once or twice a week. As soon as the divorce was final, we became good friends. She gives me excellent advice for my clients."

"She hasn't remarried?"

"Lord no. Aimee is married to her job like a nun is married to the church."

"She sounds like Tom."

"Now it's my turn to ask a personal question. Why did you and Tom divorce?"

"There are lots of reasons, but, bottom line, he worked too much. For me, it wasn't enough to be simply a trophy wife?"

"A trophy wife? That's an English phrase I haven't heard."

"It refers to someone he could parade around to show the world he had a bright, well-connected, and, arguably, beautiful woman on his arm. I needed more than a part-time husband."

"Have you considered marrying again and having a family?"

"Not really."

"You don't want children?"

"It's not children. It's family. When I look back on the divorce, it was probably my unwillingness to get pregnant that was, as we say, the straw that broke the camel's back. I didn't want my kids to grow up with an always-absent father. My dad was never around. He literally worked himself into an early grave."

"Your mother didn't object?"

"If she did, it wasn't in front of me. They rarely fought. She had a child. I had a nanny. And because my father worked all the time, she lived the good life. Thank God I had my grandmother. I'm closer to her than I'll ever be to Madeline."

"Madeline?"

"My mother. When she was growing up, my grandmother and grandfather were overly-indulgent. I always asked myself why, but after reading Oma's journal, I realized it was because she didn't want *her* daughter to suffer like she had during the Occupation. Of course there's no basis for comparison, but my grandmother couldn't see that. She was going to be sure Madeline didn't have a care in the world. As always, Grandfather Robert acquiesced. The two of them demanded nothing from her, and Mother never had the gumption to exceed their expectations."

"Yet it appears your mother expected *you* to succeed?"

"Not really. She'd be happy if I were a Hamptons housewife playing bridge and tennis and doing my charity work—not so much for charity's sake, but for show. It was my grandmother who made demands. Why she skipped a generation, I don't know. She may have realized what Mother had become and didn't want me to turn out the same way."

"She wanted you to have a purpose."

"Yes, but I also have the resolve my mother lacks. In that way, I'm like my grandmother. Perhaps she saw that in me. But enough talk about my life. What charities do you support?"

"Among others, I raise funds for Doctors Without Borders. My closest friend, Doctor Victor Janne, gives up his vacation every year to work for the organization wherever they need him. He also volunteers when there's a call for help during natural disasters or medical emergencies."

"That's admirable."

"Victor's a great guy. I'd like for the two of you to meet."

"If not this trip, the next time I'm in Paris. You said among others—"

"I also raise funds for Catholic Relief Services."

"My grandmother gives generously to Catholic Charities as well as to Hadassah, the Women's Zionist Organization of America. She donates in her mother's memory."

⌒○

"Remember, we agreed dessert is a must," Arnaud said after the waiter removed the luncheon plates and offered a dessert menu.

"True, but suddenly I crave chocolat noir ice cream from Berthillon."

"Okay, but mango's the best—"

"You're wrong *Nothing's* better than chocolate."

"I disagree. The check please," he said before Anne could comment.

"So moving on," Anne continued as the waiter left to prepare the bill. "Before we go to Berthillon, let's stop at Calixte—"

"And then L'Epicerie?"

"I think I'll forego Monleix-Wallig's delicacies, at least for today. If I'm having sinful chocolate ice cream, I doubt I'll want much dinner."

"My treat," Anne said when the waiter placed the leather folder containing the check on the table. "You paid yesterday, and I'm a modern woman who prefers to pay her own way, at least part of the time."

"And I'm an old-fashioned man who takes a lady to lunch and not the other way around. If you want to treat, have me over for dinner once you're settled."

"I'll do that if there's Chinese takeout on the Île, and you won't be dining on the priceless Limoges. I'll be dishing the Chinese noodles onto paper plates."

"As far as I know the closest Chinese restaurant is Mirama on rue St. Jacques near Notre Dame. I haven't eaten there, but I hear it's okay. I have no idea if they have takeout, and whether we eat on china or paper plates makes no difference, though I imagine you're a better cook than you're willing to admit."

"I used to cook, but like everything else, being good takes practice. Since Tom and I separated, I don't do much entertaining."

"But you cook for yourself."

"Cooking for one isn't easy, so I usually pick up prepared foods at the store like I'm doing at Calixte."

"Then I'll invite myself over, and we'll cook together, if only to get you back into practice."

"It's a deal, as long as I can figure out a way to make you do most of the work."

"I'll think about your generous offer," Arnaud said, smiling. "Shall we go?"

On the way to Berthillon, they stopped at Calixte. At Arnaud's suggestion Anne picked up a bottle of 2003 St. Chinian, Château Bousquette Prestige, that, he said, was "full-bodied, well- balanced, and a little on the peppery side."

"If it tastes good, that's all I care about," Anne said. "I gather, among your many other talents, you're also a wine connoisseur."

"I'm a Frenchman, and before you comment, collecting fine wine is one of my hobbies. I have a rather extensive cellar I love to show off."

"So in France you don't ask a woman to come over to see your etchings, you ask her to come view your extensive wine cellar."

"I have etchings, too, if you'd like to see them as well."

"I'm sure you do."

Anne picked up a piece of Brie de Meaux cheese and a mushroom tart. "No you don't," she said when Arnaud reached for his wallet. "I'm buying my own dinner, so put your money away."

"All right," Arnaud said in feigned horror. "I would never argue with a woman whose face exudes determination bordering on anger."

"Smart move, my friend. Because you made a wise decision, you may live to see another day. So, how about ice cream. My idea! My treat!"

"If you insist on emasculating me—"

"Arnaud—"

"Kidding. My father taught me to be gracious, so thank you."

"The line's not three blocks long like it was when I came during a particularly hot May afternoon," Anne said as they neared Berthillon.

"Because it's April, and it's still cool. But we still may have to wait for ten minutes or so before we get to the window."

"For chocolate, I can wait."

"Good to know. And now that we've finished lunch and our moratorium on talking business is officially over, I have news. This morning while you were signing papers, I contacted Giles Gaudrieu's housekeeper. He's in London on business, but she expects him back Friday evening. Realizing you'd be busy with the mason on Saturday and thinking your grandmother might want to see Giles, I arranged a tentative appointment for Monday morning."

"Excellent, and before I forget to ask, I hope you'll join Oma, Henri, Renee, and me for dinner Saturday night?"

"Will you be cooking?"

"Of course not, but I doubt Oma's new chef will start before Monday."

"She already hired a chef?"

"Probably, and she'll have lured him away from some fabulous Parisian restaurant, but I asked about Saturday evening. Will you join us?"

"To eat Chinese takeout?"

"Seriously? I doubt my grandmother knows there's such a thing as takeout, and Chinese food. . .? We'll go out. So you'll come?"

"If it's all right with your grandmother, absolutely."

When they finally got to the window, Arnaud ordered a cone with a scoop of pistachio and a scoop of mango. Still protesting that chocolate was best, Anne stuck with her first choice. "Mmmmm," she said as she licked the thick gooey ice cream. "I repeat. Despite your innuendos, there's nothing better than chocolate, and I won't entertain an argument on the matter."

"Then I'll eat my special cone that knows no equal and refrain from further comment."

Carrying the grocery bags, enjoying their ice cream, and window shopping, they strolled along rue St-Louis-en-l'Île toward the hotel. "You have a decision to make," Arnaud said at the entrance. "I can leave you here, or come in—"

"What, and give Corinne more fodder for the gossip mill? I think not."

"If I can't persuade you otherwise, thank you for the tour of your apartment." Leaning down, he kissed her lightly on cheek. "This was for you, not Corinne. I'll call tomorrow to hear how your meetings went."

"Sounds good." Anne reached out, squeezed Arnaud's hand, turned and entered the lobby.

"Are you officially a homeowner?" Corinne asked when Anne stopped at the desk for her key.

"I am," Anne said, wondering how long it would take Corinne to trumpet the news to all her friends on the Île. "I still intend to move Wednesday, but I wasn't able to schedule three meetings on Tuesday. Realizing the posted check-out time is noon, could I push mine to one? I'll pay for the additional day."

"There is no need. The cleaning staff works until three. I will put your room at the end of the schedule."

"Thanks. "Anne held up the bags from Calixte. "I'm eating in, so I doubt I'll be back down."

"I am not on duty in the morning, so I will tell you now. Good luck at your meetings."

"Thank you. Have a good night."

Once in her room, Anne wasted no time. She went upstairs to change, came back down, and connected her phone to the computer. After downloading the pictures, she attached them to a message and wrote,

Dear Oma,

When I got to my apartment, I expected to see bare walls. Instead I walked into THE most beautiful room I've ever seen. I can't believe what you accomplished—and from New York at that. As far as I can tell, I could move in today, but however tempting, I'm sticking to my original plan. Perhaps you have more work scheduled, though I can't imagine how you could improve on perfection. I could go on and on, but words won't do justice to what you and your decorator have created. So I'm sending pictures. If Elisabeth's home looked anything like mine, it was truly spectacular. I may spend all my time moving from window to window enjoying the amazing vistas below.

Guess what? You were right! There is a brick fireplace in my bedroom. Arnaud says the bricks are old, so maybe we're in luck. We'll know Saturday when the mason comes.

Speaking of Arnaud, he made a tentative appointment for us with Giles Guidreau Monday morning at nine. But I'm not sitting around waiting for you to arrive. I'm hard at work. Thursday morning Arnaud's taking me to see Bertrand. At one, he's going with me to see Jacqueline Bouffard. He figures she'll be more comfortable with someone she knows. He thinks she speaks English, but if not, he'll be there to translate for me. I may be able to understand what she's saying, but when it comes to answering—okay, no comment. At three, Gus and I are meeting with Isabelle Doyan and Isaac Thibault. The Nazis arrested their parents—and I believe Isaac— and seized their art collections during la rafle du Vel d'Hiv. Over the years, both Isabelle and Isaac have recover most of their families' treasures. Hopefully they'll be able to provide information that will help in our search.

I almost forgot to ask. What did you tell Mother? I can't keep saying I'm busy and that's why I'm not responding to her emails in more detail. Once I know what, if anything, you said, I'll know what to write.

Let me know what you think of the attached pictures. I can't wait for you to see the apartments in person. Now I'll open Henri's email and then prepare for my meetings. Wish me luck.

Anne opened Henri's message and read.

Hi, Anne, I doubted you'd have time to contact Gregoire Drouin, so I set up an appointment for Monday morning. Go with me or, if you have plans, I'll go alone. Hopefully he will provide names of people to contact and they, in turn, will do the same.

When the mason finishes at your apartment, he will accompany me to rue Gît to meet with Thomas Bisson, the owner of Renee's childhood home. Thomas says we can do whatever's necessary to find what, if anything, Jules left beneath the entry tiles. I'm hoping we can begin the project early next week. I'm not telling Thomas about the electrical box on the roof until we're together. I don't want him going upstairs to see what's there before I arrive.

Your grandmother is excited about our trip. I advise you to get a lot of rest. You'll need all the energy you can muster to keep up with her. She told me to say you don't have to open the door Thursday morning. She hired a security company. A guard will be on duty throughout the day.

I've never seen Veronique so busy—not even in Paris when we were young and she had energy to spare. I can't imagine what her phone bill will look like. She spends much of her time talking with one person or another in Paris. Oh well, two weeks ago we thought she was beyond help. Now she's like a teenager going out on her first date. If I didn't know better, I'd think she's Betty White's little sister. She has that much energy. Expect anything.

I'm ready for you, Oma. Anne opened the email from John, who wrote,

Good morning, Anne. During a conference call last evening, the committee voted unanimously to eliminate Impressionist paintings featuring men— that is if the museums give us what we've requested. If any one of the curators tells you a particular painting is unavailable, feel free to take a look at others he or she might be willing to loan. You're aware of our needs. Should you need to talk with me during any of your meetings, you have my cell number. Good luck!

Throughout the afternoon, Anne worked. She checked the museums' websites, making lists of alternative works in the event those the committee wanted to borrow were unavailable. "This is about as far as I can go," she said as she looked over her work for the final time, attached the document, and sent it to John.

Satisfied she was ready to conduct the Met's business at all three museums, she poured a glass of wine, retrieved her mushroom tart from the refrigerator, sliced some cheese, and cut a piece of bread. While she ate, she made yet another list, this one of potential questions for the curators.

She had barely finished packing her briefcase for the morning meeting when her cell phone rang. "I've got to stop worrying that every call will be bad news about Oma," she whispered, seeing an unidentified number on the caller ID. "Hello," she answered tentatively.

"How was your mushroom tart?" Arnaud asked.

"Delicious. And the wine was superb—though I didn't taste the pepper."

"I believe I said the wine's on the peppery side, not that it's seasoned with pepper. How's work coming?"

"I just finished."

"Then how about a walk? I'll pick you up in ten minutes?"

"What? And have tongues wagging yet again?"

"If you're worried about the gossips, then meet me. There's a little square at the southeastern end of the Île."

"Square Barye. Gus pointed it out when he took me on a short tour of the island. May I take a rain-check?"

"Of course I'm disappointed, but I understand. Your mind is on Met business. Good luck tomorrow."

"Thanks. Both for the offer and the call."

Sighing, Anne pushed end, turned off the computer, and went up to her bedroom. "Damn, I'm getting old," she grumbled. "It's only nine-fifteen."

She almost hit redial to a tell Arnaud she had reconsidered, but she quickly changed her mind. *As pleasant as it sounds, Square Barye will have to wait for another day."*

CHAPTER 20

Anne didn't need the alarm. She got up early, showered, and dressed in black slacks, a red blazer, and a red and navy-blue silk blouse. At eight-fifteen she checked her briefcase one final time, took the elevator down, turned in her key, and went outside to meet Gus.

Pont de la Tournelle was no problem, but as soon as they reached the Left Bank, the traffic slowed to a crawl. "It may seem like we aren't making progress," Gus said. "But we are better off going this way. The traffic on the Right Bank would be much worse."

Twenty-minutes later he pulled up to the museum entrance. "How long do you expect your meeting to last?" he asked as he opened Anne's door.

"I have no idea. We could finish quickly, or I may have to negotiate. I'll call when I'm ready to leave. My next meeting isn't until two, so we should have time for lunch. You pick the place."

"There is not much near the museum, but. . . I have a great idea."

"Tell me."

"It is a surprise. Good luck with Madame Malet."

There was already a line forming outside the ticket office as Anne gave the guard on duty her name. He checked the list and opened the door into a light-filled lobby filled with statues of robust maidens and eager men where railroad tracks once ran. As she neared a bronze sculpture appropriately named *La Danse*, a tall rail-thin woman with short red hair, made redder by dye, approached. Though not exactly masculine, her tailored suit did nothing to flatter her figure, and the dark thick-rimmed glasses didn't help either. "Bonjour, Madame French," she said. "Welcome to the Musée d'Orsay."

"I'm happy to be here." Anne extended her hand. "And please call me Anne."

"And I am Claire." The curator shook hands and motioned toward a door on the far side of the lobby. "We will talk in my office. Would you like coffee or tea?"

"Thank you. Neither at the moment. Maybe later."

In the office Claire pointed to one of two black leather chairs opposite her desk. Anne sat down and removed the folder containing the committee's selections from her briefcase. "These are the paintings the Met would like to borrow from the Musée D'Orsay," she said. "But before you look, you should know we're flexible and open to suggestions. If, for whatever reason, one piece doesn't work, perhaps another will do equally well."

"There was a fax from John waiting on my desk when I arrived earlier. Seeing what you had in mind prior to our meeting will allow us to expedite the process."

"At John's suggestion, I prepared a second list for your consideration." Anne passed the committee's original selections and the addendum across the desk.

Claire studied both lists, looked up, and said, "I believe most of your requests are doable. Shall we address your original list first? I will tell you what I already know. We will loan *Bal du Joulin de la Galette*. When we finish our discussion, we will stop by room thirty-two so you can take a look."

"The painting is one of my favorites," Anne said. "I'm eager to see it again."

Claire's eyebrows arched. "I'm confused," she said. "John wrote that you arrived Friday. Did you have time to visit the museum prior to our meeting today?"

"No, but in the spirit of full disclosure, I'm familiar with all but one or two paintings on the list. I majored in art history at Wellesley. During my senior year, I spent a semester studying in Paris."

"Excellent!" Claire said. "With your background and knowledge of our collection, our task just became easier. When I received your email asking for an appointment, I was working on tentative plans for a Toulouse Lautrec exhibit we hope to open here next spring, so I failed to check your credentials. Some museums send novices or, worse, attorneys to negotiate, which can make the selection process difficult. You and I will not have to bother with the usual preliminaries. Did you bring your initial design for the exhibit?'

"I did, but before we begin that discussion, I hope you will consider borrowing several Lautrec paintings from the Met Collection."

"I have already spoken with John about *Divan Japonais, The Street Walker,* and *Aristide Bruant at his Cabaret.*"

"You might also want to consider *Woman Before a Mirror.* It's another of my favorites."

"I will." Claire made a note. "And thank you."

Anne removed the organizational chart from her briefcase and handed it to Claire. "Of course this is only a first-draft," she said. "Once the pros know which paintings we'll feature, my plan will be out-of-date."

"Believe me. I am familiar with the process. There have been many times when I thought I had come up with the perfect blueprint for an exhibition or a new display, only to find the final groupings were nothing like I originally envisioned."

"Then you know the categories and subcategories I've created will be refined. But this should give you an idea of what we're thinking. I'm sorry the design is hand-drawn and not computer generated. I'm staying at a small hotel without a business center, so I don't have access to a printer."

"Which hotel?"

"The Hotel du Jeu de Paume on Île St-Louis. My grandmother was raised on Quai de Bourbon. Several weeks ago she purchased two apartments in what was once her mother's mansion. And speaking of Great-Grand'Mere Elisabeth, if time permits, when we complete our business, I would like to speak with you about a personal matter that has to do with her art collection."

"Certainly," Claire said. "I have blocked off the entire morning, so if we get to work, there should be plenty of time to talk. Shall we begin?"

"Absolutely."

Claire perused the list again, looked up, and said, "As I said, we will give you *Bal du Joulin de la Galette,* but *Liseuse Vert* is currently on loan. Before you arrived, I checked on *Sur la Plage.* It is available."

"What about Manet's *Le dejeuner sur l'herbe*? Besides being a great fit for the show, it's a personal favorite."

"You are not alone. The painting is one of the most popular in our collection. For that reason, I am not authorized to make a decision. I have submitted your request to my superior, but I have yet to hear back. If I receive word before you leave the museum, of course I will let you know. Otherwise, I will email John with our answer."

Claire again turned her attention to the list. "Let's see," she continued. "We will also loan Degas's *L'absinthe* and *Les Repasseuses*."

"When we began to plan, we were only going to feature works by French Impressionists. But after looking over our list, we decided that paintings by Mary Cassatt would enhance the exhibition. Americans enjoy seeing art created by their fellow countrymen alongside those of European greats."

"I agree. And I see you have included the French female Impressionist Berthe Morisot among the paintings of her fellow male artists. Adding Mary Cassatt means you are including a second woman."

"Which may be a draw for women viewers."

"Precisely. You are asking to borrow Morisot's *Femme Cousant* as well as *Jeune Fille au Jardin*. I do not foresee problems in their regard. Both paintings were rotated out of the exhibition several months ago, so neither is currently on the floor. I will call and arrange for you to see them if you would like."

"No need, but thank you. I'm familiar with both works. I wrote a paper on Morisot for my Impressionist class. Both paintings were on display at the time."

Anne sat quietly while Claire continued to examine both the original list and the addendum. After a few minutes she looked up and asked, "What about Renoir's *The Swing*? The setting and central figure would fit into your grouping of women enjoying the outdoors."

Anne jotted a note on her pad. "May I get back to you on that one?" she said. "I admire the painting, but we may have too many Renoirs. We're asking the Musée de l'Orangerie to provide four works from their collection. Once I know if they'll honor our request, I'll revisit your offer."

"Then I will write 'tentative' on my list. What about Manet's *Beer Waitress?*"

"Absolutely!"

"Good. There's a Morisot, *Femme a sa toilette*, that isn't on your initial list or the addendum."

"We're already hanging several paintings of women at their toilette, but I'll run your suggestion by John and the committee. Are there other works I should mention when I email him this evening?"

"I have three additional Pissarros that might fit into your plan: *Woman with a Green Scarf, Jeune fille a la baguette,* and *Woman Hanging Laundry.*"

"May I take a look at all three before I make my recommendation?"

"Of course, and ask John about Degas' *Women on a Café Terrace.*"

"If it were up to me, I would give you an immediate yes on that one. I imagine John will agree, but let me ask. One of us will get back to you by Thursday."

"Very good." Claire stood and motioned toward the door. "Shall we take a look at the paintings on our final list? We can add or delete as we go. After that, we will speak about your personal matter."

For the next two hours, Anne and Claire walked from room to room looking at the paintings on display and several in storage, eliminating some, adding one or two others, and working out how those selected would work into Anne's initial organizational plan.

"I'm feeling like the exhibit's coming together," Anne said as they walked back toward Claire's office. "I'm happy now, but if you add *Le dejeuner sur l'herbe*, I'll be thrilled."

"I will see what I can do. Our attorneys can haggle and come up with a final contract. So now that we have concluded our part in the selection process, shall we have coffee and talk about your great-grandmother's art?"

"Yes, thank you," Anne said, smiling.

"How about a croissant?" Claire asked when they were once again seated in her office.

"No thanks, just coffee."

Claire nodded, picked up the phone, and ordered coffee and one croissant. "So," she said. "While we wait for our refreshments, tell me how I can help."

For the next fifteen minutes Anne told Claire as much as she knew about Elisabeth's art. When she finished, Claire leaned back in her chair. Her brow creased in thought, she said, "It sounds as if Madame Boulet had an impressive collection."

"She did."

The conversation momentarily ceased when a waiter from the café arrived with coffee. "Now," Claire said when the young man left the room, "Though I am not certain Madame Boulet's paintings were transported to the Galerie Nationale du Jeu de Paume, that would be my assumption. From 1940 to 1944, the museum was the primary storage facility for plundered works of art. Many of the pillaged pieces were intended for the planned Fuehrermuseum in Linz. Others the Nazis deemed unworthy were sold on the international art market. Paintings not purchased, including masterpieces by Picasso and Dalí, were destroyed in a massive bonfire on the grounds of the museum on the night of July 27, 1942."

"Ten days after the Nazis seized Madame Boulet and everything of value remaining in the house."

"She was arrested during la rafle du Vel d'Hiv," Claire reflected, her brow again creased. "I am so sorry. I have heard horrific stories about the raids. Was your grandmother also taken? If so, she was one of the lucky few who survived."

"Fortunately she escaped arrest. That afternoon her mother sent her to spend the night with a friend, Renee Paquet, in Saint-Germain-des-Prés."

"So that's how she escaped the night of terror—she was away from home."

"Right. The next day she, Renee, and Renee's fiancé, Henri Marsolet, aided by the French Underground, fled Paris. After a harrowing experience crossing the Line of Demarcation, they were flown to England and then relocated to the United States. We recently learned that Madame Boulet sold two pieces from her collection to a dishonest French bureaucrat to buy their freedom. Prior to that, at her insistence, other paintings were hidden, thought we don't know where. We're also searching for those works."

"I wish you luck in all of your endeavors. Does Madame Ellison know which paintings her mother sold?'

"We believe *Madame Stumph and her Daughters—*"

"By Corot."

"Yes and *The Work Table* by Bonnard."

"I have not heard of those painting in years, though I know both existed. How far along are you in your search, both for the art your grandmother sold and the pieces the Nazis took from the house?"

"We're only beginning the process. I'm hoping you have ideas or suggestions that will help us get started."

"Of course. Forgive me if I repeat things you may already know."

"Please don't omit anything. Assume I know nothing and you'll be close."

"I doubt that, but I understand what you mean. Fortunately for future generations, Hitler demanded accurate records be kept of all seized European cultural treasures, including those owned by Jews. To accomplish this enormous task, he established the Special Staff for Pictorial Art, the ERR. The Jeu de Paume became the organization's Paris headquarters. For four years, a woman named Rose Valland worked at the museum."

"My grandmother gave me a handwritten biography of Rose that details her efforts to keep track of and eventually help recover the stolen art."

"For more information about her and the catalogued works, I suggest you google *The Documentation Project* website." Claire jotted the name on a piece of notepaper, handed the note to Anne, and continued. "During the Occupation, high ranking Nazi officials such as Reichsmarschall Hermann Göring regularly visited the Jeu de Paume. During his twenty or so visits, he selected hundreds of so-called abandoned artworks for his and Hitler's private collections."

"I hope I'm not being discourteous, Claire," Anne said hesitantly. "But I don't understand why knowing about the art Göring removed from the museum will help in our search."

"Perhaps I failed to make a clear connection. Throughout the Occupation, members of the ERR not only catalogued confiscated cultural property, they also organized museum-like exhibitions for important visitors like Göring. You can actually see some of these displays on the website."

Claire picked up the phone. Though she spoke in French, Anne understood most of what she said. "Yes," she finished. "Right away."

She hung up and said. "Before the papers arrive, if you would like, I will continue to provide what I believe is pertinent background information."

"Please do," Anne answered.

"In 1940, Hitler ordered the ERR to seize art abandoned by wealthy Jewish families who had escaped Paris ahead of the Occupation. Because they were forced to flee so quickly, most were unable to ship their collections to England or America. To locate the art, the ERR searched warehouses of shipping firms where these emigrated Jews might have stored their treasures as well as shipping manifests and art catalogues. They also raided private homes of French gentiles suspected of hiding the collections."

"The Gaudrieus were gentiles."

"The Gaudrieus?"

"I apologize. I was thinking out loud. Denis Gaudrieu was a long-time family-friend. Soon after the Nazis annexed Austria, and especially after the invasion of Poland, Great- Grand'Mere Elisabeth began to meet with Austrian and Polish friends who had personally lost, or who knew someone whose art had been seized during Nazi raids."

"So Madame Boulet realized what could happen to her collection."

"She did. Immediately after the Nazis issued the first anti-Jew edicts, Denis Gaudrieu and his sons began to remove her most valuable paintings from the house."

"Did Monsieur Gaudrieu keep the art in his home or move it to another location?"

"We have no idea. That's the problem."

"If the Nazis suspected the Guidreaus were hiding Madame Boulet's art, their house would have been thoroughly searched, if not ransacked. Did that happen?"

"Not that I know of. I recently learned that Giles, Denis's youngest son, still lives on Île St-Louis. Both Denis and Edouard died long after the Liberation."

"If the Guidreaus survived the Occupation, I doubt the Nazis knew about their efforts on Madame Boulet's behalf. But continuing with what I was saying, beginning in early 1941, the Nazis raided two hundred-three Paris locations. When the art reached the Jeu de Paume, it was inventoried and packed for transport to the Reich. Between March 1941 and July 1944, the Special Staff sent twenty-nine shipments in one hundred thirty-seven freight cars to six shelters in Germany. Once there the art was photographed, catalogued, and stored in bomb-proof installations."

There was a knock on the door. Without waiting for a response, a young man entered. He acknowledged Anne and put a folder on Claire's desk. "This is for you, Anne," Claire said. "The first page breaks down the categories of the plundered art."

Anne took the folder from Claire's outstretched hand and perused the list. Twenty-one thousand, nine hundred-three works of art were catalogued including:

5,281 paintings

684 miniatures, glass and enamel paintings, books and manuscripts

583 sculptures, terra-cotta medallions and plaques

2,477 articles of furniture

583 textiles (Gobelins tapestries, rugs, embroideries)

8,825 hand-made porcelains, bronzes, faïence, majolica, ceramics, jewelry, coins

1,286 East Asian artworks (bronzes, sculptures, porcelains, paintings, folding screens, weapons)

259 antiquities (sculptures, bronzes, vases, jewelry, bowls, cut stones, terra-cotta)

"The extraordinary artistic and material value of the art must be incalculable," Anne said. "The numbers are hard to comprehend."

"There is no way to estimate the value. Among the seized paintings were works by Rembrandt, Rubens, Hals, Vermeer, Velasquez, Murillo, and Goya, as well as Impressionist masterpieces and eighteenth and nineteenth century English paintings by Reynolds, Romney, and Gainsborough. You can view many of the stolen paintings on the *Documentation Project* website. In the folder, I have also included an inventory of paintings and other *objet d' art* the Nazi VIPs, including Göring, removed from the Jeu de Paume for their own private collections, and a list of websites that should help as you begin your search."

Anne flipped through the pages. "This information will be extremely helpful," she said. "Thank you, Claire." She removed her card from her purse. "This is my contact information if you need to reach me."

Claire took the card and stood. "I will let you know when I have an answer regarding the Manet. If we are finished, at least for now, may I call you a cab?"

"No need. I'll contact my driver and then stop by the ladies' room. By the time I've freshened up, he should be here. Thank you for your efforts on behalf of the Met as well as for the suggestions you've provided my grandmother and me as we begin our search for Great-Grand'Mere Elisabeth's paintings."

"It is my pleasure," said Claire. "I am sure we will talk again soon."

On her way to the ladies' lounge, Anne called Gus. "Have you thought of a place for lunch?" she immediately asked.

"I have. I'm five minutes away."

"You won't tell me where we're going?"

"And ruin the surprise?"

"Will you be dishing the dirt about the place while we drive?"

Chuckling, Gus said, "My dirt-dishing cap is firmly in place."

CHAPTER 21

"How was your meeting," Gus asked as Anne settled into the back seat.

"Great. If you'll tell me where we're going, I'll give you the details over lunch."

"I will provide one clue. After he was appointed Military Governor in 1944, General Dietrich Von Choltitz was unhappy with his accommodations, so he moved his entire command from the Hotel de Crillon to our mystery destination."

"La Meurice."

"You guessed, so my clue was too obvious."

"I only knew because I recently read an article about Van Choltitz. He was the officer who defied Hitler's order to burn Paris before it fell into Allied hands."

"He was. Have you read *Is Paris Burning?*"

"Years ago, but I don't want a history lesson—just the hot gossip."

"Fortunately, this time I am prepared. While I waited for you, I googled Le Meurice. There were hundreds of sites about the infamous hotel, too many to share during our short drive, so I decided to concentrate on the one person who stood out above the rest—Salvador Dalí. I am convinced the man was crazy."

"Of course I'm familiar with Dalí's work, though I can't say I'm a fan. And I know nothing about his personal life, so dish the dirt."

"There is too much dirt to dish, so I will narrow my presentation to several outrageous episodes. Dalí's antics are real and well documented. They are not gossip."

"But they're juicy."

"Juicy?"

"Titillating."

"I suppose so, but I am only reporting. You will have to be the judge. One time when he was staying long-term at Le Meurice, Dalí's ordered the staff to bring a flock of sheep to his room?"

"Why would he do that?"

"I am looking in the rearview mirror," Gus said, chuckling. "I see the grin on your face. You are expecting *real* dirt. Sadly, I cannot oblige. It seems he wanted to fire blanks at the sheep, and please do not ask me why. The article did not say. On another occasion, he paid the staff five francs for every fly they could catch and bring to him from the Tuileries Garden across the street."

"You're kidding."

"How could I make that up?"

"Point made. What did he do with the flies?"

"Again, I have no idea. But I learned that one of his regular tricks was to open his window and dangle a lobster from the end of a fishing pole over the heads the pedestrians walking on rue de Rivoli. I do not frequent Le Meurice, but I have read that, though years have passed, the hotel still maintains a Dalí-like air of decadence that sets it apart from other high-priced Parisian gilt trips."

"Pun intended?"

"Absolutely, and, again, I borrowed that brilliant insight from an article on the internet; I cannot claim the pun as my own."

"A truly honest man is hard to find these days."

"I suppose so," Gus said pensively

෴

"Now I know what you meant by gilt trip," Anne said under her breath as they pushed through the revolving door into an opulent lobby filled with intimate furniture groupings, exquisite eighteenth and nineteenth century art on the walls, large marble pillars topped by crystal chandeliers, and a spectacular art nouveau glass roof.

When they reached the entrance to the dining room, they had to wait to be seated. "This room is more my style," Anne said. "I love the silver décor and the light pouring in through all those floor-to-ceiling windows. They make the space feel so open and airy."

"A reservation for Madame French," Gus said to the formally-dressed Maître d' as he approached the desk.

"Bonjour, Madame French," said the man. "Welcome to Le Meurice. This way please."

"If I don't stop looking around, I'm going to trip and make a fool of myself," Anne whispered to Gus as they crossed the room to a table by one of the windows.

The Maître d' held out Anne's chair, put a menu at her place, and handed another to Gus. "Your waiter will be with you immediately," he said. "Enjoy your lunch."

"Do you like foie gras?" Anne asked Gus as she studied the menu. "My grandmother says Le Meurice serves the best. Shall we share?"

"I would like that," Gus said timidly.

A few minutes later the waiter returned. Anne looked at Gus, who said nervously, "We will share a single order of foie gras."

"Very good," said the waiter. "And for your entrée?"

"I'll have the truffled scallops," Anne said.

"And I will have uncooked shrimp served with crispy tails and a sea urchin gelee," said Gus.

While they waited for the foie gras, Anne talked about her meeting with Claire. "Then you and Madame Malet are in agreement about the art the Musée d'Orsay will loan to the Met," Gus said when she finished explaining.

"For the most part. She's checking with her boss about *Le dejeuner sur l'herbe*, and I have to get the go-ahead from my committee about several Pissarros that weren't among our initial selections or on the addendum."

"Did you have a chance to speak with Madame Malet about Madame Boulet's missing art?"

"I did. She provided a wealth of information."

The waiter arrived with the foie gras, interrupting the conversation. Anne spread a small amount on a toast point and took a bite. "Oh my," she said. "This is delicious. Gus, try it."

"I would say the foie gras lives up to its reputation," Gus said to the waiter, who stood by, seemingly waiting for judgment to be pronounced.

⁓

"Lunch is my treat," Anne announced while they sipped their coffee. "I won't embarrass you by asking for the check, but I'll throw a fit if you don't give it to me as soon as the waiter leaves the table."

"You would really make a scene?"

"Do you have doubts?"

Anne discreetly paid the bill, and they walked back through the opulent lobby. The valet brought the car around and opened the back door. While Gus got behind the wheel, Anne checked her phone. "Hang on, Gus," she said. "I had my ring on silent during lunch. I know you can't stay here blocking the entrance, but there's a message from Monsieur Roberge, the curator at the Musée de l'Orangerie. Could you pull over for a minute?"

Gus stopped near the exit to the hotel and waited while Anne listened to the message. "Unbelievable," she said as she pushed end.

"Is everything all right?"

"It is. Monsieur Roberge cancelled our meeting. That's the bad news. The good news is the museum will loan all four Renoirs. Now I'm sorry I didn't make an afternoon appointment with Madame Simoneau at the Marmottan. I'm wasting precious time."

"You could call to see if she can meet today."

"Nothing ventured. . ."

Anne removed the Marmottan file from her briefcase and punched in the number listed on her contact sheet. On the second ring, a woman answered. "Bonjour," Anne responded to her greeting. "May I speak with Madame Simoneau?"

"Speaking," the woman replied in English.

"Madame, this is Anne French. We're scheduled to meet tomorrow morning at nine to discuss the paintings the Metropolitan Museum hopes to borrow from the Marmottan. As it happens, Monsieur Roberge from l'Orangerie had a conflict and cancelled today's meeting. Realizing it's short notice, are you available now or perhaps later this afternoon?"

"Actually meeting today would be better for me. It sounds like you are calling from a car. Would you like to come now?"

"I'm just leaving Le Meurice. Depending on traffic—."

"Fifteen minutes," Gus whispered.

"My driver tells me we can be there in fifteen minutes."

"That gives me ample time to complete my current task. It is a lovely day, so I will meet you outside the entrance."

During the short drive Anne perused her notes one last time. She had just reread the addendum when Gus stopped in front of the museum. As he opened Anne's door, a woman approached the car. "Madame French." She extended her hand. "It is a pleasure to meet you."

Madame Simoneau is Claire's antithesis, Anne thought. Shaking the curator's hand, she said. "Please call me Anne."

"And I am Jeannine. I wish the Marmottan had a courtyard so we could continue to enjoy the warm sunshine. Since that is not the case, shall we go to my office?"

While they walked toward the museum door, Anne studied Jeannine Simoneau. She was short; about five foot two, with curly brown hair and an infectious smile. Though she wasn't obese, she obviously liked her food, making her round face appear even fuller.

"May I order tea and perhaps something sweet?" Jeannine asked when they were seated in two comfortable chairs in an area to one side of the room. "We have a small café on site."

"No thank you," Anne said. "I just finished a fabulous lunch at Le Meurice."

"Ah, Le Meurice. Last month my husband and I celebrated our anniversary in the exquisite dining room. The foie gras—"

"Is to die for. I cleaned my plate."

"Something we already agree upon. That bodes well for the business part of our meeting."

Anne handed Jeannine the folder and said, "This is my committee's wish-list."

"Last night I received a fax from John, but because you and I were originally scheduled to meet tomorrow, I have only taken a cursory look. He says you are flexible and will consider alternate works if one or more paintings on your list is unavailable."

"The addendum I prepared is stapled to the back of our initial request."

Jeannine flipped through the several pages. "I see," she said. "Excellent, but before we begin, Claire Malet called after you left the Musée d'Orsay. Hoping you would not object, she thought it might expedite matters if she told me about your personal search for Madame Boulet's art. Though she thought we were meeting tomorrow, she wanted me to be ready with supplementary information when you arrived."

"Of course I don't object. I'm grateful for Claire's assistance. She was kind to provide me with a list of websites cataloging the art the Nazis seized, as well as information about works that have been restored to their rightful owners."

"So she said. Another reason she called was to tell me to be sure to mention *The Lost Museum* by Hector Feliciano."

"I bought the book before I left New York, but coping with jet lag and dealing with Met business, I haven't had time to take it out of my suitcase, let alone take a look."

"I was privileged to meet Feliciano in New York years ago."

"If you have time, I'd like to hear about your meeting as well as any thoughts you might have as my grandmother and I begin our quest."

"Then we should get down to business. We can continue this discussion when we finish. Being a smaller museum, our board would prefer to limit our contribution to between five and eight paintings." Jeannine perused Anne's list. "I see you have crossed off several works that were on John's fax."

Anne pulled out a copy of her plans for grouping the paintings and spread the sheets out on the desk in front of Jeannine. "Last night I worked on this preliminary exhibition design," she said. "For the moment, though I'm waiting for confirmation from the committee, I've divided the show into three major categories. The paintings in each division will depict women and children engaging in everyday activities."

"Then you are not planning to hang landscapes or paintings of men?"

"As of now, no. However, depending on what we end up borrowing, that may change."

Anne waited quietly while Jeannine examined the lists, making marginal notes as she read. Five minutes later she looked up and, smiling, said, "We will loan the three Morisot paintings as well as *Girl with the Greyhound,* a painting not on either your original or supplementary list."

"I'm not familiar with *Girl with the Greyhound,*" Anne said. "May I take a look before I decide to make a recommendation to the committee?"

"Of course. I am a Morisot fan, so, naturally, I believe her paintings will add depth to your exhibition." Jeannine again directed her attention to the list. "Renoir's *Portrait de Madame Renee Monet Reading* is available, as is *Portrait de Julie Manet.*"

"I know both works are on our initial list, but we may have more Renoirs than we need. I'll check with John and one of us will get back to you. Shall we address the Monets?"

"Fine," said Jeannine as she again studied the list. "Let's see. You are asking to borrow *Promenade à Argenteuil* and *Les Cousines on the Beach at Trouville.* I will check with our board, but I believe we can loan both. What about *Michael Monet wearing a Boulle?*"

"An excellent suggestion." Anne made a note. "We're borrowing *Renee Renoir in Clown Costume* from l'Orangerie. We could hang the two works side by side."

After a twenty minute back and forth about the various paintings, Anne closed her folder. "That was incredibly easy," she said. "Unless I decide differently when we view the actual paintings or the committee vetoes one of my choices, I think we're all set."

Jeannine stood. "If so, shall we take a look at your preliminary selections?"

For the next forty-five minutes, Anne and Jeannine walked through the museum, viewing the paintings they'd discussed and determining how each would fit into the categories Anne had created. Before they finished, Anne had decided to recommend *Girl with a Greyhound.* "I'm elated, and I imagine John and the committee will be equally thrilled," she said as they walked back toward Jeannine's office.

"Good." Jeannine gestured to one of two overstuffed chairs under the window. "Now that we have concluded our official business, we can be more comfortable while we talk."

Anne sat down, put the Met folder in her briefcase, and removed a notepad.

"I met Feliciano in New York in 1997," Jeannine began. "At the time, he was launching a world-wide book tour. But before I continue with specifics, allow me to put his research in context. When he began his interviews, Feliciano met intense opposition from French museums. Most vehemently refused to cooperate."

"Because they were knowingly displaying questionable works and had a vested interest in maintaining their silence."

"Yes. They realized they could be forced to forfeit priceless paintings and other valuable artifacts."

"But if the victims actually *saw* their family possessions hanging in a museum, wouldn't they try to claim them? I know I would."

"There are many reasons why that did not happen. When Feliciano began his research, though the war had ended forty-plus years before, the politics of the time continued to play a key role in the recovery—or lack thereof. As he began his investigation, the Berlin wall was still standing, and the cold war dominated world politics."

"How did those two set of circumstances affect his work?"

"They made it difficult for him to get answers. One of his principal goals was to determine why so many Jews refused to initiate searches for their art. When he interviewed German Jews, most said they were dealing with more important issues."

"That makes sense."

"True, but in November 1989 when the wall came down and Germany was reunited, they still didn't look. Most said—or rather gave the excuse—it was enough they had survived the Holocaust. Those who lived in East Germany under brutal Communist rule explained that the pain of everyday living had kept them from needing or wanting material possessions."

"So they still weren't helpful."

"Most were not. In the book, Feliciano deals with this common phenomenon among the victims. They felt guilty because they survived."

"After talking with my grandmother, I believe I understand their thinking, though I doubt anyone who hasn't lived through what they did will ever truly know what they felt. After the Liberation, she wasn't interested in recovering her mother's art. Only now, after seventy years, has she begun to talk about that terrible period in her life."

"Claire said Madame Boulet was arrested during la rafle du Vel d'Hiv."

"On July 17, the second night of the raid. She was initially taken to the Velodrome d'Hiver and then transferred to Drancy. Several days later, she was packed into a cattle-car and transported to Auschwitz. To this day, my grandmother feels guilty because she wasn't arrested at the same time."

"Hers is not an uncommon response. Many other children who lost parents during the Holocaust feel the same way. We could talk about this for hours, but since our time today is limited, I will again be specific. In amassing material for his book, Feliciano conducted more than two-hundred interviews with art dealers, art historians, and surviving relatives of families who were victimized. He concluded his research using documents from German looting inventories and papers that had recently been declassified."

"Are the documents and papers you mentioned available to the public?"

"They are. I will have copies delivered to your hotel."

"Since we're meeting this afternoon, I hope to move into my apartment tomorrow morning—number forty-five Quai de Bourbon, fifth floor. Could you send them there?"

"Of course." Jeannine wrote down the address and continued. "Initially, the French governmental ministries and museums refused to let Feliciano search their records. However, they finally gave in to pressure from the victims' families."

"Do you have specific family names? Maybe my grandmother will recognize one or more of her friends or acquaintances."

"I will send the list along with the other papers. There is also a wealth of information in Feliciano's book. Because he persisted, the French government was compelled to display nearly two thousand looted works the museums had quietly integrated into their collections."

"Have the paintings been returned to the lawful owners?"

"Many have, though, ironically, some families turned around and sold their painting back to the museums where they had been on display."

"They didn't want the paintings after all?"

"Feliciano's book will explain their reasoning. Claire told me she provided you with a list of websites to aid in your search. I hope our discussion this afternoon along with the information I will be sending to your apartment will be of equal benefit."

"Please know how much my grandmother and I appreciate your help."

"It is my pleasure." Jeannine looked at her watch. "Unfortunately, I must bring our meeting to a close. Tomorrow I will ask the board to approve the decisions you and I have made. I do not foresee a problem."

Anne stood. "Either John or I will be in touch."

"Thank you for everything," Anne said at the museum entrance.

"It was my pleasure," said Jeannine. "Enjoy your evening."

"Another successful meeting?" Gus asked as he pulled into traffic.

"It was, but I'll fill you in later. I need to make a few notes. I want to email John with the particulars when I get back to my room. My mind is so full, if I don't write—"

"I understand. I will quietly dodge the maniacs while you work."

꿍

Back at the hotel, Anne picked up her key from the young girl on duty behind the desk, went to her room, and, without stopping to change clothes, turned on her computer. She sent John a lengthy email about the two meetings, asking for a decision on the works in question by Thursday morning so she could notify Claire and Jeannine, unless he wanted to contact them directly.

Next she wrote to her grandmother, providing an overview of what she'd learned from Claire and Jeannine about looted art. She listed two website addresses among the many Claire had supplied and wrote: *If you have time, here are a couple of sites to explore. At first glance, they seem more current than those I provided before I left for Paris.*

She clicked send and then responded to an email from her mother, addressing only the work she was doing on behalf of the Met. Finally, she wrote to Meg, briefly relating why she hadn't written and what was going on in Paris.

Finished with the tasks at hand, she opened the *Documentation Project* website and looked down the list of Parisian Jews whose collections were seized during the Occupation. "I don't believe it!" she exclaimed when she got to the middle of the first page. There between Ball and Braun was the name Boulet."

She picked up the phone and called her grandmother.

CHAPTER 22

Veronique answered on the second ring. "Hi, darling," she began. "I just got your email."

"I clicked send less than a minute ago. Are you sitting at the computer?"

"As we speak I'm looking at the first page of *The Documentation Project*. You *did* tell me to get to work."

"I don't think I put it quite that way. I believe I said when you have time. That doesn't mean right this second."

"Laura has me packed and ready to go, so I had a few spare minutes. Do you have news?"

"I do. Immediately after I sent the email, I started to peruse the list of Parisian Jews who lost their art collections during the Occupation. Are you sitting down?"

"I told you I'm at the computer, so, yes, I'm sitting down.

"If I'd called fifteen minutes later, you'd have seen what I did. The name Boulet is listed between Ball and Braun."

"What does that mean?"

"It means the night of the raid the Nazis took whatever paintings Dennis hadn't already hidden."

"We knew that."

"Yes, but now we know the stolen art was initially transported to the Jeu de Paume. When you have time, enlarge the photographs on the website. If we're lucky, you might recognize one or two of the paintings that were still there when you left that afternoon."

"I'll begin immediately, but I don't think there were many left. Remember what I wrote in my journal?"

"You said the walls were bare. But look anyway— *when you have time*. We've waited this long—"

"Because of my stubborn refusal to talk about the Occupation."

"We agreed to move ahead, remember? See what you can find on the *Documentation Project* website and then look at other sites on Claire's list. Your fax is up and running?"

"Of course it is."

"If Corinne has a machine, I'll transmit the complete list."

"Give me time to add paper. I wish I'd paid closer attention to the paintings in Mother's collection."

"There you go again. Forget what you didn't do then. Take a look. Maybe something will jog your memory. If not, we're in better shape today than we were yesterday. I'll be busy all day Thursday, so I'll bring you up to date when I see you Friday morning."

"Are you coming to the airport with Gus?"

"With the three of you and your luggage, there won't be room. I'll be here eagerly anticipating your arrival. Safe travel."

As soon as she pressed end, Anne called Arnaud. "I know it's late—"

"It's early. Remember, you're in Paris, the city that never sleeps."

"I believe that's a moniker for New York."

"Oh yes. Now I remember. Paris is the City of Light. How was your day?"

"Fantastic. If you aren't busy, I'd love to collect on that rain check and take a walk. I can tell you my news in person."

"I'll be there in ten minutes."

"Make it thirty."

"Why so long? I didn't figure you for a woman who spends hours in front of the mirror trying to look beautiful for her man."

"You figured it out. That's why I need extra time. I want to be sure to put on a shade of makeup that makes me look good under streetlamps, and, of course I'll be changing out of my jeans into a designer dress just for you."

"I knew it."

"I hate to further damage your already fragile ego, but I need thirty-minutes to fax twenty pages to my grandmother, that is if Corinne has a fax machine."

"Don't bother to ask. I'll bring the papers home and fax them, or, better yet I'll scan them and email the file."

"A fax would be better. Despite the late hour, I'm sure Oma is already standing by her machine, and I mean that literally. She professes she's computer literate, but I'm not sure she knows how to open a pdf file. That said, when you two eventually meet, please don't quote me. She'd be mortified if she thought I questioned her technological skills. She believes she's a real geek."

Arnaud laughed. "Then I'll send a fax and return the original papers to you in the morning."

"Before going down, I'll email Oma and let her know to check her machine in the morning. Thank you. I'll see you out front in ten minutes."

"Obviously you want to avoid the wagging tongues."

"How'd you guess? Corinne wasn't behind the desk when Gus dropped me off, but just in case—"

"Ten minutes it is."

Anne sat back down at the computer and emailed her grandmother.

Oma, Arnaud volunteered to fax the lists so I don't have to bother Corinne. We (Arnaud and I) are going for a walk. Do not jump to any conclusions. *I've been cooped up inside all day. I could use the exercise, and I want to tell him about my meetings. The fax will be there when you get up in the morning. Get some rest!*

Arnaud was waiting when Anne exited the lobby. "Where to?" he asked, as she handed him the file containing the papers.

"Definitely Square Barye. I must see this world famous site."

"World famous?"

"It must be. Henri talked about it, and Gus said to 'take time from my busy schedule and find romance in Square Barye.'"

"Is that such a bad idea?"

"All I'm saying is there's no way the square could possibly live up to all the hype."

"For once, I'll keep my thoughts to myself and let you decide."

As they walked along the Seine, Anne watched the flower-decked Bateaux Mouches carrying tourists along the river. *How far I've come since my first boat-ride on the Seine,* she mulled. She turned to Arnaud and said, "Tell me about the square. Why's it so special?"

"Probably because it's a place where one can, if only for a little while, escape the craziness of the modern world. Parisians come to sit on grassy lawns or on benches beneath rows of chestnut trees overlooking the Seine. Some come just to see the fountain. Though it's April in Paris, which means many Parisians are outside enjoying the spring air, we might happen upon an empty bench by the river."

"Why is it that every time I hear the words, 'April in Paris,' I feel an urgent need to break out in song? And speaking of singing, I should add crooner to Gus's adjective list."

"Crooner?"

"Gus and I were having coffee in a small café at the airport when he mentioned the glories of April in Paris. Of course we sang for the noticeably thrilled crowd."

"You didn't!"

"We did. We even bowed as the masses clapped with great adulation."

"I'm afraid you you'll never put crooner in my adjective column. I only sing in the shower when there's no one around to hear me."

"Someday you'll have to sing and let me be the judge."

"Only if we're in the shower."

"Arnaud—"

"Okay, too forward. The square was named after the sculptor, Antoine Louis Barye. You must have heard him about him during one of your art classes."

"I recall he sculpted animals during the Romantic Period."

"He was one of the great animal-life artists of the French school."

"That's why they named a square after him?"

"I doubt that was the reason. Late in life he had the honor of serving as the keeper of plaster casts at the Louvre. He was also a professor of zoological drawing at the Musée National d'Histoire Naturelle. In all probability the latter distinction is why he received the honor. So here it is—the famous Square Barye. There *is* an empty bench over by the Seine. Shall we enjoy the river while you tell me about your day?"

They claimed the bench. For the next half-hour while they listened to the water gently lapping against the shore, Anne told Arnaud about her meetings at the Musée d'Orsay and the Marmottan as well as her lunch with Gus at Le Meurice.

"It sounds like you had a successful and pleasant day," he said when she finished her account. "Congratulations."

"Thank you, and since I have no more scheduled appointments, at least for the moment, I'd like to move tomorrow morning. Realizing you volunteered to help in the afternoon—"

"What time do you want to start?"

"Meet me in the hotel breakfast room at eight-thirty. A good meal is the least I can do for the man I'm asking to lug my heavy bags across the Île."

"An excellent idea. I'm sure I'll be hungry, but, beyond that, we haven't given the gossips anything scintillating to report since Saturday. They're due. To perfect our act, shall we practice?" He leaned over and kissed Anne softly on the lips. When she didn't object, he kissed her again. Drawing back and grinning, he said, "Now wasn't that better than chocolate?"

"Without a doubt!" Sighing deeply, Anne put her hand on Arnaud's neck, pulled his lips to hers, kissed him again, abruptly let go, and said, "I needed another taste."

"And?"

"I'll definitely come back for more."

Hand in hand and quietly enjoying the sounds and scents of spring, they strolled along Quai de Anjou toward the hotel. "Thanks for a lovely evening," Anne said as they neared the entrance.

Arnaud looked from side to side—once, and then again.

"Care to tell me what you're doing?" Anne asked.

"I'm looking for gossips?"

"Do you really think there are hordes of women lurking around waiting for us to come back?"

"You never know, but I have to be sure before. . ." He bent and kissed her on the lips. "I'd kiss you again, but—"

"You don't want to take a chance."

"Right! I'll fax the papers to your grandmother as soon as I get home and see you in the morning at nine."

CHAPTER 23

Anne woke up a little before seven, showered, put on a robe, and, hoping to find a message from John, went to her office to check her emails. "Good," she whispered when she saw his name pop up in her inbox. She opened his message and read.

Great job, Anne. The attorneys have taken over, so, at least for now, there's no need for you to return to any of the museums on behalf of the Met. We will borrow all of the paintings you and the curators agreed upon as well as Renoir's The Swing *from the Musée d'Orsay. We are also taking the three Pissarros from the Marmottan, as well as the Renoirs that were on our original list. We're still waiting to hear about the Manet. While we're selecting the paintings we want to display from the Met collection and preparing requests for the National Gallery, the MFA in Boston, and the Walters in Baltimore, our publicity team is working on final titles, and the design group is deciding how the painting will be grouped into sub-categories. I'll get back to you when there's an update.*

Anne responded, asking John to keep her in the loop, and telling him she was available to meet again with any of the curators should the need arise. With nothing else that required her immediate attention, she dressed in jeans, packed her cosmetics, and went down to meet Arnaud.

"I just made a fresh pot of coffee," Corinne said when Anne entered the breakfast room.

"Would you like a cup?"

"Definitely," Anne answered. "Thanks."

"While she poured, Corinne continued. "I haven't seen much of you over the past few days. And when I do, you're rushing off. Your meetings went well?"

"They did. I completed my business yesterday afternoon, so I'll be checking out this morning. I hope you haven't altered the cleaning schedule on my account."

"As I said before, it is no problem. Will Arnaud be helping you move? I ask because William would be glad to assist."

I'm sure that's why you're asking, Anne mused. *More fodder for the gossips.* "He is," she said. "I invited him to join me for breakfast before I put him to work. I hope that's okay."

Corinne's eyes brightened. "Arnaud is always welcome." She handed Anne a cup of the steaming brew and gestured toward the buffet. "There is cream over there, the sugar is on the table, and there is a copy of the *International Herald Tribune* on the stand by the door if you care to catch up on the news while you wait for Arnaud."

"Thanks. When I'm through eating, I'll stop by the desk and settle my bill."

"That will not be necessary. Madame Ellison took care of everything."

"That's my grandmother. She's *always* a step ahead."

Anne was pouring a second cup of coffee when Corinne, grinning and blushing, ushered Arnaud into the room.

"Good morning." He kissed Anne on the cheek. "I hope you slept well. I certainly did."

"Actually, I didn't," Anne said, frowning. "I tossed and turned all night."

"Because you were excited?" Arnaud looked at Corinne, then back at Anne. "About moving into your apartment, of course."

"I'll leave you so you can finish breakfast and get started with your task," Corinne said.

"Why do think she left so fast?" Arnaud teased when Corinne started up the stairs.

"No doubt to call Madame Turmel. She'll want to know about your excitement and my tossing and turning. So much for my sterling reputation."

"You're really irritated—"

"Of course I am. Were you *trying* to make the Île's leading gossip think something happened between us last night?"

"It didn't?"

Without comment, Anne put several slices of ham and cheese on her plate, filled a bowl with fruit, and selected a delicious-looking, definitely-fattening pastry from the tray.

"Bertrand's eager to meet you," Arnaud said, as he put his plate on the table. "Sophie too, though she doubts she'll be able to help in your search. So, if you'd like to cancel—"

"I get it. You're looking for an excuse to rescind your invitation. "You're afraid Sophie will inadvertently expose some deep, dark secret."

"Not at all. I have no secrets. I'm the perfect brother. I'm always reminding Sophie she's a lucky woman to have—"

"Oh Lord—"

"Well, maybe I'm not perfect, but if you ask, she'll tell you to put 'great brother' on my adjective list."

"We'll see about that, and speaking of Sophie, other than to say she went to Stanford and is married to an American businessman, you haven't said much about her. Is she older or younger?"

"She's three minutes older. We're twins. She never lets me forget she's my big sister, which is ironic because she's half my size—if that. You remind me of her. Both of you are beautiful, intelligent, single-minded, and stubborn women."

"I don't know whether to say thanks or be insulted."

"Consider it a compliment. So, am I forgiven for giving Corinne fodder for the gossip mill? Regardless of what I did or didn't say, you know she was going directly to the telephone. Why not give her titillating to talk about."

"I may forgive you, but only for practical reasons. If I don't, I'll have to lug my suitcases across the Île."

"Or call a cab."

"If I were you, I'd quit while I'm ahead—"

"Good advice."

"Welcome to my home away from home for the past few days," Anne said as she opened the door to her suite. "It's not the George V, but the rooms are clean and comfortable."

Arnaud glanced around the room. "Not bad, he said. "I only see two suitcases and a briefcase by the door. "Is this all you want me to move? You didn't bring much—"

"When I packed for the trip I intended to stay two weeks. I didn't bring my entire wardrobe, but now—"

"You may have to do some shopping."

"Or a load of laundry. Did you see a washer and dryer in the apartment?"

"No, but there were louvered doors in the kitchen. They're probably behind there. If not, I'm sure there's a laundromat on rue—"

"Forget that! I'm like my grandmother. If the washer and dryer aren't there now, they will be tomorrow."

Arnaud picked up the large bag and Anne's carry-on, while she grabbed her briefcase. "You can wave to Corinne while I turn in my key," she said when the elevator door opened into the lobby.

"You're afraid I'll say something to damage your reputation—"

"*Further* damage. I'll meet you by the door."

Anne gave Corinne the key, thanked her, and joined Arnaud outside. "Expect for feeling I'm living in a glass bowl, this is a nice hotel." She looked back at the entry. "I would stay here again."

"Even with the Île's chief gossip at the desk that's positioned, most likely intentionally, with a view of everyone who comes and goes?"

"Point made. Privacy, here I come."

"We're driving?" Anne asked as Arnaud remotely opened the trunk of a white BMW sedan.

"I thought you'd have a lot of luggage, so I brought the car. It's a beautiful spring morning—"

"Please don't tell me it's April in Paris."

"Will you let me finish? I was going to say I almost brought my convertible."

"You have two cars!"

"I do—one for work, and one strictly for fun." Arnaud put Anne's bags in the trunk and held open the passenger door for her to slide in.

"Do you think we'll find a place to park near the house?" she asked as they pulled away from the curb.

"Parking's not an issue. When I jogged over to meet you Monday morning, I noticed an entrance to an underground garage below the house, so keep your keycard handy. You'll need it to open the gate."

"An underground garage? That's a modern concept."

"True. Having underground parking isn't the norm on the Île. About twenty years ago, when parking became an issue, several owners converted their basements to garages."

"I can only imagine how much it cost to reinforce the massive structures and create driveways leading down."

"Trust me, in Grandpapa's case, the price tag was almost prohibitive."

Five minutes later, Arnaud parked below the building in one of the two spaces designated fifth floor. They took the elevator to the lobby and another to Anne's apartment. She inserted her keycard, opened the door, stepped into the living room, and paused. *If I didn't know better, I could almost believe Great-Grand'Mere Elisabeth is here watching me move into her home,* she mused. *I truly feel her presence—*

"Should I put the suitcases in the bedroom?" Arnaud asked, interrupting her thoughts.

"In a minute." Anne quickly passed through the dining room into the kitchen, and opened the louvered doors. "*Yes!*" she exclaimed. "The washer/dryer. Now all I need to make the kitchen perfect is food. Is there a supermarket within walking distance?"

"Fortunately, no."

"Fortunately?"

"It's been a battle, but we Lousiens, which is what those of us who live on the Île call ourselves, won. Why ruin the small-town feel with a gigantic supermarket? For major shopping, you'll have to cross to the continent. I'm actually driving over there now—a last minute trip to buy perishables for tonight's dinner. If you'd like to go—"

"Thanks, but I have no idea what I need."

"Then I'll take you whenever you're ready. But now, if I expect to earn my excellent-chef adjective— which I do—I have a lot to accomplish. I'll pick you up at seven and give you a tour of the apartment before Sophie arrives"

CHAPTER 24

Anne laughed as she hung several pairs of slacks, six blouses, and two dresses in the huge walk-in closet. When she finished putting the cosmetics in the bathroom cabinets, she looked over at the Jacuzzi tub. "Why not," she said. She wrapped her hair in a towel, put in a measure of French bath salts, laid her head against the back, and soaked in the steaming water.

Twenty minutes later, the water tepid, and with things to do before dinner, she got out, put on a lounging robe, went to her office, and opened a message from her grandmother that began,

Thanks for sending the pictures, darling. I'm glad you're pleased. A warning, expect an email or a call from your mother. I told her I bought two apartments on Île St-Louis—one for you and one for me. I said I'd explain when I get back, or since I'll be in Paris for a month or more, she can visit me. I insisted she give me at least a five day heads-up before she travels. She hasn't responded.

I spoke with the security company. I think Henri told you, but I'll reiterate. The guard will be there early in the morning. There's no need for you to check in unless you're curious. My new chef, Andre Pasquier, will arrive Saturday morning. I borrowed him from L'Ambroise, where he's been working under a Michelin three-star chef. I'm told he's good. I hope so. Lord knows I'm paying him enough. He's taking a temporary leave of absence for as long as I'm in Paris. He'll prepare breakfast Saturday before the mason arrives and return Sunday morning to fix brunch before starting full-time on Monday. Plan to eat out on Friday, Saturday, and Sunday, though I doubt I'll join you Friday. I believe Henri would like to eat at Brasserie de l'Île St-Louis. Perhaps you'll indulge him. I'll see you soon, my darling granddaughter. I'll be shutting down my computer at noon tomorrow New York time.

"I can't wait to read this," Anne said as she opened an email from her mother. Without a greeting, Madeline wrote,

For God's sake, Anne, either call or email me immediately. What the hell's going on with Mother? She just told me she bought two apartments in Paris. Has she lost her mind? Last week she was dying, and now she's traveling to Paris for an extended stay? How long have you known? Why didn't you tell me? I could have talked her out of this nonsense. I'm committed to a bridge tournament next week but am making reservations to come Paris a week from Tuesday.

"Your priorities are still in order, Mother," Anne muttered. "Play in your bridge tournament and then come to Paris to see your mother." She hit reply and wrote.

Mother, Got your email. Too much to explain. Oma is eager to return to the home where she was raised, and you know she never does things halfway. I moved into my apartment this morning. Hers is being readied for her arrival. She and I will spend the next few weeks exploring the Paris she knew as a young woman. If you want to join us, fine, or wait until we get home and come to the city. I'm sure Oma will explain everything when you two get together. There's no need to back out of your bridge tournament to rush over here. If there's a problem, I'll let you know. How's your tennis game coming? Keep in touch.

My sarcasm will undoubtedly go unnoticed, Anne mulled as she turned off the computer.

⌒⊙

Anne was watching a Bateau Mouche filled with people glide by when Arnaud arrived in a silver Mercedes convertible with the top down.

"Merely an ordinary second car to fill the empty space in your garage?" she teased.

"You don't like my Silver Streak?"

"What's not to like?"

"You were joking."

"I would say more like conveying my extreme envy. I thought you'd walk over."

"I didn't have time. A master chef can't be away from his stove for too long. You wouldn't want my culinary creations to burn."

"Of course not," Anne said with just a hint of sarcasm. "So what delicious dish is the great Chef Lessard preparing?"

"You'll have to wait."

"Patience, I'm afraid, is not my forte."

"You want instant gratification—"

"Which house is yours?" Anne asked, ignoring Arnaud's comment.

"Number twenty-six. Realize I'm now attempting to earn my historian adjective. Louis Le Vau built the house for Nicholas de Sainctot."

"Who? Remember, you're talking to an ignorant American."

"Ignorant isn't an adjective I'd put on your list."

"You're clearly obsessed with adjectives."

"If you haven't figured it out by now, I like to win. At the moment, I'm losing out to Gus. So, yes, I'm obsessed with adjectives. Nicholas was Lord of Vemars. From 1655 to 1659 he was Steward of the King and Master of Ceremonies of France. After that his job was to introduce ambassadors to Louis XIV's court."

"That's it? Do you think you're entitled to the prized historian adjective for that presentation? First, it was too short, and, more importantly, you failed to dish any dirt."

"You're saying I have more work to do," Arnaud said, feigning dejection.

"Much more."

"I'll keep at it, but not now. This is my home. There's traffic approaching from behind, but I'll stop long enough for you to take a quick look."

Anne gazed up at overhanging balconies on each floor. "Gus said Quai de Bethune was once called Quai des Balcons after its famous wrought-iron balconies."

"Gus is correct, and you know how I hate—"

"I do, but could we forget about adjectives—at least for now. Tell me about the house. Was the façade recently restored?"

"Not since the late eighteenth century. When Grandpapa and I converted the mansion to apartments, we had the front cleaned. I'll tell you more about the building later. That horn you just heard means we have an irritated driver waiting to move on."

Arnaud rounded the corner, entered the underground garage, parked next to the BMW, and opened Anne's door. At the elevator, he inserted a keycard in the fifth-floor slot on the end of the row.

"Oh my!" Anne exclaimed when the elevator door opened directly into Arnaud's apartment. "Before we go any farther, give me a minute."

Arnaud waited while Anne looked around the room that was a splendid blend of the traditional and the modern. Rustic-red floor tiles were topped with antique beige Oriental rugs containing splashes of cardinal red and cobalt blue. Two groupings of beige sofas opposite patterned overstuffed chairs in geometric and floral designs accentuated the colors in the carpet and gave the large space an intimate feel. Opposite the front door, a gilded eighteenth-century mirror-topped a marble fireplace, and an ornate chandelier hung from the ceiling in the center of the room. Natural light flooded the space from three large floor-to-ceiling windows, and a smaller stained-glass window enhanced the charm of the room. She walked to one of the windows, gazed at the panorama below, turned back, and said, "I don't know what's more stunning, your living room or the view."

"I'm glad you approve. Would you like to see the rest of the apartment before Sophie arrives?"

"Need you ask?"

They passed through open French doors to the right of the elevator. "This is the dining room."

"I never would have guessed," Anne teased.

"Then I'm glad I explained. When Grandpapa moved to the home, he couldn't take the furniture with him. I initially thought about buying something new—more modern and more comfortable—but all of this was my grandmother's, and, in the end, I couldn't part with it. The Limoges in the chiffonier and on the table belonged to her mother."

Anne walked over to take a closer look at the simple but elegant antique china, ornate sterling silver, and sparkling Baccarat crystal. In the center of the table, was a matching crystal vase filled with tulips, iris, and daffodils. "I'm definitely impressed," she said, "Though I doubt you could top what I've already seen, would it be invading the great chef's space if I asked to see the kitchen where he's creating whatever smells so enticing?"

"My pleasure. I'm especially proud of my kitchen. When Grandpapa moved out, I designed what you're about to see."

Anne followed Arnaud through a swinging door into a kitchen with cream cabinets, blue, cream, and beige granite countertops, and a large island topped with the same granite. "Even I might be motivated to cook in here," she said. "And what a cozy breakfast nook. Are the windows the real thing?"

"If you mean are they the originals, they are. Like my grandmother's dining room furniture, I couldn't part with them, though I had them sealed to keep out the drafts. If you look down, you can see my private gardens in the courtyard."

"You garden?"

"Of course. Any chef worth his salt cultivates his own herbs and vegetables."

"That's bad."

"I thought it was pretty good."

"Did you grow the flowers in the vase on the dining room table?"

"I planted the bulbs. I seem to have what you Americans call a green thumb."

Anne stepped behind the table and looked down at uniform rows of emerging herbs, vegetables, and blooming spring flowers. "Clearly you enjoy tending your garden," she said.

"I do. For me, digging in the dirt is the ultimate relaxation, and I don't mean what you call dishing the dirt."

"I knew what you meant."

Back in the center of the room, she paused in front of a fireplace covered in blue Delft tiles. "This is definitely a work of art."

"Because it is, I remodeled the room around it. I'd have preferred brown granite countertops—"

"But the blue hues compliment the design in the tiles."

"Exactly. My great-great-grandfather purchased the tiles in the city of Delft shortly after he bought the mansion."

"They're exquisite." Anne ran her hand over the smooth blue and white design and then turned back. "I'm also jealous of your Viking stove."

"I can't imagine why you would be."

"Right, because I don't cook."

"No comment. I've quickly learned to stop talking when I see that sort-of-frown on your face. So moving on, unless you want to stand here admiring my stove, I'll show you the rest of the place."

Arnaud crossed the room and opened a door leading to a central hallway. "This way," he said, gesturing toward the rear of the apartment. Halfway down the hall, he stopped in front of two closed doors. "These are my guest rooms." He opened one and then the other, allowing Anne to see two tastefully decorated suites.

"They're both lovely," she said.

"Thank you. I'm working on my decorator adjective." Before she could respond, he said, "Through that last door on the right is my office. Take a look."

Anne stepped into a room that resembled an old-world, very-exclusive men's club. She went to one of the mahogany bookshelves lining three of the walls. Removing one of the volumes, she caressed the cover and carefully leafed through the yellowing pages. "This room and this book conjure up one of my best childhood memories," she said wistfully. "Whenever my mother and father traveled together, which was often, I stayed with Grandfather Robert and Oma. Every night after dinner, my grandfather took me by the hand, lead me into his library, sat me on his lap in his huge leather chair, and read to me from books that were Mother's—a twelve-volume collection entitled *My Book House.* When I was very little, he read poems from the first volume, *From the Nursery.* Later, when I was too old for nursery rhymes, night after night he read my favorite story, *Princess Nellie and the Seneca Chief.* Oma gave me the books after he died. Even today I occasionally pick up Volume 9—"

"And read about Princess Nellie."

"Right! Wow, I can't imagine why holding this book made me think of the 'olden-days,' as my grandfather called them."

"Because they brought back good memories. When I look at the Delft-tiled fireplace in here, I think about my great-great-grandfather who brought the tiles from Delft, and then of great-grandfather Auguste, who, I'm sure, spent wonderful hours in this room listening to his father tell stories. Naturally, I never met either man, but they're here with me every day."

"Of course they are. And speaking of fireplaces, I hope you're still coming to watch the mason remove the bricks from above the mantle—"

"I'm baffled—"

"Why? I invited—"

"Not by your question—only that suddenly you stopped reminiscing about the past, looked at my fireplace, and immediately thought of the invitation you issued to join you on Saturday. Yes, I'll come, but have you asked your grandmother how she feels about having a stranger hanging around while the mason works? Whatever she does or doesn't find, I'm sure she'll experience a multitude of emotions. If Elisabeth *did* leave a message, reading what she wrote will be difficult, and if she didn't—"

"I can't *begin* to wrap my mind around that possibility. Oma would be devastated, and we'd be back to square one."

"Not really. We know whatever paintings were left in house when the Nazis came for Elisabeth were taken to the Jeu de Paume, and you have upcoming appointments with Grandpapa, Giles, and, Madame Bouffard."

"And I'm also meeting with Isaac and Isabelle. Though they won't be able to help in our search for the art Denis hid, they may be able to give us direction by telling us how they went about recovering the art the

Nazis took from their families' collections. All this aside, it would be so much easier if Elisabeth left a message."

"Hopefully she did, and, if your grandmother doesn't object, yes, I'll join you Saturday morning."

"Good. Plan to be at my apartment by seven forty-five. We'll go down together."

"I thought the mason was coming at nine."

"He is, but Oma's new chef is serving breakfast at eight."

"Then she *did* hire a chef."

"I told you, she works fast. I think his name is André Pasquier. He's taking a leave of absence from L'Ambroise for as long as Oma's in Paris. He's coming in Saturday morning and then starting full-time on Monday."

"I like L'Ambroise, though given a choice, I prefer Taillevent."

"I asked you to join us for dinner Saturday night. If you recommend Taillevent, would you reserve a table for five at eight—that is if you can book a reservation on such short notice? If all goes well, we'll have reason to celebrate."

"If I'm able to accomplish this nearly-impossible feat—and I assure you I will succeed—what adjective—"

"You know somebody."

"The head chef."

"Work your magic and I'll add magician to the list."

"Have I pulled ahead of Gus?"

"By far, but please don't brag. I want to keep him happy, and, before you comment, of course, I want to keep you happy too."

"You want to *keep* me happy or *make* me happy?"

"It's not the same thing? Make a reservation, mighty magician. And now, will you show me the rest of your apartment?"

"Besides the three bathrooms that, due to lack of time, I skipped, there's only one more room to see."

Arnaud opened the door opposite his study and stepped aside, allowing Anne to enter a large bedroom decorated in browns, reds, terracotta, and cream. Against the wall was a large king-size bed with a spread that matched the drapes on the two floor-to-ceiling windows. "This is the master suite," he said. "It was once my great-grandmother's room. She and my grandparents are another reason I wanted to live here instead of in New York. I love that my home was once theirs. It seems right that it became Grandpapa's and now it's mine. But enough sentimentality. The chef must return to the kitchen."

"You mean the tour's over? What about your etchings and the wine cellar you bragged about?"

"My etchings are hanging in my office, and the wine cellar is off the kitchen. I'll work on my collector of fine art and sommelier adjectives later, but, now, I must don my chef's hat and apron."

"So I can add culinary genius to dirt-disher, historian, and fantastic kisser."

"I like the third adjective, but I should probably refresh your memory." He quickly walked to where Anne was standing, kissed her softly and then again with growing passion.

"Is there a stronger word than fantastic," she murmured when Arnaud stepped back. "How about fabulously fantastic?"

"That works for me." He'd leaned down to kiss her again when a buzzer sounded. "Bad timing, Sophie," he groaned.

"Good timing," Anne said, smiling.

"Come on." Arnaud took Anne's hand. "I want you to meet my big sister."

"Buzz me up," Sophie ordered when Arnaud pushed the intercom button. "The traffic's terrible, and you know how I hate to be late. Is Anne with you?"

"And hello to you too. Yes, Anne's here, and your timing's atrocious."

"You can do your charm thing later. Push the button."

Minutes later the elevator door opened. A much-smaller, more-feminine Arnaud bounced into the room. "Hi, little brother," she said, standing on tiptoes to give Arnaud a kiss.

"Sophie, this is—"

"Of course," Sophie said, her green eyes sparkling. "It's a pleasure to meet you, Anne. You're everything Arnaud said and more."

"Must you," Arnaud began.

"Of course I must."

"It's nice to meet you, Sophie," Anne said, realizing in less than thirty seconds that she liked Arnaud's sister.

The initial greeting over, Arnaud poured wine and excused himself, leaving Anne and Sophie in the comfortable living room. Over the next thirty minutes, Anne learned about Sophie's college days at Stanford, how she met her husband on an airplane traveling from Paris to Palo Alto, her failed efforts to have children, their recent venture into artificial insemination, her home in the sixteenth arrondisement, and her passion for the ballet. When Arnaud opened the French doors from the dining room to announce that dinner was served, Anne felt like she was talking to an old friend.

"I have no idea what you're serving," Anne said. "But I'm impressed even before the food arrives."

"Look at the Limoges menu card at the end of the table."

"Amazing," Anne said as she read aloud,

Potage Saint-Germain
Poulet au vinaigre a L'Estragon
Pommes Anna
Haricots verts a la Vapeur
Salade verte avec croutes de Roquefort
Pots de Crème Javanaise

After pouring white wine into one of three wine glasses set at each place, he said, "If you'll excuse me, I'll serve the Potage Saint-Germain."

"Hurry," Sophie urged. "I'm starving."

"You're always in a hurry," Arnaud said. "Why don't you sit back, relax, and enjoy the presentation."

"I'm always in a hurry because I have important things to do."

"You two make me sad I didn't have a brother or sister," Anne said after Arnaud left the room.

"I realize a lot of siblings fight, but Arnaud and I rarely do. He's the best brother a girl could have, and I say that in all honesty, not merely to impress the woman he loves."

"Excuse me," Anne burst out. "I've know your brother for three days, and—"

"He's in love with you. He's glowing. Does that phrase only apply to pregnant women? I can't figure out how you feel about him, but I know you like—"

"Like what?" Arnaud said as he served the pea soup.

"You're cooking." Sophie smiled at Anne. "And your presentation. The swirls of crème add a decorative touch. Are you trying to impress me? Oh, I get it. You want Anne to think you're a culinary genius."

"Culinary genius. That's what I agreed to put on your brother's adjective list."

"Adjective list?"

"Arnaud's trying to catch up with my driver, Gus. When I introduced the two of them, I gave Gus rave reviews calling him an historian, great driver, etc. I didn't say anything nice about Arnaud."

"And now he's trying to amass adjectives beside his name."

"So when I introduce him to my grandmother on Friday—"

"She'll be impressed."

"I'm really in trouble," Arnaud groaned. "You're already finishing each other's sentences."

"Be very frightened," Sophie said, her eyes shining. "Anne has now become my new bff. So try the list on me, Anne. I'll decide whether or not your grandmother will be impressed."

"I'll tell you what I have so far. Of course I'll be adding additional adjectives during my stay on the l'Île."

"As you get to know my brother, I'm sure some of the adjectives you add will be less than complimentary.

"Thanks a lot."

"Anne would expect her new bff to tell only the truth. So, Anne, what adjectives have you put on the Arnaud Lessard list so far?"

"Let's see, dirt disher."

"I beg your pardon?"

"He's a good gossip. He tells me about scandals and intrigues that happened here on the Île."

"He's talking about the past. I can tell you what's going on now."

"Then maybe I'll have to start an adjective list for you too, beginning with 'gossip queen.'"

"I prefer 'knower-of-all,'" Sophie joked. "So what other adjectives are on my brother's list?"

"He already has so many, it's hard to recall, but, at this point, I believe he qualifies as a gardener, flower arranger, historian, magician, mover, and culinary artist."

"Aren't you forgetting number three?"

Sophie cocked her head. "What's number three?"

"I can't recall," Anne said. "Shall we move on?"

"Let me jog your memory." Arnaud stood, walked to Anne's chair, lifted her chin, kissed her on the mouth, and grinning, said, "Now do you remember?"

Sophie laughed. "Now I understand—"

"I'm not sure you do—"

"Oh, I think she does," Arnaud said, smiling. "Shall we eat?"

"If it means we can stop this inane conversation, absolutely," said Sophie.

"My compliments to the obnoxious chef," Anne said, after tasting the soup. "I'd ask for the recipe, but you know I only cook Chinese takeout."

"How do you cook Chinese takeout? "Sophie asked.

"I reheat—which means I don't cook."

"Then you should definitely marry a man who does."

"Anne, try to remember your bff's words," Arnaud said.

"So suddenly I'm the good guy, or girl if you want to get picky."

"You always were—at least that's what you've always insisted."

The remainder of the dinner was equally enjoyable, both for the food and the company. "I'm afraid tonight has been all about me," Anne said when Arnaud went for the dessert.

Like it was about me before dinner. We'll share time equally next time we get together."

"It's a deal—"

"What's a deal?" Arnaud asked as he placed a champagne flute at each plate.

"You seem to appear at the end of every conversation," Sophie said. "If you must know what we're discussing, stick around. I was telling Anne the next time we get together *I'll* do all the talking."

"Trust me, she will." Arnaud poured the champagne and raised his glass. "To my new friend and neighbor. Here's to you and your new home, Anne."

"And to you and my new bff. Thank you for a wonderful time."

~~~

It was after eleven when Sophie stood to leave. "It's been lovely meeting you," she said as she removed a card from her purse. "Here are my numbers and my email address. Let me know if you can meet for lunch. I know you're busy."

"I'll make time."

"I'm doomed," Arnaud groaned as the two women hugged. "Sophie, call me when you get home. You know I worry."

"That went well," Arnaud said as the elevator door closed.

"Your sister's delightful."

"Another plus in my column?"

"So now you have a column as well as an adjective list."

"If it means I'm beating Gus, I do. Would you like a glass of wine before I drive you home?"

"Thanks, but no thanks. It's already late, and I need to make a few notes before we meet with your grandfather. Thank you for inviting me. Sophie's great."

"I agree, though the two of you together scare me."

"As well we should," Anne warned. "Be very afraid."

CHAPTER 25

"Thank God I'm finally over jet lag, Anne whispered when the alarm went off at seven. While she waited for the coffee pot to do its magic, she sat at the breakfast table and scanned the notes she'd made the night before. When the pot beeped announcing the coffee was ready, satisfied she was prepared for her meeting with Bertrand, she poured a cup and, taking it with her, went to shower and dress.

I may be forced to shop, she thought as she stood in the huge closet looking at her sparse wardrobe. She finally selected a pair of beige slacks and a white silk blouse with a navy-blue, red, and yellow geometric pattern. Looking in the mirror, she suddenly remembered Gus's tales about Le Meurice. "This time I look like a walking Salvador Dalí painting," she muttered as she turned off the light.

With ten minutes to spare, she poured a second cup of coffee and, cup in hand, went to her office. *Funny, I was just thinking about Gus,* she mused when his name popped up in her inbox. She opened the message and read.

Hi Anne, At two-thirty I will be out front waiting to drive you to Madame Doyon's home on rue Vieille-du-Temple. Unless there is an unusual amount of traffic, it should only take ten minutes to get there. If you are running late, please call so I can let Madame Doyon know when to expect us. I will tell you what I discovered about Didier when I see you. Gus

Anne wrote back,

Two-thirty works for me. If Madame Bouffard and I aren't finished, I'll tell her I'd like to meet again when my grandmother can join us. Thanks for arranging the get-together with Isobel and Isaac and for your super-sleuth work regarding Didier. I can't wait to hear what you have to say. Oh, and I strolled through Square Barye. You were right! It's lovely. I finally understand what you were trying to tell me about April in Paris. See you later. Anne

None of the other emails required an immediate reply, so she picked up her purse, locked up, and took the elevator to the lobby.

Arnaud pulled up just as she exited the building. "I don't know about you, but I'm hungry," he said as she slid into the passenger seat. "If we're going to be at Grandpapa's by nine, we don't have much time, so what about a quick bite at La Charlotte de l'Île—aka, calories galore?"

"And then, rather than drive, we'll run to Bertrand's to burn off—"

"Maybe one bite of a chocolate croissant and two sips of hot chocolate."

⁓

"Finding a parking place so close to the café is definitely a good omen." Arnaud said as he maneuvered into a spot that was vacated seconds before.

"Oh my God!" Anne exclaimed as she got out of the car.

"Oh my God, good? Or oh my God let's get out of here; the aromas are too tempting?"

"Definitely the former. In my dreams this is how heaven smells."

"You'll soon know how manna tastes."

"Look at all those goodies," Anne said as they entered the shop. "This is the way a grandmother's kitchen should smell. If I close my eyes, I can picture a cheery elderly woman standing by her stove in her ruffled-top apron covered with flour and sprinkles of sugar. Her silver hair is pulled back in a bun, and there's a smile on her face as she bakes tray after tray of gooey chocolate-chip cookies and buttery fudge brownies."

"It was like that at your grandmother's house?"

"Are you kidding? The minute you see Oma, you'll know she wasn't your typical grandmother. I doubt they sell designer aprons. Yes, there were usually chocolate chip cookies around, but her chef baked them."

"You sound disappointed."

"Not really. I never knew any better. None of my life was what you'd call normal. Did your grandmother bake chocolate chip cookies for you?"

"Grandmamma died several years before I was born."

"What about your mother? Did she bake?"

Why bother to bake with places like La Charlotte de l'Île around?"

"Point made."

Anne passed by case after case, each filled with a chocolate dream—chocolate figurines, tarts oozing chocolate filling, and chocolate frosted cakes. "I've walked into a warm, cozy, chocolate-filled dream," she murmured. "I have no idea what to order."

"If it helps, Sylvie makes *the* best chocolate-filled croissant I've ever tasted. But if you really want to think you're in heaven, order her hot chocolate."

"I'm not really a hot chocolate fan."

"I'm willing to bet my apartment that you've never tasted hot chocolate like this. It's really more like a warm soft chocolate bar than a chocolate drink. It's so thick that Sylvie adds whipped cream so it's drinkable. Even that doesn't work for me. I usually buy a bottle of water and take a drink between sips so the chocolate sludge doesn't stick in my throat."

The three tables in the front of the store were taken, so they entered the back parlor that resembled a tiny Victorian sitting room with dim lights, an assortment of pattered armchairs, carnival masks, and dried flowers. "Do you know what you want," Arnaud asked as Anne sat down.

"I'll try the chocolate-filled croissant you raved about."

"Hot chocolate?"

"I'll pass. I'm sure I'll be able to swallow Jasmine tea."

"It's your loss. I'll be right back with your boring drink."

Five minutes later Arnaud put a tray on the table. "That's the only drink I've ever seen that doesn't slosh around in the cup," Anne said.

"Try it so you can tell Grandpapa you tasted Sylvie's melted chocolate bar."

Anne took a sip, and then another. "You're right," she said. "Oma would love this place."

"You'll bring her here before she returns to New York?"

"You mean *if* she returns. I'm already drawn to the Île. Imagine how she'll feel when she sees her childhood home. And no, I won't submit her to this torture. Her doctor has her on a reduced salt, low fat diet, so unless Sylvie serves fat free croissants, Oma won't hear about La Charlotte de l'Île from me."

"And yet she hired a top-rated Parisian chef. Does she think he'll prepare low fat meals?"

"I'll let Renee handle that battle when it comes, and believe me, it will." Anne took a bite of the croissant. "Again, you're right. This *is* manna from heaven."

They were almost finished eating when a Kimono-clad woman entered the room. Arnaud rose and greeted her with a kiss on each cheek. "May I introduce Madame Anne French?" he said "Anne this is my favorite café owner, Sylvie Laroquet."

"I am sure he says that to all the ladies on the Île," Sylvie said, blushing. "Bonjour, Madame French. Are you here in Paris for business or pleasure?"

"A little of both," Anne said, realizing that less than a week ago her answer would have been different.

"Anne moved into an apartment in her great-grandmother's home on Quai de Bourbon," Arnaud said.

"Then you will be living here on the Île?" Sylvie asked.

"My home is in New York, but I hope to visit Paris several times a year."

"Perhaps Arnaud will find a way to convince you to stay."

"I'm working on it," Arnaud said, chuckling.

"I will leave you to enjoy your breakfast," Sylvie said. "Come back to see us soon, Madame."

"That's strike two," Anne said as Sylvie returned to the front of the café. "And don't give me an I-don't-understand look." You lived in New York, so you know about baseball, at least the basics. I'm sure the rivalry between the Mets and the Yankees was front page news. Are you *trying* to give the island gossips more to talk about, or is it just my imagination?"

"Would I do that?"

"Of course you would, and wipe that I-have-no-idea-what-you'r e-talking-about look off your face. I bet Sylvie is already on the phone telling every one of her friends to spread the word that Arnaud Lessard is having breakfast with the American woman."

"I'm merely trying to build on our supposition that everyone living here will think your grandmother is arriving for our marriage at Église Saint-Louis-en-l'Île."

"That's taking place next weekend," Anne said, her annoyance lessening.

"Saturday night." Arnaud laughed. "Shall we go tell Grandpapa?"

⟳

"Was that rue de Fleurus?" Anne asked as Arnaud passed the entrance to the Luxembourg Gardens.

"It was. Let me guess. You want me to dish the dirt on Gertrude Stein's salon."

"Not this time. I recently learned that Didier Duplessis owned a house on rue de Fleurus during the Occupation."

"Duplessis is the man Gus mentioned when—"

"I forgot to tell you about Didier during our celebratory lunch."

"Right. We spent most of our time talking about Madame Monleix-Wallig's delicacies. So who's Didier?"

Anne spent the next few minutes telling Arnaud about the clues in Jules' letter and what Gus had learned from his sources. "And he may have new information," she finished.

"He didn't provide specifics?"

"No. He said we'd talk later today. I can't wait to hear what he has to say."

About a kilometer up the road, Arnaud pulled into the driveway of what appeared to be a newly-restored group of buildings. He parked in the guest lot and led Anne through a shaded courtyard to the door of a ground-floor apartment.

While they waited for a response to Arnaud's knock, Anne looked around at the well-kept grounds. "Without going inside, I see why your grandfather likes living here," she said.

"I was skeptical at first, but it turns out, for him, it's the perfect place. He eats his meals in the community dining room, and there are all sorts of organized activities—bridge tournaments, day trips to historic places, and field trips to the city. He has all the comforts of home, and I feel better knowing he's monitored by professionals. If he doesn't check in several times a day, a staff member comes running. He wears a medical-alert necklace, but please don't mention it during our conversation. Grandpapa is a man's man. A necklace is something a woman wears."

"Mum's the word," Anne said as a tall, thin, silver-haired man answered the door.

"You're here!" Bertrand said. "I haven't seen you lately."

"It's not entirely my fault, Grandpapa. The last few times I've called, you've been busy with your new friend."

"What my grandson won't say is I am usually with my girlfriend." Bertrand hugged Arnaud and then reached for Anne's hand. Kissing it gently, he said, "You must be Madame French."

"Please call me Anne, sir. And chivalry, at least in your case, is definitely alive and well."

"Always, and please do not call me sir. That mode of address, though polite, makes me sound like an old man. I am Bertrand, or, if you prefer, Grandpapa. Welcome to my home, Anne."

"I'm impressed," Anne said as she entered a large tastefully-decorated suite. "Arnaud says you call this the home. I've never seen an assisted living facility this luxurious in the United States."

"I am glad you like my place. I brought the furniture from the Quai de Bethune apartment. Arnaud wanted to get rid of it—too old fashioned for his modern tastes."

"Grandpapa—"

"Admit it. You thought my apartment looked like an elderly retreat."

"I never did. Before I forget, Anne and I had breakfast at La Charlotte de l'Île. Sylvie sends her love."

"Ah, Sylvie, "Bertrand said wistfully. "What delights—"

"Isn't Madame Monleix-Wallig the one with delights and delicacies," Anne said, laughing.

"Did I say something humorous?" Bertrand asked.

"Inside joke, Grandpapa. I'm sure you and your girlfriend have secrets."

"Anne's your girlfriend?"

"Your grandson is teasing, Bertrand."

"I am not so sure, but there is no reason to argue. Please sit." Bertrand pointed to a couch opposite an overstuffed chair. "Unfortunately, without a kitchen, I am unable to brew coffee or tea."

"I just had cup of Sylvie's delicious jasmine tea," Anne said. "So I'm all set."

"In that case, tell me how I can help, my dear."

Glancing occasionally at her notes, Anne spent the next fifteen minutes telling Bertrand what she'd recently learned from Renee, Henri, and Veronique about Elisabeth's arrest and their subsequent escape from Paris. Bertrand listened attentively while she talked about her grandmother's newfound wish to find the art Denis Guidreau removed from the Boulet mansion and the pieces the Nazis took from the house during the July 17 raid.

"So Veronique is *finally* coming to Paris," Bertrand said when she finished her account. "I knew her, though I doubt she would remember a boy who was ten years old in 1942. She knew my father."

"Henri told me about Auguste and Anton," Anne said. "Both were special men."

"They certainly were. And speaking of Henri, yesterday I received an email saying he and Renee are also coming to Paris."

"When did you start emailing?" Arnaud asked. "And for that matter, when did you buy a computer?"

"Months ago. I *may* give you my email address, but I will definitely give it to Anne. I want to know if you are behaving properly." He leaned forward and whispered, "If you have a Facebook page, Anne, send me a friend request."

"You're kidding, Grandpapa. *I'm* not on Facebook."

"Then I suggest you join the age of social media, my dear grandson."

When Bertrand looked back at Anne, his green eyes had lost their twinkle, and his chiseled jaw was tightly clamped. "I am not sure how much

I can help you," he said. "But I will share what I know. The Occupation was a terrible time, so my childhood was anything but normal."

"Henri told me how brave you were."

"Perhaps stupid is better word. I had no idea what I was doing was so dangerous. I did what Papa asked."

"You knew," Arnaud said.

"Well perhaps," Bertrand said thoughtfully. "But back to what I was saying about that grim period in my life. With the Nazis marching up and down the Champs Élysées and the German flag flying from all our public buildings, there was little laughter. Conversations were hushed, or in Papa's case, probably because he was a member of the Resistance, there were no conversations at all. But I am speaking too generally. On the night of July 17, Anton and Papa sent me to Madame Boulet's."

"You saw what happened?"

"I arrived just as two soldiers were lifting her into the back of a canvas-covered truck. As soon as that truck pulled away, another arrived. Several soldiers jumped out and went inside. I waited around the corner, occasionally peeking to see what they were doing."

"Wasn't it dangerous for you to be watching?" Anne asked "You were out in the open and vulnerable."

"Probably so, but I was young and invincible—or so I believed. When the soldiers finished removing furniture and boxes from Madame Boulet's house, they draped a yellow tape across the door. I knew the stars on the tape meant no one could enter the house because it belonged to a Jew. The Nazis hated the Jews, but, to me, Madame Boulet was just a nice lady. I didn't know why anyone would hate her. I ran home to report to Papa and Anton. Looking back, I think it was the only time I saw Anton cry. He rushed out the door. When I asked Papa where he had gone, he said 'to find Madame Boulet.' All night we waited for news. I know Papa was worried. He walked back and forth. Back and forth. He never went to bed."

"When did Anton return?"

"About seven the next morning. He said nothing. There was no need. His face told the story. He was agitated, and his eyes were red from crying. Throughout the rest of the day, he was fixated on getting Henri, Renee, and Veronique out of Paris. Over and over he said it was *vital* that Henri survive the war."

"He used the word 'vital'?"

"He did."

"May I digress for a moment?"

"Of course you may."

"During the Occupation, my grandmother kept a journal. On Bastille Day 1940, about a month after the Germans marched into Paris, she wrote that her mother was across the Île visiting Denis and Lili Guidreau. You lived near the Guidreau's. Did Madame Boulet call on your family?"

"Before the Occupation she came by regularly, usually with Anton. But after the Nazis issued the first restrictive edicts and it was no longer safe for Christians to associate with Jews, she stopped coming. I remember Anton was angry that friends could no longer meet without fear of reprisal. He ignored the new regulations and continued to visit Madame Boulet at her home."

"How do you know?"

"I often heard Papa say to Anton, 'If you *must* visit, you *must* be careful.'"

"It sounds like Anton and Elisabeth were good friends."

"They were all friendly, but, honestly, Anne, I wasn't paying attention. However, I do know Madame Boulet was close to Denis and Lili Gaudrieu. Before she married and moved to Quai de Bourbon, they were next-door neighbors."

"My grandmother says when she lived on the Île, everyone knew everyone else's business This closeness among neighbors is why I'm wondering if you know whether Elisabeth sold her childhood home prior to the onset of the Occupation?"

"I am not sure, though I doubt it. Before the Occupation, I was too young to realize what was going on in the neighborhood, though I do recall my father saying it was a shame such a beautiful place stood vacant.

It may just be sheer happenstance, but in 1949, Henri and Renee came to Paris to sell her family home. I never asked, but I assume he also sold the Quai de Bethune mansion during that trip."

"What makes you think so?"

"Because about a month after they left for New York, a family with a teenage son moved into the mansion."

"What can you tell me about the new owners?"

"Not much. Martin, the son, and I were about the same age, but we never became friends. He attended a private school and spent his summers and holidays in the country, so he was rarely around. After his parents died, sometime in the late 1970s, he stayed in the house when he came to Paris, I assume for business, though he continued to spend the majority of his time in the country. Jumping ahead about forty-five years, after Martin's wife Christine died, it was difficult for him to remain in their home, so he deeded the farm to his grandson and moved permanently to the Île. I dined with him several times before I moved to the home. He seems like a fine man, but he is very quiet—he keeps his thoughts to himself. He does not share details about his life. I wish I could tell you more."

"Thank you for sharing what you *do* remember. If you're up to it, I have a few more questions."

"Of course."

"Were you acquainted with the Huards or the Siegles? My grandmother said Monsieur and Madame Siegle sent their children to the country shortly before la rafle du Vel d'Hiv."

"I knew *of* the Siegles. I assume my father was acquainted with the family. If the parents remained behind, I am sure they, too, were arrested during the raid."

"Do you know if the children moved back to the Île after the Liberation?"

"I do not, but if you tell me where they lived, I will find out."

"I have no idea, but it's not that important. What about the Huards?"

"I remember meeting Madame and Monsieur Huard, but that is all. I am sorry I cannot provide additional information. I was only a boy—"

"As I said before, I'm grateful you've shared what you *do* recall."

Realizing there were no more questions to ask about Elisabeth's neighbors, at least that Bertrand could answer, Anne directed the conversation to Denis Gaudrieu and the hidden art. Bertrand couldn't offer much new information, though he said in the months before the Nazis raided Elisabeth's house, he had heard Anton and his father talk about selling several paintings.

"Did you ask *why* they were selling the art?" Anne asked.

"It was not my place to question."

"What about the other paintings, the ones Elisabeth didn't sell?"

"Other than I heard Papa say Denis was hiding them where the Nazis would not think to look, I know nothing about them. I assumed Denis was transporting them to the continent by boat under cover of darkness. That would have made sense. The Nazis could monitor the ponts but not the river—at least not all the time." He sighed. "I suppose we will never know what happened all those years ago."

"I hope you're wrong in that regard," Anne said.

⌒◯

Fifteen minutes later, Bertrand looked at his watch. "I am afraid I must bring our delightful time together to an end," he said. "It is nearly time for lunch, and I have a date. Please come again very soon." His eyes twinkling, he added, "But call before you plan to visit. I am a very busy man."

"Your grandfather's amazing," Anne said as Arnaud pulled out of the parking lot.

"Another adjective for my list?"

"Like what? I can't imagine—"

"I'll get back to you on that one. Are you hungry? We don't have time to stop at a restaurant, but—"

"Let's go by Calixte and pick up something light. We can eat at my place before our appointment with Madame Bouffard.

⌒◯

After a snack of crusty bread and cheese, Arnaud and Anne walked around the corner to number forty-seven. A woman, who, despite her age, looked spry, opened the door.

"Bonjour, Madame Bouffard," Arnaud said.

"Bonjour, Arnaud." Turning to Anne, in heavily-accented English, she said, "You are Veronique's granddaughter. I see the resemblance."

"Merci, Madame. Thank you for seeing me."

"Please come in. My daughter Cecile is making tea."

Madame Bouffard escorted Anne and Arnaud into a large parlor and pointed to a velvet-covered settee. Anne and Arnaud sat down. She sat opposite them and, without engaging in small talk, began. "I know you are eager to learn about the night the Nazis took Madame Boulet. I am not sure how much I can say that you do not already know. I was only ten in 1942."

A middle aged woman carrying a tray with a teapot and four cups entered. Arnaud stood, took the tray, and set it on the coffee table. "May I introduce my daughter, Cecile Hebert," Jacqueline said.

Anne stood and extended her hand, "Bonjour, Madame Hebert."

"Bonjour and welcome." Cecile shook hands with Anne and then turned to Arnaud. "I have not seen you since your father's funeral. How is Bertrand?"

"As ever, he's enjoying life."

"Please give him my best when you see him."

"Thank you, and please tell Luc hello." He looked at Anne and explained, "Luc is Cecile's son. He and I attended school together." He again addressed Cecile. "I hear you have a new grandchild."

"And I, a great grandchild," Madame Bouffard announced. "I only wish my precious grandson and his wife lived closer so I could see them more often."

"They don't live in Paris?" Anne asked.

"My son is in the diplomatic corps," Cecile explained. "He and his family live in Washington, but they come home several times a year."

"And you live here on Quai de Bourbon?"

"I do. After my husband died, I moved in with Mama."

"I'm sorry for *your* loss."

"Thank you. Francis was ill for several years so, in some ways, his passing was a blessing."

Jacqueline poured tea for everyone. "What would you like to know, Madame French?" she asked.

"Would you call me Anne?"

"Certainly, and please, call me Jacqueline. In these modern times, I am told we no longer stand on formality. How may I help you, Anne?"

"You saw the Nazis take Great-Grand'Mere Elisabeth the night of July 17?"

"I did. Until I saw Mother sobbing uncontrollably and Papa trying unsuccessfully to comfort her, I did not realize something horrible was happening next door."

"Would you tell me what you saw?"

"Of course. I watched through a slit in the draperies in this very parlor. Take a look. You will see the view I had of the events taking place at Madame Boulet's home."

Anne walked to the window and peered out. Because Elisabeth's house was on a curve, Jacqueline had a clear view. "You really *could* see everything," she said as she sat back down.

"Unfortunately, yes. It has been decades, but I vividly recall everything that occurred. A man wearing a black coat and a red arm band with a large black swastika on the front knocked on Madame Boulet's door. When she did not answer, the soldiers went back to the truck and retrieved a large heavy beam. They returned and, after several tries, battered down the door. All three men went inside. About ten minutes later, the soldiers came out dragging Madame Boulet between them. They hoisted her up to a third man who was waiting at the back of the truck, turned, and went back into the house."

"Though this may be a foolish question, how did Madame Boulet seem?"

"She was very weak—so frail I could see her bones through her gauzy dress. I am sure she would have collapsed on the walkway had the men let go of her arms. Her condition surprised me. I knew my parents and our other neighbors had been leaving meat and vegetables on her doorstep several times a week. With more to eat, I thought she might be stronger."

"What happened next?" Anne asked.

During the next ten minutes, Jacqueline repeated the same story Bertrand had told that morning. She finished, "And it was not until I received Veronique's note that I realized she was away from home that evening and not arrested along with her mother. The morning after the raid we saw Madame Boulet's friend standing in front of the house. He looked distraught. A few minutes later Papa went out to speak with him, but he was gone."

"A man came to Elisabeth's home on July 18?" Anne asked. "It wasn't Veronique's friend Henri?"

"I would have recognized Henri. This man was older. I did not know who he was, though I had seen him before. I once heard Mother say he was not from the Île. Is the man important?"

"Maybe. I don't know."

Realizing Jacqueline knew nothing more about the mysterious man, Anne changed the subject. "Did you know Madame Huard?" she asked.

"I did. She died about ten years ago."

"Did she have children?"

"Yes, two boys and a girl. The boys left Paris immediately after the Liberation, and they never moved back. Several years later, her daughter, Francoise, married an Île resident, Louis Laplante. They live abroad for many years, but when Madame Huard became ill, they moved back to the mansion so Francoise could care for her mother. After Madame Huard died, Louis reconfigured the mansion. He made a single apartment of the first and second floors and converted the rest of the house to multiple units. Louis died last year, but Francoise chose to remain in the apartment."

"Do you think Madame Laplante would see me?"

"I am sure she will."

"Francoise and I are good friends," Cecile said. "If you would like, I will be glad to arrange a meeting."

"Thank you," Anne said. "I'm sure my grandmother would like to speak with Francoise, but, at this point, I don't know when. I'm not privy to her schedule, other than we have an appointment with a mason Saturday morning."

"A mason?" Jacqueline said quizzically.

"We believe Great-Grand'Mere Elisabeth left a message for Veronique behind the bricks over her bedroom fireplace—perhaps a letter to help us locate the art Denis Guidreau took from the house."

"I was always excited when Monsieur Guidreau came to call," Jacqueline said.

"I don't understand—"

Jacqueline's eyes twinkled. "Though he was much older, I was infatuated with Charles Guidreau. Perhaps, as we say today, I had my first crush.

"Where's Charles now?" Anne asked. "My grandmother and I are meeting with Giles Monday morning, but being older, Charles may know more about what was going on."

"Unfortunately, he died during the Occupation. He was randomly executed in retaliation for the assassination of a Nazi officer by members of the Resistance. As you might imagine, the family was devastated by his death."

"I'm sure they were."

❧

Twenty minutes later, Anne glanced at her watch. "We've taken up enough of your time," she said. "Jacqueline, it is truly a pleasure to meet you, and you, Cecile."

Jacqueline stood. "I hope you and Veronique will call after she is settled."

"We definitely will. Enjoy the rest of your day."

"Thank you." Jacqueline turned to Arnaud and held out her hand. "It is good to see you," she said. "I hope you, too, will come again very soon."

Arnaud kissed her outstretched hand. "Ah, the good old days," she reminisced. "Thank you for reminding me of a more polite world, young man."

CHAPTER 26

Gus was parked in front of Anne's building when she and Arnaud rounded the corner. He got out of the car as they approached. "Am I late?" she asked.

"You are right on time."

"Arnaud, thank you for taking me to see both Bertrand and Madame Bouffard," Anne said.

"You're welcome. Our part of the day went well. I hope you and Gus have equally good luck this afternoon. I'll call later for an update."

"All right," Anne began as soon as Gus pulled away from the house. "I've been waiting all day. What did you discover about Didier?"

"Surprisingly, though it has been decades, a great deal. Didier was corrupt—"

"We knew that—"

"Yes, but he was dishonest in a way we had not considered. Didier purchased art from desperate Jews who believed they were buying their freedom. He then resold the paintings and kept the money for himself. He rarely paid his partner—the printer who prepared the papers—and he often withheld payment from the guards at the Line of Demarcation. Your grandmother and the others were fortunate to make it to the escape point without being detected. Once they were in place to cross the Line, they were at risk again—"

"Because Didier hadn't paid the guards to look the other way. Did that happen to many escapees?"

"To at least five I know of, and there were probably others."

"Yet the Jews kept using Didier's services. Surely they heard—"

"I am sure they understood the dangers involved. Perhaps they felt they were risking more by remaining in Paris."

"As it turns out, they were," Anne said, thinking about la rafle du Vel d'Hiv. "What happened to Didier after the Liberation? And what about Leon? In his letter to Renee, Jules said if they couldn't find Didier, they should look for his son."

"One of my sources learned that the Nazis arrested Didier in February, 1944."

"For what? For forging false documents?"

"For assisting Jews. That was the most serious of the accusations against him."

"Now isn't that the ultimate irony?"

"It is. Most of the people I spoke with believe Leon was also arrested. However, his wife and their son Damien escaped."

"How do they know?"

"Because Damien now owns what was once Didier's house on rue de Fleurus. That in itself is not unusual. Homes on rue de Fleurus, like the mansions on the Île, are often passed down from generation to generation. However, this is curious. Damien *bought* his grandfather's home. He did not inherit it. The French government seized the house after the Liberation. Several years ago Damien purchased it from the descendants of the family who bought it in the late 1940s. My source says he paid far more than the house is worth to buy it back."

"With crooked money, no doubt."

"That is not true. According to my contacts, Damien is a well-respected businessman."

"Really!"

"So I am told."

"Were you able to find out anything about the paintings Didier bought from Jews who were trying to flee France?"

"Not yet, but my contacts' contacts are still working their leads."

"I don't suppose we could show up at Damien's front door and ask him what happened to the paintings his grandfather sold."

"That would be unwise. Be patient a while longer. I hope to learn something definitive before long. It may not be the news you wish to hear, but at least Madame Ellison will have answers. However, that is all I can say for now. This is Madame Doyon's home."

Gus parked in front of an old three-storey home. Together he and Anne climbed the stone steps to the front door. Gus knocked. Minutes later an elderly man dressed in a suit opened the door. "Madame Anne French for Madame Doyon," Gus announced.

The man stood aside, allowing Anne and Gus to enter the foyer. Once inside, he motioned to an open door on the right, and said, "Please follow me."

As Anne entered an ornately decorated parlor, an elderly gentleman rose to greet them. "Welcome, Madame French," he said. "I am Isaac Thibault." He shook hands with Gus and gestured toward the woman seated on the couch. "May I present Madame Isabelle Doyon?"

"Bonjour, Madame Doyan," Anne said.

"Good afternoon, Madame French," said Isabelle. "Welcome to my home." She turned to Gus. "It is nice to see you again. Would either of you like tea?"

"Thank you, no," Anne said.

"Not for me," said Gus.

Isabelle addressed the man who had brought them to the parlor. "That will be all for now, Martial. Thank you."

When Martial left the room, she motioned to two chairs on one side of a marble top coffee table. "Please make yourselves comfortable," she said, as she and Isaac sat down on a green-velvet Victorian settee. When everyone was settled, she said to Anne, "Gus told us you and your grandmother, Madame Ellison, are beginning a search for art the Nazis removed from Madame Boulet's home during la rafle du Vel d'Hiv."

"That's my primary reason for this visit, Madame, but I have another request. I hope I'm not being rude by asking, Monsieur Thibault, but before we talk about the art, time permitting, would you tell me about la rafle du Vel d'Hiv. On our way over, Gus said the Nazis arrested your entire family during the raid, yet somehow you survived. I know my grandmother would appreciate hearing your story."

"Of course," said Isaac. "Though Madame Ellison will likely be upset by what she learns. It is true. Along with the rest of my family, I was taken during the raid. Thank God, I only spent one night in the velodrome."

"You escaped?"

"In a way, but not on my own. I had help from a mysterious stranger."

"Will you tell me what happened?"

Isaac looked at Isabelle for approval. "Yes, share your story with Madame French," she said.

"Very well," said Isaac. "On the night of July 16, 1942, my parents, my sister, and I were literally dragged from our home in the Marais, yanked into the back of a canvas-covered truck, and taken along with about twenty other Jews to the Velodrome d'Hiver. I was only five at the time, but my recollections of that night and the following day remain vivid, terrifying, and mystifying. To be sure I was remembering correctly, when I was old enough to do so, I interviewed many individuals who, like me, lived through the experience. Later when I learned how to use a computer, I did some online research. Those I spoke with and the articles I read made me realize my memories of that night are quite accurate."

"I'm surprised someone so young could recall so clearly."

"I have often thought about that—perhaps I remember because the velodrome was such a dreadful place. Not a day goes by when I don't wonder why I was one of the lucky few who survived. But back to your question. My first recollection of the velodrome was the roof. In places I could see it had been painted dark blue. I asked one of the soldiers herding us into the building why—"

"You actually spoke with one of your guards?"

"I did—one time. I was an innocent. . ." Isaac paused and then said thoughtfully, "Though that was certainly the last vestige of my childhood naiveté. My father quickly pulled me away, but not before the man said the blue paint was to keep us hidden from view so the allied pilots wouldn't drop their bombs and kill us all. Every few minutes I looked up, terrified a bomb would suddenly crash through the roof and send glass and debris raining down. I vividly recall the almost-unbearable heat, and the stench in the building was nauseating. The windows were screwed shut to keep us from escaping, so there was no ventilation. On top of that, five of the ten lavatories had windows that were blocked to prevent escape. Most of the time the toilettes that were open were running over with excrement. I remember asking Mother why the soles of my shoes were so sticky. She didn't respond, but minutes later my question was answered—I saw a man urinating on the floor."

"What about food and water?"

"During my interviews I learned the only water source was a single fire hydrant pumping filthy contaminated water from the Seine. Some drank—the result being diarrhea that added to the stench and the filth. The Red Cross was allowed in, but there wasn't enough food to feed even a small portion of all the people stuffed into that small space—up to thirteen thousand at a time. I recall there were moments when I was unable to breathe. To this day, I am claustrophobic in crowds. Some detainees tried to escape the horror. I watched a guard shoot two men and one woman as they attempted to go out the door while another group was being herded inside."

"How horrible," Anne said, shuddering.

"There are no words to describe what occurred in that infamous sports arena. I, for one, thank God it was destroyed. I cannot imagine people enjoying themselves in a place that brought so much pain to so many."

"I am sure everyone who was incarcerated at Drancy would agree," said Isabelle. "But if you go off on a tangent, we will never get to the primary purpose for Madame French's visit."

"You are right," Isaac said, smiling at his friend. "I will quickly finish my story. I will never forget the terror I felt when a man, who said his name was Yves, dragged me away from Mother. The anguish on her face and her arm reaching out to me as I turned to look one last time still haunts me after all these years. When the Nazi records were finally made public, I learned that three days after my escape, she, my father, and my sister were bused to Drancy. Two days later, they, along with fifty other Parisian Jews, were packed into a boxcar and transported by train to Auschwitz. Had I been taken with them, I would have been immediately gassed. I was too young to work."

"Did any of your family survive Auschwitz?"

"Upon their arrival, my mother and sister were immediately marched to the showers to be deloused—and we know what that meant. Father was forced to work eleven hours a day, digging ditches and clearing land for more facilities to house the ever-increasing Jewish population. For several years he lived—if you can call it living—in an overcrowded blockhouse swarming with rats and other types of vermin. He slept with one or two other prisoners on a foul-smelling bedbug-infested mattress, endured a leaky roof that let in the rain in the spring and summer and the snow in the winter, and used overflowing toilets that produced an ever-present fetid odor. Worse, he watched men die from illness. From beatings inflicted by the Nazi guards. From a bullet to the brain for no apparent reason. After suffering such unspeakable horrors, the fates were unkind. He died during a severe outbreak of dysentery in November, 1944—just two months before the Soviets liberated Auschwitz in late January, 1945. In all, I lost him, my mother and sister, an aunt, and two uncles in the camps."

"The words I'm sorry hardly express how I feel," Anne said. "I hope you understand what I'm about to say. Though my great-grandmother's immediate death in the gas chamber was tragic, if she had to die at Auschwitz, I'm glad she didn't suffer like your father."

"I agree with you, Madame French, but it seems I owe you an apology. You are obviously distressed by my graphic explanation."

"There's no need to apologize. I asked, and you answered my question. You said you remained at the velodrome for a short while before meeting a mysterious man."

"My savior. As I was saying before I began talking about Auschwitz, on the morning of July 17, Yves, wearing a French policeman's uniform, took me through an unlocked door. He quickly handed me over to a man who was hiding in the shadows. I never saw Yves again, but I am sure he was a member of *la Résistance française*. Without explanation, the mysterious man lifted me up, put me in the cab of his truck, and drove me to his farm, about seventy kilometers—"

"You could judge the distance?"

"Not at the time, but I have returned many times since the Liberation. The house sat on six hectares—that would be close to fifteen acres—and was about seven kilometers from the nearest village. So it was literally and figuratively off the Nazis' radar. When we first drove into the tree-lined approach, through the fog of fright, I remember thinking what a contrast from the velodrome. The setting was soothing and quiet. The truck windows were wide open. I could hear birds singing and the sound of running water from a nearby watermill. The air was warm and smelled sweet. It almost washed the stench of the velodrome from my nostrils."

"Did you remain at the farm, or was that your first stop on your journey out of France?"

"I stayed for nearly two years. I became one of Papa Pierre's and Mama Josette's many sons and daughters—Jewish children who, like me, they saved from sure death. During those years, Papa Pierre's love and Mama Josette's care and good food helped me heal. Along with my 'brothers and sisters,' I slept in the barn Papa Pierre had converted to a dormitory, but we all ate our meals together in the large kitchen in the farmhouse. For all intents and purposes, we became a close-knit family. Each of us had our chores, and our work kept the farm running smoothly. From time to time, one of the older children would depart, and Papa Pierre would bring some-one else to join us."

"Except for the circumstances of your being there, it sounds like you had a wonderful life with Papa Pierre and Mama Josette," Anne said.

"I did—so much so that when it came time for me to leave, I was dis-traught. Though Paris was liberated in August, 1944, the war in Europe continued until May 1945. In June of that year, Papa Pierre located my aunt, my mother's sister. She came to Paris from Nice to care for me in my family home in the Marais."

"What happened to Papa Pierre and Mama Josette?

"Over the years, we remained close. Every six months I joined them and their other charges for a weekend at the farm. As time passed, we began to bring our spouses and our children to the gatherings. Papa Pierre died in 1987, and Mama Josette followed him—I am sure to heaven—several years later. I still see their other 'children,' though, sadly, our numbers are dwindling. I was the only one of my family to sur-vive the Holocaust, but despite the horror our family faced, Papa Pierre taught me there are many good souls in the world. He and Mama Josette risked everything to save over fifty Jewish children in the two years I was with them."

"What an inspiring story in the midst of such horror," Anne said. "Great- Grand'Mere Elisabeth also experienced acts of kindness during that terrible time. At their own peril, her friends and neighbors provided food, and one friend, Denis Gaudrieu, hid her art collection, thus preventing the Nazis from seizing her most valuable paintings during la rafle du Vel d'Hiv. Denis, along with Elisabeth's other friends, sold two paintings to facilitate my grandmother's escape from Paris."

"It is always good to hear about kindheartedness in a time of evil and tragedy." Isaac took a deep breath, exhaled, and said, "And now shall we talk about the art the Nazis took from my family? Gus believes Isabelle and I can provide direction as you begin your search for your great-grandmother's art."

"When did you begin to look for your family's paintings," Anne asked.

"In 1989, immediately after the fall of the Berlin Wall. At the time, I used resources offered by the Israelis."

"Have you reclaimed all of your art?"

"Unfortunately, no. My son recently took over the search, though I had already recovered several pieces including *Still Life with Sleeping Woman* and *Woman Seated in an Armchair* by Matisse and Maurice Utrillo's *Restaurant des Quatre Pavillons*."

"I saw slides of all three paintings in one of my art history classes," Anne said. "Where are they now?"

"*Woman Seated in an Armchair* hangs in the Indianapolis Museum of Art. I saw it several years ago when I visited the United States. *Still Life with Sleeping Woman* is in the National Gallery in Washington. *Restaurant des Quatre Pavillons* now hangs in the Israeli Art Museum. There has been much controversy surrounding the painting. I will not bore you with the details, but if you are interested, there is information on line. But I have dominated the conversation for too long. I can see Isabelle is eager to tell her story."

"It is about time you let me speak, and, yes, you do go on." Smiling at Isaac, Isabelle turned to Anne. "Understand, I was just a baby during the Occupation, so I cannot claim firsthand knowledge. In 1941, my mother and father were seized while at their art gallery in the Marais.

Prior to the Occupation, Papa was a successful art dealer who bought and sold what Hitler later termed 'degenerative art.' Though the Nazis closed the gallery when they enacted laws prohibiting Jews from owning businesses, my parents continued to hide their most valuable paintings in a safe behind a false wall in the then-empty building. When the Nazis arrested them, they were placing two additional paintings into the safe. Though I cannot be sure, I believe someone, perhaps a fellow Jew hoping to buy his freedom by revealing information to his oppressors, reported they had left the house carrying packages that could contain paintings."

"In her journal, my grandmother wrote about an informant on the Île."

"I have heard horror stories of Jews betraying Jews in order to save their own lives—lives the Nazis took anyway. I suppose desperate men and women do desperate things."

"Fearing something like this could happen, had your parents sent you away—perhaps to the country?"

"Several days before they were arrested, they placed me with Catholic friends in the Latin Quarter. I am told we had several close calls as the Nazis searched for Jewish children living with Gentiles, but we made it through the war. Soon after the Liberation, my grandparents came to Paris from Provence, and we moved into this house. We never thought we would see Mother again, but several months later she miraculously came home from Ravensbruck, the notorious women's death camp in Northern Germany. She was a walking skeleton, but she was alive. It was a long process, but my grandparents nursed her back to health. When she was well, they hired an agent to find the art the Nazis took from both the gallery and our home. We have yet to recover all of the paintings, but we have had some success."

"That's my hope," Anne said. "I want my grandmother to have at least a part of her heritage."

"When Gus first spoke with us about your quest, I prepared a list of names and addresses of individuals who continue to assist us as our search progresses, though, like Isaac, my son has now taken over the investigation. I have also provided his contact information. When I told him we were planning to meet, he said he would be glad to speak with you."

"Thank you," Anne said. "I'll tell my grandmother. I'm sure she'll call."

"Good," Isobel said. "I also recommend a handbook by a man named Charles Hawley. His primary reason for writing the book was to help descendants reclaim Nazi spoils and to make restitution easier, but he also hoped to force German museums to research the provenances of the art they put on display. Several of our paintings were hanging in museum collections here in Paris and in Germany."

"Thank you for the suggestion," Anne said, taking the list. "I'll order the book as soon as I get back to my apartment."

"I think it may help, but I warn you, it is over five-hundred pages in length. Most of it is filled with case studies of valuable *objet d'art* the Nazis pilfered from private collectors, though several chapters deal with paintings sold at below-market prices, allowing the owners to finance their own escapes or to buy freedom for their family members. I hope the book will provide leads as you try to recover your great-grandmother's art."

"Could you tell me about a few of the paintings you've recovered?" Anne asked. "I have a degree in art history. I might recognize the titles."

"My favorite painting from my parents' collection is Courbet's *Nude Reclining by the Sea*. We have yet to learn where the Allies found it after the war, but it was returned to the family in late 1940. It now hangs in the Philadelphia Museum of Art. My grandparents sold most of their paintings, but if they had not done so, I would have. Today one does not keep priceless works of art around the house. My son keeps me informed as he searches for the remaining works."

"What delightful people," Anne said thirty minutes later as Isaac and Isabelle waved goodbye at the door.

"Then you feel the meeting was worthwhile?"

"Absolutely. If nothing else, I can tell Oma more about her mother's final days—that is if she wants to know—and we have new leads to follow."

"Speaking of your grandmother, shall I pick you up on the way to meet her plane?"

"I'll wait for her at home. Oma doesn't know the meaning of the words 'pack light,' so I doubt they'll be room for the three of them, me, and the luggage. Call when you get to Pont Marie and I'll come down."

I should stop on the fourth floor and check the progress the workers are making in Oma's apartment, Anne thought as she entered the lobby. But with a lot on her mind, she decided to look in later and took the elevator straight to the fifth floor. She entered her apartment, kicked off her shoes, and went to her office to check for phone messages. The red light was blinking. She pushed play. "Join me for dinner," Arnaud said. "I'd like to hear about your interview with Isaac and Isobel. If you're in a rush, we can stay local."

She pushed redial "May I have a rain check?" she asked. "I have a lot to do before Oma arrives."

"For her?"

"Yes, in a roundabout way. I'm working on a theory. If I'm right, her life as well as Henri's will be turned upside down."

"You haven't mentioned a theory."

"Because I'm still tying up loose ends. I'll call when my grandmother gets settled. If you're free, will you join us at Brasserie de l'Île St-Louis tomorrow night? Oma says she's coming, but I doubt she will. Renee will choose to stay home with her, so you'll likely be dining with just Henri and me. I don't relish the thought of animals looking down from the walls while I eat, but this isn't about me. After dinner, if I've worked out the kinks and you have time, I'll explain my theory and possibly ask for your help—"

"Will I earn another—"

"You'll earn my thanks."

"I was joking. Whatever you need."

"Good to know. You were almost tagged with the dreaded pain-in-the-ass adjective, and you definitely don't want that."

"Apparently not. So, as you Americans say, before I put my foot in my mouth any farther I'll say good night and see you tomorrow."

"Yes you will," Anne said. "Sleep well."

Before I say anything to Arnaud, let alone to Oma, I have to be sure I know what I'm talking about, Anne thought as, notepad in hand, she went to the kitchen, poured a glass of wine, sat down at her desk, and began to write.

It was after midnight when she finally turned off the kitchen light and went to bed. She tried to fall asleep, but it seemed that every time she shut her eyes, a new thought popped into her mind. Afraid she'd forget by morning, each time she woke up she turned on the light and jotted down her latest thought.

At seven, after only a few hour of deep sleep, she dragged herself out of bed, went to her office, and checked Flight Tracker. Her grand-mother's plane was thirty minutes early, so, with little time to spare, she made coffee. While it dripped through, she showered, dried her hair, and dressed in slacks and a sweater.

With time to spare, she picked up the tablet, went to the kitchen, and took a cup of the still-too-hot-to-drink coffee with her to the office to put her random thoughts in some sort of order. "Damn, my theory makes sense," she reasoned twenty minutes later when the phone rang.

"We're crossing Pont Marie," Gus said.

"How's Oma?"

"I'm fine," Anne heard coming from the backseat.

"Tell her I'm headed down right now."

"You can tell her. I am switching to Bluetooth."

"Good morning, darling," Veronique said. "Is my apartment ready?"

"Welcome to Paris, Oma. I haven't been down since I checked with the guard yesterday morning. I didn't go in, but the place was swarming with workmen."

"We'll soon see if everyone did his job. Gus says we should be there in five minutes."

Anne had just reached the curb when Gus pulled up. Henri exited the passenger seat and enveloped her in a smothering bear-hug. "You look beautiful, honey," he said, stepping back and holding her at arm's distance. "Paris agrees with you." He leaned in and whispered, "Or does that smile on your face have something to do with Arnaud Lessard?"

"Don't be ridiculous. I'm glad to see you—that's all."

Anne quickly turned to greet her grandmother, but Veronique had looked away. Clearly lost in her private thoughts, the old woman gazed up at the house she hadn't seen in decades. Choosing to let her be, Anne hugged Renee. "Is Oma okay," she whispered.

"She's been unusually quiet, but I know she's glad to be here."

"You don't have to talk for me." Veronique walked to Anne and the two women embraced.

"How are you doing?" Anne asked as Veronique wiped the tears from her eyes.

"As well as I can be under the circumstances, darling. The memories come rushing back, as I'm sure you can imagine. Shall we go up and take a look at what my efforts have produced?"

"I'll help Gus with the bags," Henri offered.

"You go up with the ladies," Gus said. "The elevator is small. There will not be enough space for the four of you and the luggage. I will bring the bags up in several loads."

When the elevator reached the fourth floor, Anne inserted her key-card in the slot by the door and escorted Veronique into an exquisitely decorated apartment—similar to hers though a little more elegant and definitely more formal. "The living room is stunning," Oma," she said, awestruck. "You and your decorator *have* been busy. The poor woman must be exhausted—so much so that she'll have to rest for months before accepting a new client."

"After what I paid her, she may stop working and retire to a villa in Tuscany." Looking around, Veronique whispered, "The place is Mother."

"I don't know about that," Anne said softly. "But it's definitely you." She put her arm around her grandmother's shoulder, and they stood quietly, soaking in the ambience.

Veronique finally broke the silence. "I truly feel Mother in this room," she whispered. "It's as if she's standing right here beside me."

"I'm sure she'd be delighted with what you've done with her home. Would you like to explore your apartment on your own?"

"Don't be silly. Come with me—all of you."

They all passed through the lovely dining room into a kitchen that, without the desk, looked much like Anne's. "Even with an expert decorator, I have no idea how you orchestrated all this from thirty-five hundred miles away," Anne said. "Chef Pasquier will appreciate having two ovens and an Imperial stove. I don't believe I have an Imperial. What am I, chopped liver?"

Veronique smiled when she heard the phrase she and her granddaughter often used when protesting their insignificance. "The very fact that you don't *know* if you have a top-of-the-line stove is the reason you don't. Why would I put an Imperial or a Viking in the apartment of a woman who thinks heating Chinese takeout is cooking? I hope you noticed you have a state of the art microwave."

"As a matter of fact, I did, but you don't. Why is that?"

"Because no respectable French woman would reheat leftovers or pop one of those frozen dinners in a microwave oven."

"But a respectable American woman definitely would."

"So it appears." Veronique laughed at the frown on Anne's face.

"This is a great place," Henri said, as they left the kitchen and wandered down the hall. "I, too, am surprised by what you've accomplished, Veronique."

"Thank you Henri." Veronique opened the first door on the left and announced, "This is my office."

"And there's your fax machine," Anne said. She looked around and added, "As well as every other electronic device known to man."

"I'm a modern tech-savvy grandmother, didn't you know?"

"If I didn't, I definitely do now."

"Good. Shall we take a look at Renee and Henri's suite?"

They crossed the hall. Veronique opened the door and stood aside so Renee could enter first. "I hope you're pleased" she said.

"Oma, when I was here Monday after I signed the papers, this was two bedrooms.

How did you have a wall taken down and the space reconfigured in just three days?

"I'm a miracle worker, though I suppose I should give my decorator a little credit. Her workmen have been laboring feverishly around the clock since Monday afternoon."

"But you didn't know you were coming to Paris until last Saturday."

"Truth be told, I decided the day I bought the apartments. I just didn't know when."

"This is a lovely suite," Renee said. "Henri and I will be very comfortable here."

"Good," said Veronique." Taking Henri by one arm and Renee by the other, she guided them out the door and into the hall. "Now," she said. "Shall we take a look at my bedroom?"

"Spectacular!" Anne said as they entered the master suite. "You've outdone yourself, Oma." She hesitated and, smiling, added—"But there's one problem."

Veronique's eyes flashed. "I'm sorry," she said, indignant. "Did I hear you say there's a problem with the room?"

"There is, but certainly not with the décor. What I mean is there's no way you can be sick. You can't be lying around on that exquisite satin bedspread or leaning against the polished wood on your headboard. And they'll be no lounging on the chair. Oma, I love what you've done with the apartment."

"I knew you were kidding." Veronique chuckled. "Thank you, darling."

"I was going to invite you to come up to see your handiwork in my apartment, but you look exhausted. Why don't we postpone your visit until later? While you sleep, I'll walk to Calixte to pick up lunch and snacks. I'll be back around two with everything you'll need to survive until Andre arrives tomorrow morning." She looked over at Henri. "You and Renee look like you could use some rest too."

"It's times like this when I realize I'm an old man," Henri complained. "I slept on the plane, but I'm still tired."

"You're not an old man. It took me days to get over my jet lag. What about you, Renee? Will you take a nap?"

"After I hang Veronique's clothes."

"I've invited Arnaud to join us for dinner at Brasserie de l'Île St-Louis," Anne said. "Henri, are you up to eating out, or would you rather stay in?"

"If we're dining at my favorite restaurant, I'll be ready."

Anne turned to her grandmother. "Oma, will you come? We'll eat early."

Veronique shook her head. "Thank you, darling, but not tonight. Tomorrow will be a busy day. I want to be well-rested."

"How about you, Renee?"

"I'm happy to stay back with Veronique. I don't like pork knuckles. And I don't appreciate having animals staring down at me from the walls while I dine."

"Maybe I'll stay home, too," Anne said, wrinkling her nose.

"Go and have a good time," Veronique insisted. "And speaking of Brasserie de l'Île St-Louis and your dinner companions, when will I have the pleasure of meeting Arnaud Lessard?"

"Tomorrow. Assuming you'd be too tired to go out, I asked him to join us for breakfast. Unless you object, he'll stay while the mason removes the bricks. He's been so helpful. I thought—"

"You thought right. I want to meet the young man who so quickly caught your eye."

"Oma, Arnaud's a friend who's helping us find your mother's art—nothing more."

"You can't fool me, my precious granddaughter. You're always telling me how perceptive I am. Yes! Bring the father of my great grandchildren to breakfast in the morning."

Anne rolled her eyes. "The overseas flight must have rattled your brain," she said. "Don't get your hopes up, and *please* don't make embarrassing comments when I introduce you to Arnaud."

"Would I ever say anything to embarrass you?" Veronique kissed Anne on the cheek. "Go shopping. I'm glad to see both you and Paris."

⌒⊙

Before walking to Calixte, Anne went back up to check for messages. The red light was blinking on her answering machine. "You have two new messages," the computerized voice flatly droned. "First message."

"You must be waiting for your grandmother," Arnaud said. "I'll be tied up with a client for most of the day. My cell will be off, so call my landline and leave a message about dinner. See you tonight."

Anne paused the messages and immediately called, confirming that dinner was a go and asking Arnaud to make a seven-thirty reservation for three at Brasserie de l'Île St-Louis.

That accomplished, she pushed the button to hear the second message. "I am on my way home," Gus said excitedly. "I just listened to my voicemail. When you have a minute, please call my cell."

Anne immediately pushed redial. "It's me," she said when Gus answered. "What's up?"

"I wanted you to know I have an appointment with Damien Duplessis this afternoon."

"You're kidding! How'd you manage that? I can't believe Damien would agree to see someone who'll be accusing his grandfather of stealing valuable art."

"I was surprised. When I told him *why* I wanted the meeting, he seemed eager to see me. I think he is trying to make things right with the people his grandfather wronged. Before I forget to ask, what are the names of the two paintings Madame Boulet sold? I have a pad and paper beside me in the passenger seat."

"We believe *Madame Stumpf and Her Daughter* by Corot and *The Work Table* by Bonnard. This is unbelievable, Gus. Will I hear from you again today?"

"Probably not until tomorrow. When I am through with Damien, I will join two of my sources for dinner. They may have located the son of Didier's principal buyer, but please do not get your hopes up, and wait before you say anything to your grandmother."

"Hopefully your hard work will pay off. We may never recover the paintings, but maybe we'll find out where they went."

Anne hung up and walked to Calixte. She filled two baskets, then another at the cheese shop, and a third at the patisserie. "This should feed Oma, Henri, and Renee for a week," she said as she put the perishables in her refrigerator.

⸙

At one forty-five, Henri called. "Need help with the groceries?" he asked.

"I do. Is Oma up?"

"She's still asleep, but Renee wants to make lunch. Will you buzz me up?"

"You're lucky you're asking today. Yesterday I would have had to meet you in the lobby. I finally figured out how to get from floor to floor."

"I'll be there in two minutes."

"Would you like to see what Oma's done with my apartment?" Anne asked as Henri entered the living room.

"Sure. Let's see what else your grandmother accomplished from three thousand miles away. Lead the way."

"Well, what do you think?" Anne asked when the tour ended.

"Pretty special. Working with her decorator to fix up both your apartment and hers has been therapeutic for Veronique. When she first said she wanted to 'go home,' we thought she was returning to the Île to die. It turns out she's here because she wants to live."

"The day I came to the apartment and met with Doctor Richmond, I thought she was giving up. Thank God we were all wrong."

"Amen. And so you know, one of the reasons she's so eager to live is her wish to bequeath her mother's home to her great grandchild."

"And she's picked Arnaud to be the child's father."

"She has. He's handsome. He's rich. He's French. That makes him the perfect man for you."

"Interesting, since she hasn't even met him."

"What can I say? Maybe you should warn Arnaud. In spite of what she told you earlier, your grandmother won't keep her thoughts to herself. Come on, join us for lunch."

By the time Veronique came to the kitchen forty-five minutes later, the groceries were put away and lunch was waiting on the dining room table. While they ate, Anne brought them up to date, though she didn't mention Gus's afternoon plans. Henri talked about his scheduled meeting with Gregoire Drouin and his luncheon date with Claude.

"I made an appointment, too," Veronique announced proudly. "Anne and I will visit Madame Huard's daughter, Francoise Laplante, Saturday afternoon. I called before my nap. And that's not all, Anne. Monday morning at nine, you and I are having breakfast with Giles Guidreau. Arnaud had already spoken with Giles's housekeeper, but I confirmed the meeting. I believe I'll ask Arnaud to join us. Giles might be more comfortable if someone he knows is there, and I want to spend as much time as possible with my future grandson."

"That's not going to happen, Oma, so please don't say anything to embarrass me or Arnaud."

"I'll try to refrain, darling, though I can't make any promises."

"Would it help if I beg?"

"Begging didn't help when you were a child—it certainly won't now." Veronique smiled at Anne's apparent frustration. "So now that this matter is settled, shall we take a look at your apartment?"

"Sure." Anne shrugged in resignation.

"I'm impressed with my accomplishments," Veronique bragged when the tour of the fifth floor was over. "Perhaps I missed my calling—I should have been a decorator."

"You would have been a good one," Anne said, smiling at the delighted look on Veronique's face. She turned to Henri. "Since I haven't heard otherwise, I assume Arnaud made a seven-thirty reservation at Brasserie de l'Île St-Louis. I'll come down at seven-fifteen. If you're up to it, we'll walk to the restaurant."

"I'm more than up for a walk. I can't wait. I've had pork knuckles with lentils on my mind since our plane touched down at Charles de Gaulle. Wait till you try them."

"Yea, like that's going to happen. See you later."

⌒⊙

Anne thought she saw a smirk on the owner's face when she seated them at Arnaud's table and put a menu at each place. *She probably thinks Henri's part of the wedding party,* she mused while looking around the tavern-style room decorated with mounted animal-heads, wood-paneled walls, antique fixtures fashioned from barrels, and painted Alsatian folk-art. "Is this *really* your favorite restaurant," she whispered to Henri.

"It is, honey. Would you believe this place hasn't changed since I first ate here fifty-years ago?"

"Oh, I'd believe it."

"What? You don't appreciate the well-worn floors and tables, the tin ceiling, and the years and years of paint peeling off the walls."

"I can't say I'm impressed, though I do like the gigantic antique espresso machine. It looks like it popped right out of a Toulouse-Lautrec painting."

A gruff-looking waiter about Henri's age approached the table. "Henri Marsolet!" he declared, extending his hand. "I haven't seen you in a while."

"This is my first time back in several years." Henri grasped the waiter's hand. "Anne, this is Marq Hobart, the best waiter in Paris."

"And the oldest," Marq joked.

"Nice to meet you, Marq." Anne looked beyond the waiter and waved.

Marq turned to see who Anne was greeting. "Arnaud Lessard is joining you?" he asked.

"He is," Anne said. *And you already knew he was coming.* She motioned Arnaud to the table. Before sitting, he shook hands with Henri, kissed Anne on the cheek, and asked, "How are you, Marq?"

"As good as an old man can be, Arnaud. How's Bertrand? We miss him around here."

"He's well. I'll bring him to dinner sometime soon."

"Very good. Your preferred wine?"

"Please, unless you prefer something else, Henri."

"Whatever you choose is fine with me."

"I suppose you'll have your usual entree," Marq said.

"Of course." He handed Marq the menu. "I didn't need this."

"And you, Henri," Marq said. "You're having pork knuckles with lentils?"

"You remembered."

"Of course. Have you decided, Madame?"

"Not yet," Anne said, "But I'm close."

"Bring the wine, Marq. By then Anne will be ready to order."

"What's your usual?" Anne asked when Marq left the table.

"Choucroute garnie. That's sauerkraut studded with ham, bacon, and pork loin."

"I'd love to say it sounds delicious, but—"

"Do you see anything you can stomach," Arnaud asked. "Pun intended."

"I'll try the coq au Riesling."

∽⌒◦

The chicken was excellent, and the conversation was filled with stories and laughter. When the meal was over, Anne saw Henri in a different light. At Brasserie de l'Île St-Louis, he was home.

Despite Henri's objections, Arnaud paid the bill. "My way of welcoming you back to the Île," he said.

The conversation continued during the short walk back to the mansion where Henri shook Arnaud's outstretched hand and hugged Anne. "I'll see you both tomorrow."

"At eight," Anne said. "Let's hope it's a good day for Oma."

CHAPTER 27

"Would you like to come in?" Anne asked at her apartment door. "How about a glass of wine while I explain my theory?"

"You aren't too tired?"

"I'm wide awake."

"In that case. . . Arnaud took her in his arms, kissed her, and then again more passionately.

"Forget the wine," Anne whispered.

"My thoughts exactly."

"This is probably a bad idea. . ."

"I know, but—"

❧

They made love with an urgency Anne had never felt before, both wanting to give the other pleasure, but unable to curb their intense desire. "Please! Now!" she urged, when, her body on fire, she didn't think she could endure one more moment of the exquisite agony.

"I love you," Arnaud whispered as he pulled her on top and eased her down. Moments later, her body tensed. She cried out; overcome with wave upon wave of intense rapture.

"Oh my God!" Anne groaned as Arnaud turned her over and began to move, slowly at first, and then with increased ardor. When he began to moan, she raised her hips and met his passion with equal intensity.

"Could we do it again?" she murmured as he rolled off and took her in his arms. "Right now?"

"As soon as I catch my breath. Could I have maybe ten minutes—"

"That's not what the book says." Anne ran her fingers through the hair on his chest and kissed his damp cheeks.

"What book?"

"The one you studied—"

"I'm sorry."

"The book that taught you how to make me feel so good."

"Oh, that book." Arnaud grinned. "I didn't have to read—I'm a born expert. Add that to my adjective list."

"I'll also add the ass-who-just-ruined-the-mood," Anne teased. "But back to the book. I believe it says we should be cuddling and murmuring sweet nothings after incredible sex—"

"Or doing it again right now," Arnaud whispered, caressing her breast and kissing her lightly on the lips. "You know, I may not need ten minutes after all."

"But you've already spoiled the mood."

"Didn't you just say—"

"Are you really going to keep this up?"

"Oh, it's up—"

"Then *it* can wait. Tempting though it may be to test your self-proclaimed prowess, I think I'll use your down time to—"

"Down time?"

"Poor choice of words. I hope your ego isn't too bruised because I'm thinking of something besides making mad, passionate love. I—"

"You want to share your theory. Though begrudgingly, I understand. It's why you invited me in—"

"Not really. Okay, I confess I had an ulterior motive."

"Which, believe me, we'll get back to very soon. So talk to me."

Suddenly serious, Anne propped her head on her elbow. She inhaled, exhaled deeply, and said, "If what I believe is true. . .Lord, I can only imagine. I'm merely speculating, but I *know* I'm on the right track. When Oma and I first talked about the Occupation, she said she felt lucky. While her friends' parents traveled, her mother stayed home. That alone isn't significant, but minutes later she qualified her statement. She recalled a four-month period in 1932 when Elisabeth embarked on what she called a grand tour. Apparently one day she announced she was leaving, and, true to her word, she departed several days later."

"I assume Veronique was upset that she was being left behind with the servants. Did Elisabeth explain why she was leaving?"

"She only said that World War I and its aftermath had kept her from seeing Europe after passing her *baccalaureate* exam. I gather that was something a young girl of her stature and class would do."

"I haven't heard the entire story, but from what you've already said, Veronique's reaction seems reasonable. All her life she'd been raised without a father around to made demands on her mother's time. Clearly, she wouldn't like the idea—"

"True."

"I hear hesitation—"

"You do, but not about Oma and her response to Elisabeth's sudden revelation. Remember when Jacqueline offhandedly mentioned a man who regularly visited the Boulet mansion—the same man who came by the house the night of July 17?"

Arnaud didn't immediately respond. Anne waited, giving him time to process her words. Suddenly he blurted out, "You can't be serious—"

"I am. I don't believe Elisabeth set of on a grand tour."

"You think she went away with the mysterious man—her lover."

"Not exactly."

"Then what?"

"I'm getting to that. Renee recently told me that Elisabeth and Anton introduced her and Henri to Veronique."

"Okay, but what does that have to do with the man. . .? Oh my God! That's your theory! You think Anton was the man Jacqueline saw—that he and Elisabeth were lovers."

"I *know* they were, and here's why. Anton wanted Oma and Henri to meet because he felt they had a lot in common."

"I don't see anything unusual—"

"Because you don't know Oma. She and Henri are *nothing* alike. So why would Anton suddenly want them to meet—and that's a rhetorical question. When I pressed Renee for a possible ulterior motive, she had nothing to offer. Since I wasn't ready to share my developing theory, I quickly backed off. I don't believe Elisabeth and Anton were casual acquaintances looking to introduce three young people who *might* get along. Why make the effort or take the time? If they all lived on Île St-Louis, perhaps, but Henri and Renee lived in Saint-Germain. As I said to Renee, they were hardly next door neighbors who might run into one another from time to time while strolling along rue St-Louis-en lÎle. No, this was a long-planned meeting. Elisabeth and Anton wanted their children to be friends—and close friends at that."

"Okay, but—"

"You're still not convinced. Be patient. That's only part of my premise. I'm slowly building my case. My theory is reinforced by another odd occurrence. Why would a homebody, which Elisabeth clearly was, come down one morning and, out of the blue, announce she's going away for an extended trip—something she'd never done in the past. Oma wasn't just anxious about her mother's impending departure. She was also worried. Elisabeth hadn't been herself for months, but when she came home four months later, though she was still tired, she was once again, 'normal.' My word, not Oma's."

"If, as you believe, Elisabeth and Anton were lovers—and I'm still not totally convinced—maybe she left Paris to forget him—to end the affair. Was Anton's wife alive?"

"She was, though she'd been ill and bedridden for years."

"So, in effect, Elisabeth was Anton's mistress—she was the other woman."

"I guess you could call her that, but—"

"Oh my God!" Arnaud blurted out. "Elisabeth didn't leave Paris to forget Anton. She was pregnant with his child. She had a difficult time during her first trimester—"

"Causing her to appear tired and 'off.'"

"And when she couldn't hide her condition from Veronique any longer. Saying she wanted to travel, she went away to have the baby."

"All the clues fit."

"Then why didn't Grandpapa say something? All the major players in the drama are dead, so he wouldn't be betraying a confidence."

"He didn't know. The child was born in 1932. Bertrand was ten when he helped his father and Anton with Resistance operations—"

"In 1942, so he and Elisabeth's child were about the same age."

"True. But Auguste and Denis had to know."

"I imagine they did, but keep talking. This is getting interesting."

"I told you Oma said her mother always put her to bed at night before going out for the evening with friends—"

"Friends meaning Anton."

"Exactly."

"All right. I'm almost sold."

"Then let me seal the deal. After he graduated from college, my uncle George, though he wasn't really my uncle, but rather Great-Grandfather Samuel's friend who eventually befriended Elisabeth. . .Understand?"

"I'll sort it out later. Go on."

"After graduation, Uncle George bought a farm in Brittany. As conditions under Nazi rule became increasingly difficult for Parisians—especially for the Jews who, even with ration cards, couldn't get food—he would bring whatever he could spare from the farm. In one or more of her entries Oma noted—or perhaps complained—that whenever she tried to join the conversation, Elisabeth would suddenly stop talking and banish her from the room. She went on to confess in the journal, and later to me, that she sometimes disobeyed her mother's order and hid just around the corner, her ear to the wall as she tried to hear what the adults were saying."

"Did she say what she heard—perhaps something to confirm or negate your theory that her mother gave birth to Anton's child?"

"No. For the most part, she wrote about conversations that took place early-on in the Occupation. During those discussions, Uncle George shared unsettling news about Jews in some of the annexed countries. Later on she mentioned that Uncle George was coming to Paris more frequently. Those visits occurred after Elisabeth's grand tour."

"You're assuming Uncle George raised Elisabeth and Anton's child on his farm?"

"Yes, and because Elisabeth couldn't go to Brittany for news of the child's progress, especially after the Nazis came to power, he came to Paris to report to her in person. He probably couldn't be sure a letter would arrive uncensored. It makes perfect sense."

"Maybe, but you'll need more proof before you say anything to your grandmother. You can't surprise her with this kind of news based on mere speculation. You have to be sure of your facts."

"I agree. That's why I pray Elisabeth left a message that will do the talking for me."

"Hopefully she did, but you don't have to figure out *everything* now. In my opinion, there are more important things to think about." He pulled Anne to him and, murmured, "Or better yet, don't think."

⚬

Light was pouring through the windows when Anne rolled over and reached for Arnaud. She patted the bed, but he wasn't there. She threw back the covers, got up, and put on a robe. Nearing the bathroom, she heard water running in the sink. "Don't tell me you're one of those I can't face myself in the morning men," she called out.

Arnaud shut off the water, turned around, and toweled the water off his face. "I found an unwrapped toothbrush," he said. "Did you buy one in the off chance I decided to spend the night?"

"Of course. I had known you less than an hour when I stopped by the local pharmacy to ask the clerk if she knew what brand of toothbrush you prefer. She went right to the shelf and selected the one you're brushing with now."

"I imagine she saw what I used the last time she and I made passionate love all night long You don't think I remained celibate while I waited around for you to come into my life."

"I don't know why not. I was pure as the driven snow. . .I take it you're heading home."

"I am. I can't appear at breakfast in the same clothes I wore to dinner last night. What would your grandmother say?"

"First of all, she won't know what you wore. She stayed home, remember? And secondly, it won't make any difference what you have on. Within seconds she'll know you spent the night."

"Unless she has access to the security camera feed, how could she?"

"Even *she* wouldn't go that far—at least I don't think she would—but there won't be a need. I guarantee, she'll know."

"She may, but if I don't change, Henri will *definitely* figure it out. I'll be back in an hour."

"Make it an hour and forty-five minutes."

"You're going back to bed?"

"That's why I want you to wait. It will be too late—"

"For what?"

"For me to rip off your clothes and drag you back to bed. If you arrive at seven—"

"When I saw you standing outside the bathroom door, I wanted to pick you up, carry you over to the bed, and—"

"But you were dressed, and it was too much trouble."

"How did you guess?"

"It wasn't hard."

"Oh but it was, and it will be again when I return at seven forty-five. Since I'm meeting your grandmother for the first time, I'll behave. Though I won't be as easy tonight."

"I hope you *will* be easy."

Arnaud leaned over and kissed her softly. "I could be easy now without much persuasion."

"Though tempted, I should look presentable, and after last night, I have a lot of work to do."

"Why bother? You're sure your grandmother will know what we've been doing."

"But we don't have to flaunt it. So leave. I hope she's not having security call her to report my every move."

"Do you think—"

"No. See you in a while."

∽◯

Promptly at eight, Henri answered Anne's knock. "Morning," he said cheerily. "You two look happy."

Anne turned to Arnaud. "I told you," she said. "We don't even have to wait for Oma—"

Veronique entered the room. "Wait for me for what? Why would you have to wait for me? I've been up for hours."

"Morning, Oma," Anne said, dreading her grandmother's comment. "This is Arnaud Lessard. He's—."

"Yes he is." Veronique smiled, her eyes twinkling. "I'm delighted to meet you, Arnaud. Henri and Renee have been singing your praises, and it's obvious my beloved granddaughter wholeheartedly approves." She paused and, smiling, added, "Though clearly not in the same way."

"See?" Anne whispered.

Ignoring Anne's remark, Arnaud smiled at Veronique. "It is nice to meet you, Madame Ellison."

"Please call me Veronique, young man. I expect you and I are going to be *very* good friends."

Anne rolled her eyes as Renee joined them. "Arnaud, it's good to see you again," she said. "How's Bertrand?"

"He's well. Thank you for asking."

"It smells great in here," Anne said, eager to change the subject. "Chef Pasquier must be doing his magic."

"He arrived an hour ago with his arms full of groceries." Looking sideways at Arnaud, she said, "I imagine you're hungry, young man."

"Oma—"

"Oh stop, Anne. "I merely meant I've never met a man who didn't enjoy breakfast."

⤳

"My compliments to the chef," Anne said when Andre poured hot coffee. "Your omelets are better than those at Mere Poulard on Mont-Saint-Michel. Until now they've been my favorites."

"Merci, Madame." Andre bowed. "That is indeed great praise."

"I agree with my granddaughter." Veronique folder her napkin. "I'm going to freshen up before we meet the mason."

Arnaud quickly stood, pulled out Veronique's chair, and helped her stand. "Thank you, young man," she said. "Anne knows I appreciate a man with good manners. My beloved Robert was very polite."

She winked at her granddaughter, turned, and left the room.

⸺◦

Promptly at nine, the intercom buzzed. "That must be the mason, Monsieur Aubin," Henri said. "I'll go down and meet him. Before we get started, I want to be sure he's going with me to rue Gît this afternoon. Buzz us in when you're all gathered in your apartment, Anne."

Anne went to the box by the door, pushed the intercom button, and said, "Monsieur Marsolet will be down to bring you up, Monsieur Aubin."

Minutes later, looking tense and on-edge, Veronique joined the others in the living room. "Did I hear the intercom?" she asked tentatively.

"You did, Oma. Henri went down to meet Monsieur Aubin. Are you ready to see what your mother left behind the bricks?"

"As ready as I'll ever be."

Renee took hold of Veronique's arm and led her to the door. "Whether or not your mother left a message, it's going to be fine," she said firmly.

"Renee's right, Oma. Even if we don't find anything behind the fireplace bricks, we have other leads to pursue."

"We do, Veronique," said Arnaud.

"But you admit a letter would help."

"Of course it would," Anne said. "So let's go take a look."

"I'm ready," Veronique said—though with little conviction.

They took the elevator to the fifth floor. Anne unlocked her apartment and immediately pushed the intercom button. "We're ready, Henri," she announced. "Come on up."

Five minutes later Henri escorted the mason into Anne's bedroom. "Madame Ellison, this is Joseph Aubin," he said.

"Thank you for giving up your Saturday morning to help, Monsieur Aubin." Veronique extended her hand.

"It is my pleasure." Aubin gently shook Veronique's trembling hand. "And please call me Joseph." He held up his tool box. "As you see, I am ready to work."

"Do you mind if we watch?" Veronique asked.

"Not at all. Monsieur Marsolet said you wish to locate a message your mother hid during the Occupation."

"We *hope* she did. We're not sure if there's actually a hiding place. We're merely speculating."

"Shall we find out?" Joseph walked to the mantle, ran his hands over the bricks, and opened his box of tools.

Veronique and Renee sat in the chairs on either side of the drum table while the others stood nearby. As he worked, Joseph appeared to sense Veronique's impatience. "I am sorry this is taking so long," he apologized. "I am trying to preserve the original bricks."

"No need," Veronique replied testily. "I can buy antique bricks to replace the ones you're forced to break. Please open the mantle as quickly as possible."

"Oma," Anne admonished.

"I'm sorry, Joseph," Veronique said sheepishly.

"No need to apologize, Madame. I know you are eager to see what the bricks hide. However, it takes time."

In what seemed like an eternity, Joseph removed three bricks in the center of the fireplace just below the mantle. Shaking his head, he turned to Veronique. "There is nothing here."

"Then please open the next row," Veronique softly ordered, her tone echoing the apprehension on her face.

"Oui, Madame." Joseph turned back and began to open the next row of bricks.

"I hope there's something there," Anne whispered to Arnaud. "If not, we only have four rows left before the fireplace opening."

"They sat silently while Joseph worked. *You could cut the tension in the room with a knife*, Anne thought when, fifteen minutes later, he turned back and frowning, said, "There is nothing in the second row either. Shall I open the next?"

"Of course," Veronique snapped. "If need be, knock down the entire fireplace."

"Oma!"

Veronique took a deep breath and said, "Again, I apologize, Joseph."

"And as before, there is no need."

The electric tension continued to build as Joseph chiseled the bricks. In the third row down, he stopped working and looked back at Veronique. "I believe I have found a hollowed-out space, Madame."

"Oh, I hope so." Veronique clasped her hands in her lap and squirmed nervously.

Anne sat on the floor in front of her grandmother's chair and took her hand as Joseph removed the two center bricks. He turned back and, grinning, said, "I have found a hollow space."

With Anne's help, Veronique rose and walked slowly to the fireplace. "Please stand aside, Joseph," she said, "I appreciate your hard work, but I would like to be the first to look."

"As you should be. Here is a flashlight to help you see what is inside."

Henri joined Veronique by the fireplace and held the flashlight while she peered into the space. "Is there something there?" Renee asked from across the room.

Tears in her eyes, Veronique looked back at her friend. "There is," she cried. "Mother left letters."

"I'll take them out," Henri offered. "We've been patient this long. It won't hurt to be careful. Remember, these papers are almost seventy-years old."

"Is there anything besides papers in the hiding place?" Anne asked.

"There are only three envelopes." Henri handed them to Veronique. "Messages from your mother, my friend."

Veronique took the letters and, holding them to her breast, returned to her chair. "The envelopes are numbered," she said. "I assume in the order they're to be opened."

"Would you like to be alone?" Renee asked. "This can't be easy—"

"No thank you, my dear. I want the people I love most in the world with me."

Arnaud stood. "I'll make a pot of tea—"

"Please stay," said Veronique.

"I have several calls to make." Joseph picked up his tools. "I will join your chef in the kitchen."

"Thank you, Joseph," Veronique said.

"Okay, Oma," said Anne. "Let's see what your mother wrote."

CHAPTER 28

Veronique sat for a few minutes holding the envelopes in her hands and caressing the paper as if touching something sacred. The rest of the group waited quietly until, finally, her face pale as a ghost, she said uneasily, "Anne, I've been dreaming about finding a second message since you solved the riddle of Mother's poem, and now I'm afraid to open the envelope. I don't know if I want to read what she wrote."

"You can do this, Veronique," Renee encouraged. "If you're still blaming yourself for not returning to Paris years ago—"

"It's not that. . .I don't know why I'm so hesitant." Taking a deep breath and letting it out slowly, she carefully opened the first envelope and took out the letter. She scanned the first page, looked up, and, with frustration on her face and in her voice, said, "It's another poem. I've only read a few stanzas, but—"

"Don't worry, Oma. We'll figure it out together, but you read. My French—"

"Is better than you let on. You read my journal entries."

"I could translate this poem too, that is if you have a French dictionary handy and want to sit here for several hours."

"I'm afraid I don't have that kind of patience. I'll read this time, but when you move to Île St-Louis, you'll have to relearn the language."

Without giving Anne a chance to respond, she said, "The letter is dated May, 1942. It begins,

From here, from there, from everywhere,
Our friends provide relief.
By day and night they come
To bring us food and keep our treasures safe.

How times have changed for worse in recent years.
The rabbits that ran free in happy scenes
Now give us life and hope. And we survive
To ponder smiles and happy, joyful times
That now lie buried deep within our hearts.

No longer do our childhood jewels bring joy.
They now are cloaked by mantle of the night
In happy, joyful habitat of youth;
Still closeted in deepest, darkest thoughts.

And in this time of sadness and despair,
Old friends no longer come and linger here.
And children dwell alone in private rooms
Where parents bid them stay for safety sake.
We long to keep them close, but must let go,
For young or old alike, they are not ours.

And lovers nevermore will join in joy.
Great ecstasy grows dim as days drag by.
Pray God, my love, you always will remain
The steadfast star that guides me on my path.

No sun will shine again on us, my love.
Now nights of joy live only in our hearts.
Pray God, our own will come to understand
Our lasting love—a joy that has no end.

And never fear beloved. Your care is our concern.
The faces, scenes, and colors bright
Will do their part to lighten-up your life,
And bring you happiness in years to come.

I wish that life were kinder, love; that people understood,
So you would know the joy of Paris lights.

But country walks are so much safer now:
No unkind men around to cause you harm.
No vicious tongues to turn your smiles to frowns.
New friends and kin must satisfy your needs,
And give you love I now so long to give.

Few sunsets will I see beyond today.
No fear of death; but what I leave behind
Now troubles me and leaves me sad in heart.

Live well, my darling loves, and think of me.
Would God my dearest friend live on beyond
The darkness and travail you all must face,
And bring you safely home to live in peace
In bright and sunny days that lie ahead.

Be strong, my dears, for someday you will know
The reasons; choices we are forced to make,
The absence, sacrifice, is all for you.

My prayer: Please, God, that all of you live well.
Your lives, your hopes, your dreams are in your hands.

"I don't understand any of this," Veronique said, her brow furrowed.

"It certainly is strange," Renee agreed. "Portions of the poem make sense, but other sections are ambiguous."

"I think I know what Elisabeth is cryptically saying, Oma, and, if I'm correct, it's not going to be easy for you to hear—for you either, Henri. I've shared my theory with Arnaud. He thinks I'm on the right track."

"You never mentioned a theory," Veronique said uneasily.

"I didn't broach the subject because, until yesterday, I hadn't come to a definite conclusion. I also suppose I was also waiting to see if your mother left a message behind one of the bricks. It turns out she did.

I'm hoping *her* words—not mine—will explain. So shall we interpret the poem? Let's take it apart slowly, stanza by stanza."

"Why should we do that?" Veronique countered.

"So you can see *why* I believe what I do. Oma, you read a few lines, and then I'll tell you what I think Elisabeth is really saying. If I want you to stop at any point, I'll tap your knee."

"All right," Veronique unenthusiastically agreed. "But I'm not sure we'll ever figure this out."

"Just read," Anne said. "And in English please."

"Okay,

From here, from there, from everywhere,
Our friends provide relief.
By day and night they come
To bring us food and keep our treasures safe.

"We know what that stanza means," Renee said. "Denis Guidreau and his sons are the friends who came from Quai de Bethune to removed Elisabeth's treasures—her paintings. Madame Huard and other neighbors who lived close by provided food. There's nothing new or extraordinary in these lines."

"Mother could also mean Uncle George," Veronique argued. "He didn't have anything to do with removing her art—at least I don't think he did. But he *did* travel to Paris from the farm, especially at the onset of the Occupation. Later, when he was required to send a portion of his crops to Germany, and with the Nazis watching the train stations for smugglers, it became increasingly difficult for him to visit."

"Elisabeth may be referring to all of the above," Anne said. "Certainly everyone you mentioned helped you survive. And there might be other friends, too, like Auguste or Anton. Could it be they also stopped in from time to time?"

"It's possible," Veronique said, looking flustered. "Oh, Anne, I'm already confused, and I've only read a few lines."

"Perhaps if we keep reading, everything will eventually be clear."

"I hope so." Veronique sighed and read.

How times have changed for worse in recent years.
The rabbits that ran free in happy scenes
Now give us life and hope. And we survive

Anne tapped her grandmother's knee. "Not hearing your mother's poem until a few moments ago, I haven't had adequate time to give these three lines any serious thought, but —"

"She must be referencing the rabbits Madame Huard raised in her courtyard," Veronique said. "She's echoing the line in the first stanza—the one where she says our friends 'bring us food.'"

"I agree, but there may be more. I think Elisabeth is providing a clue to help locate the paintings Denis hid."

"But surely she isn't alluding to paintings in those lines."

"She may be. Didn't you say Elisabeth owned a version of Manet's *Le déjeuner sur l'herbe*?"

"She did. I remember the painting—not because I liked it, but rather because I wondered why she found it so appealing. To me, it seemed sort of off balance."

"Many others would agree, but that's another story. I believe this is where Elisabeth first refers to her art collection."

"Were there rabbits in Manet's painting?" Renee asked. "When I visited Veronique, I paid little attention to the art hanging on Madame Boulet's walls. All I cared about was having my best friend help me plan my wedding."

"That makes sense. Your marriage to Henri was uppermost in your mind. Answering your question, I don't believe there are rabbits running free on Manet's canvas."

"Maybe Elisabeth is talking about rabbits in the picture in a happy scene *and* rabbit meat," Henri interjected.

Veronique suddenly brightened. "I think I understand what Mother means, and my interpretation makes sense in light of what you said about

Le dejeuner sur l'herbe. In the lines before, Mother wrote that friends came to keep her treasures safe and out of harm."

"Yes, we've already figured that out."

"But let's take it a step farther. Could it be that Madame Huard also took something *away* when she came to bring food—perhaps something Mother left outside the front door? Could she have hidden the Manet in *her* home? I recently read an online article that said many Christians acted as trustees for Jewish art during the Occupation—often at great personal peril."

"Again, it's conceivable, though I seriously doubt that's what Elisabeth means. However, at least for now we're not rejecting any ideas. Together we're interpreting Elisabeth's words, so, all of you, share whatever far-out ideas come to mind. Let's keep plugging away. Please read the next two lines, Oma."

Veronique sighed and began to read. "'*To ponder smiles and happy, joyful times/That now lie buried deep within our hearts.*' Mother is undoubtedly referring to the days before the Occupation—the 'happy, joyful times.' I hadn't smiled in quite a while."

"I'm sure she missed your smiles and the happier days, but there's more to what she's saying. Listen. '*That now lie buried deep within our hearts.*' Note, she doesn't say '*my*' heart. She uses a plural pronoun."

"'Our' undoubtedly means her and me," Veronique said. "Perhaps she's still talking about the paintings. They're hidden somewhere in a dark place, and we're remembering them in our hearts—though I don't know why she'd think I'd miss them. Honestly, until Denis began to take them from the house, I took for granted they were there."

Anne smiled at her noticeably-nervous grandmother, who seemed to realize she was rambling. "I'm sure everything you say is true, Oma, but I don't think your mother is referring to your smiling face before the Occupation or, for that matter, about any of her paintings."

"Elisabeth uses the word 'buried,'" Henri pointed out. "That implies out of sight. Could she be referencing a secret hiding place where Denis took Elisabeth's art, perhaps an underground vault or room?"

"Possibly," said Anne. "But the line could also suggest something Elisabeth and whomever else she is referencing were keeping to themselves."

"What could that be?" Veronique asked, her brow creased.

"I believe we'll soon know. Let's move on to the next lines."

Veronique found her place and began again.

No longer do our childhood jewels bring joy.
They now are cloaked by mantle of the night
In happy, joyful habitat of youth;
Still closeted in deepest, darkest thoughts.

"Now, despite what you said earlier, I'm sure Mother's referring to the paintings. She's telling me they're hidden away. She's not thinking about them every day, though they remain in her memory."

She paused, and Anne let her ponder. "But where are they?" she asked minutes later. "Oh, I don't know, Anne. With every line I read I'm more perplexed."

"And I'm trying to clear the cobwebs. Let's talk about the words 'childhood jewels.'"

"What could the jewels be?" Henri asked. "Could Elisabeth be referring to the paintings that no longer bring her joy because Denis has taken them from the house?"

"That makes sense," Renee said.

"And finishing my thought—Elisabeth is obviously writing about her home on Quai de Bethune,"

"That's what I'm thinking. The 'habitat of youth' is her childhood home. But, again, look at Elisabeth's pronoun choice."

"She used 'our,' not my," Veronique said pensively.

"Keep that in mind."

"Could there be a brick fireplace above a mantle in Elisabeth's childhood home?" Renee pressed on, not questioning Anne further about Elisabeth's pronoun usage.

"Possibly, but I don't believe she's referring to another small hiding place. She says the jewels are 'cloaked by the mantle of the night.' And note, she uses the word 'closeted.'"

"Do you think Denis took the paintings and hid them in a closet? That would explain Mother's use of the word 'closeted.'"

"A closet, yes, but more likely a closet within a closet—a dark space that can't be seen— perhaps an area just large enough to hold the paintings Denis removed at her request. When Arnaud and I visited Bertrand, he mentioned that Elisabeth's Quai de Bethune home hadn't been lived in for some time. Denis Guidreau, or maybe Anton, could have taken Elisabeth's paintings to the empty house and built some sort of space to hide them."

"But how would Mother know that? When I asked where Denis was taking the paintings, she said she hadn't asked. She didn't *want* to know. I think I wrote that in my journal."

"Maybe she changed her mind. Again, I'm only speculating, but as life under Nazi rule grew increasingly difficult, she probably realized if something happened to her, you wouldn't be able to locate the paintings. But we're getting ahead of ourselves. Let's keep deciphering the poem."

"All right. Mother writes, '*And in this time of sadness and despair/old friends no longer come and linger here.*' Clearly the Occupation brought hardships to the Jews. Friends rarely visited, and if they came to call, they didn't stay long. I remember asking her why. Her answer was short and to the point. She said, '*C'est le temps dans lequel nos vivons*'—It is the time in which we live. In the weeks prior to her arrest, even Renee and Henri stayed away."

"You know why, Veronique. It was a mutual decision."

"I know that, dear. I wasn't criticizing. As the Nazis continued their relentless persecution of the Jews. . . Well, it was a terrible time."

"I don't think Elisabeth is referencing old friends, Oma—hers or your. I think she means Anton. He no longer lingers when he comes to visit."

"That can't be right," Veronique argued. "Anton rarely came to call."

"I think he did. You just didn't know. We'll get to that in a moment. First, Henri, I know I asked before, but I'm asking again. Did you ever wonder *why* your father was so eager for you to befriend a Jewish girl who lived on Île St-Louis?"

"I never thought to ask. Why? Do you think he had some mysterious ulterior motive?"

"Perhaps—"

"What—"

"In a minute." Anne turned to Renee. "Henri says he never questioned Anton's reason for introducing you to Oma. Did you ever ask yourself why it seemed important that you make friends with the daughter of casual acquaintance—and a Jew at that?"

"Absolutely not. I was glad we met. That was the extent of my reflection."

"Back to you, Henri. During your first meeting with Elisabeth and Oma, your father said something strange. I don't recall his exact words, but it was an admonition to hold each other close. Did he ever explain what he meant?"

"He didn't need to. I understood. He was saying that during difficult times, we all should care for one another."

"Under the circumstances, didn't you think that was a strange thing to say? Think about it. You and Renee were Gentiles. Consorting with a Jew was against the law in Nazi-occupied Paris. Why would he make such a request? Why would he, in effect, put your lives in jeopardy by asking you to hold each other close—in other words, not just to be friendly, but to be good friends?"

"I have no idea. Where are you going with this, Anne?"

"You'll soon know. Oma, please read the next part of the poem."

Frowning, Veronique began again. *"And children dwell alone in private rooms/Where parents bid them stay for safety sake.'"*

Henri and Renee reacted at the same time. Renee nodded her consent, and Henri spoke first. "No one was hidden away in rooms," he argued. "My father admonished me to be careful, but he never restricted my movements. Except for his staunch refusal to allow me to join the Resistance, there were no limitations regarding what I could or couldn't do or where I was or wasn't allowed to go. Even in July 1942, he never ordered me to stay away from Veronique." Looking puzzled, he hesitated, and then said. "As a matter of fact, thinking back, despite the increasing danger, he *urged* me to visit."

"Interesting," Anne said. "What about you, Renee?"

"The same goes for me. My father cautioned me to be careful, but he never made me stay in the house for, as Elisabeth put it, 'safety sake.' Mother hated it when I went to see Veronique, but she knew we were good friends, so she never forbade me from going."

"Even in the worst of times, Mother didn't hide me from view," Veronique said. "Unless she wanted to talk privately with friends."

"I don't think Elisabeth is referring to you, Oma. Nor is she writing about Henri or Renee. I believe the lines refer to a person hidden from the three of you."

Veronique's brow quickly puckered. "I don't understand," she said tentatively. "Mother has to mean Henri. She's speaking metaphorically. We all know Anton wouldn't let him fight for the Resistance."

"Oma, I want you to give extra thought to the next stanzas. Elisabeth is writing more cryptically and, I'm sure, symbolically."

"I'm doing the best I can," Veronique protested.

"I know, and you're doing a great job. Please tell us what Elisabeth says next."

"All right," Veronique said, though not appeased. "She writes, *We long to keep them close, but must let go/ For young or old alike, they are not ours.*"

"That's a strange line," Renee said. "I'm not sure how to word this, and my interpretation may be confusing, but could Elisabeth be saying that Veronique is not 'hers' in a figurative sense? Could she mean, though Veronique is her own flesh and blood, she is also her own person? Does what I'm suggesting make sense? Maybe she's saying that, despite the dangers, she wants her daughter to live her life without excessive restrictions?" She paused and then said, "It seems I'm as confused as Veronique."

"What you say makes perfect sense," Anne said. "Now listen to the second line of the stanza. 'For young or old alike, they are not ours.' Elisabeth uses the words 'young *or* old.' Though Henri is a few years older than you and Oma, you're all basically the same age, and, again, she uses a plural pronoun, 'ours,' not mine."

"Who's Mother referring to," Veronique pleaded.

"Pay close attention and see if what she says makes sense."

"I think we've done quite enough analyzing," Veronique said crossly. "Instead of presenting your theory piecemeal, Just tell us what you're thinking."

Anne knew her grandmother had figured it out. She wasn't angry. She was lashing out because she was afraid to hear the words. "Indulge me a little longer, Oma," she said. "We're working this out together. It won't help if I tell you what I think. Please read. You'll soon understand."

Frowning, Veronique continued.

And lovers nevermore will join in joy.
Great ecstasy grows dim as days drag by.
Pray God, my love, you always will remain
The steadfast star that guides me on my path.

"Lovers," Henri said, stunned. "Elisabeth had a lover?"

"It's out of the question," Veronique argued with mounting distress.

"She did, Oma. Before I heard your mother's poem and, granted, we've only analyzed a few stanzas, I suspected that Anton and Elisabeth were lovers. Now I'm certain."

Renee gasped, and Henri took a deep breath. When he responded, the tone of his voice and the look on his face exuded anger, disbelief, and denial. "There's no way," he argued. "My father was an honorable man. He would never cheat on Mother. He loved her."

"He cared for her like Elisabeth cared for Samuel all those years he was sick. But was he in love with her? You've often said she was ill, and her condition worsened during the years before she died—I think you said in 1933."

"But—"

"Please hear me out. What I'm saying makes sense in light of everything we know. Though I'm not sure, I believe Auguste Lessard introduced Anton and Elisabeth."

"Why would you think that?" Veronique asked.

"It's just a hunch. For our purposes, let's assume he did. But whoever brought them together knew Elisabeth was lonely. She had a child and no husband—no man in the house to care for her and satisfy her needs. Your father was married to a woman, who, in the strictest sense of the word, couldn't be his wife. Anton was young—a man's man. I'm not passing judgment, Henri. Both Anton and Elisabeth were vulnerable. They needed each other and understood what it was like to care for an ill spouse. For those reasons, and probably more, they fell in love."

Anne paused, waiting for Henri to respond. For a few moments he was quiet. When he finally spoke, he was no longer angry—his voice and facial expression expressed resignation. "You may be right," he said. "If my father and Elisabeth *were* lovers, it would explain a few things I've often found puzzling. Beginning in the late 1920s and early 1930s he began to travel more often, especially during the year before Mother died."

"You said she passed in 1933."

"Right. I recall one morning in particular. After breakfast he suddenly announced he'd be leaving that night and would be away for about a week."

"Why does that one conversation stand out in your mind?" Anne asked.

"Probably because it was the first time I asked to go. He said no—now that I think about it, perhaps a little too adamantly. It was also the first time he said he *needed* me to stay home with Mother—not something like, 'For me, would you please stay home,' or 'I'd like for you to be here for your mother.' No, he '*needed*' me to remain behind."

"Didn't you have servants who could care for your mother?"

"We did, including a fulltime nurse who lived in the room next to hers. His refusal to take me with him on that trip was just the beginning of a difficult time in our relationship. His ever-increasing demands prompted many heated arguments."

"Tell me about them," Anne said.

"Each one was like the one before. It was like we were using the same script over and over. I'd ask if I could go out with friends. If he was staying home, it was okay, but if he planned a night out, I had to remain at the house. With all the servants and the nurse around, I couldn't figure out why one of us had to be there. Now I'm wondering if maybe he was ashamed of his behavior, and, in some way, was assuaging his guilt by having me stay home with his mother—his wife—while he making love to his mistress. I'm sorry, Veronique. I could have chosen a kinder way of expressing my feelings, but I don't know how else to explain—"

"No apology necessary," Veronique said.

"You're doing fine," said Renee. "Keep talking."

"Very well." Slowly and deliberately choosing his words, Henri pressed on. "I loved Mother, but, at times, I also hated her. Can you possibly understand?"

"I can," Anne answered. "I've felt the same way about my mother, though not for the same reasons and not to the extent you harbored your negative feelings. I think all children have a love/hate relationship with their parents."

"Of course they do," Renee agreed. "And you had good reason to feel as you did."

"Thank you." Henri smiled at his wife and said, "As I aged and was required to shoulder more and more of the burden, I was furious with my father for depriving me of my freedom, and I grew more and more hostile toward Mother. I blamed her for my unhappiness—for making me miss out on life. Like you said, Anne, she was *always* ill. I can't remember a time when she was a 'normal' mother. Now, as I hear Elisabeth's poem, I realize why he might—"

He paused.

"Now what are you thinking?" Renee asked. "I know this is hard for you to hear, my love."

"Of course it is. What boy—or, for that matter what man—would want to know his father cheated on his mother? But suddenly, after all this time, I get it. If *I* felt angry for being saddled with Mother's care, imagine the frustration and resentment my father must have felt—the burden he carried. Though I still can't justify his behavior, perhaps I can understand why he and Elisabeth fell in love. He must have been so lonely."

"As was she," Anne said. "And you're right. How can we judge either of them? To use yet another cliché, we never had to 'walk in their shoes.' What about your mother, Oma. Did you ever imagine she had a lover?"

"Never in my wildest dreams. I told you before, Anne. She was always here when I went to bed at night, and she joined me the next morning for breakfast. How could I know she was meeting a man—that is if she really was? And if what you say is true, though I'm still not convinced, where did they meet?"

"To answer your first question, I'm sure they were discreet. And in your defense, back then what young woman would think her widowed mother had taken a lover? As for where they met, until now I hadn't thought about it—maybe in the house on Quai de Bethune."

"That's not possible," Veronique argued. "You know we were a tight-knit community. Everyone knew everyone else's business."

"True, but it makes sense. The Quai de Bethune house was vacant. Elisabeth and Anton could have left their homes after dark, probably after both you and Henri had gone to bed, and returned long before you got up. With shades or draperies at the windows, no one would have realized anyone was inside the mansion. Even if they lit candles, a casual passerby wouldn't have seen the dim light, especially if they met in an interior room."

"Did you share your theory with Bertrand?" Veronique asked.

"No, but I listened very carefully to what he said, and I read between the lines. His responses to my questions support my theory. He told us when Anton learned of Elisabeth's arrest, he was distraught. With little to no hope of finding her, he raced to the Velodrome d'Hiver. Hours later he returned to the Île. Bertrand said when he entered the house his eyes were red and puffy and his shoulders were slumped in grief. He and Auguste talked privately for a few minutes, and then, 'almost miraculously'—Bertrand's words—'at least outwardly,' his sorrow vanished. He began to focus all his energy on getting you, Henri, and Renee out of Paris. According to Bertrand, he was 'a driven man.'"

"That's an understatement," Renee said. "When he came to my house to break the news of Elisabeth's arrest, he kept repeating the same line. 'Henri must survive. It is 'vital'—"

"He used the word 'vital'?"

"He did. In fact so many times the word is indelibly etched in my memory."

"Anton's reaction to Elisabeth's arrest isn't surprising," Arnaud said. "According to Grandpapa, he and Elisabeth were good friends. Henri, when you first emailed me that Anne was coming to Paris and wanted to speak with Bertrand, I called him to determine whether or not he had enough pertinent information to merit a visit. During the conversation, I asked if he remembered Madame Boulet. He said he did—and rather well. Apparently, before the onset of the Occupation, she visited regularly, usually with Anton. However as the Occupation continued and the Nazis issued edicts forbidding Christians from associating with Jews, she stopped coming altogether. He thinks it was she who decided it was best to stay away, not Auguste or Anton."

"She probably thought she'd be putting them in danger if she continued to visit," Veronique said pensively. "That fits with my theory."

"Your theory?" Henri said. "You have a theory?"

"Yes. I told you. When Mother sent me to Renee's, I believe she knew she would be arrested, likely that night."

"I'd say that's one theory we can all agree on," Anne said.

"That's good," said Veronique, "Because I can't accept *your* theory, Anne. Nothing you've said so far convinces me that Mother and Anton were lovers. I'm sorry, darling. You're wrong."

"I'm not through, Oma. Read the next stanza."

"All right, but—"

"Just read!"

"Okay. . ."

No sun will shine again on us, my love.
Now nights of joy live only in our hearts.
Pray God, our own will come to understand
Our lasting love—a joy that has no end.

"Who's Elisabeth addressing?" Henri asked.

"*Me*, of course," said Veronique. 'Us' refers to her and me."

"No, Oma. That doesn't make sense. Please read the stanza again."

Under duress and clearly irritated, Veronique slowly read the lines to herself. When she finished, her frown deepening, she put the letter in her lap. "You're right, Anne," she said. "'My love' can't be me, but I don't understand what Mother means when she writes about nights of joy. I told you she rarely went out."

"Elisabeth is speaking to Anton, Oma. He's the 'love.' Think about it. By process of elimination, it can't be anyone else. We know it wasn't Auguste. I don't think you mentioned him more than once in you journal, so he wasn't significant—at least in your eyes. Jules and Denis were married and off limits."

"But Anton was married too."

"He was. We'll talk about that when Elisabeth brings it up—if she does."

"And if she doesn't?" Henri asked.

"I'll tell you what I think and let you decide. In these lines, Elisabeth senses the end is near—that she and Anton won't be together again. The sun is symbolic of the love they share—of happy times. '*No sun will shine again on us, my love.*' I don't think that means actual sunlight. Elisabeth knows she won't live through the Occupation—that she and Anton will never be able to celebrate their love in the open for all to see. The 'nights of joy' that now live only in her heart means she knows they will never again make love, and though it may be shocking for you to imagine, likely in your home in your her room after you'd gone to bed."

"No!—It's impossible!"

"Actually, it's likely. Of course 'our own' is you, Henri, and Renee. she wants you to know about her and Anton—to 'understand.' She uses the word 'pray' because she realizes what you're hearing for the first time will be difficult to accept."

"If you're right and, mind you, I'm still not totally convinced, 'our lasting love' must mean, though she and Anton will never be together again, either in daylight or darkness, their love will survive—even beyond this life."

"Exactly, Oma. Now, please read the next line. Elisabeth's choice of pronouns is important. One word in particular will solve at least part of the mystery."

"All right," Veronique said. "Mother continues, *'And never fear, beloved. / Your care is our concern.'*"

"If, as I'm beginning to believe, Anton and Elisabeth *were* lovers, Elisabeth is probably addressing him again," Renee said.

"I don't think so, Renee. She says 'Your care is *our* concern.'" Anton, too, cared about whomever she's addressing. *Our* concern—not *my* concern. Oma, please keep reading.

Veronique inhaled, exhaled deeply, and read. *"'The faces, scenes, and colors bright/*

Will do their part to lighten-up your life, / And bring you happiness in years to come.'"

"Clearly Mother means her paintings," she said.

"I agree, but this time the scenes, faces, and bright colors were sold to lighten the *beloved's* life and to bring happiness in the *beloved's* future."

"How many times do I have to say this, Anne? Mother sold her paintings to facilitate my escape. She wanted me and my friends to be happy and free in the 'years to come.' Certainly this time she's referring to Anton."

"Veronique's right," Henri said. "My father didn't need Elisabeth's money. He had plenty of his own. Elisabeth didn't sell her paintings to provide for him."

"That's just it, Henri. The art wasn't sold to help your father. He's not the 'beloved' Elisabeth is referencing. 'And beloved' is singular. Elisabeth didn't use the plural, beloveds, so she can't mean you, Renee, and Oma. She also says 'life,' not lives."

"A singular noun," Renee said.

"Yes. She's talking about one person. Realizing this is becoming a redundant request, Oma, please keep reading."

Obviously frustrated, Veronique continued.

I wish that life were kinder, love; that people understood
So you would know the joy of Paris lights.
But country walks are so much safer now,
No unkind men around to cause you harm.
No vicious tongues to turn your smiles to frowns.
New friends and kin must satisfy your needs,
And give you love I now so long to give.

"Oh my," Veronique said, startled. "She's talking to a child, and she's addressing him or her as 'love.'"

"You're right, Oma. Remember what you said? Your mother was always home. Then, out of the blue and using the excuse she hadn't been able to see Europe after graduation, she set off on a grand tour."

"That's true. She was gone over four months. When she finally came home, she was more like her old self, though she still seemed tired—I thought from traveling from country to country."

Anne noted her grandmother's sudden pained expression and knew she understood.

"I'm almost afraid to ask," Veronique continued hesitantly. "You don't believe Mother set off to tour Europe. Do you believe she went away to give birth to Anton's child?"

"I do."

"When did Elisabeth leave?" Henri asked.

"Early in the spring of 1932," Veronique answered offhandedly, her furrowed brow reflecting her endeavor to process Anne's shocking assertion.

"In that case, the pieces of a puzzle that, in my mind, has remained unfinished for years are falling slowly into place. As I said before, around that time, my father began to travel more frequently. One time he was away for several weeks. I remember that particular trip because Mother was very ill. I was worried if she died while he was away, it would be my fault."

"But I don't understand. Henri. If what Anne believes is true, why didn't Mother and Anton tell us about their relationship after your mother died?"

"Because people wouldn't have understood or accepted them as a couple," Anne said. "Elisabeth was a Jew, and Anton was Catholic. They were unmarried with a child, who, for all intents and purposes, was a bastard."

"But a marriage would have reunited the family. That was Mother's fervent wish."

"Even before the onset of the Occupation, both families would have been disgraced by such an announcement," Arnaud said. "And after June 1940...Well, we all know what happened to Christians who married Jews."

"Arnaud's right, Oma. If it was dangerous for Henri and Renee to visit you, how could Anton and Elisabeth have married and openly lived together?"

"I see your point." Veronique again hesitated, and then contemplating aloud, said. "But where was the child all this time? Do you think Elisabeth and Anton asked Uncle George to care for him or her? Mother doesn't say whether they had a boy or girl."

"At first I thought with Uncle George, but now I tend to believe he or she lived in the country somewhere near George's farm. We know the child wasn't in the city. Elisabeth writes *'so you would know the joy of Paris lights.'* She goes on to say that *'country walks are so much safer now.'* Go back to the many conversations your mother had with George, Oma. Do you remember anything pertinent?"

"Maybe, though at the time it didn't seem unusual or strange. Mother always cried when George came to visit. I thought she was happy to see him. When he left, she cried again. I assumed she was sorry to see him go."

"That's a logical supposition."

"I guess, but it doesn't negate the fact that I was blind. I accepted my premise as the reason for mother's sadness and never looked for another answer. I often heard her refer to her 'precious child,' but I assumed she was talking about me. Before I gave you my journal, I read an entry from November 1940, a day when Uncle George and Mother spent all afternoon talking privately. When she called me to dinner, I recall her face was flushed, and her eyes were red. She apologized for the sparse meal. I thought that was why she was so upset—she was worried we might starve."

"But now we know that wasn't the case," Henri said. "The 'unkind men' blocking the path were the Nazis."

"Or, as Arnaud suggested, it may have been society before the Nazis occupied Paris."

"You're right, Renee. In all probability Elisabeth is referring to the Nazis as well as to her neighbors and friends who wouldn't understand."

"Anyone who lives on the Île knows there are vicious tongues in our small community," Arnaud said. "And the gossips could turn a child's happiness to sadness."

"So friends and relatives were caring for the child," Veronique said, talking more to herself than to the others. "Uncle George never had children, so it has to be someone who lived nearby."

"And it seems Elisabeth never went to visit," Anne said. "At least not after the onset of the Occupation. She says she wishes she could give him love—"

"Him?"

"Or her. For our purposes, let's use the pronoun him."

"I believe the stanza also explains Mother's reluctance to flee the country. Remember what I wrote in my journal, Anne? Over and over I begged her to leave Paris. I wanted to live with Uncle George in Brittany until Paris was liberated. I couldn't understand why she always said no."

"There's another possible explanation for her refusal to live with Uncle George," Anne said. "If her child was nearby and she had access, she might have found it difficult to keep the secret, thereby putting him in danger."

"Or it could be something else altogether," said Arnaud. "Simply put, she may not have wanted to disrupt the child's life."

"I suppose it could be all of the above," Anne said. "But whatever her reason, Elisabeth knew she was about die."

"I agree," Veronique said. "She says,

Few sunsets will I see beyond today.
No fear of death; but what I leave behind
Now troubles me and leaves me sad in heart.

Tears welled in Veronique's eyes as the put the poem on her lap. "I was such a fool," she said softly. "I *chose* not to see the darkness around me. I never understood the depth of Mother's misery."

"But, Oma, you were young—"

"I can't blame my blindness on my age, Anne. I need to admit the truth, both to myself and to all of you. I didn't question, probably because I didn't want to hear answers that would force me to face reality. I was a coward."

"Oma—"

"Please let me finish. This declaration—or perhaps I should say confession—has been a long-time coming, though I doubt the truth will assuage my guilt. For the first time in decades—no perhaps from the moment the Nazis marched into Paris—I'm finally acting like an adult. I'm facing the truth." She sighed and said, "I feel like all I've done for the past thirty minutes, or for that matter since I arrived in Paris, is sigh."

"Under the circumstances, you're response is appropriate, Oma. Sigh all you want."

"Thank you, darling. Perhaps I'm sighing because I suddenly feel like a befuddled old woman. And no comment please. Mother goes on to say,

Live well, my darling loves, and think of me.
Would God my dearest friend live on beyond
The darkness and travail you all must face,
And bring you safely home to live in peace
In bright and sunny days that lie ahead.

"This part of the poem is easy to interpret," Henri said. "Elisabeth hopes Anton will survive the Occupation. My father is her dearest friend." He paused momentarily and then said, "But he didn't live to bring their child home."

"No, my love, but now you know why he forbade you from joining the Resistance. He realized he might not survive, but if you were alive—"

"You would reunite the family," said Veronique. "Joy and peace in bright and sunny days would come after the Nazis were defeated.

Mother's last lines need no interpretation. In light of what we just discussed, they are very clear. She writes,

Be strong, my dears, for someday you will know
The reasons; choices we are forced to make,
The absence, sacrifice, is all for you.
Your lives, your hopes, your dreams are in your hands.
My prayer: Please, God, that all of you live well.

Veronique folded the poem and looked up at Henri. Inhaling and then exhaling deeply, she said, "We have a brother or sister somewhere out there."

"You do, Oma, but you need to know the sacrifices Elisabeth and Anton made weren't simply for their child. They were for both of you and for you, Renee. Oma, your mother didn't want you to suffer humiliation. And Henri, Anton was afraid you'd think badly of him."

"What happens now?" Veronique pleaded. "Henri, after all this time how do we possibly find our brother or sister. Uncle George is dead, and he didn't have children. He left his farm to me. Believing I would never return to France, Robert eventually sold the property."

"Maybe there's a message in the second letter," Anne said.

"Perhaps," said Veronique. "But before we look, I need to take a short break."

Renee stood and said, "I'll make tea. The rest of you wait in the living room while Veronique freshens up. Come back in twenty minutes."

At the door Anne paused and looked back. Veronique hadn't moved. She was still sitting in her chair staring at the fireplace.

CHAPTER 29

When they all returned and were settled in Anne's bedroom, Veronique picked up the second letter from the table beside her chair. Glancing at the name on the envelope, she looked up and, in utter bewilderment, said, "This isn't addressed to me. It was left for you, Henri."

"Really?" Henri said.

"Yours is the name on the front."

Henri walked over to Veronique and took the letter from her outstretched hand. "My father wrote this," he said. "He left a message for me just as Elisabeth left one for you."

"Would you like to be alone when you read your father's letter?" Veronique asked.

Henri nodded no. "Please stay," he said. "Like you, I want my family close."

"Of course we'll stay, my friend." Veronique motioned to the chair on the other side of the table. "Sit here by me."

Henri sat, wiped a tear from the corner of his eye and began to read.

August 22, 1942

My Dear Son,

I wish there had been time to talk before you left Paris. To be honest, we should have talked years ago, but I continued to put off what I knew would be a difficult discussion. Unfortunately, la rafle du Vel d'Hiv necessitated immediate action on my part. I had to make arrangements for you, Renee, and Veronique to flee Paris—and right away. There was no time to call you aside and begin a conversation we might not have been able to complete. You may be wondering why I found it hard to reveal what you will now read. The answer is simple. I was afraid you would think less of me—that I would lose your love and respect. But I cannot face the months, or, God forbid, my death, without confessing a sin that has, ironically, brought me great joy.

Let me begin by telling you about my life with your mother. I cared deeply for Victoire. Despite her debilitating illness, I remained faithful to her and honored our vows. As I am sure you understand, doing so was not easy, especially as the years took their toll on her health. I know how my demands affected you. We both suffered—I, because I knew Victoire's pain was far worse than mine, and you, because you are the son who, despite the constraints I placed on your life, always did as I asked.

In the summer of 1928, my resolve to be a good husband suddenly evaporated. My friend Auguste Lessard introduced me to one of his neighbors, a beautiful widow with a young child. I confess my sin. I strayed. My one love—my life's partner—is and always will be Elisabeth Boulet. Shortly after Elisabeth and I were introduced, we began a love affair that ended a month ago when the Nazis took her from me. Please understand, Henri. I am not apologizing for the affair, only that I did not have the courage to share my joy—and my shame—with you before now.

Last night I finally mustered the strength to return to my dearest's home. Under the cover of darkness, Auguste, Denis, and I entered the house through the window she always left unlocked—my means of access after Veronique and the servants had gone to bed. How agonizing it was to be back in the room where we had known such bliss. Denis pried open the bricks above the fireplace, our hiding place, and I put this letter beside the one Elisabeth left for her adored daughter. Just weeks before she died, she told me about a poem she wrote in April 1942—a cryptic message about our child, and the Swiss bank accounts we opened to provide for your futures.

If you are reading my letter, you already know everything. It is my prayer that you and Veronique will find your brother after the Nazis are defeated.

"A brother! Henri. We have a brother."

"So it seems." Henri said, tears again welling in his eyes as he read.

Since his birth, he has been living on a farm in Brittany with a Catholic family, neighbors of Elisabeth's friend—the man Veronique knows as Uncle George. At Elisabeth's request, I sold two of her paintings to pay for safe passage out of France for you, Renee, and, of course, for Veronique. My sources in the Resistance say you made it safely to New York. I Thank God! Not long before my beloved was taken from me, we sold two more paintings, a self-portrait by Fantin-Latour and a Degas, to Didier Duplessis, the same bureaucrat who purchased the other works. The money we received from the sale was placed in the Swiss bank account we created for your brother's new family— his caretakers until you find him and make him part of your lives. Whether or not you are reunited, when he comes of age, he will have his inherit- ance. I have deposited the remainder of my money in the same bank in your name. The password and access codes for both accounts—yours and the one Elisabeth left for Veronique—are in a third envelope behind the bricks.

I am told your brother is a fine boy. Perhaps you questioned why I felt it important that you and Veronique be friends. Now you know. There is an enduring connection between Elisabeth and me—one that lives on despite her death and perhaps mine. After your mother died, I begged my dearest to be my wife. She refused. She had Veronique to consider, and the shame of having a child out of wedlock was too much for her to bear. She could not tell her cherished daughter she had a brother, and, respecting her wishes, I could not tell you.

Weeks after the Nazis occupied Paris, assuring her that I could make the necessary arrangements for Veronique, you, Renee, and your brother to accompany her to Vichy France, I pleaded with Elisabeth to leave. Not able or willing to believe her life was in jeopardy and vowing not to be driven from her home, she refused my offer. I reluctantly accepted her explanation, though in my heart I knew the true reason she was choosing to stay—she would not leave me behind.

"That's it!" Veronique interrupted. "That's why Mother remained in Paris! She wouldn't leave Anton!"

"So it appears," Henri said. "We're *finally* getting answers to questions we've been asking for seventy years—both aloud and to ourselves."

Renee reached out and patted her husband's hand. "You're right, my love," she said. "Tell us what else Anton wrote."

Henri nodded, took a deep breath, and continued to read.

I believe she would have acquiesced had I agreed to go with her, but I am too proud. I believe a true Frenchman should stand and fight for his country—not run like a coward. When the first anti-Jew laws were enacted and she realized hers and Veronique's lives were at stake, I again asked her to leave, but, as before, she refused.

On the afternoon of July 17, learning from my resistance connections that a raid on Parisian Jews was imminent, I urged her to send Veronique to Saint-Germain to visit Renee. When Veronique arrived safely, Jules sent me a message, and I went to the Île. These were the last hours I spent with my beloved. How poignant it was knowing she would never again lie in my arms. We were both aware of what would soon occur. Realizing she was too weak to travel, I begged her to let me take her to a safe place on the continent, but fearing for my life if I were caught helping a Jew, she again refused. The process was in place for your escape. She worried if we altered the plan, you would refuse to leave.

I know you yearned to join me in the struggle against our oppressors. Looking back, I suppose I was being hypocritical when I refused to let you remain behind to fight by my side. Like me, you understood what it means to be a Frenchman who, beyond all else, feels it his duty to defend his country. I know how difficult it was for you to watch your friends, some younger by years, fighting the Nazis while you sat idly by. How proud I am of you, Henri. Your arguments for joining the Resistance were valid, but I could not permit you to participate. You are the older son, and you must take care of Renee, Veronique, and your brother. They will need you. Auguste, Jules, and I are working tirelessly to drive the Germans out of France. God willing, that day will soon be here.

When my dearest Elisabeth was taken from me, I struggled to hide my excruciating pain and overwhelming despair. Had I shown even the slightest emotion, you might have believed I was having second thoughts, and I could not let you remain in Paris. Auguste and Jules know my story. If I die, they will tell you everything.

Do not judge me, Henri. Instead, use all your energy and join with Veronique to find your brother. Be a family. This is what Elisabeth wanted. It was her greatest desire. Through your efforts, our love will live on.
With great affection and respect,
Your father, Anton

For several minutes, Henri sat silently. When he looked up, his cheeks were wet with tears. "Are you all right, my love?" Renee asked.

When he didn't respond, Veronique took his hand and said, "None of this was easy to hear, dear friend, but you're always telling me we should look to the future. Anton and Elisabeth had a boy, but neither revealed his name or anything about the couple who cared for him. Why?"

"For the same reason Elisabeth left her message to you in a cryptic poem," Anne answered. "If the Nazis discovered the letter, there would be nothing said that could lead them to their son. I assume both Anton and Elisabeth thought you would return to Paris immediately after the Liberation. Even if Jules and Anton were killed fighting the Nazis, George could have provided additional information."

"How stupid I was." Veronique slumped in her chair.

"Please, Oma. Less than a minute ago you told Henri we have to look to the future. It's time to reunite your family."

"Anne's right." Renee reached out and squeezed Veronique's hand. "God willing, your brother's alive. If not, we'll try to locate his family. For now, let's finish this business. Henri, what's in the third envelope?"

Henri carefully opened the seal. "Is it the information we need?" Veronique asked anxiously.

"It appears to be. There are two numbered accounts in the private bank of Lombard Odier Darier Hentsch & Cie in Geneva. One may be accessed by Veronique Boulet or her heirs. The other by Henri Marsolet or his heirs. There are passwords and numbers. There's also this." He held up a key to a safe-deposit box.

"I should be relieved," Veronique said. "But suddenly there's so much to think about. I still can't believe my mother and your father were lovers."

"I guess that makes us a real family," Henri said.

"We always were, my friend." Veronique turned to Anne. "Now what?" she asked.

"We have a lot to do. When we finished here, Henri and Joseph will go to Renee's, and this afternoon you and I are calling on Francoise."

"I have several appointments on Monday," Henri said. "Including a ten o'clock meeting with Gregoire Drouin. If all goes as planned, Joseph will remove the tiles in Renee's entry hall Tuesday afternoon."

"Oma, you and I are joining Giles Gaudrieu for breakfast Monday morning. Hopefully he'll add more to what we already know. I'd like to leave for Geneva on Tuesday—"

"There's no need," Veronique said. "We can access the account from here by phone. I'll call the bank in the morning."

"That may not be possible. You'll need to show proper identification before the bank grants access—"

"But I can't travel—"

"I know. That's why I'm going."

"I agree with Anne," Arnaud said. "I doubt you'll receive answers over the phone, at least not the first time you make contact."

"And we're not talking about just the money in the account," Anne said. "The safe-deposit box can't be accessed from here. Maybe we'll open it and find another letter from your mother, or maybe her jewels."

"And the bank records may provide additional information," Arnaud added. "Since I know people at the bank, I'll go along—"

"How thoughtful of you, young man," Veronique said, a faint smile crossing her still-troubled face. You're right. Anne should go, and I'll feel much better knowing my granddaughter is traveling with a strong, protective man."

"Oma, I've traveled by myself since I was sixteen. I spent three weeks in Rome when I was nineteen, and I lived in Paris for four months when I was twenty."

"Still, you want me to feel comfortable. After all, you're traveling to a foreign country on my behalf."

"It's the first time I've heard Switzerland referred to in quite that tone. You'd think I was traveling to someplace dangerous, like Iran. I'm crossing an open border."

"Maybe so, but I'll rest easily knowing Arnaud is with you. If you leave Tuesday, Catherine Labbe will have time to prepare and overnight my power of attorney and whatever other papers the bank requests."

"The lawyer I used for the sale of the house still practices in Paris," Henri said. I'll see him Monday afternoon and sign whatever papers are necessary for you to access my account information."

"You have your account number," Anne said. "You could call to get your balance."

"I know, but let's do this my way. I want *you* to tell me what my father left, not a bank manager I've never met."

"Then I'll call as soon as I have something to report."

"While you and Veronique are at Francoise's, I'll make the flight and hotel reservations," Arnaud said.

"You do that young man. There's a lovely Four Seasons in Geneva—"

"How would you know, Oma? As far as I know, you haven't been to Switzerland recently—if ever."

"Remember German Victory? When I decided to come to Paris, I researched five-star hotels—"

"Okay, but why in Geneva? You knew your mother opened an account in a Swiss bank, but unless you know something I don't, you had no idea where—"

"I didn't know for sure, but Geneva seemed like the logical place. Look at a map of France during the Occupation, and you'll see why."

"What's German Victory?" Henri asked.

"Not what, but who," said Veronique. "He's the banker who established Mother's, and, I assume, Anton's accounts."

"His name was German Victory?"

"No, his name was Gardiner Vachon. I wasn't sure I'd remember, so I gave him a codename."

"I doubt your German Victory is still alive, Veronique."

"That shouldn't be a problem for Anne and me," Arnaud said. "Both my grandfather and I have accounts at Lombard Odier Darier Hentsch & Cie. I know all eight partners."

"See, Anne?" Veronique smirked. "It's good that Arnaud's going with you."

"Now you expect me to believe you knew Arnaud maintains an account in the same bank where your mother put her money?"

"You didn't know? I'm psychic!"

"I don't recall hearing you brag about that talent during any of our past discussions."

"You're wrong, my darling granddaughter. Only yesterday I told you I can see the future. Would you like for me to elaborate?"

"I'll pass."

"I'd like to hear," Arnaud said.

"My grandmother has nothing to say! Do you, Oma?"

"Evidently not—at least not now. So, Arnaud, you'll make a reservation at the Four Seasons?"

"I will. That's where I usually stay when I'm in Geneva on business."

"When I was surfing the web, I saw the hotel has lovely suites."

"Oma!"

"What? I'm talking with Arnaud about a hotel. I can't imagine why our conversation would be problematic for you."

"I won't disappoint you, Veronique."

"I'm sure you won't." Behind Arnaud's back, Veronique winked at Anne.

"Let's go down to our place, and I'll fix lunch," Renee offered. "It's been an emotional morning. Veronique, you should rest before your appointment with Francoise."

"Renee's right, Oma. Take a nap. I'll be down to pick you up at two-fifteen."

"I'll be ready." Veronique turned to Arnaud and said, "Tonight at dinner, you can tell me if you were able to book a suite in Geneva."

"I'll be sure to let you know how I fare." Arnaud bent and kissed the smiling woman on both cheeks.

"My grandmother has never been known for her subtlety," Anne groaned as she stuck her keycard in the slot and opened her apartment door. "I hope you weren't embarrassed."

"Not at all. And you're right—subtlety isn't a word I would put on Veronique's adjective list."

"Sit for a moment and tell me what adjectives you *would* use."

Arnaud sat on the couch, and Anne sat beside him. "Let's see," he began. "She's perceptive, charming, funny, bright, loving, frightened—"

"Frightened?"

"Absolutely. Despite what she says, she can't find a way to put the past behind her. She feels guilty because she didn't come back to Paris after the Liberation. She's convinced it will be her fault if she and Henri don't find their brother. She already believes she could have saved Elisabeth if she hadn't gone to Renee's on the afternoon of the seventeenth. Now those feelings of guilt are exacerbated because she has a sibling out there somewhere—a brother Elisabeth wanted her to know and love."

"I think she's going to find him," Anne said. "I have yet another theory."

"My guess, we're thinking the same thing."

"I think the couple who moved into Elisabeth's house on Quai de Bethune was caring for her son. What was the boy's name?"

"Martin Fontaine."

"Right. Bertrand said he, meaning Martin, was about seventeen when the family came back to the Île, so the age would be right. This was their city home, but he spent weekends and holidays in the country. Now he spends most of his time on the Ile."

"Will you share your theory with Henri and Veronique?"

"Not until I have definite proof."

"While you're visiting with Francoise, I'll see what I can find out."

"How about lunch? I have a state of the art microwave."

"So you're reheating—"

"One of the marvelous meals from Calixte."

"I would love to join you, but——."

"You're going to meet a woman who cooks."

"You guessed my secret. I'll be back to pick you all up at seven forty-five." He kissed her lightly on the lips.

"Saving your energy and passionate kisses for the other woman?"

"Now you know." Without further comment, he walked out the door.

Anne put several slices of cheese and part of a baguette on a paper plate. She took her lunch and a bottle of water to her office, opened her laptop, and checked her email. There were messages from Meg, Tom, and John. She began with John.

Hi Anne, The contracts for the Paris paintings are being drawn and will soon be signed, sealed, and delivered. I'm hoping we have as much success with the museums in the U.S. The paintings from the Musée d'Orsay will arrive on December 1 and those from the Marmottan and the Musée de l'Orangerie on December 7. Our design staff is working on the groupings. Email your fax number, and I'll transmit the tentative plans. We're creating permanent titles for the categories and planning three subcategories. I'll email when we come to a consensus. John.

Anne wrote back.

John. Thanks for the update. Glad you got most of what we want. I can't wait to see the final plans. My fax number is 33 (0) 1 49 52 71 12. I check my email several times a day. My best to the committee. Anne

She opened the message from Meg.

You won't believe what I read on the society page in the POST. Tom is marrying Susan. Did you know? I'm attaching the article and the picture. Good luck to the new trophy wife. LOL. Write when you can.

"Okay, Tom," she whispered. "How did you break the news of your pending nuptials?" She opened his email and read. *Hi Annie, I tried to call you yesterday, but you weren't home, and I didn't want to leave a message. By now you probably know, I'm getting married.*

Without reading on, Anne hit reply and congratulated her ex. *Good luck,* she ended, sorry Tom couldn't hear the sarcasm in her response.

She replied to several other emails, then changed out of her jeans and dressed for her appointment. At two-fifteen she went down to meet her grandmother. "Shall we find out what Francoise knows," she said when Veronique came to the door.

Before turning toward Madame Huard's home, Veronique crossed the street and gazed down at the Seine. "When I was young, I didn't appreciate what I had," she said somberly.

"Do any children realize how lucky they are, Oma? You keep beating yourself up for things you think you should have done. Instead, let's live in the moment. Three weeks ago I didn't think we would have *days* together, yet look where we are now. You're in Paris. You've learned you have a brother. And we're close to finding your mother's paintings—"

"And you're in love."

"Oma—"

"Can you deny it?"

"I'm very much in like. Will that do?"

"It's a matter of semantics. I know what I know."

"A profound statement. Thank God we're at Francoise's so this conversation can come to an abrupt end."

"There's nothing more to be said. I'm merely waiting for you to admit your feelings for Arnaud."

Anne rolled her eyes and rang the bell. Minutes later a middle-aged, impeccably-dressed woman opened the door. "Madame Ellison," she said. "How nice to see you." Turning to Anne, she nodded politely. "And you are Madame French. Please come in."

"Thank you for seeing us, Madame Laplante," Veronique said. "I remember your home. During the Occupation, I came by several times to leave notes of thanks from Mother. Without Madame Huard and the other neighbors, she would have starved to death long before the Nazis came for her."

"I was too young to understand what Mother was doing or why, but I knew she was fond of Madame Boulet. Please join me in the parlor, and we will talk. Would you like tea?"

"No thank you."

"Madame French?"

"No thanks, and please call me Anne. I understand your mother raised rabbits and shared the meat with my great-grandmother."

"She did." Francoise pointed to a window across the room. "Look out there. You will see a space that once teemed with rabbits. Mother often said it was the one time she was grateful the animals reproduced so prolifically."

Anne walked across the room. There, amid lovely flowers and a vegetable garden, was an ancient, rusty rabbit-cage. She turned back to Francoise and said, "You kept one of the cages."

"At Mother's insistence. It became a poignant reminder of a horrible time in her life—a memory of the Occupation and what all Parisians were forced to endure. I also think she meant it as a memorial to Madame Boulet. To the end, my mother spoke of yours with great affection and great sorrow, Veronique. She never understood why Madame Boulet remained in Paris. She often pleaded with Auguste and Jules to help her escape."

"Your mother knew Auguste and Jules?" Veronique asked.

"She did. I believe Auguste introduced Madame Boulet to Anton."

"So we recently learned," Anne said.

Francoise continued. "As the Nazis intensified their campaign against the Jews, everyone feared Madame Boulet would be arrested if she did not leave immediately."

"I knew the Siegles sent their children to the country," Veronique said. "Were Aaron and Margery taken by the Nazis?"

"On the seventeenth—the night your mother was seized."

"Did the children survive the war? Did they return to the Île?"

"The oldest son came back to sell the house. I last heard he and his siblings live in New York. Perhaps knowing what happened to their parents made moving back too difficult."

"That, I understand," Veronique said. "This is my first trip back to Paris since the day after the raid."

"Mother always believed the Nazis arrested you too. Imagine my surprise and joy when I learned you had somehow avoided arrest."

"Thank you," Veronique said. "One of my reasons for returning to the Île after so many years is to locate the paintings Denis Guidreau removed from the house prior to la rafle du Vel d'Hiv. Did you and Madame Huard ever speak about my mother's collection?"

"Actually we did. Were you aware that, for a time, Mother was a trustee for two of Madame Boulet's paintings, a Degas and a portrait by Fantin-Latour? She said Denis Guidreau delivered the art to her for safekeeping sometime in December 1941. She always wondered where they went after they left our home."

"Why?" Veronique asked.

"Because one night in late June 1942, Anton and Denis came for them. Anton told Mother he was selling the art to provide security for his son."

"Did she mention Henri by name?"

"I do not believe so. I knew Henri was an only child, so I assumed. . .But now that I think about it, why would Anton be selling Madame Boulet's paintings to care for *his* son?"

"The sale was for *their* son," Veronique said. "Anton and Mother's."

For the next fifteen minutes, she and Anne told Francoise what they had recently learned about Elisabeth and Anton's love affair and the child that was born of that union.

"Now some of what Mother said makes sense," Francoise said when they finished explaining.

"Do you think she knew about the affair?" Anne asked.

"If she did, she never said anything to me. But Madame Boulet was correct. At that time, people would not have understood. Social mores began to change during the war, but before the Occupation. . .Well, I doubt your friends and neighbors would have been sympathetic, Veronique."

"Do you know *why* your mother helped mine?" Veronique asked. "I'm not exaggerating when I say she put herself in mortal danger by doing so."

"Mother often said that no one on Île St-Louis had a problem because Madame Boulet was Jewish. Fortunately for our family, the Nazis never knew my grandmother, too, was a Jew. When she married my grandfather, a Catholic, she converted. That may be one reason Mother was so eager to help. I imagine she thought what was occurring in your life could be happening to us. I also know she liked Madame Boulet and took great pride in organizing the ladies of the neighborhood. When they could, they took from their own meager rations to supplement yours. Mother arranged the deliveries so no one brought food more than once a week."

"In case the Nazis were watching?"

"Though Mother never said so, I assume the neighbors were concerned. Nothing made her happier than to see Madame Boulet's health begin to improve. Toward the end of her life, she and I spent precious hours talking about her childhood, my father, and their struggles during the Occupation. I will always treasure the memory of those last days we spent together. One afternoon when we were talking about the Occupation and, specifically, your mother, she said that some nights when everyone had gone to bed and the streets were deserted, knowing Madame Boulet was alone, isolated, and needed a friend, she would visit. I assume they talked about personal matters, but, to the end, Mother never betrayed her friend's confidence. After listening to you, it occurs to me there were times when I felt she was leaving something out. She talked about Madame Boulet's devastated family, not solely about Veronique."

"Implying there could be another child."

"Possibly. I wish I could tell you more—"

"You've been very helpful," Veronique said.

Anne could tell her grandmother was tiring. "It's been a very long and emotional day," she said to Francoise. "Thank you so much for talking with us."

"I hope you will call on me," Veronique said. "I expect to be in Paris for several weeks."

"I will do that," Francoise said, smiling. "Please come again, or call if you have additional questions."

"I wish I could thank your mother and our other neighbors for their kindness and generosity."

"I am sure they all knew how you felt. Perhaps our mothers are looking down and see us together. It makes me happy to think so."

"I hope they are," Veronique said, extending her hand. "And thank you again for your time."

During the short walk back to the apartment and on the elevator ride up to the fourth floor, Veronique was unusually quiet. "I have an idea," Anne said when they were back in her grandmother's living room. "We're both tired. Let's postpone dinner at Taillevent until Wednesday evening. It would be better for me. I still have work to do for the Met."

"Fine, if you're sure you aren't disappointed."

Before Anne could reassure her grandmother, Renee entered the room. "I thought I heard you two," she said. "How was your meeting with Francoise?"

"It went well," Veronique said, almost in a whisper.

"It did," said Anne. "But it's been a long day. Would you and Henri be disappointed if we postpone dinner until Wednesday evening?"

"Truth be told, I'd rather wait. I'm still suffering from jet lag."

"Do you think Arnaud will be disappointed?" Veronique asked.

"I'm sure he's flexible. And if we postpone until Wednesday, we can tell you about our trip."

"And Henri and I can talk about what we found at rue Gît."

"Then it's decided. I'll call Arnaud."

"Thanks for making me feel like it's your fault we're not going out," Veronique whispered.

"You're welcome," Anne whispered back. "I'll see you in the morning."

"Brunch at eleven?"

"Absolutely."

"Why don't you invite Gus to join us? He's been so helpful."

"Are you sure you want all of us to invade your space?"

"Of course I do. I won't be doing any of the work—which is how it should be."

"I'll come see how you're doing in a minute," Renee said as Veronique started down the hall toward her bedroom. "Anne, your grandmother looks exhausted."

"She is—both physically and emotionally. Dinner tonight would be too much for her."

"Then you don't have work to do?"

"No, it was the only excuse I could come up with, but she knew I was cancelling for her."

"She must be tired if she didn't argue."

"My sentiments exactly."

"I'll call Arnaud and see if he wants to go out for a bite. Do you think Henri would like to join us?"

"I'll send him up to talk with you when he gets back. I'm sure he'll want to share his news.

"Great, I'll expect him. You know, Renee, my grandmother's a fortunate woman. She's blessed with two wonderful friends. Who could want for more?"

Renee put her hands together prayerfully, looked upward, and proclaimed, "Thank you, Anton."

CHAPTER 30

Anne entered her apartment, went straight to her office, and called Arnaud. "Good, you're home," she said.

"I am. How was your meeting with Madame St-Hilaire?"

"It went well, though she didn't have much to add beyond what we already know. But this is interesting. Francoise told me to look out the window above the courtyard. There, sitting among a well-tended garden teeming with spring flowers, was a rusty rabbit cage with the front dangling by one hinge—a memorial to Elisabeth, or so she said."

"Madame Huard cared that much for her neighbor?"

"Apparently so. When I asked why her mother would risk so much to bring rabbit meat to Elisabeth and Veronique and later keep one of the cages, she said her mother's mother—her grandmother—was a Jew who married a Catholic and converted."

"Thus the empathy."

"So it seems. There but for the Grace of God—"

"Amen to that!"

"So, yes, it was a good visit, which brings me to the reason for this call."

"You didn't phone because you miss me and need to hear my voice?"

"That too."

"Am I to understand there's a more important reason?"

"There is, so be serious. Today was difficult for Oma. She's physically and emotionally exhausted. I could see she was too tired to go out, so I made an excuse so she wouldn't have to be the one to cancel. I told her I have museum business that requires immediate attention."

"But you don't."

"No. Unless something unexpected happens, I've finished what I need to do."

"Then I'll call Taillevent and cancel. How about you?"

"If you mean am I tired, yes. But not enough to turn in for the night."

"Damn. I was going to come over and turn-in with you—"

"Arnaud—"

"Just kidding—or maybe not. Anyway, how about dinner? That is unless you want to stay in and re-heat Chinese."

"I'm sorry I ever mentioned Chinese takeout."

"But you did, so you'll have to live with the consequences. I'll reserve a table at l'Orangerie—the restaurant, not the museum. It's sort of a mini-Maxim's."

"As long as no animals are staring down at me while I'm forced to inhale the sickening aromas of pork knuckles, I'm game."

"Pun intended?"

"I wish I could take credit. The words simply slipped out."

"Eight?"

"Eight is great. But don't make the call until we see if Henri wants to go along. Renee's sending him up as soon as he gets back. Are you busy now?"

"I just finished a conference call with Aimee and a client."

"Aimee?"

"I told you. She often gives me investment advice."

"Right, you did. I forgot."

"And yes, I'm free, why?"

"Could you come over now?"

"Because you miss me?"

"Yes, please hurry. I plan to rip off your clothes, throw you down on the living room floor, and—"

"I'll be there in five minutes, and that includes the two minutes it will take to put on my running shoes. But, seriously, is there a problem?"

"I told you Henri's coming up. I thought you might like to hear what he has to say."

"I would. I'll see you soon."

On her way to change, Anne stopped by her office to check her email. She had just turned on the computer when she noticed the red light blinking on her answering machine. Figuring it was an earlier message from Arnaud, she pressed play. "Whatever the hour, call me," she heard Gus say. "If it's not too late, I would like to come by. I have important news."

She pushed redial. "Gus," she said. "What's up?"

"I have something to share."

"Should I be worried?"

"No, but that is all I will say for now."

"Ah, a mystery. Sure, come on over, that is if Arnaud and Henri can hear. They're both on their way."

"I would like for them to be there."

"Then buzz me when you get to the lobby door, and I'll release the elevator."

Ten minutes later the intercom buzzed. Anne pushed the button. "I'm here," Arnaud said.

"You *did* mean soon. You're the first to arrive."

"I beat Henri?"

"And Gus. Come on up."

"Gus is coming?"

"He should be here shortly. He says he has something important to share, but only in person, not over the phone."

"Should we uncork the champagne?"

"Not yet. I'll see you in a minute."

Anne had barely greeted Arnaud when the intercom buzzed again. "I looked out the window and saw Arnaud's car parked out front," Henri said. "Is it safe to come in?"

"Not you too. Yes, Arnaud's here, and yes, it's safe—as you put it. What do you think we do up here?"

"Well, let's see—"

"In case you don't know, that was a rhetorical question, which means no response required. Arnaud's here for the party."

"What party?"

"Gus is joining us. The elevator is free, so come on up and we'll explain."

"Why's Gus coming by?" Henri asked as he entered the living room.

"I only spoke with him for a moment. He says he has news."

"Should I call Veronique? Oh Lord, What if it's *bad* news? I hate to think—"

"Not yet. When I asked if I should be worried, he said no. Where's Oma in case we need her?"

"She's asleep. Renee says dinner's off."

"Postponed until Wednesday." Anne pointed to a chair opposite the couch. "Have a seat. While we're waiting for Gus, tell us your news."

Henri sat and said, "Joseph will remove the tiles in Renee's foyer Tuesday afternoon. If we accurately interpreted Jules' letter, there are only nine squares beneath the chandelier, so taking them up shouldn't be a problem."

"You'll call us in Geneva when you're finished?"

"Of course. Let's hope I have something champagne-worthy to report."

"I'll keep my fingers crossed. What else? Renee said you were out. Since you were alone, I assumed you weren't strolling through Square Barye."

"Not today, but ah. . . the hours Renee and I spent in that lovely spot. I know the Seine has seen all—"

"I get the picture—no need to elaborate. So where'd you go?"

"To see Micha Begin."

"Really?"

"Who's Micha Begin?" Arnaud asked.

"Five-year-old Micah, his three-year-old sister Sarah, and their parents, Levi and Miriam, crossed the Line of Demarcation with Renee, Veronique, Robert, and me."

"Did they accompany you to England?"

"No. We parted ways soon after the crossing. They were taken to Spain. I googled Micha and discovered he owns a successful business in the Marais. I sent an email, and he agreed to see me. He and his family remained in Spain until 1950 when they returned to Paris. The government returned their home and the family business. Micah took over after Levi died in the early sixties. Miriam passed a few years after her husband. Sarah majored in political science at the university. For years she was an attaché to the French embassy in Madrid. She recently retired."

"She never came back?"

"Not for an extended stay. She remained in Madrid to be near her children and grandchildren."

"I know the Begins sold several paintings to purchase exit papers," Anne said. "Have they recovered any of their other art?"

"Micha didn't have much to offer in that regard, but though he was only five, he remembers the arduous journey from Paris to the Line of Demarcation. A few years ago he found one of the stops on the Underground Railroad. If we have time, Renee and I will try to visit the children of the farmer who did so much for us."

"Do you think there's a need for me to make an appointment with Micha?" Anne asked.

"Not unless Veronique wants to see him, and I doubt she will. She was traumatized by Elisabeth's arrest. Except for the time when Sarah made too much noise and the guard gave her a stuffed animal to keep her quiet, I doubt your grandmother paid much attention to the Begins."

"Then why don't you tell Renee and not her—at least not now. She doesn't need to worry about finding time to meet with Micha Begin."

"I agree."

"So, Anne, tell us about *your* day," Arnaud said.

Anne had scarcely begun to talk when the buzzer sounded. "You'll have to hear about our appointment with Francoise later," she said. "That's Gus. Would you believe my hands are cold and clammy? I'm not sure if I'm anxious about what he *will* say or what he *won't* say." She pushed the intercom button. "Come on up, Gus."

When Arnaud opened the door, Gus entered, carrying a brown paper-wrapped package about forty-five by thirty-five inches. "What's that?" Anne asked tentatively.

"Take off the wrapping and take a look, but be careful."

Anne took the package and cautiously removed the paper. "It's *The Work Table*!" she gasped. "How in the world—"

"Damien Duplessis gave me the painting."

"I beg your pardon," Henri stammered. "Did you say—"

"You heard right. Damien has made it his life's work to return the paintings his father kept for his private collection. He did not know your grandmother was alive. When he googled Veronique Boulet—"

"He hit a dead end. He didn't realize Oma had married an American and stayed in New York."

"You're saying Damien Duplessis handed over the painting, just like that!" Henri said skeptically.

"Not exactly. I did not simply walk into his home and say, 'That particular painting belonged to Elisabeth Boulet.' When I told him my story, I mentioned the two pieces Madame Boulet sold to Didier, who, I guess, was as meticulous in his recordkeeping as the Nazis. Damien went to his desk and removed his grandfather's ledgers and journal. He looked carefully at the entries. There they were, four paintings Elisabeth and Anton sold to Didier, two for your escape, Henri—"

"And two to care for our brother."

"Your brother?"

"It's a long story, Gus. Finish telling us about your visit with Damien, and then we'll tell you what we've learned since we last met—that is if you have hours to spend."

"Unfortunately, I do not have time. I have an appointment with a buddy who worked with someone who worked with Rose Valland. Though second or third hand, he may have pertinent information about the art Denis did not hide."

"Back to the paintings Elisabeth sold," Anne said. "Did Damien say anything about the Corot?"

"You will not be able to recover *Madame Stumpf and Her Daughter.*"

"Because he doesn't know where it is?"

"Actually, he does, but because Madame Boulet sold the painting—"

"It wasn't stolen, so we can't make a claim."

"That is true, but you can see *Madame Stumpf* —perhaps you already have. It is hanging in your National Gallery."

"You're kidding," Anne said, incredulous. "I can't believe I walked by Great-Grand'Mere's painting and never stopped to give it a second look."

"Blinders?"

"No. I wasn't a Corot fan—at least until now."

Henri extended his hand to Gus and said, "Thanks to you, Veronique will have one piece of her heritage."

"Shall we take *The Work Table* up to Oma?" Anne asked. "She'll be ecstatic."

"You will have to go without me," Gus said.

"Absolutely not! You recovered the Bonnard. You're giving it to my grandmother. How about tomorrow morning? Oma asked me to invite you to brunch. She wants to thank you—"

"I would be pleased to join you."

"Good. Brunch is at eleven. Come here at ten forty-five. We'll go down together—and thanks, Gus."

"You are welcome. I hope I am as lucky tonight as I was with Damien."

⌒

"What an amazing day," Anne said when Gus and Henri left, and she and Arnaud were alone. She leaned her head against the pillows on the back of the couch. "Did you make a reservation for dinner?"

"I did. You don't want to go?"

"I'd rather pour a little wine, add foaming bath salts to the Jacuzzi tub, get in, and soak. Care to join me?"

Instead of answering, Arnaud began to unbutton his shirt. "You get the wine and I'll add the bubbles." He paused. "But if you tell *anyone* on the Île that Arnaud Lessard took a bubble bath—"

"Your secret's safe with me until—"

"No 'until.' I'm invoking the sanctity of the confessional."

"You must be concerned about your reputation. Cross my heart, but *you* pour the wine and *I'll* fill the tub. I wouldn't want bubbles pouring out all over the floor because you added too many scoops of bath salts. Can you imagine Oma's expression if she looked up and saw white froth raining down from the ceiling?"

"Or hear her comments. Okay, you add the foam. I don't want her rushing up here to interrupt what I have planned."

"You have plans?'

"Oh yeah! I'll be with you in five minutes."

"I'll be waiting." Anne began to unbutton her blouse, gave Arnaud a leering look, and went down the hall.

CHAPTER 31

The evening was amazingly romantic. Anne and Arnaud soaked in the Jacuzzi, sipped wine, and made love. They snacked on cheese and bread, drank more wine, slept, woke up, and made love again.

As the sun came through the open window, Anne awakened to the smell of coffee coming from the kitchen. She rolled over and looked at the clock. *So early,* she thought and pulled the pillow over her head.

Arnaud came into the room carrying a tray that held a coffee pot and one cup. "I assumed you prefer café au lait to the real thing," he said as he placed the cup on the nightstand.

"I do, but I don't want to get up. Last night was perfect." She reached out. "Come back to bed. Let's see if it's possible to improve on perfection."

"So I earned another adjective."

"Absolutely, and I finally know what everybody means about April in Paris. When I landed at Charles de Gaulle, Gus tried to convince me that April was the perfect time to be here. He quoted Henri Miller. Now I truly understand what Miller meant."

"And you're going to share?"

"If I must." She patted the bed. "But I'd rather tell you when you're back under the covers."

"I'm afraid that's not going to happen—at least not now."

"You're already tired of me?"

"That's it. I'm going to meet one of those other women we talked about, but not before you quote Miller."

"Okay, but—"

"Tell me!"

"All right. He wrote, 'When spring comes to Paris the humblest mortal alive must feel that he dwells in paradise.' That's how I feel right now."

Arnaud leaned over and kissed her on the cheek. "I'm glad I'm adding to your idea of paradise, but I have things to do. I'll meet you at your grandmother's apartment at eleven."

Anne sat up. "You're really leaving? What's going on? Surely you aren't working on Sunday morning."

"Using another phrase I learned when I lived in New York, 'There's no rest for the weary.' Stop frowning. I'll see you later."

Instead of drinking her coffee, Anne rolled over and went back to sleep. When she woke up two hours later, the coffee was cold. She put on her robe and slippers and went to the kitchen. "I'll take a microwave over an Imperial stove any day," she mumbled as she placed the cup on the carousel and pushed reheat. When the beeper sounded, she took the steaming brew to her bathroom and turned on the shower. She took several sips, put the cup on the counter, and thinking of the night she and Arnaud has spent making love in the Jacuzzi, stepped under the hot spray pouring from the ceiling.

⌒◦

At ten forty-five, Gus arrived. "The Bonnard's over there," Anne said, pointing to the couch.

"You rewrapped it."

"I did. I want Oma to have the pleasure of unwrapping it herself. I can't wait to see her face. She'll be thrilled."

"I hope so, because *The Work Table* is all I have for now. The friends I met for dinner last evening were not much help. They are still checking their sources, but I do not think we should count on them for additional information. The websites Madame Malet provided will likely be more beneficial as you search for the stolen art."

"I'm surprised the thought even crossed my mind, but it's *possible* I can convince Oma to stop looking for the pieces the Nazi's took from the house, especially if, as we expect, Elisabeth's finest paintings are hidden here on the Île."

"You believe they are?"

"There's a strong likelihood."

"That would be wonderful, but if what you presume is true, where have the paintings been all these years. And why has no one found them before now?"

"The clues Elisabeth left in her letter point to a hidden compartment in a closet in Elisabeth's childhood home on Quai de Bethune, though at this point we have no idea if the art is there or, if it is, in which of the many closets. As to why the paintings haven't been found, again, this is only a possibility, but we assume because the mansion was never converted to apartments—"

"The floor plans would not have been altered," Gus mulled aloud. "Was this information in the message Madame Boulet left for your grandmother?"

"It was. After brunch I'll share the poem Elisabeth wrote. Oma won't mind. She invited you to breakfast, so you're part of her in-crowd."

"So next you must obtain permission from the current owner to look through the closets for a hidden space."

"Yes, but it may not be that difficult. You'll soon know why. Shall we go down and surprise Oma? You bring the painting."

⌒◯

"Morning," Anne said when Veronique opened the door. "It smells great in here."

"Chef Pasquier is a genius." Veronique leaned toward Anne and whispered, "And I'm speaking from experience. While he isn't looking, I sneak tastes." She looked up and said, "I'm glad you could join us, Gus. Thank you for what you're doing to us help find Mother's paintings."

Henri glanced at the package in Gus's hands. I'm glad to see you too," he said.

"There's something going on," Renee said. "I know it. I see surprise written all over my dear husband's face. He was never one to hide his feelings."

Gus looked at Anne for approval.

"It's your show."

"What show?" Veronique asked. "What are you talking about? Am I missing something?"

"Come on," Henri urged. "Let's not stand here discussing whether it's time—"

"Time for what? Gus?"

Gus placed the package next to Veronique. "For you, Madame Ellison."

"It's Veronique. I told you I don't want to feel like an old woman."

"Veronique then. I hope this pleases you."

"I can't imagine. . ." Veronique pulled aside the brown wrapping and stared at the painting. "*The Work Table,*" she choked out. "Oh my! But how?"

"It's a long story, Oma. Gus will explain over brunch."

"For once in my life I don't know what to say." Veronique wiped a tear from her eye. "Gus, I doubt you could understand what this painting means to me. It was one of two pieces Mother sold to purchase our freedom."

"I know," Gus said. "I am glad you have it now."

"Where shall we hang *The Work Table*?" Anne asked.

"Over there." Veronique pointed to the fireplace. "Henri, would you please remove the painting that's hanging above the mantle."

"Sure." Henri crossed the room to the hearth. "The two paintings appear to be about the same size," he said as he took down the nineteenth century landscape and placed it on the floor. He took *The Work Table* that Gus was holding, carefully hung it on the protruding hook, and turned back. "I think Elisabeth's painting looks great," he said. "What do you think, Veronique?"

"Surely *The Work Table* was meant to hang just where it is." Veronique clasped her hands in glee. "I'm so happy. Gus, words can't express my thanks and my joy. I only wish my dear Robert could be here to see Mother's painting hanging in what was once her home."

"I'm sure both he and Great-Grand'Mere Elisabeth are looking down on all of us and smiling."

"I hope so, darling," Veronique said, pensive. "I truly hope so."

Veronique looked from the painting to the clock on the mantle below and then back at the gathered group. "Where's Arnaud?" she asked. "It's eleven-thirty. I want him to see the painting."

"He saw it last night," Anne said. "And I don't know where he is. When he left this morning—"

"When he left *this morning*," Veronique repeated, smiling at the flustered look on Anne's face. "I assume he knows brunch will be served at eleven."

"He does, and since he hasn't called to tell us otherwise, I'm sure he'll be here soon."

"Shall we have Mimosas while we wait?" Renee asked. "We can toast the return of *The Work Table*."

"An excellent idea," Veronique said. "But I don't understand why Arnaud's not here."

Ten minutes later the group was gathered in the living room sipping Mimosas when the buzzer sounded. Anne walked to the door and activated the intercom. "I was beginning to worry—"

"Everything's fine," Arnaud said. "I brought a friend along."

"Then come on up. I'm releasing the elevator. We're all eager to meet your new friend."

"Arnaud brought someone with him?" Veronique said. "Did you know, Anne?"

"Not really, but I may know who it is."

"Who?" Henri asked.

"I'll let Arnaud explain."

Minutes later they heard the elevator stop on the fourth floor. Anne took a deep breath and opened Veronique's front door. "Come in," she said. "You're both welcome."

Veronique rose and started for the door. When she saw the man to Arnaud's right, she stopped. For a moment she seemed confused, but suddenly she covered her face with her hands and began to sob.

"What is it," Henri asked. "Veronique?"

"He has Mother's eyes."

"What are you talking about?"

Arnaud closed the door and turned to the stunned group. "May I present Martin Anton Fontaine? Henri and Veronique—your brother."

"Anton is my father's name," Henri said, clearly flustered.

"And don't forget, it's also your middle name," said Renee.

"Of course." Henri walked to the door and enveloped Martin in a bear-hug. "Until yesterday Veronique and I didn't know about you, my brother."

"I only recently learned I have a brother and a sister," Martin said, escaping Henri's lengthy embrace.

"Come sit with me." Veronique said, motioning toward the sofa. "Will you have a Mimosa?"

"Yes, thank you, "Martin said. "It appears we have reason to celebrate."

Before going to the kitchen, Renee crossed the room to where Martin was standing. "I'm your sister-in-law, Renee," she said. "And this is Anne French, your grandniece. You already know Arnaud, and this is our good friend, Gus Ruel."

"Saying it is great to meet all of you would be an understatement," Martin said.

"You mentioned you only recently discovered you had a brother and sister," Veronique continued as she and Martin sat on the couch.

"Perhaps 'recently' isn't the appropriate word, though in terms of my advancing age, I would say three years qualifies as being recent."

"I agree," Veronique said, smiling. "How did you learn about us?"

"It is a long story. I will present the short version and elaborate another time. My wife Christine died a little over three years ago—"

"The same time you discovered you had a family?" Henri said.

"Yes. Because of my dear wife's death, I found out about you and Veronique."

"I don't understand," Veronique said.

"If the two of you would stop asking questions, I'm sure Martin will explain," Renee scolded.

"Of course," Henri responded sheepishly. "Martin—"

"Christine and I spent all of our married life on our farm in Brittany. We came to Paris from time to time, but we both preferred country life.

As you might imagine, remaining on the farm after her death was difficult. Everywhere I looked, there she was. When I was unable to get beyond my initial grief, my son Eric urged me to spend more time on the Île."

"I understand how it feels to lose a beloved spouse," Veronique said. "I felt the same way when I lost my dear Robert ten years ago."

"I am sure you did. A few months before Christine died, our grandson married a lovely woman. At the time, he and his new bride were renting an apartment in the town of Quimper. I knew how Eric Anton loved the farm—"

"Your grandson's middle name is Anton," Henri interrupted.

"It is. He was named after his father and given my middle name, though at the time I didn't know I was named after my real father. As I was saying, I believed Christine would have wanted Eric Anton and Emme to have the farm, so I gave it to them as a belated wedding gift from his grandmother and me."

"How lovely," Veronique said. "I'm sure Christine would be pleased."

"I believe so. When I was packing to move back to Quai de Bethune, I discovered two letters among the legal papers my father—or should I say my adoptive father—Charles Fontaine left for me. They were in Mother's diary. He had put the box aside with her things when she died. When he passed, I went through the legal documents, but I left her personal letters and the diary for another day."

"That sounds familiar," said Renee. "Last week I came upon letter Papa placed in the family Bible he put in my satchel before Henri, Veronique, and I escaped Paris."

"And we just found the messages Elisabeth and Anton left for us," Veronique said. "Letters explaining that you were living with a family somewhere near Uncle George."

"That is what Arnaud said. There are so many coincidences. I loved Uncle George. He was always coming around."

"And reporting back to Mother and Anton."

"When you found the letters, did you look for us?" Henri asked. "Maybe you thought we weren't interested in finding you."

"I never thought that, and, yes, I did look for you. No one I spoke with on the Île knew where you were. Many old-timers remembered that your—I mean *our*—mother lived at number forty-five Quai de Bourbon, Veronique, but most of them thought both you and she were taken by the Nazis during la rafle du Vel d'Hiv. Of course they had no idea why I was inquiring."

"No one questioned your motive?" Veronique asked.

"A few did, but I kept my reason to myself. A few weeks ago I saw a transaction note in the newspaper. Veronique Ellison, an American from New York, had purchased two apartments at number forty-five. I knew my sister was alive and coming home. I usually take two walks a day—one in the morning and another after dinner. Each time I set off, I made it a point to walk by the house There were workmen there during the day, but the place was dark in the evening. I assumed you had yet to move in—if, in fact, that was your intent. This morning Arnaud came to my door."

"Bertrand Lessard told Arnaud and Anne that you and he have had dinner together several times in recent years," Veronique said. "Did you ask about Henri or me?"

"When Bertrand and I dined together, I was not ready to share the story of my adoption or that I had recently learned I have a brother and sister with a neighbor I hardly knew. Looking back, I realize, had I asked, he would have told me about you and Henri and how to find you. These precious years would not have been wasted."

"Maybe not," said Veronique. "But as Henri often says, we should look to the future, not dwell on the past."

"True, but we must remain in the past for a while longer." Martin reached into his pocket and held up two envelopes. "I brought two letters. Mother wrote the first in April 1932, shortly after my birth, and the other just weeks before the Nazis took her away."

"Will you read them to us?" Veronique asked.

"Please wait," said Renee. "I'll tell Andre to put the brunch in the warming drawer. He can leave. I'll serve when we're ready to eat."

"Thank you, Renee." Veronique turned to Martin. "Unless you want to eat before we talk."

"Whatever you prefer."

"I'd like to hear the letters," Anne said.

"So would I," said Henri.

"In that case, would you please bring the champagne and the orange juice back with you, dear friend? Now we have more reason to drink a toast."

Five minutes later Renee returned with the champagne and a pitcher of orange juice and refilled everyone's glass.

"I think we're ready," Veronique said. "Would you please share Mother's letter, Martin?"

"Of course." Martin began to read.

April 2, 1932

My Precious Child,

Welcome to the world. Had things been different, you would have been born in joy, spending your youth with your dear sister on Île St-Louis. Always know you are a child of love. The flesh is weak. I fell in love with a married man. Whatever you think as you read this letter, always know your father, Anton Marsolet, is an honorable man. He is my best friend. My lover. My protector. My all.

Because I must, I have placed you with two lifelong friends, Charles and Marcelle Fontaine. I wish I could watch you grow, but a baby born out of wedlock—even if that child was is deeply cherished— is scorned. I cannot have that for you. Nor can I embarrass your sister. She knows nothing about Anton and me. We have been discreet.

Charles and Marcelle have accepted my offer of a home in the country. I purchased the farm where they will care for you. It will someday be yours, as will my childhood home on Quai de Bethune. My attorneys are drawing up papers that will be delivered to your new family. I grew up in this idyllic place. I pray one day you will raise your family on Île St-Louis.

I yearn to hold you in my arms, but I know this cannot be. I lack the strength. Your mother is a coward. How could I see your smile and hold your tiny hand

and then leave you behind? How could I be with you and not say, "I am the mother who loves you with all her heart and soul?"

My dear friend, a man you know as Uncle George, will tell me about you. How tall you are. What you like to do. If you are happy. God willing, some-day in the future—though only He knows when— we, along with Henri Marsolet, your brother, and Veronique Boulet, your sister, will find a way to be together—to be a family. That is my most fervent wish.

I have vowed not to reveal my secret until Charles and Marcelle feel the time is right. It would be unfair to ask them to love and raise you as their own, and then take you from them because I am ready to make you a part of my life. I gave this letter to Marcelle, who promises to leave it for you among her personal papers. Your father and I believe you deserve to know about your family. Never feel shame, my son. You are a treasured result of a great love.

Your loving mother, Elisabeth Boulet

When Martin finished reading, Veronique was crying. "I don't want to upset you," he said. "Should I read the second letter?"

"Definitely," Veronique said. "I want to hear."

"You realize Elisabeth just answered another of our questions," Anne said.

"Which one?" Henri asked. "We have so many."

"We couldn't figure out why she steadfastly refused to move to Brittany to live with Uncle George."

"Mother's letter explained why," Veronique said. "She wouldn't go and leave Anton behind."

"True, but now we know she made a promise to the Fontaines. She put Martin in their care and would not take him from them."

"When I learned I was adopted, I wondered why my real parents never tried to find me," Martin said. "By the time I read Mother's letter, I had raised Eric. He was married and he had a son of his own. Loving both Eric and Eric Anton as I do, I could not imagine giving either one of them into the care of others. At first I was angry, feeling Mother had abandoned me, but when I thought about the sacrifice she made to ensure my safety—how she must have suffered—"

"Anton, too," Henri said.

"Of course. I meant both Mother and Father."

"What did Mother say in the second letter?" Veronique asked.

"The letter is dated ten years later, on April 1, 1942. It begins,

My Dear Martin,

Thanks to Uncle George, I know you are a strong, loving boy. You are a living testament to a love that will ever endure, though I may soon depart this world.

I fear the end is near. How glad I am that you are far away. God keep you safe, my son. As I write this letter, the Nazis are commencing a campaign to rid the city of Jews. I am a Jew. For that reason, though your father has repeatedly asked me to be his wife, I cannot accept. In this hate-filled world, I must think of him.

I hope to live, but I am preparing to die. There is so much I want to say. Would that I had the strength to travel to Brittany to see you—if only from afar. I do not know what the future will bring. My greatest wish would be to watch you and your brother and sister meet—to be privy to the decisions the three of you make in the years ahead. That, I know cannot be. I am not afraid to die, but I wish I could live, if only to be a part of your lives.

Your father fights bravely for the Resistance. Henri begs to join, but Anton and I agree—he must live. As the oldest child, it is his duty to care for you and Veronique. I pray they will return and find you when Paris is finally liberated, If my prayers are not answered and my beloved Anton is killed in the fight to defeat the Nazis, speak with Denis Gaudrieu—number thirty Quai de Bourbon, or Auguste Lessard at number twenty-seven. If both men are gone, I have left a message behind the bricks over the mantle in my bedroom. Remove them and you will know everything.

Martin stopped reading. "Did it?"

"We believe so," said Veronique.

"Where are they?"

"In your home on Quai de Bethune."

Martin shook his head. "I assure you, Veronique. There are no valuable works of art hidden in my house."

"We believe Denis, perhaps with Anton's help, created a space in the back of one of your closets. Would you let us look?"

"Of course, but the mansion has five storeys and many closets. Did Mother provide a clue to help locate the closet she was referencing?"

"No, but Anne and I are seeing Giles Guidreau tomorrow morning. Perhaps Denis, fearing he, too, might not survive the Occupation, left a clue that will help us narrow the parameters of our search."

"I am leaving for the country early in the morning. Emme is petite, so the doctors have decided to deliver the baby by Caesarian. I would like to be there when my great grandson is born, but if you think it necessary, I will cancel my trip."

"Of course you should be there," Veronique said. "We've waited seventy years to find the paintings; a few more days won't matter."

"How long will you be gone," Henri asked.

"I plan to return late Wednesday morning. Shall we begin our search Wednesday afternoon?"

"Perfect," Anne said. "Arnaud and I leave for Geneva early Tuesday."

"If you plan to visit Lombard Odier Darier Hentsch & Cie, I will be glad to give you the name of my account manager."

"We appreciate it," said Veronique. "You suddenly stopped reading your letter to ask if Mother's poem provided clues to locating the paintings. Is there more we should hear?"

"Only a brief paragraph in which she professes her love for me and for you."

"I'm sure it was hard for her to give you up—"

"Undoubtedly," Martin said. "She loved and sacrificed for both of us. Her love somehow gave her the strength to place me with the Fontaines—"

"And to send me to see Renee the afternoon of July 17. She knew she would never see me again."

"I don't understand—"

"It's a long story that will wait for another time." Veronique stood. "Shall we eat? I don't know about the rest of you, but suddenly I'm very hungry."

CHAPTER 32

The pleasant and enlightening conversation continued throughout brunch and into the afternoon while they had coffee in the living room. Veronique and Henri shared Elisabeth's poems and Anton's letter with Martin. He, in turn, talked about his life in the country, his amazing adoptive parents, his son and grandchildren, and Uncle George. They were finishing their coffee when Arnaud's phone rang. "Will you excuse me for a minute," he said.

"If you'd like privacy, use my study," Veronique offered.

"Is everything okay?" Anne asked, seeing the puzzled look on Arnaud's face when he returned several minutes later.

"I guess, though when it comes to my sister, one never knows. She invited, or perhaps I should say ordered you and me to come to dinner. Her words were, 'You're coming. No excuses.'"

"You have a sister?" Veronique asked.

"I do. Sophie's my twin."

"Really? Do twins run in your family?"

Anne shot her grandmother a don't-go-there look. "I'd love to go," she said. "That is unless Oma needs me."

"Go enjoy yourself," said Veronique. "I'm not some old woman you have to babysit."

"Then it's settled."

"Anne, what time do you and Arnaud return to Paris on Wednesday?" Martin asked.

"If everything goes as planned and the plane's on time, a little after one."

"My train arrives at eleven-forty. Shall we all meet at my place at three?"

"Perfect! If there's a problem, we'll text you Wednesday morning."

"Would you like a ride to the airport?" Gus asked.

"No thanks," Arnaud answered. "Our plans aren't firm, so I'll drive and leave the car."

"Gus, you've been unusually quiet," Anne said. "So quiet I almost forgot you're here."

"I have been listening to your stories with great interest. I am happy for all of you."

"That makes it unanimous." Veronique turned to Martin. "I'm so glad we found you, brother. Our meeting has taught me a lesson I wish I'd learned decades ago. For whatever time I have left, I intend to live every minute to the fullest."

"I agree, Veronique." Martin stood, kissed his sister on the cheek, and shook hands with Henri. "I will see you all on Wednesday."

"Please give Emme our best," Anne said. "Text us when the baby comes."

Veronique walked to the entry table, removed a notepad from the drawer, wrote her cell number and email address, and handed the paper to Martin."

"Thank you," Martin said. "I will attach a picture of Martin Eric Anton Fontaine to my text."

"Another Anton," Henri said. "Our father would be so proud."

"Of all of you," said Anne. "This meeting took place later than he or Elisabeth expected, but it happened. That's what's important."

"No more sentimental talk," Veronique said. "Safe travel, Martin, and in the event I forget to ask, will you join us for dinner at Taillevent Wednesday evening? We already have a great deal to celebrate. We found you, and, thanks to Gus, I have one of Mother's paintings. Who knows? After we search your home, we may have even more reason to rejoice."

"I would like to join you," Martin said. He turned to Anne. "If you have a problem at the bank, text or call. I will see what I can do. I am a very good client." He removed three business cards from his wallet, handed one to Anne, one to Henri, and the third to Veronique. "If you need me, you now have my contact information."

"I should be leaving too," Gus said.

"Will you join us Wednesday evening?" Veronique asked.

"If you do not feel I am intruding."

"Don't be ridiculous. I'm forever indebted to you, as I am to Arnaud."

"In that case, it is my pleasure. Will you need the car tomorrow?"

"I'll drive the ladies to the meeting with Giles," Arnaud said.

"Then unless you need me before then, I will see you Wednesday evening."

"We'll have to take two cars to the restaurant," Anne said. "As soon as I know, I'll text you with the particulars." She rummaged through her purse and handed Gus a keycard. "If we're late getting back from Martins', you can park in the garage and wait in my apartment. Over the past few days, I've seen the maniacs racing around on the Île. I don't want you to risk your life circling the quais until you find a place to park."

"Maniacs? I don't understand."

"Maniacs, Oma. Remember why you hired Gus?"

"Because his resume said he'd published books about the Occupation."

"That and because you thought he could keep me safe from, and I quote, 'the homicidal maniacs who drive around Paris.'"

Veronique grinned. "I did say that, didn't I? Well, whatever my reason at the time, I made a wise selection."

As Gus walked toward the door, Veronique approached the fireplace and looked up at the Bonnard. "I never believed I would live to see one of mother's paintings hanging in her home," she said. "Somehow a simple thank you isn't adequate—"

"It is enough," said Gus. "I am glad you have at least one of Madame Boulet's paintings."

"Perhaps we'll find several more at Martin's."

"I hope you do."

"Do you really think Mother's paintings are hidden somewhere in Martin's home?" Veronique asked as the elevator carrying Gus headed down.

"If we interpreted her poem correctly—and I think we did—I believe they are."

Arnaud looked at his watch. "We should go," he said. "Sophie expects us at five-thirty."

"Dinner so early?" Veronique asked.

"Probably a lot of talk before we eat. My sister's anything but shy and reserved. In many ways Sophie reminds me of you, Veronique. You're both get-it-done fireballs, and that's a compliment."

"I'll take it as one."

"You're sure you don't need me, Oma?" Anne asked as Veronique walked her and Arnaud to the door.

"No, darling. I'm tired, but it's a happy tired. I'm going to relax, and when I get my second wind, research websites that deal with stolen art that's been returned to the rightful owners."

"Why not forget the art the Nazis took from the house—at least for now. If there *are* paintings in Martin's closet, you may not want to initiate what would undoubtedly be a long search."

"We'll see, but there are a few things I want to know. We have the Bonnard, and we know *Madame Stumph* is on display at the National Gallery. I would like to locate the Degas and the Fantin-Latour."

"You do realize Elisabeth *sold* those paintings to Didier—"

"And I can't claim them, but I may be able to see them."

"True, and along with your investigation, you have countless decisions to make Will you hang three, four, or who knows how many other valuable paintings here in the apartment? We're talking about millions of dollars' worth of art. The insurance costs alone will be prohibitive. I know we have an incredible security system, but—"

"I haven't gotten that far, Anne. Yesterday morning I had little hope of ever seeing Mother's paintings again. Now. . . Perhaps I'll gift them in her memory—"

"To the Met? What about the Musée d'Orsay? Paris was Elisabeth's home."

"I'll consider both—that is *if* we find the paintings—."

"*When* we find them."

"Okay, *when* we do."

"You'll have plenty of time to decide. Personally, I can't wait for Wednesday."

"Time will pass so slowly while we wait for Martin to return."

"It will speed by because you'll be busy." Anne turned to Arnaud. "What time are you picking us up in the morning?"

"How about eight-forty-five?"

"I'm glad you plan to drive," Veronique said. "I don't think these old legs would take me all the way to Quai de Bethune."

"I don't like walking the cobblestones either," said Anne. "I'll come down for you at eight-thirty. We'll meet Arnaud downstairs so he doesn't have to park."

"I'll be ready. You two have a lovely time this evening. Arnaud, bring Sophie and her husband to meet me very soon."

Anne held her breath waiting for her grandmother to finish the sentence with a suggestion they'd soon be family. Veronique stopped short of commenting, but she gave Anne a knowing smile.

"Thanks for allowing me to be a part of a great day," Arnaud said, bending down and kissing Veronique on both cheeks.

"Thank you for doing your part to make it so," said Veronique. "I'm certain there will be many more good days in our future."

"Bye, Oma," Anne said. "It's definitely time for us to leave."

⌒◯

"Is everything all right with Sophie?" Anne asked as she and Arnaud took the elevator to the fifth floor.

"I assume so, but our conversation was rather cryptic. There was no 'please come to dinner.' Rather it was, 'Be here at five-thirty, and bring Anne.'"

"I wonder what she wants."

"We'll soon know."

"You're right. Call when you're on your way, and I'll meet you downstairs."

Anne washed her face, applied fresh makeup, and fixed her hair in a French braid. She put on gray slacks, black heels, and a red, gray, and black silk blouse. She had just switched purses when Arnaud called. "I'm on the way." he said. "Are you bringing a scarf? I brought the convertible, and we'll be moving faster than we do on the Île."

"I won't need one. I pulled my hair back. I hope Sophie doesn't have a house full of people. I look like a teenager."

"I'm sure you're gorgeous."

"Yea, right! I'm walking out the door. See you in a few minutes."

Arnaud drove up just as Anne exited the lobby door. "Good timing," she said as she slid into the passenger seat.

"And I was right. You look beautiful."

"And you are very handsome, Monsieur Lessard. Where does Sophie live?"

"In the Sixteenth Arrondissement in what was once the fifth and sixth floors of a stone building constructed in the early 1930s. If I weren't an aficionado of the Île, I could be very happy living in her neighborhood."

"It's that special?"

"For me, yes. I'm a student of architecture, and, architecturally, the sixteenth is one of the most interesting parts of the city. The northern part of the district has broad avenues that converge at Place de l'Étoile and Avenue Foch. The Bois de Boulogne takes up a good part of the western half of the arrondissement. The rest encompasses two former villages, Passy and Auteuil. Sophie and Lionel live in Auteuil near the Castel Beranger."

"How long will it take to get there?"

"Door to door the apartment is sixteen kilometers from mine. If the traffic's not too bad, about twenty-minutes."

"Then she's really not *that* far from the Île."

"In terms of kilometers, no. But she thinks she's worlds away, at least she did when she first moved. I initially thought she'd have a terrible time leaving Île St-Louis. Fortunately, the adjustment wasn't too difficult. I'm sure she'd move back if she could, but so far she hasn't found a place to her liking or one she and Lionel can afford. When I put the fourth floor apartment on the market, she and Lionel planned to make their home California. If I'd only known. . .But enough talk. Enjoy the scenery while I serve as your personal tour guide. In several places along the way, you may think you're back in New York. We just crossed Pont Marie. We'll soon drive through Place de la Concorde, famous, as you know, for the Egyptian obelisk."

"I do, and so did Oma. In her journal, she wrote about meeting a friend at the obelisk. She had ridden her bike to the continent, though I don't recall why. I remember the entry because she mentioned the unusual number of bicycles on the streets. Paradoxically, she was glad there was less traffic to impede the riders, but realizing why there were so few cars, she was sad. Does that make sense?"

"It does. Grandpapa also rode his bike around the city. He said the same thing."

"There aren't many bikes out there now, and there's definitely a lot of traffic. At first I thought that was what you meant when you said I'd feel at home during the drive. Now I understand. You were referring to street names. We're on Avenue de New-York."

"Which will soon become Avenue du President Kennedy."

"Without the 'de' and the 'du,' I *could* be back home."

"I love this part of Paris," Anne said as they entered the sixteenth. "The area's busy and bustling, but it still has a certain feel. What I mean is, if I close my eyes, I can almost picture Auteuil the way it was when Monet and Degas painted here."

"Sophie's neighborhood reminds me of the Paris of old. I suppose that's another reason I find it so charming."

"Five minutes later Arnaud parked in front of a six-storey stone apartment building on a tree-lined street. At the entrance to the lobby, he pushed the button by the intercom to the right of the door. "You're here," Sophie quickly responded.

"Since we're talking, I think that's a reasonable assumption," Arnaud rejoined. "So do we keep standing out here, or are you going to buzz us up?"

"Anne's welcome, but I'm not sure you are. I'm releasing the elevator now."

Sophie was standing at the open door when the elevator reached the fifth floor. What a great space," Anne said as they entered a large light-filled room.

"The apartment's nice, but Sophie prefers modern—"

"My brother means I don't go for old fashioned—or maybe just old. Come on. I'll give you the grand tour of the downstairs. Lionel's still upstairs dressing. He's rarely on time."

"He's always on time," Arnaud argued. "You're perpetually early—so much so that you usually have to drive around the block so your hosts can finish their final preparations."

"I'm not that bad."

"Oh but you are, my darling sister."

Sophie led Anne through the dining room into a large, rustic-style kitchen. They took a look at Sophie's sitting room and Lionel's office, as well as a guest room with a private bath and a powder room on the first floor. "We have three bedrooms upstairs, but Lionel's still up there, so—"

"Lionel's right here." A tall, handsome, dark-haired man descended the stairs. "I'm sure my wife said I'm never on time, but if you'll all look at the clock on the mantle—especially you, Sophie—you'll note that Arnaud and Anne are early."

Arnaud walked over and enveloped his brother-in-law in a bear hug. "Good to see you, my friend," he said. "Clearly my sister is still driving you crazy."

"As ever. And you're Anne French," he said, smiling. "My wife has been singing your praises non-stop ever since she got home the other night."

"And you're, Lionel."

"Well now that we all know who we are, come sit down," Sophie said. "Wine, Anne, or perhaps something stronger?"

"Wine would be great, but let me help."

"No need. I've made a few hors d'oeuvres, but not too many. I cooked, which, if you're wondering, is rare. I usually have my parties catered."

"Is someone else coming?" Arnaud asked.

"It's just us. I'll be right back."

Minutes later Sophie returned with a tray of cheese and crackers and wine for Arnaud, Anne, and Lionel. "You aren't joining us?" Arnaud asked. "Are you sick? You could always drink me under the table."

"That was in the past. My doctor tells me wine isn't good for a pregnant woman."

For a moment Arnaud didn't respond. "You're pregnant," Anne said. "Congratulations to both of you."

"You're pregnant," Arnaud finally said. "That's why the command performance."

"You're a little behind in the conversation, dear brother. The word's been used twice in the past fifteen seconds. And yes, I'm pregnant. I wanted you to know before we tell our friends. I'm a little more than three months along."

"Then you knew when you were with us the other night?"

"I did, but I didn't want to say anything until after my doctor's appointment yesterday. You didn't notice? I wasn't drinking. I took a glass of wine but never touched it. Oh, now I remember—you only had eyes for Anne."

"I'm so happy for you," Anne said, letting Sophie's comment pass. "And everything's fine with you and the baby?"

"More than fine. The only thing we don't know for sure is whether we're having two boys, two girls, or a boy and a girl."

"Twins?"

"Two for the price of one."

"That's fantastic! I'll be the best uncle two kids could ever have."

"I'm sure! Lionel and I are looking for an apartment on the Île. Why don't you move in with Anne and give us your place?"

"I recommend you keep looking," Anne said. "I've known your brother for a week."

"We'll see." Sophie continued. "And Arnaud, so you know, I'm ready to move as soon as your things are out, or you can leave everything there. I don't mind your outdated décor."

When Anne looked at the clock, it was already ten. Though Lionel rarely got a word in edgewise, he didn't seem upset—in all probability, Anne decided, because he was used to being second-fiddle to his wife. During the delightful meal, they discussed art, Anne's semester in Paris, Sophie's college days at Stanford, how she and Lionel met, Martin, Arnaud and Anne's upcoming trip to Geneva—even Arnaud's marriage to Aimee.

"Coffee in the living room?" Sophie asked when they'd finished dessert and there was a break in the conversation.

"Unfortunately, I have to work," Arnaud said.

"So now that's what they call whatever it is you intend to do."

"Realizing I don't have to explain my actions to my sister, I will anyway. I was scheduled to meet with a client Tuesday afternoon. Anne and I will be in Geneva, so I had to cancel. That, however, doesn't mean I can postpone the business at hand. I need to transmit timely information and receive instructions about how to proceed."

"Okay, I get it, but so you know, life is too short to waste it working."

Lionel shook his head. "My lovely and sometimes not so brilliant wife thinks money to buy an apartment on Île St-Louis will fall off the chestnut trees into our laps."

"Won't it?" Sophie teased. "You see, I've learned something new this evening. What time's your flight?"

"Eight," Anne said.

"Eight in the *morning*? I didn't know anyone was up at that ungodly hour."

"In point of fact, some of us who live in the *real* world get up earlier than that," Arnaud said.

"Really! You'll have to tell me about those people someday."

"She thinks I go to work at noon," Lionel said. "I'm gone every morning by eight."

"No!" Sophie declared. "I had no idea."

"You'll soon be getting up early, Arnaud said. "That is if you get any sleep during the night with two crying babies to keep you awake."

"I can't wait."

"How long will you be in Geneva?" Lionel asked.

"We're due back around one on Wednesday," Anne said. "Wednesday evening my grandmother is hosting a celebratory dinner at Taillevent for family and close friends. Will you and Sophie join us? I know she'd be delighted."

"We would *love* to have dinner with family," Sophie said.

"Good. I'll call with the time," Anne said, ignoring Sophie's comment and Arnaud's grin. "Congratulations again. If I'd known about the babies, I'd have knitted booties."

"You knit?" Arnaud said.

"Let me qualify my last statement. I should have said I would have *purchased* knitted booties."

"Bring them next time. I never turn down gifts, do I Lionel?"

"You wouldn't believe the presents I've given my wife—gifts I didn't buy."

"Who knows better what I want?"

"Night, Sophie." Arnaud kissed his sister and shook Lionel's hand.

"What a great evening," Anne said. "We'll see you Wednesday."

"Good luck in Geneva and at Martin's. What a story. It would make a great novel."

"Who knows," Anne said thoughtfully. "Perhaps someday I'll write a book."

CHAPTER 33

"You're right on time," Veronique said, as Renee ushered Anne into the living room. "And you look happy. Did you and Arnaud have a good night?"

"I don't know if Arnaud did, but I slept well. Sorry to disappoint you, Oma, but he dropped me off about eleven."

"And you think I'm disappointed."

"Aren't you? Are you ready to go?"

"I will be as soon as I get my pocketbook." Suddenly all business, Veronique said, "Thirty minutes ago Henri and I faxed our notarized papers giving you access to the safe-deposit box and the two accounts."

"I didn't know notaries made house calls."

"I'm sure most don't. Madame Labbe came by on her way to work. I'll follow through with a phone call to Julien Odiet, my account manager. While we're out, Henri will overnight the hard copies of the documents to the bank."

"Apparently you've thought of everything."

"I hope so. Shall we go? I imagine Arnaud's waiting."

"How was dinner at your sister's?" Veronique asked as Arnaud pulled away from the house. "I believe you said Sophie's invitation was a command performance."

"It definitely was. Long ago I learned, when my sister says jump—"

"You say how high?" Veronique chuckled. "I've always felt that's the way it should be between a man and a woman."

"I'm sure we could argue that point for days and never agree."

"True, so tell me Sophie's reason for issuing an order."

"She wanted us to be the first to know she's pregnant with twins."

"So I guess twins *do* run in your family. You had no idea?"

"None whatsoever. She and Lionel have been trying—until now, with no success."

"Please congratulate both of them for me."

"You can do it yourself," Anne said. "I invited Sophie and Lionel to join us at Taillevent."

"An excellent idea," said Veronique. "And since we're sharing news, I have something to tell you, though it isn't as exciting as your announcement, Arnaud. Last night I told you I planned to research the paintings Mother sold—the ones for Martin—"

"I didn't think you'd go straight to the computer." Anne paused and then said, "Okay, as you often say, procrastination isn't a word in your dictionary. You evidently discovered something significant?"

"I did. The Fantin-Latour is in the Bührle collection in Zurich. I would like to see it as soon as possible."

"What about the Degas?"

"I googled Degas and recognized the painting that hung in Mother's bedroom. It's entitled *Dance Class at the Opera* and it's hanging—"

"In the Musée d'Orsay."

"You've seen it?"

"Many times. In fact I walked by it last Tuesday morning. We'll go see the Degas before I leave for New York. If we don't have time, I'm sure Arnaud or Gus will drive."

"You've already made reservations to fly home?" Arnaud asked.

"Not yet, but I will in the next day or so. First I want to see what we find at Martin's."

"But—"

"It doesn't appear there's a place to park," Veronique interrupted, ending the conversation.

"You're right," Arnaud said. "I'll leave you two out front, park in my garage, and walk back."

"Are you okay, Oma?" Anne asked as they waited for Arnaud to join them on the sidewalk. "If you prefer, we can wait inside."

"Contrary to what you may think, Anne, I am not a feeble old lady. Though my body may be weaker than it once was, my mind is sharp, and my powers of observation are excellent. Arnaud Lessard is in love with you. I saw how disappointed he was when you said you're going back to New York. That's why I changed the subject. Has he asked you to stay in Paris?"

"No, but it wouldn't do any good if he did."

"You're sure?"

"Positive."

Just as Anne emphatically uttered the word 'positive,' Arnaud came into hearing distance.

"Positive about what?" he asked.

"Positive Giles will have information to help locate Elisabeth's paintings," Anne quickly answered.

"Then why waste time?" He held out his arm and Veronique took hold. "Shall we see what Monsieur Guidreau has to say?"

They had barely knocked when Giles opened the door. "It has been so long." He reached out and kissed Veronique on both cheeks.

"I would say so," Veronique said. "I noticed you failed to say I haven't changed a bit."

"Nor did you say the same to me. It is good to see you, Veronique. Until I heard from Arnaud, I assumed the Nazis arrested you when they took your mother."

"Earlier in the day I went to visit a friend in Saint-Germain, but had I been there—"

Noting her grandmother's trembling hands," Anne said, "Bonjour, Monsieur Gaudrieu. I'm Veronique's granddaughter Anne."

"Bonjour, Anne, but such formality is unnecessary among friends. Please call me Giles." He extended his gnarled hand in Arnaud's direction. "Bonjour, Arnaud. Seeing you all grown up suddenly makes me feel quite old."

"Forgive me for using an absurd American phrase, but 'welcome to the club,'" Veronique said, as Arnaud and Giles shook hands.

"If that means you feel the same way, then we are truly kindred spirits," said Giles. "Shall we all go in and make ourselves comfortable?"

Giles led the group to the sitting room and gestured toward a settee. "Ladies, please make yourselves comfortable." He turned to Arnaud and then pointed to one of the chairs opposite Anne and Veronique. "Please sit," he said.

As Arnaud and Giles settled in their chairs, Veronique folded her hands in her lap. "Forgive me, Giles," she said. "Realizing it would be polite to begin with niceties, I would rather not."

"Because you have more important things on your mind."

"I do, so I'll get right to the point. There will be time for reminiscing later."

"I understand." Giles leaned forward, giving Veronique his complete attention. "And now," he said. "What would you like to know?"

"You said you weren't sure whether or not I escaped Paris. Did you think to search for Henri after the Liberation? He and Renee returned to Paris numerous times over the years. He could have told you how to find me."

"No, Veronique. I did not try to find Henri. Although my father was friendly with Anton. I barely knew Henri, so I had no reason to seek him out. Frankly, I had other things on my mind. At first, the peace was as confusing as the years during the Occupation. Years later when Paris and Europe returned to normal, all I wanted was to forget that horrible time and get on with my life."

"That's understandable, but what about searching for me—Elisabeth's daughter?"

"We all knew what happened to the Jews who were seized during la rafle du Vel d'Hiv. As I said earlier, when you failed to return after the Liberation, I assumed you were dead. I saw no reason to initiate a search."

"I guess that makes sense."

"I assure you, Veronique, had I known—"

"I know, Giles. I apologize. I didn't mean to suggest—"

"There is no need to apologize. I am not easily offended. What else is on your mind?"

"Do you have any idea where your father hid Mother's paintings?"

"Sadly, no. Even after Madame Boulet was arrested, respecting her wishes, my father would not disclose the hiding place."

"Do you know where the paintings were initially taken?"

"I do. They were brought to our home. As far as I know, only my father, Auguste, Anton, and, perhaps Jules, knew where they ended up. I would tell you if I knew. Back then, being secretive was for everyone's protection. If we did not know—"

"You couldn't be forced to tell the Nazis. I believe that's why Mother kept so much from me."

"In Nazi-occupied Paris, everyone kept secrets."

"And speaking of secrets, did you know Elisabeth and Anton were involved?" Anne asked.

"Involved?" Giles said. "I don't understand—"

"They had a son—"

"Really? I never knew." He hesitated and then said. "But thinking back, one afternoon I stood guard outside Madame Huard's house when Papa and Anton removed two of Madame Boulet's paintings—"

"I apologize for interrupting," Anne said, "But if I don't ask now, I may forget later. Do you have any idea why your father left the paintings at Madame Huard's? You said his usual practice was to bring them to your house before moving them to their hiding place."

"None whatsoever. I never asked, though I assume he had his reasons."

"I'm sure he did. You were saying?"

"As we left Madame Huard's house, paintings in hand, I heard Anton say, 'These should take care of the boy for life.' I assumed he meant Henri. After Madame Boulet was arrested, Anton was like a man possessed. He had to get you, Henri, and Renee out of Paris."

"He wanted us out of harm's way so we could return and find our brother, Martin Fontaine."

"Martin Fontaine is your brother?" Giles said, stunned.

"He is. You and my brother have been next-door neighbors for years."

Before Giles could comment further, a woman entered the room, interrupting the conversation. "Breakfast is served, sir," she announced.

Giles stood, took Veronique's arm, and helped her off the couch. "Perhaps you will tell me the entire story while we eat," he said as they walked toward the dining room.

During the meal, Giles described his role in the removal of Elisabeth's paintings, answering each of Veronique's queries to the best of his ability. With no more questions to ask, she, Anne, and Arnaud told him about Martin and what else they'd discovered in the preceding days.

"So you believe my father and his friends hid the paintings next door in what is now Martin's home," Giles said, as they sipped their coffee.

"In a closet within a closet," said Anne. "But figuring out which one could be problematic."

"Perhaps I can narrow your search. Because Louis Le Vaux designed many of the mansions on the Île, they have similar floor plans. Elisabeth was an only child, so I expect her bedroom was on the fourth floor. It was likely the one with the view of Saint-Germain-des-Prés."

"My room was on the fourth floor, and Mother's was upstairs," Veronique said.

"Then that's where we'll begin our search," Anne said. "Thank you, Giles."

"You are welcome. I wish I could offer more suggestions, but perhaps this will help." He stood up, walked to the buffet, and opened a drawer. "Last night I looked through my father's journal." He presented Veronique with the worn leather book and continued. "I do not know how much this will assist you in your search, but I thought perhaps you, Henri, and Renee would find it interesting. Not long ago I reread the entries. There are no specific references to the paintings or the Resistance, but perhaps Papa's words will help you understand what he and other resistance fighters did to drive the Nazis from Paris. He wrote a great deal about Auguste, Anton and Jules, though he used their code names, Andre, Dillon, and Alexandre."

Veronique took the book and held it to her chest. "Thank you, Giles," she said, tears in her eyes. "I'll take good care of your treasure, as will Henri and Renee. I'm sure they will come by to thank you in person. Everyone was so secretive in those days, so we all know so little about our parents and their struggles. My journal helped Anne understand. Perhaps your father's journal will provide additional insight."

"What a delightful man," Veronique said, as Arnaud drove toward Quai de Bourbon.

"That he is," Arnaud said. "And if he's right about Martin's floor plan, he's saved us hours of searching for the closet Elisabeth alluded to in her poem. So, what will you two do for the rest of the day?"

"I never thought I would say this, but I want to visit Drancy. Will you go with me, Anne?"

"Of course. Henri's busy, but I imagine Renee will want to come along."

"Arnaud, will you join us?" Veronique asked.

Arnaud shook his head. "I'm afraid business forces me to refuse your invitation."

"Then perhaps Gus will drive. Anne, would you please call and tell him we need the car after all?"

"Right away." Anne took her phone from her purse, scrolled to Gus's number, and pushed talk. "Gus," she said, "Realizing this is short notice, do you have time to drive three women to Drancy this afternoon?"

For a minute there was silence on the other end of the line. "Gus," Anne persisted. "If you're busy—"

"I can reschedule," Gus responded tentatively. "Are you at the apartment?"

"We're pulling up now."

"Then I will leave as soon as I make a call."

"Great! Oma and I will freshen up and get Renee. Let us know when you're crossing Pont de la Tournelle. We'll be waiting out front."

෮෨

Thirty minutes later, with the women in the car, Gus crossed Pont Marie. "A private guide, Zachary Barron, will meet us at the entrance to Drancy." he said. "Zachary will explain the significance of the memorial sculpture and personally take you on a tour of the grounds."

"How did you manage that with such short notice?" Anne asked.

"As soon as we hung up, I called. To visit the Drancy museum, one must have an appointment. I hoped Zachary could arrange for a guide to meet us. Instead, he offered to lead the tour."

"I take it Zachary is important," Anne said.

"He is, but not just because he is a Drancy and Auschwitz survivor. He was instrumental in establishing the Drancy Memorial. I told him Veronique's mother, Madame Boulet, was held at Drancy. Perhaps that is why he offered to meet us."

Few words were spoken during the remainder of the drive. Assuming her grandmother was thinking about Elisabeth and nervous about what she might learn at the memorial, Anne left her alone. Instead, she looked out the window, all the time wondering if they were following the same route Elisabeth had taken so many years before— if the images she was seeing were the final impressions Elisabeth had of Paris. *What was she thinking?* Anne mulled. *Was she terrified, or, as Oma believes, resigned to her fate? Did she know she was going to die?* "Of course she did," Anne whispered.

"Did you say something?" Veronique asked.

"No," Anne said. "I was just thinking aloud."

"About Mother?"

"Yes and what she was feeling as she traveled the route we're taking today."

"It pains me to think how she must have felt, and I am sure this is just the beginning of what will likely be a heartbreaking day."

"We can turn back—"

"No, darling. Not if I'm going to move ahead."

When they arrived at the memorial entrance, an old man approached the car and opened Veronique's door. "This is Zachary Barron," Gus said, as he helped Veronique out of the backseat. "As I told you, Zachary is a Holocaust survivor. He is also a friend."

"It's nice to meet you, Zachary." Veronique extended her hand. "Thank you for showing us around Drancy."

"It is my pleasure, Madame Ellison." Zachary gently shook Veronique's hand. "Gus says your mother was detained here."

"She was taken from her home during the second night of la rafle du Vel d'Hiv, transported to the velodrome, and, several days later, bused here to Drancy. Not long after she arrived, she was herded into a cattle-car and taken to Auschwitz."

"I assume she was not one of the lucky few who returned to Paris."

"Unfortunately no. Zachary, meet my friend, Renee Marsolet. She and her husband Henri escaped Paris with me in July 1942. They have visited the Drancy memorial several times in recent years."

Zachary doffed his hat. "Madame Marsolet."

"It's nice to meet you, Monsieur Barron."

"I would prefer it if you would all call me Zachary."

"Thank you, Zachary," Veronique said. "This is my granddaughter Anne French."

"Bonjour, Madame French."

"Bonjour, Zachary," Anne said. "We are grateful you offered to be our guide. Gus says you are in-part responsible for the creation of the Drancy Memorial."

"I played a small role, Madame. I was among those who insisted that commemorative plaques pointing out the involvement of the French State in the fate of French Jews be placed on the site. Until recently, the official stance of the French government has been that the Vichy regime was illegal and therefore separate from the French Republic."

"So they could deny any responsibility for the atrocities committed against the Jews," Anne said.

"Correct. It was not until July 16, 1995, that President Jacques Chirac finally accepted responsibility for the carnage on behalf of the French people. At that time, he particularly noted the brutality and inhumane actions of French police, who organized and carried out la rafle du Vel d'Hiv."

"You became interested in the project because you were incarcerated at Drancy?" Veronique asked.

"I did. Unlike your mother, I was one of the lucky ones. I was a young man, so when I arrived at Auschwitz, I was assigned to the labor force. It was a horrible experience. Though there were many times I was sure I would not make it another day—I lived."

Zachary motioned to seats near the entrance. "Gus told me you wish to know about Drancy," he said. "I thought you might be more comfortable sitting here while we talk—that is, if you would like for me to provide a short overview before we look at the Memorial."

"We would, thank you," Veronique said.

"Please stop me if you are uncomfortable."

Veronique nodded and Zachary began. "Arguably, Drancy was the most notorious concentration camp in France. When it was built in the 1930s, it was poetically named *La Cité a de la Muette*—the Silent City—for its perceived peaceful ideals."

"That's rather ironic," Anne said.

"I would say *bitterly* ironic. *La Cité de la Muette* was initially designed to be a public housing project, a collective living space, but when the Nazis took over, they turned it into a camp for prisoners of war. In 1942, it became a regroupment camp under the authority of the French police. Here the Jews of France were held until they could be deported to the extermination camps." Seeing Veronique shudder, he asked, "Would you like for me to stop or to choose my words more carefully, Madame? I do not want to upset you more than you already are being in the place where your mother was detained."

"No," Veronique insisted. "Though what you're saying is difficult for me to hear, I must."

Zachary nodded. "Very well then," he began again. "When the initial anti-Jewish raids began in 1941, the victims were brought here to Drancy. Everyone who survived tells the same story. The French police and Nazi guards were brutal and inhumane, and the general living conditions were bleak. There was very little food. The place was overcrowded. The facilities were filthy."

"It's difficult for me to imagine Mother in such a place."

"I am sure she experienced a terrifying few days. I will be glad to tell you more, but—"

"Please continue," Veronique said. "Forgive me if I'm emotional from time to time."

"I understand. During the rafle du 11 arrondissement, on August 10, 1941—"

"I'm not familiar with the rafle du 11 arrondissement," Veronique interrupted.

"It was a raid that occurred eleven months prior to la rafle du Vel d'Hiv. During the operation, 4,232 Jews were arrested and transported to Drancy. Originally built to hold seven hundred, the camp was not equipped to handle such a large number. During the early years, almost all of the inmates were men, though beginning in July 1942, women and children were also interned here."

When Zachary mentioned July 1942, Veronique shuddered again. Noting her grandmother's strong reaction, Anne took her hand. "Are you certain you want Zachary to go on, Oma," she asked. "We've already learned a great deal."

"I am, darling. I believe I made it clear. I am *determined* to know everything before I see the memorial." She turned to Zachary and said, "On July 17, the second night of la rafle du Vel d'Hiv, the Nazis dragged Mother from her home and transported her to the Velodrome d'Hiver."

"I doubt the Nazis were the ones who took your mother away," Zachary said.

"Of course they did," Veronique said huffily. "The other day Anne met with one of Mother's neighbors who witnessed the entire episode. She positively remembers a man wearing a red armband bearing the Nazi swastika."

"The Nazi with the armband may have been in charge, but the operation was coordinated by the French police," Zachary insisted. "Our fellow countrymen made most of the arrests those two horrible nights."

"But others have said the same thing as Madame Bouffard," Veronique argued. "I know Mother was arrested by Nazi soldiers."

"Jacqueline may have been wrong, Oma. She was only ten. She saw an SS man in a black coat with a red arm band, but she wouldn't have known if the soldiers with him were German or French."

Veronique sighed. "Maybe Jacqueline *was* mistaken," she said. "If I was rude, I apologize, Zachary. I suppose, to a child, a soldier is a soldier. For me, hearing this makes Mother's arrest even more troubling—if that's possible."

"I have always felt that French involvement made the atrocities committed against the Jews even more despicable," Zachery said. "That is the reason I have fought most of my adult life to force the government to admit its role in the deportations. But let me return to the raid of July 16 and 17. The doomed souls were transferred to the Velodrome d'Hiver and kept up to five days with little food or medical attention. From there, some were transported to Beaune-la-Rolande or Pithiviers. Others, like your mother, were brought here to Drancy. In 1973, the French-Israeli artist Shelomo Selinger designed and sculpted a memorial to those who passed through here on their way to Auschwitz."

"I recall hearing about Selinger in my sculpture class," Anne said. "Though I know little about his life or his art."

"His is an amazing story. If you are truly interested, there is a great deal of biographical and artistic information on line. Briefly, Selinger survived nine German death camps as well as two death marches. On May 8, 1945, when the Red Army liberated the Terezin camp near Prague in what was then Czechoslovakia, he was discovered still breathing, on a pile of dead bodies. A Jewish military doctor pulled him out and transported him to a military field hospital. There he regained his health, though for the next seven years he had no memory of what he had been through—of the horrors he had faced."

"Under the circumstances, that might not be such a bad thing," Veronique said.

"I have always thought that," Zachary said. "Shall we look at Selinger's creation? He aptly titled the Drancy sculpture *The Gates of Hell*."

Anne took her grandmother's arm to steady her as she rose. "You're sure you want to do this, Oma?" she asked.

"I am, darling." Veronique turned to Zachary and said resolutely, "I am ready."

"My husband and I took pictures of Selinger's sculpture from all angles," Renee said as they neared the memorial. "We recently showed the photographs to Anne, but I'm afraid we weren't able to provide a satisfactory explanation."

'Then let me briefly point out the various parts." Zachary handed Veronique a small guidebook and said, "If you want more in-depth information about Selinger, his sculpture and its significance to Jews, perhaps this will help. Gus said you married a Catholic and converted to your husband's faith."

"That's true," Veronique said. "I am Catholic. And I'm ashamed to say, I don't remember much about the religion of my youth. We weren't orthodox—"

"I understand. Please do not think I am judging you. I asked because, rather than elaborate now, if you do not understand what I am saying, the book you are holding will provide detailed information. We could spend hours out here, but I know you would like to see the exhibit in the boxcar. There is another bench over there. Perhaps you would like to sit while I talk."

Veronique walked to the bench, sat, and nodded she was ready.

"The Shoah Memorial, like it's counterpart in Paris, is a place for meditation and contemplation," Zachary explained. "In Hebrew, 'Shoah' means catastrophe. Many scholars and historians believe it is a more appropriate term for what most today call the Holocaust."

"Why's that?" Anne asked.

"Because, historically, the word has been used to describe assaults upon *Jews*, while holocaust, broadly speaking, refers to the mass destruction of humans by other humans. Scholars now use 'Ha Shoah'—the Shoah— or 'Final Solution,' a phrase coined by the Nazis, when describing the fate of the *Jews* at the hands of the Nazis."

"And Holocaust?" said Veronique.

"Denotes atrocities committed against *all victims* of Hitler's regime."

"Interesting," said Veronique. "Thank you for explaining, Zachary."

"You are most welcome. And now about Selinger's sculpture. The three granite columns represent the Hebrew letter *shin*, which can stand for the name of God, *shaddai*, and for the flame of divine revelation. It is the symbol used in the mezuzah displayed next to the front doors of Jewish homes. Madame Ellison, I imagine you had a mezuzah next to your door when you were growing up."

"When I was a young child, we did, but later—."

"Of course it would have been foolhardy for Jewish families to flaunt their faith during the Occupation. I was concentrating on what I planned to tell you about the memorial. I was not thinking—"

"I wasn't offended."

"Good. Then I will continue to explain the significance of the monument. The seven steps leading up to the columns denote the elevation of the souls of the victims. They also represent other more complicated Jewish beliefs that are described in the book. In the center column, there are ten tortured human figures. That is the number required for a minyan—a quorum for prayer. The head, coif, and beard on the two front figures are meant to make up the Hebrew letters *lamed*, or thirty, and *vav*, six."

"Thirty-six," Veronique interjected.

"Yes. In the Jewish faith, this is the minimum of honorable and moral individuals necessary for the continued existence of the world."

"I see," Veronique said. "The sculpture is very impressive and would obviously be quite meaningful to a practicing Jew. I'll read the book, so when I return to see the memorial—as I'm sure I will—we can enjoy a more profound discussion."

"I would like that," Zachary said. "When you come back, be sure to visit the new Shoah Memorial Center. In September 2012, fifty years after the deportation of Jews from Drancy to the concentration camps, then French President Hollande inaugurated the building which is now managed by the French Shoah Organization."

"Were you involved in the project?" Veronique asked.

"I was and I still am, "said Zachary. "The center is a place where the French people can learn about this terrible time in our history. Engraved on the front of the building are the words, 'Passer-by, Meditate and do not forget.' Would you like to take a look when we finish here."

"I think I'll wait until my next visit," Veronique said. "I am tiring. While I'm still able, I would like to walk to the boxcar. I'm told it is one of those used to transport the Jews to Auschwitz."

"That is true. It became part of the memorial in 1988. Inside are exhibits detailing the deportations. Shall we walk over now?"

Veronique nodded and, with Anne's help, stood. "It's possible I'm walking the exact path Mother once walked," she said somberly.as they approached the railroad track leading from the memorial sculpture to the boxcar.

Without comment, Anne linked her arm through her grandmothers', and Renee took her friend's other arm. Veronique leaned heavily into her granddaughter as they walked slowly along the track. The closer they got to the railroad car, the tighter she clung to Anne's arm. At the entrance, she paused. "There's the sign Henri mentioned," she said. "See Anne?" This car was built to hold eight horses. It was intended to transport animals. . ."

"This must be terribly difficult, Oma."

"It is, darling. If you don't mind, I'd like to spend a few minutes alone inside the car."

"Of course. Renee and I will wait out here with Zachary and Gus. Call if you need us."

While Gus and Zachary conversed nearby, Anne and Renee stood close enough to the door so they could respond if Veronique called. "I'm beginning to worry about your grandmother," Renee said after twenty minutes had passed. "I hope she's all right."

"I'll check on her."

"Okay, but she won't be happy. She ordered you to wait outside."

"I know. I'll tell her I want to see the exhibits. That's the truth. Wish me luck."

"Oh I do." Renee smiled knowingly.

"I hope you don't mind if I interrupt your musings," Anne said, as she entered the railroad car. "I'd like to see the exhibits."

"Fine, as long as you're not in here because you're worried about me."

"Why would I worry about you? Like I said, I want to see the displays so when you talk about them, I'll be able to relate."

Without responding, Veronique moved slowly, stopping to study each picture and piece of memorabilia. Anne went from one display case to the next, all the while keeping a close eye on her grandmother. "Henri told us he was claustrophobic in this car with ten other people," she said, pausing in front of a photograph of a similar railroad car with Jews being herded inside. "It's hard to imagine fifty people were stuffed into this small space."

"Or more, as I learned when I saw the exhibit over there." Veronique pointed to one of the lighted cases. "That display contains a series of photographs showing Jews—men, women, and children— beginning their final journey. Seeing the horror and fear in their eyes as the Nazi guards violently shove them inside a cattle-car, helps me understand—if anyone can—what Mother must have felt that horrible day. It's almost too much to bear." She turned toward the door, her head bowed in grief and immeasurable anger.

Anne waited, not knowing what to say.

At the door, Veronique took a deep breath, raised her head, and with hardening resolve, stood erect. "Shall we join the others?" she said doggedly. "I've seen everything I need to see in here—perhaps more than anyone should ever witness."

"So have I." Anne took her grandmother's arm and they exited the car.

Veronique remained silent as they slowly walked back to the memorial entrance. Pausing before they got into the car, she asked for an address where she could mail a contribution for the upkeep of the memorial. Seemingly anticipating her request, Zachary handed her a sheet of paper. "Everything you need to know, including my contact information, is written here," he said. "Please call anytime you would like to come back for another tour, a visit to the Memorial Center, and an in-depth discussion of the Shoah sculpture."

"You will be hearing from me," Veronique put the paper in her pocketbook. "Thank you again, Zachary."

"Zachary took off his hat, bowed and said, "You are welcome, Madame."

Still lost in private thoughts, Veronique said little during the ride back to the Île. Respecting her tacit wishes, the others made no attempt to engage her in conversation.

As they crossed Pont Marie, she finally spoke. "Thank you for driving us to Drancy, Gus."

"I hope the experience was not too difficult," Gus said.

"Seeing the place where Mother spent her last days wasn't easy, but it was something I needed to do."

"I understand. You mentioned other places you wish to visit. Will you need the car tomorrow?"

"My first inclination is to say no, but perhaps I may. Anne mentioned a memorial behind a church in the Marais—one commemorating Parisian Jews who died during the Occupation. I would like to take a look. And I want to visit the Deportation Memorial on Île de la Cité."

"If that is what you wish to do, let me know when to pick you up."

"I will," Veronique said. "And thank you again, Gus."

CHAPTER 34

Anne left her grandmother and Renee on the fourth floor. "Uggs and sweats, here I come!" she said as she rode the elevator to the fifth. She entered her apartment and, without stopping to check for messages, went to her room. "But first a bath," she whispered as she turned on the water in the tub and added a measure of foaming bath salts. By the time she finished undressing, the tub was full. She stepped into the steamy water. As the bubbles caressed her chin, she lay back, closed her eyes, and thought about Arnaud's caresses the night before.

For the next twenty minutes, though the Jacuzzi jets spouting water refreshed her body, they couldn't wash away her jumbled and contradictory thoughts. One moment she wished she'd never met the man who, in such a short time, had complicated her life. The next, she rued the day she she'd be leaving Paris and him behind. "It's definitely time to get out of here and face reality," she grumbled as she pulled the plug and watched the now-tepid water begin to run rapidly down the drain.

"There," she said. "No more water! No more thoughts of Arnaud!"

Still covered with froth, she stepped into the shower to rinse the remaining bubbles from her skin. Five minute later, dry and wrapped in a bath towel, she went to the kitchen and poured a glass of wine. "Oh Lord," she groaned, suddenly remembering she'd forgotten to pick up the documents she would need to access Veronique and Henri's accounts and Elisabeth's safe-deposit box. Irritated with herself, she picked up the phone, scrolled to her grandmother's number, and pushed talk.

"Hi, honey," Renee answered on the second ring.

"You knew it was me?" Anne asked. "Caller ID?"

"No. By process of elimination. Who else in Paris would be calling your grandmother's landline this late? I imagine her army of decorators and haute couture designers have closed up shop for the night—if not forever after what she put them through. What's up?"

"Nothing important. Is Oma close by?"

"She's napping. I'd rather not disturb her. Can I help?"

"I hope so. I forgot to pick up the documents I'll need in Geneva tomorrow. If you know where they are, I'll get dressed and come down."

"They're on the entry table, but don't bother to dress. I'll have Henri bring the folder up, put it by your door, and knock so you know it's there. Listen for him in about five minutes."

"Thanks."

"You're welcome. Good luck at the bank, and safe travel. We'll see you Wednesday afternoon at Martin's."

A few minutes later, Anne heard a rap on the door. She waited until she heard the elevator move again, stepped into the hall, and picked up the folder. "I'd hate to forget these yet again," she whispered as she went to her office and immediately tucked the folder into her briefcase.

"What the hell am I going to do now," she muttered, feeling just a little sorry for herself. *Maybe I'll take a walk. I could use the exercise. And what self-respecting adult goes to bed so early?* "That's ridiculous," she said. "If I don't have the energy to get dressed and go down to Oma's, I'm certainly not going to make the effort necessary to stroll around the Île."

Unable to shake her foul mood and hoping that reading Feliciano's book might take her mind off Arnaud, she took the tome off the shelf. But once in her bedroom, instead of sitting down to read, she put on a lounging robe, opened the balcony door, pulled a chair outside, and sat down. As she gazed out at the twinkling lights of Paris, Feliciano's research was no longer uppermost in her mind. All she could think of was what was she going to do about Arnaud Lessard.

Half an hour later, even more conflicted and growing more and more irritated because she had let Arnaud complicate her life, she stood, moved the chair inside, closed and locked the balcony door, and returned to her office. "There's only one way to solve my problem," she grumbled as she sat at the computer. "I'm going home."

She googled Air France and reserved a seat for Saturday morning. Unhappy, yet relieved she'd made a decision, she returned to her bedroom and packed her carry-on for the overnight in Geneva. Though it was still early, she set the alarm for five and turned out the light.

⌒◯

The shrill ringing of the phone beside the bed jarred Anne awake. She rolled over, looked at the clock, and, groaning, removed the receiver from the charger. "What," she answered sleepily. "I thought you were my alarm blaring. Is it five already?"

"And good morning to you, too." Arnaud said cheerfully. "It's four forty-five. I called to make sure you're up and about."

"I would have been in fifteen minutes. Are you still coming at six?"

"I am. You'll be ready?"

"I'll be waiting out front."

Without waiting for a response, Anne hung up.

⌒◯

Still annoyed—though she really wasn't sure about what—Anne was waiting by the curb when Arnaud arrived. He popped the trunk and put her carry-on inside. When he leaned down to give her a kiss, she abruptly turned. "What's wrong?" he asked as he opened the passenger door.

"Nothing!" Anne said sharply.

"Suddenly that silly saying I learned during the months I lived in New York comes to mind. Let's see, how does it go? Ah yes. If you believe that, I have a bridge—'"

"To sell." Anne finished the statement and, despite her still-foul mood, she smiled. "I'm sorry. I don't function well without several cups of coffee to wake me up. I keep telling myself to buy a Keurig, but so far I haven't had a minute to shop. I was in a rush to get ready this morning and. . . But you don't need to hear me complain."

"Are you sure caffeine will cure what ails you?"

"I don't know. Hopefully. I have a lot on my mind. I keep wondering what we may or may *not* learn in Geneva today and, beyond that, what we'll find at Martin's tomorrow. Oma will be disappointed if you and I come home empty-handed and devastated if her mother's paintings aren't hidden in Martin's closet—if there *is* a closet within a closet. I could have been totally off base when I hastily interpreted Elisabeth's poem. Maybe I should have given the verses more thought before pressing my theory. Now Oma and the others may suffer the consequences of my haste while I'm sitting in New York—"

"You're going home?"

"I am. Regardless of what we find today in Geneva or tomorrow at Martin's, I'm leaving Saturday morning."

"Why? Either way, your grandmother will need you here."

"She'll have Henri and Renee."

"True, but it's not the same thing. She won't admit it, but she depends on you. I assumed you'd be staying at least another week to see that she's settled. Whether she finds her mother's art or not, didn't you say you want to see '*her* Paris?'"

"I did but—"

"But you're going home anyway." Arnaud reached over, put his hand on Anne's leg and said, "You can make all the excuses you want, but we both know this is about you and me. And before you comment—no, this isn't my ego talking. I've been unavailable for two days, and suddenly you believe all I do is work."

"Okay, I admit the thought crossed my mind. Chalk it up to past experience, but that's not it."

"What then?"

"It's not that easy to explain." Anne reached in, grabbed a Kleenex from her purse, and daubed her eyes.

"Try."

"I love you—that scares me."

"And I love you. What's so frightening about that?"

"Can you honestly say you aren't nervous about where this could lead?"

"If by '*this*,' you mean us, why would I be apprehensive?"

"Maybe I'm jumping the gun. If so, I apologize, but you asked. Yes, I love you, but there are so many problems—"

"Like what?"

"We could *drive* to Geneva and I'd still be talking. And those problems aside, there's more. It's impossible for two people to fall in love in less than a week."

"I fell in love with you during lunch at Le Tastevin—or rather when I left you at the hotel I was very much in like. Maybe I didn't *really* fall in love until the next day. Veronique fell in love the minute she saw Robert at the Hotel du Jeu de Paume."

"She told you that?"

"She said she knew she loved him before they left for the Lambert."

"She couldn't have known. She was in shock. Her mother had just been arrested, and she was being forced to flee the only home she had ever known."

"Yet somehow she knew, and she and your grandfather were happily married for nearly sixty years."

"But they didn't have our problems."

"We haven't even begun to discuss our problems, let alone look for possible solutions."

"I realize I'm overusing the word, but that's another problem—there aren't any solutions."

"Anne—"

"Please, no more." Anne wiped her eyes. "If we keep this up, I'll turn into a blubbering idiot, and I don't want to arrive at the bank with a swollen face and runny makeup."

"Then we'll talk tonight in Geneva."

"I don't want to discuss anything serious tonight. When I got in the car, I was determined to spend the evening as friends."

"But now?"

"Now I realize I can't pull it off. I was incredibly rude when you called to be sure I was up. You saw a side of me I struggle to keep in check. When I'm anxious, or feel my back's against a wall, I lash out."

"You were irritated because I didn't let you sleep for fifteen more minutes?"

"You know that's not it."

"Then will you please tell me what's going on in your head?"

Anne inhaled and exhaled deeply. "Remember when we talked about your split with Aimee—"

"If my past with Aimee's the problem, then—"

"Aimee's not the problem. *I* am. You said her simmering anger ruined your relationship."

"I did, but you're simplifying matters. There were *many* factors that caused our marriage to end in divorce."

"I'm sure there were. The same holds true for Tom and me. It wasn't *just* that he was a workaholic. And before you ask—no, workaholic isn't an adjective I'll be adding to your ever-growing list. Anyway, when it comes to being nasty and hostile, I can beat Aimee in spades. When I feel cornered or pressured, I'm the Mr. Hyde of Doctor Jekyll and Mr. Hyde fame. Once you see my Mr. Hyde side, you'll run like hell, or if you don't, you should. I'll be back to Paris from time to time. We can meet for lunch or dinner as good friends. If I stay now, though I may try to keep my nasty side at bay, it will eventually emerge and drive you away."

"It couldn't."

"Trust me, it could—and it will."

"So, giving you that—at least for now—what's your plan?"

"We'll take care of business at the bank and enjoy this afternoon and evening. It may be bittersweet, but I want to live the fantasy one more night and face reality tomorrow when the sun comes up."

"You don't want to talk about what that reality could be?"

"No. I simply want to enjoy the dream a few more hours. Can you do that for me?"

"If that's what you want, I'll try. But it won't be easy."

"For either of us," Anne said introspectively. "That's for sure."

During the flight to Geneva, Arnaud was unusually quiet. *I wonder if staying overnight in Switzerland is a bad idea after all,* Anne mulled, as the plane's wheels met the tarmac at Cointrin International Airport.

When they arrived at the gate and the captain turned off the seatbelt sign, Arnaud removed both his and Anne's carry-ons from the overhead bin while she took her briefcase from beneath the seat. "Are we taking a cab to the bank?" she asked.

"I hired a car. The driver will meet us on the next level down."

They deplaned, took the escalator to the baggage claim area, and immediately saw a man holding a sign with 'Lessard' written in bold black letters. "I am Paul Demers," he said as they approached. "Do you have checked luggage?"

"This is it," Arnaud said.

"Then please follow me. The car is parked in the lot across the street. If you do not mind walking a short distance, it is easier to leave from there instead of the front of the terminal building where parking is difficult."

"We'll walk," said Anne. "We've been cooped up breathing stale air. A little exercise will feel good."

As they entered the crosswalk, Arnaud took Anne's hand. "Are you okay?" he said softly. "You're awfully quiet."

"Nerves, I guess. I'm sure Oma's already sitting by the phone waiting to hear about the millions of dollars in her account and the incredible jewels in her safe-deposit box."

"Maybe you'll be able to deliver good news. Why all the negativity?"

"I'm not being negative. I'm being realistic."

"Okay—"

"See what I mean about my nasty side? I overreacted. I'm sorry."

"This is the car." Paul said, interrupting the conversation. He remotely unlocked the back door of a sleek BMW sedan and continued. "I will put your bags in the trunk."

"I'll keep my briefcase with me," Anne said.

"Very well, Madame. You are going to Lombard Odier Darier Hentsch & Cie on rue de la Corraterie?"

"We are," Arnaud answered as he slid in the backseat next to Anne.

During the drive, Anne checked the papers in the folder Henri had left outside her door. When Paul stopped in front of the hotel, she quickly got out, and, without waiting for Arnaud, walked swiftly toward the bank entrance. He finally caught up at the reception desk in the lobby as she was saying, "Anne French for Monsieur Odiet."

"Oui, Madame French," said the woman. "I will let Monsieur Odiet know you are here."

Minutes later two men approached the desk. The taller of the two extended his hand. "Madame French," he said. "I am Christian Hentsch."

"It's a pleasure to meet you, Monsieur Hentsch. May I introduce Arnaud Lessard?"

"Arnaud and I are old friends." Christian shook Arnaud's outstretched hand. "It has been too long since we last met."

"That's only because I'm able to manage my account online, as you know, Christian. Frankly, I'm surprised you're still working with private clients. Running the Technology and Banking Unit must take up most of your time."

"Sadly, I no longer have clients, but today I came out of my cave to personally introduce Julien Odiet, who will take care of you, Madame French."

Anne shook Julien's hand. "It's a pleasure to meet you, Monsieur Odiet," she said.

"Julien, please." He shook hands with Arnaud and again addressed Anne, "Madame French, yesterday I spoke with your grandmother. An hour ago we received the pdf file—a duplicate of the notarized hard copies you are carrying that allow you to access Madame Boulet's account, her safe-deposit box, and Monsieur Marsolet's information. As Madame Ellison has requested, I have prepared a document for you to sign in the event she chooses to have the contents of her safe-deposit box couriered to Paris."

"She won't have to come to Geneva and open the box in person?" Anne asked. "Isn't that unusual?"

"That is our customary procedure, but due to circumstances—"

"Circumstances?"

"Because Madame Ellison is a Holocaust survivor, and considering her advanced age, we have decided to make an exception. When you sign the document, I will have two bonded and insured employees inventory the contents of the box—in your presence if you desire. They will prepare a list and have it checked by another employee, a notary. After that, should you wish, we I will make arrangements with our courier service to fly the items to Paris. But before we get to the safe-deposit box, shall we go to my office and discuss Madame Ellison's and Monsieur Marsolet's accounts?"

"Certainly," Anne said, feeling more unnerved by the minute.

"I leave you two in good hands," Christian said. "Technology calls. If I don't get to work, Arnaud, you will no longer be able to manage your money online. Madame French, Julien will set up an online account for Madame Ellison before you leave. She requested that you be given unlimited access, and she named you her executrix and sole heir, with her remaining assets going to your children after your death."

Nice try, Oma, Anne thought as Christian was saying. "Monsieur Marsolet will have his own online account. You will be able to access his information today, but after that, unless he specifically authorizes you to complete a transaction, his information will be kept private."

"Thank you." Anne extended her hand.

"You are most welcome." Christian shook hands with Anne and again with Arnaud, turned, and left the room.

"This way." Julien led Anne and Arnaud along a hall lined with photographs, Anne assumed, of past bank executives. Halfway down he stopped, opened a door, and stepped aside, allowing Anne and Arnaud to lead him into a spacious mahogany-paneled office. He closed the door behind them and gestured toward two burgundy leather chairs facing a mahogany desk. "Make yourselves comfortable," he said. "When we finish discussing the accounts, I will take you to Madame Boulet's safe-deposit box."

"Though I think I already know the answer to my question, I'll ask anyway," Anne said. "To your knowledge, did Madame Boulet ever come to the bank?"

"I do not believe so, but let me check again to be sure." Julien removed a signature card from the folder on his desk and looked carefully. "Auguste Lessard seems to be the only person who ever accessed the box. He always brought the key."

"Auguste opened my great my grandmother's lock box?" Anne said, taken aback.

"He did." Julien looked closely at the card. "Apparently Monsieur Lessard opened the box seven times—"

"But how?" Arnaud asked, dumfounded. "With so many Nazi guards patrolling the border, how could Auguste make his way across the Line of Demarcation and then into Switzerland so often? One such journey would have been daunting, but seven—"

"I have no way of knowing how he accomplished the seemingly impossible," Julien said. "But, clearly, the same individual signed the card each time."

Anne turned to Arnaud. "I knew Auguste was Anton's friend and partner in the Resistance, but I had no idea he and Elisabeth were close friends. If they were—and it appears that's the case—I doubt my grandmother knew. I may be wrong, but I believe she only mentioned Auguste once in her journal, and then she only referenced him in passing."

"Yet it appears my great-grandfather and your great-grandmother were good friends—so much so that she entrusted him with her money and whatever is in the safe-deposit box."

"So it seems." Anne sighed and turned to Julien. "I apologize for interrupting," she said. "You understand all of this comes as a shock—"

"Of course. It is also hard for me to believe Monsieur Lessard could so easily cross the border into Switzerland during the Occupation—yet he did."

"And carrying this key."

"Now I am surprised," Julien said. "Madame Ellison actually had the key in her possession all these years?"

"No. Until recently she had no specific information about her mother's dealings with your bank. She knew a Swiss account existed, but nothing else. With more than sufficient money to live comfortably, she chose not to seek information about the account."

"It may also be that memories of the Occupation and her mother's death were too painful to deal with," Julien offered. "That, we have learned, is not unusual among victims of the Holocaust. If you do not mind my asking, how did Madame Ellison eventually learn that Madame Boulet's money and safe-deposit box were in *our* bank?"

"Before the Nazis took her away, Madame Boulet hid the key to the box and a letter containing a cryptic poem behind several bricks above the fireplace in her bedroom. Last Saturday a mason removed the bricks. We found the key and, working together, my grandmother, Monsieur and Madame Marsolet, Arnaud, and I solved the riddle of the poem."

"That is how you knew to come to Geneva. What a fascinating story. However, even without a key, with proper identification, which you have, we would have given you access to the box. After the Holocaust, the bank eased its regulations requiring a key to open boxes rented prior to 1938. As you might imagine, the change was necessary. Many of the Jews who trusted our bank to protect both their money and their valuables were slaughtered in the Ghettos and in the Nazi death camps. In the chaos following Germany's defeat, most of their heirs were unable to locate their relatives' account information, let alone the small key required to open a personal safe-deposit box."

"A fact I hadn't considered," Anne said. "It was only recently that I *began* to understand—if one who hasn't lived through the Occupation ever could—the impact the Nazis had on the lives of Parisian Jews. What happened to Madame Boulet and to my grandmother is horrific."

"It was," Julien said. "I am the youngest of eight children. I was born fifteen years after VE Day, but throughout my life, particularly when my parents were still alive, I heard gruesome and shocking stories of Holocaust victims. My father, who was also in banking, was an Austrian Jew, and my mother a Swiss Catholic. Fortunately, they moved to her home here in Geneva in early January of 1938, two months before Hitler's armies annexed Austria."

"Your father's family stayed behind when he and your mother emigrated?" Anne asked.

"Yes. Like Madame Boulet, they, too, chose to remain in their homes. As a result, over twenty of Papa's relatives—his mother and father, a brother, a sister, as well as cousins, aunts and uncles—died during the Holocaust."

"So you understand the pain the Jews suffered."

"Unfortunately I do. However, you are not here to listen to tales of the horrors my family experienced. Shall we continue with the specifics about Madame Boulet's account? With proper identification and legal authorization, Monsieur Lessard leased the box in her name and that of her daughter Veronique Boulet in perpetuity. Let me see. . ." He rifled through the papers in the folder until he located the one he was seeking, read for several minutes, and then said, "When Madame Boulet died, all of her assets reverted to said daughter."

"And if my grandmother hadn't survived the war or if she died in later years without accessing the account, then what?"

"If she had children, the money and the contents of the safe-deposit box would have been divided equally among them. If there were no children, all of her assets were to pass to Monsieur Anton Marsolet or his heirs."

"Really?"

"You are surprised, Madame? Do you doubt the authenticity—"

"Not at all. I'm merely taken aback—which seems to be the rule of the day. You were saying about Auguste Lessard?"

"He opened the account on June 23, 1940, and made the last deposit on June 23, 1940. In all, he made seven deposits—"

"Which I find hard to believe," Arnaud said.

"The date Auguste opened the account doesn't surprise me," Anne said. "I recall a journal entry my grandmother made in early June 1940. Worried that French banks were no longer safe, her mother had just transferred the majority of her money to your bank, Julien. In her Paris account, she left only what was absolutely necessary to maintain the household."

"Madame Boulet was correct about the instability of the French banking system."

"So Great-Grandfather Auguste last came to the bank on July 11, 1942," Arnaud said, seemingly not hearing the last part of the conversation. I wonder why Grandpapa never mentioned—"

"Maybe Bertrand knew Auguste was away, but not where he had gone," Anne said. "Or if he did know, he might not have thought the information was relevant to our search for Elisabeth's art."

"Perhaps if you ask a specific question, he will be able to shed more light on the subject," Julien said as he removed two sealed envelopes from his top desk drawer. "Each of these contains account information—one for Madame Boulet, and the other for Monsieur Marsolet. As a matter of protocol, to verify you are who you claim to be, may I see the account numbers and the password Madame Ellison said she was sending with you?"

Anne took an envelope from her briefcase and handed it to Julien.

"Everything appears to be in order," he said. "Including the password."

"May I see?" Anne asked.

She took the card from Julien, glanced at the letters and numbers, and then looked again—this time more closely. Suddenly she reached out and grabbed Arnaud's arm.

Arnaud jumped at Anne's intense reaction and the unexpected pressure on his arm. "What?" he snapped. "Is there a problem?"

"Look at Elisabeth's password." Anne handed him the card containing the letters and numbers. "You won't believe what you see."

Arnaud looked carefully and then read aloud. "EBM09071942. I don't understand. Do you think there's a message in Elisabeth's choice of letters and numbers?"

"Definitely. Look at the first three letters. They're Elisabeth's initials."

"EBM," Arnaud read. "Elisabeth Boulet—"

"Marsolet. Elisabeth Boulet *Marsolet*. And the numbers in the password represent a date—9 July, 1942—"

"My God!" Arnaud gasped. "You're right! When she was arrested, Elisabeth and Anton were married. But in the letter he left for Henri, he wrote that he'd proposed—not once, but several times. On each occasion she refused."

"Maybe the last time he pled his case, she accepted."

"Then why didn't he mention the marriage in the letter?"

"I don't know. Maybe Elisabeth asked him not to. Perhaps she thought the password would tell the story. Julien, may I see the signature card?"

"What are you looking for?" Arnaud asked.

"This." Anne pointed to the first line on the card.

"Okay. It's Auguste's signature, and there's a memo that says on July 9 he changed the password."

"It's the memo I find puzzling. Julien, how was Auguste able to alter the password? Madame Boulet was a Jew living in Nazi-controlled Paris. In a journal entry—I believe in early January, 1942—my grandmother wrote that the Nazis had disconnected their telephone, so her mother couldn't have called to authorize a new password. And I doubt she had an attorney on hand to prepare a notarized power of attorney so Auguste—"

"Monsieur Lessard had Madame Boulet's power of attorney from the time he first established the account." Julien removed a yellowing paper from the folder on his desk and held it in Anne's direction. "As you see, he had her *procuration,* or proxy. That meant he had her legal authorization to deposit money, access the safe-deposit box, alter passwords, and make necessary changes to the account." He took another paper from the folder, handed it to Arnaud and continued. "As you can see, Monsieur Lessard also had Monsieur Marsolet's proxy."

Arnaud's eyebrow shot up in surprise. "That's not possible!"

"To be sure, before you arrived I double-checked the records. Each time he came to Geneva, Monsieur Lessard made deposits to Monsieur Marsolet's accounts as well as to Madame Boulet's."

"You misunderstand, Julien. I wasn't questioning the authenticity of the document. I'm just surprised Auguste had such wide-ranging authority."

"I'm not surprised!" Anne said. "I'm stunned. It will take time to process all of this. I had no idea." She paused and then with a sharp intake of breath said, "I'm sure I'll have many more questions later. But for the moment, let's return to the change in Madame Boulet's password."

"On the bank's signature card there is no mention of the combination of letters and numbers Elisabeth used," Arnaud said. "Is that what you were looking for?"

"Initially yes, though I know a password isn't normally displayed on a signature card, I wanted to check be sure. Julien, you said, by necessity, bank protocol changed after the Holocaust. I wondered if passwords were noted on the card so heirs of Jews who didn't survive could more easily make deposits and withdraw money from their deceased relatives' accounts."

"No matter how lax the new regulations, that would never happen," Julien insisted. "We have the list of passwords in our safe so, with proper papers, a family member of a person who died during the war or under any other circumstance, could gain access. However, we would never openly display account information. Could you imagine—"

"I could. That's why I wanted to check. When I did, I found something interesting. Arnaud, look at the initials beside all of Auguste's signatures."

"They're G.V.," Arnaud said. "Why is that significant?"

"G.V.—Gardiner Vachon. You remember, the man Oma nicknamed German Victory. Julien, German Victory was the codename my grandmother gave the banker who initially established Madame Boulet's account here at your bank."

"She gave Monsieur Vachon a code name? In all my years as a banker, I have never heard of such a thing."

"My grandmother is definitely unique. Her mother warned her *never* to put anything in writing. Not being one to listen to orders, she wrote Monsieur Vachon's name in her journal so she'd remember if the need arose. Then, just to be safe, she gave him a code name in English so she wouldn't forget."

"That's clever thinking," Julien said.

A frown on her face, Anne shook her head. "Or not," she said. "I've heard and then retold this story several times recently, but only now did I realize my grandmother's efforts to disguise Monsieur Vachon's name would have been to no avail had the Nazis ransacked the house and found her journal."

"Because she also recorded his true name in the book alongside the code name," Julien said.

"Right."

"You'll have to mention that small detail to Veronique when you tell her about the initials G.V.—the infamous German Victory—on the card," Arnaud said, smiling.

"Would you dare tell her?"

"I get the point. Some things are better left unsaid."

"Exactly, but what a coincidence the initials on the card would be G.V. Had I not recently read my grandmother's journal, I wouldn't have given the bank's representative a second thought."

"And speaking of remembering," Arnaud said. "That is if we've exhausted the topic of German Victory, I clearly recall the date on the letter Anton left for Henri. It was written on August 22, 1942. If—as we now believe—a wedding took place on July 9, calculating quickly, and I may be off by a day or so, he wrote his letter forty-two days after the ceremony and thirty-six days after Elisabeth was arrested. Yet he never mentions a final proposal or Elisabeth's apparent acceptance."

"Who knows why he remained silent, but the evidence suggests he finally convinced her to marry him. Realizing she didn't have long to live, she may have wanted to die as his wife. Maybe she asked him to keep the marriage a secret, and he respected her wishes. And you raise yet another question. Why didn't she leave a second letter for Oma? There were eight days between her marriage and the second night of la rafle du Vel d'Hiv."

"She could have thought about writing a note to explain, but realizing the end was near, knew there wasn't time for Denis to remove the bricks and hide another message."

"Or maybe there was enough time, but she knew the Nazis were watching the house and she couldn't put Denis at risk. And here's a possibility we haven't considered. Remember Madame Bouffard said Elisabeth looked weak and ill when the Nazis dragged her from the house? She wasn't able to stand on her own, so the soldiers dragged her to the truck, one on either side to hold her upright. She could have been too feeble to write another letter. Or she assumed Oma and Henri would return to Paris immediately after the Liberation, find the clues she had left, come to Switzerland, and, looking at the password, realize the marriage took place."

"Is it really possible Veronique didn't know her mother and Anton had married?"

"Considering she didn't realize Elisabeth and Anton had been lovers for years, why would she even *begin* to think they'd become husband and wife at the end? And here's another new mystery to solve. Elisabeth wrote her letter in a code of sorts. Her words were so cryptic they required interpretation. Yet Anton's letter was straightforward. Why's that?"

"He may have figured with Elisabeth gone and nothing of value let in the house, the Nazis wouldn't bother to return. Martin was out of harm's way—"

"So there would be no need to leave an ambiguous message."

"This unforeseen news understandably came as a surprise," Julien said. "I should have excused myself earlier, but honestly, I am fascinated by Madame Marsolet's story."

"It's strange to hear you use Elisabeth's married name," Anne said.

"I am sure it is," Julien said. "If you prefer, I will give you privacy to continue your discussion."

"No need. Nothing could be any more shocking than what I just learned." Anne opened the envelope with Elisabeth's name printed on the front and glanced through the first two pages. The document was in French, so deciding to let her grandmother translate in-full later on, she flipped to the last page. "I was wrong," she choked out. "This time I'm not shocked—I'm overwhelmed." She turned to Julien, wide-eyed. "Is this figure correct? Are you absolutely sure—"

"I am. I checked the balance in the account just this morning. Madame Ellison is a very wealthy woman."

"She was already wealthy. Now she's Fortune-500 wealthy. There are over two hundred fifty million euros in this account."

"Madame Marsolet provided well for her daughter."

"That she did. I assumed. . . No, I can't say I assumed anything. Let's see what Anton left for Henri." She opened the enveloped marked Anton Marsolet and looked at the last page.

"And?" Arnaud said.

"Henri's not quite as rich as Oma. Poor man. His balance is only one hundred twenty-five million euros."

"Poor man, indeed! I doubt Henri ever imagined he'd have that kind of money."

"I agree, and I can't wait to tell him. It won't be the amount as much as the knowledge that his father loved him and provided for his future."

"As he did for Martin Fontaine," Julien said. "Martin called this morning. Though I am not at liberty to provide specific numbers, he instructed me to say the Fantin-Latour and the Degas Madame and Monsieur Marsolet sold more than adequately provided for him and his future family."

"My grandmother and Henri only recently learned they have a brother."

"That is what Martin told me. May I wish you all much happiness as you get to know one-another."

"We're definitely off to a good start. Imagine how everyone will feel when they learn Elisabeth and Anton were married."

"I would love to see the looks on their faces," Arnaud said.

"So would I, but we're going to have to settle for how they *sound* when I give them the news. I don't want to wait until we get home tomorrow to tell them."

"If you have no further questions at the moment, we can proceed to the next task." Julien picked up the phone on his desk and said to the person on the other end, "Please bring box one hundred fifty-two to the conference room." He hung up, stood, motioned toward the door, and said, "If you will kindly follow me. Prior to your arrival, not knowing whether or not you would bring a key, I took the liberty of having Madam Boulet's box removed from our safe. It has been well-guarded at all times."

They walked further down the picture-lined hall and entered a richly-furnished conference room. In the center of a shiny mahogany table, guarded by one of the bank employees, was a large safe-deposit box. "I will leave while you to take a look," Julien said. "The guard will remain outside the door. When you are finished, press the red button on the table."

"Thank you," Anne said. "I'll let you know if we want to use your courier service."

When Julien left the room, Anne sat down at the table and opened the box. Inside were two velvet-covered jewel cases and an envelope. She removed the letter, glanced at the date, and looking up, said, "Elisabeth wrote this for Veronique on March 23, 1942."

"Really!"

"You seem surprised."

"I am, but not about the letter. I'm still amazed my great-grandfather was able to travel in and out of France on a regular basis."

"Maybe, like Didier Duplessis, he bribed the guards to look the other way."

"It's certainly possible. So, at first glance, does the letter say anything we don't already know?"

"You're asking me? Haven't you been listening? My grandmother constantly admonishes me to brush up on my French? Out of necessity, you do the honors."

"Sure, but I agree—"

"It's probably wise not to go there—"

"In that case. . ."

For several minutes Anne waited while Arnaud silently perused the letter. "Realizing you aren't finished, you know I'm not a patient person."

"Really? That's a surprise."

"Again, I suggest you quit while you're ahead, though I admit I set myself up for a possible retort. So tell me what you've learned so far."

"Elisabeth reiterates her love for Anton and says he's the reason she won't leave Paris."

"I wonder if she had second thoughts about fleeing after she and Anton were married. I'm sure Auguste could have made the necessary arrangements."

"After seeing the signature card, probably with little difficulty. But they would have had to cross the Line of Demarcation and then the Swiss border on foot. Remembering what Madame Bouffard said—"

"Elisabeth was weak—unable to stand on her own. She wouldn't have survived the journey in her frail condition. Does the letter tell us anything we don't already know?"

Arnaud read the next few paragraphs. "Most of what's in here is old news, but here's something that may be significant. Elisabeth writes, 'If the Nazis come, there will be little of value for them to take.' Apparently she sold the paintings Denis hadn't already removed."

"That has to be why Auguste came to Geneva in July. He was depositing the proceeds from the latest sales into Elisabeth's account for Veronique, Anton's account for Henri, and perhaps into Martin's account as well. He had to make the deposit in person. He couldn't wire-transfer the money."

"I agree, but you look pensive. What are you thinking?"

"Under the circumstances, I hope I can persuade Oma to stop looking for whatever else the Nazis took from the house. If there was nothing of value, why bother to continue the search? Once again I'll remind her of the journal entry, the one where she said the walls of the house were bare. If there were any paintings left, they weren't important enough for her to notice."

"You think she'll heed your advice?"

"I don't know. . .Maybe. Okay, I doubt it. But if we find the paintings in Martin's closet—"

"Suppose we do. What next? Surely Veronique doesn't expect to hang millions of dollars' worth of art in her apartment. Even if she installs the most sophisticated security system known to man, within hours, everyone on Île St-Louis will know about the paintings, and soon the press will arrive en masse. The news would be more important than Clinton's visit to Madame Monleix-Wallig to sample her delicacies."

"Will you be serious! Oma and I talked about what she'd do with the paintings if we find them. I originally suggested she donate them to the Met."

"So they could be featured in your Christmas Exhibition."

"Possibly, but we also discussed gifting them to the Musée d'Orsay in Elisabeth's name. With that kind of contribution, they might make her a trustee."

"She'd love that, wouldn't she?"

"No question, and it would give her an excuse to remain in Paris."

"You think she wants to stay?"

"I do—for at least part of the year. If she goes back to New York, it will be for Henri and Renee. I believe she thinks she's come home. But enough of this. What else did Elisabeth say?"

"Lee's see." Arnaud read for a minute, and then looked up. "She answered one of our questions. She wrote, 'With the assistance of his partners in the Resistance, Auguste risked his life to deposit additional monies into Anton's and my accounts and to see that my jewels are held in safekeeping.'"

"Shall we see what Auguste brought to Geneva?"

"Absolutely." Anne lifted the lid of a brown wooden box. "Oh my God!" she exclaimed as she stared down at a plethora of pearls—a double strand, a long single strand, and a choker with a diamond clasp. She picked up a pearl ring and the matching earrings. "I'm stunned," she said. "I wonder what's in the second box, I'm afraid to look."

"Shall I open it for you?"

"No thanks, I was joking." She lifted the lid. "Look at this," she said, pushing the box toward Arnaud.

On the dark blue velvet lining, lay a diamond necklace with a matching bracelet and earrings, several diamond-encrusted pins, a large diamond solitaire on a gold chain, and two diamond rings. Arnaud picked up a ring with a square-cut diamond and held it up to the light. "I know very little about jewelry," he said. "But even I know this is an amazing stone."

"As are all the others." Anne pulled the box back toward her and, one-by-one, picked up each piece.

"What do you plan to do with these?" Arnaud asked. "Will you sign the paper to have the box inventoried and the jewels couriered to Paris?"

"I'll sign because I'm sure Oma will want her mother's jewelry, but I'll let her contact Julien with specific instructions. I'll take Elisabeth's letter and the account information with us on the plane."

While Arnaud pushed the button to summon Julien, Anne signed the authorization document. That task completed, she put the letter in her briefcase and the jewelry cases back in the safe-deposit box. When Julien entered the room, she and Arnaud were waiting by the door. "You're finished with your business," he said. "Shall I arrange for a courier?"

"My grandmother will let you know. Here's the authorization necessary to courier the contents of the box to Paris, if that's what she decides. Do I need to return to the bank in the morning?"

Julien nodded no. "Not unless you want to access the safe-deposit box again before you leave."

"At this point I see no reason. Thank you for your excellent service."

"It is my pleasure." Julien shook hands with both Anne and Arnaud. "I hope to see you both again."

CHAPTER 35

"It's early," Anne said when Julien left them at the bank's main entrance. "If you'd like, we can go back to Paris."

"If that's what you want—"

"I want to be with you, but why prolong the inevitable? I'm not sure—"

"If you aren't sure, then let's stay. We certainly have cause to celebrate."

"Oma and Henri are the ones who should be celebrating. This is *their* good fortune."

"True, but you helped get them to this point. You delicately—and, I might add, with great skill—interpreted Elisabeth's poem. You've taken much of the burden off Veronique's shoulders while all along allowing her to think she's playing an important role in finding her mother's paintings."

"She is. I couldn't have done this without her journal and without hearing her remarkable and tragic story."

"Then enjoy your victory. You've been running around ever since you arrived in Paris. You can relax for at least one night. We'll have lunch, enjoy the rest of the afternoon, go to dinner, and then, to use another phrase I learned during my short stay in America, 'kick back.' If you want to sleep in separate beds, I'll take a cold shower and cooperate."

Anne laughed. "Okay, my friend," she said. "Let's enjoy one last hurrah."

Arnaud called Paul, who was waiting nearby. Ten minutes later they pulled up to the entrance to the Four Seasons Hotel des Bergues. "Will you need the car again this evening?" he asked as he took the luggage from the trunk.

"As far as I know, we're staying in," Arnaud said. "As soon as I book our return flight to Paris, I'll call and let you know what time to pick us up. I imagine we'll be leaving early."

Paul gave the luggage to the bellman, who led Anne and Arnaud into the lobby and pointed toward the reception desk. "You may register just over there," he said. "I will place the luggage in your room."

Registering took only a few minutes and as the bellman promised, their bags were waiting on a rack at the bottom of the bed. While Arnaud opened the drapes and the French doors leading to the terrace, Anne glanced around at the Wedgewood-blue and light-green living room furnished in Louis Philippe-style white-stained furniture. "The Hotel des Bergues and this room in particular seem out of place in Geneva," she said. "At least in the parts of the city I've seen. In my opinion, though I could be proven wrong with further exploration, this is an architecturally-bland town."

"I'm not particularly fond of modern Geneva either," Arnaud said. "But I do like this hotel."

"So far, so do I. I'll change and then, though I have mixed emotions, I'll call Oma. After that, you can take me to lunch.

⌒⟲

"Much better," Anne said when she returned to the living room ten minutes later. "A skirt and heels aren't really my thing."

"What *is* your thing?"

"Yet to be determined, but, please, let's not go there. I'll make my call—"

"I'm confused. You *want* to speak with your grandmother. Yet—and I quote—you have 'mixed emotions.' Are you afraid she'll be upset when she hears Elisabeth and Anton married?"

"I'm sure she'll be astonished—probably more so than we were—but when she has time to absorb the news, she'll be pleased."

"Then why worry about telling her?"

"I'm not anxious about her reaction to the marriage itself—rather that it took place and she didn't know. She always talks about how naïve she was during the last months of the Occupation. She was ashamed she didn't realize her mother and Anton were lovers. When I tell her they were *married*, she'll chastise herself because she didn't have a clue."

"Then wait until you get home to break the news."

"I can't. She'll be livid if I say there's nothing new to report and when I get home confess I knew about the marriage during our earlier conversation."

"You could say you wanted to tell everyone the news at the same time."

"That won't fly. By now you know my grandmother can read me like a book. The moment I open my mouth, she'll realize I'm lying. I'll tell her now." She scrolled to Veronique's number, took a deep breath, let it out slowly, and pushed call.

"Should I leave?" Arnaud asked as Anne waited for her grandmother to answer.

"I'd rather you stay and let me know if I'm leaving anything out."

Veronique picked up on the third ring. "I've been waiting for your call," she said eagerly. "What happened at the bank?"

"Hi, Oma. Yes, I'm fine. The bankers couldn't have been nicer, and the hotel is lovely."

"I'm sorry, Anne. I've been sitting here impatiently waiting. Why don't I start over? Hello, darling."

"I'm teasing. You're a very wealthy woman."

"I've been a wealthy woman for over sixty years."

"I know, but now you're outrageously wealthy."

"What exactly does that mean?"

"It means you have over two hundred fifty million euros in your account."

There was a long pause on the other end of the line.

"Oma," Anne said. "Are you still there?"

"I am, darling. When you called, I got up and began to pace, but when you provided the actual numbers, I had to sit down. Mother left that much?"

"When accrued interest and at today's currency value, yes."

"What about the safe-deposit box?"

"There was a letter for you. I'm bringing it home."

"Did it say anything we don't already know?"

"Not really. Elisabeth wrote the letter on March 23, 1942, four months before she was arrested—"

"And two months before she wrote the poem we found behind the bricks. Any idea how the letter got to Geneva?"

"Auguste delivered it."

"Really!"

"That's right. Arnaud and I were as astounded as you sound. It turns out that Auguste was the only person who ever opened the box or deposited money. He accessed it seven times between June 1940 when, on Elisabeth's behalf, he opened the account, and July 1942, the last time he came to the bank."

"But how could he have crossed the Line of Demarcation and then the border between France and Switzerland so many times without being captured? It couldn't have been easy."

"We're not sure—probably with help from his friends in the Resistance. I doubt we'll ever know."

"There's so much I wish I knew," Veronique said introspectively. "If only—"

"No more looking back, Oma. Shall I summarize what your mother wrote?"

"No need if it doesn't say anything new. I'll read it when you get home. Is there anything else?"

"There is. Are you still sitting down?"

"I am. You're frightening me, Anne."

"There's nothing frightening about what I'm going to say, but I guarantee you'll be shocked. Is Henri around?"

"Gus just drove him, Renee, and Joseph to rue Gît."

"When they get back, will you have him call?"

"Of course, but now I'm even more nervous. You won't tell me whatever it is you want Henri to know?"

"I want to hear what, if anything, he found at Renee's home, and I think I should be the one to tell him what's in his account. I wouldn't tell him what's in yours."

"That's not it, and you know it. What?"

"Before you put the notarized documents in the folder I brought to Geneva, did you look closely at Elisabeth's password?"

"No. Did you have a problem?"

"Not a problem, but between March 1942 when she wrote the letter and the time Auguste came to Geneva in mid-July, Elisabeth changed the password."

"How could she do that? She was in occupied France—"

"She didn't. Auguste did it for her."

"How do you know?"

"When he made the change, he wrote the word *procuration,* meaning letter of attorney or proxy, beside his name."

"Auguste Lessard had Mother's power of attorney?"

"And Anton's as well. The authorization was granted when Auguste made the first deposit. Though I didn't see when he opened Anton's account, I assume it was during that first trip to Geneva. If he wants, Henri can find out when he speaks with Julien."

"I'm amazed by all of this. I had no idea!"

"Your mother wouldn't even provide the name of the bank, why would she go into detail about what other legal papers she'd signed?'

"I suppose you're right. Do you have any idea *why* she changed her password?"

"I believe so. She chose a series of numbers and letters she knew she would never forget. She picked EBM09071942."

For a few minutes Veronique didn't respond. "I'm afraid I don't understand," she finally said.

"I'm going to repeat the letters and numbers, and, remember, I'm using the European method of writing a date. Do you have a pen and paper handy?"

"Hold on a minute. I'll get one. . .All right, I'm ready."

"Write down EBM09071942 and tell me what you see."

"EBM—"

"Elisabeth Boulet Marsolet."

"You can't be suggesting Mother and Anton were married."

"They were, Oma. The ceremony took place on July 9, 1942, eight days before la rafle du Vel d'Hiv."

"09071942. Oh, Anne! Why didn't I realize—"

"Because Elisabeth didn't want you to know."

"Anton finally persuaded Mother to say yes. She must have known she was about to die, and she wanted to marry her one great love. That, I understand. But why didn't she or Anton tell us about their marriage? If not in person, they could have left another letter behind the bricks. And where did they get married?"

"I assume they expected you and Henri to return after the Liberation, find the password, access the account, and realize they were married. As for where the ceremony was performed, Elisabeth didn't say. Maybe someone came to the house to marry them. Jacqueline Bouffard said Elisabeth was frail. She may not have been strong enough to leave home. Or they could have married in Église Saint-Louis-en-l'Île."

"But what priest would marry a Catholic and a Jew? It was 1942—"

"Maybe Father didn't know Elisabeth was Jewish."

"If he was from the Île, he had to know. I've told you—"

"I know, everyone knew everyone else's business. We can speculate all we want, but I doubt we'll ever know where the wedding took place. No civil servant would dare marry a Christian and a Jew with Jew-hating Nazis in control."

"And we know they didn't marry in a synagogue. Oh, Anne, I'm so ashamed. Gus teases you about wearing blinders when it comes to art. I was blind about life. I didn't even know my own mother was married to my best friend's fiancée's father."

"That's quite a mouthful, but honestly, Oma, you have no reason to feel ashamed. Those were difficult times for everyone. You were secretly meeting Renee so the two of you could talk. In April, two months before you fled Paris, you told her you couldn't be part of her wedding party. The food you needed to survive was delivered by neighbors under the cover of darkness. Why would you question something your mother was making every effort to hide? I doubt she wore a wedding ring."

"She hadn't worn a ring for years. Oh my! Now I remember! She took it off just before she left on her grand tour. I was young, but I noticed. When I asked where it was, she said her hand was swollen and didn't want it to get stuck. I don't think she ever put it back on."

"Her hands were probably puffy from the pregnancy."

"Knowing what we do, that makes sense. I hate to think the Nazis took her ring and her other jewels, so I'm almost afraid to ask—is there a pavé diamond ring in the safe-deposit box?"

"There is. Oma, Elisabeth's jewelry is amazing."

Anne spent the next few minutes describing the pieces in the two velvet boxes. She finished with, "Do you still have the paper and pen you used to write Elisabeth's password?"

"I do."

"Good. Here's Julien's contact information. Call him." Speaking slowly, Anne repeated the numbers. "I signed the appropriate authorization to have the box inventoried and the jewelry couriered. The pieces are too valuable for Arnaud and me to take with us on the plane."

"Do you think that's wise? I mean can we be sure *all* the jewelry will arrive—that nothing will be missing?"

"I'm sure it will. I've seen the bank and met the people who work there. Believe me, they won't risk their reputation for a ring or a bracelet."

"I'll have a safe installed. You've finished at the bank?"

"As far as I know."

"Are you flying home tonight?"

"In the morning, though we'll probably leave earlier. . .Arnaud just mouthed the word nine, so we should be home by eleven. Martin's train arrives at eleven forty-five. Why don't you text him and see if we can meet earlier—maybe one or two."

"I will, though I can't imagine finding anything that could amaze me more than what I just learned, and I don't mean what you said about the jewels or the amount of money in the account. Henri will be shocked about the marriage."

"Will you tell Martin?"

"Of course. I imagine he'll be surprised, but probably not stunned like I am. He never knew Mother and how stubborn she could be. Once she made up her mind—"

"No comment," Anne teased. "So if you're okay, and there's nothing else for now, Arnaud and I are going to lunch. I'll have my cell if you need me."

"I'll be fine, though I certainly have a lot to absorb. I love you."

"I love you too."

Arnaud was on the phone when Anne hung up. "Bertrand," he mouthed.

While Arnaud talked, Anne stepped onto the terrace. As she gazed out at the sparkling water of Lake Geneva, her thoughts turned from searching for missing art to the predicament at hand. *How can I leave the man I love,* she asked herself, and then answered, *But how can I not? Yes, I love Arnaud Lessard, but—*"

"Are you ready to go?" Arnaud asked, interrupting her musings.

"I am," Anne said, trying to recover. "From what little I heard of your conversation, I gather Bertrand didn't know Anton and Elisabeth got married."

"He had no idea. Nor did he realize Auguste had crossed into Switzerland even once, let alone seven times."

"He never asked his father why he'd be away for days at a time—where he'd been?"

"He said he assumed he was involved in resistance operations. He knew better than to ask for specific details. Did you tell Henri about his good fortune?"

"Gus drove him, Renee, and Joseph to rue Gît. Oma will have him call when he returns."

"While you were talking, I also phoned Paul. He'll pick us up in the morning at seven."

"In that case, with nothing left to accomplish, at least for the moment, I'm starving."

Lunch was more about what wasn't said than what was. Unlike other meals they'd shared, there was little talk. They relaxed and enjoyed the scenery. Both cautious about causing an argument. Neither wanting to push. They had just shared a dessert when Anne's phone vibrated. She checked the caller ID. "If you'll excuse me," she said. "It's Henri. While we talk I'll walk toward the lake."

"I'll take care of the check and join you."

Anne nodded, stood, and pushed talk. "How are you Henri?" she began as she left the table.

"In a state of shock."

"Because you spoke with Oma, or from what you discovered at Renee's?"

"The former. Do you really think Elisabeth and my father got married several days before la rafle du Vel d'Hiv?"

"Without a doubt. Elisabeth changed her password eight days before the Nazis battered down her front door."

"I had no idea—"

"Oma had the same response. I'm telling you what I told her. Why would you? Your father and Elisabeth were discreet—so much so that neither you nor Oma knew they'd been lovers for years."

"Veronique says she buried her head in the sand. I was different. I wanted to know *everything*."

"Yet despite your inquisitive nature, Elisabeth and Anton were able to conceal their affair, their child, and their marriage."

There was a pregnant pause on Henri's end.

"Henri?"

"I'm here honey. There's so much to absorb."

"For both you and Oma. Did she also tell you about—"

"She only discussed the marriage and her bank account."

"She didn't tell you Auguste traveled to Geneva seven times between June, 1940 and July 1942?"

"No! You're kidding! How—"

"We have no idea. We may never know."

"You're probably right. Is that it? I'm not sure this old ticker can take much more."

"Actually, there's more. Auguste had Elisabeth's power of attorney—your father's as well. Though I don't know exactly when—or if—he initially opened Anton's accounts, he freely deposited money each time he traveled to Geneva."

"Again, I'm amazed."

"I'm sure you are. If you have additional questions, we'll talk when I return to Paris, though I'm not sure I'll have answers you're seeking. For now, back to the password change. Arnaud and I believe the addition of the letter B was to celebrate Anton and Elisabeth's marriage and her new last name. The numbers tell us when the ceremony took place."

"But in his letter to me—the one hidden behind the bricks—he wrote that Elisabeth turned him down every time he asked."

"Until she realized she wasn't going to survive, either because she was too weak or the Nazis had intensified their campaign against Parisian Jews and she knew she'd soon be arrested."

"I suppose that makes sense," Henri said pensively. "What a shock."

"Oma's sentiments exactly."

"No doubt, but moving on—at least for now. Veronique said you wouldn't tell her what my father left for me."

"I thought I should deliver the news. You can share the information with her if you choose. So, care to know how rich you are?"

"Sure. Am I in for yet another shock?"

"Possibly. Are you sitting down?"

"No. I'm pacing while I attempt to absorb what I just heard. Do I need to be seated?"

"I'd say so."

"Okay. . .I'm now on the couch."

"At today's value, your account is worth one hundred twenty-five million euros."

There was silence on the other end of the line.

"Henri?" Anne said. "Are you still there? Did you have a heart attack?"

"No," Henri said breathlessly. "But it's the closest I've ever come. What are Renee and I going to do with all that money?"

"I'm sure you'll think of something. Before we hang up, did you learn anything at Renee's?"

"Nothing more than we already know, but I'm glad Joseph took up the tiles. Jules left keepsakes for Renee, including family pictures and Adele's wedding ring."

"What about the electrical box on the roof?"

"We hit a dead end. As we thought, when the house was rewired, the old box was removed, so if Jules left a message, it's gone."

"Too bad. Is Renee all right after spending the afternoon in her childhood home?"

"She is. She and your grandmother walked over to Calixte. Are you enjoying yourself in Geneva?"

"I am. It's a beautiful day. I'm going to sit by the pool. I didn't bring a swimsuit, but it's enough just to be outside."

"Well you have a good time, honey. While you're doing that, I'll be sitting right here in the living room thinking about how rich I am."

"You weren't too bad off before my news."

"No, but now the possibilities are limitless."

"They certainly are. So you dream about your vast wealth while I bask in the Swiss sunshine. See you soon."

Just as Anne pushed the end button, Arnaud came up behind her. "Did I hear you say you're going to sit by the pool?"

"You did. Will you join me?"

"I have several calls to make. I'll meet you back at the room."

Anne found an empty lounge chair by the pool. She sat down, stretched out, and closed her eyes to take a short nap. "Damn, I can't do this," she whispered, unable to drift off.

"I beg your pardon, Madame." Anne looked up at a waiter carrying a tray of water.

"I was thinking out loud," Anne said.

"It is a warm day. Would you like a bottle of water, or if you prefer, a glass of wine."

"Water please. Where do I sign?"

"There is no need. This is a courtesy we provide our guests."

You're losing revenue, Anne thought. *This little bottle would cost four or five dollars in New York.* "Thank you," she said.

When the waiter left, she took her water and strolled along the path by the lake. She had always been a water person, but even the lapping of the tiny waves on the shore couldn't ease her anxiety. "I can't stay away forever," she whispered as she turned and walked back toward the room.

Nervous and confused, she inserted the keycard in the slot and pushed open the door. "I'm back," she called out. "Arnaud?" She checked the bedroom, but he wasn't there. *Maybe he gave up on me and went home,* she mused. *That would make things so much easier.*

Looking around, she spied a note on her pillow. She picked it up and read. 'Finished my work and went out for a run. Back soon! Missed you this afternoon. Hope you enjoyed the sunshine.'

"I missed you too," Anne whispered. "That's the problem." She took a shower, dried her hair, put on the thick terrycloth robe she found hanging behind the door, and returned to the living room just as Arnaud opened the door. "Good run," she asked, half smiling.

"Good run and a good swim. I was sweaty, so I took a quick dip to cool off."

"I thought of you while I sat out by the pool. I'll miss you when I get home."

"Then don't leave."

"I have to go. That's the problem."

"Could we stop talking about problems, at least for the moment?" He took a step forward, untied her robe, gently pushed it off her shoulder, and murmured, "Can you do that?"

"I don't know," Anne groaned. "But you're making a good case." She didn't resist when he began to kiss her neck, his lips traveling to her breasts. "I don't think this is a good idea," she weakly argued.

"Stop thinking."

Their lovemaking was intense, passionate, and poignant—each wanting to give the other pleasure as if it were the last time they would be together.

"I love you," Arnaud whispered, gathering Anne in his arms and stroking her hair.

"And I love you, but let's not have this talk—at least not now. Let's savor the moment."

For the next half hour they lay wrapped in each other's arms. Both silent. Neither wanting to cause conflict by talking.

Arnaud finally broke the silence. "You know our life could always be this good," he whispered into her hair. "You keep dwelling on the negatives. What about the positives?"

"There are no positives, at least in the long run. So let's get dressed and, if only for a while longer, stop thinking about the future and live in the moment."

"If that's what you want, get dressed, but—"

"It's what I want."

⚭

Anne showered, dressed in a black dress that showed off her slender body and long legs, and put on black sling-back high heels. Arnaud stood as she entered the room. "You look beautiful," he said. "You're sure you don't want to stay in and pick up where we left off? We could order room service—"

"What, and waste my little black dress? No way!"

"You're *absolutely* sure—"

Before she could respond, Anne's phone rang. "Saved by the bell," she said. "It's Oma."

"Hi, darling," Veronique said. "I hope I'm not interrupting."

"Arnaud and I are about to leave for dinner, but I have a few minutes. What's up?"

"I reached Martin. Emme had the baby this morning, but the baby's birth isn't why I called. Emme's mother had just arrived, and though he didn't say so, I think Martin was looking for an excuse to leave. He's taking an earlier train back to Paris. If it works for you and Arnaud, we'll meet at his house at noon rather than three."

"Perfect. We land at Charles de Gaulle a little after ten."

"Is Gus picking you up?"

"No. Remember? Arnaud's car is at the airport."

"That's right. Maybe it's best you aren't expecting Gus. I tried to reach him earlier, but he didn't answer."

"Did you leave a message? I'm sure he checks—"

"I did. He just called back. He was meeting with a contact."

"About what? Did he say?"

"Not specifically, but I gather he's still looking for information about the paintings the Nazis removed from the house the night they arrested Mother. I must say, Gus was one of my better finds."

"The fates were smiling when you googled limo drivers. That's it from this end—at least for now. Arnaud's looking at his watch and giving me the evil eye. So if there's nothing else, I'll see you tomorrow. I know you're apprehensive about what we may or may not find at Martin's, but try to get some sleep."

For Anne, and, she suspected, for Arnaud as well, dinner was bittersweet. The conversation was enjoyable but not meaningful. Like at lunch, they tacitly avoided sensitive subjects, instead, talking about Arnaud and Sophie's childhood on the Île, Anne's experiences growing up in New York and the Hamptons, and her sometimes contentious relationship with Madeline.

After dinner, holding hands and soaking in the atmosphere of a lovely spring evening, they took a stroll. "I was going to suggest a nightcap on the terrace, but you look exhausted," Arnaud said as they turned back toward the hotel.

"I am, and tomorrow we have to get up early for yet another day of adventure. Lately my entire life consists of one escapade after another. After we finish at Martin's—"

"We agreed—tonight we're not talking about the future, and that includes what we may or may not find tomorrow. Let's go to bed."

Arnaud checked his messages and returned two calls while Anne got ready for bed. She was almost asleep when he slid beneath the covers. "I love you," he whispered.

She snuggled against him, and murmured, "I love you too."

CHAPTER 36

Wrapped in Arnaud's arms, Anne slept soundly. When she felt him roll out of bed, she lifted her head and looked at the clock. "It's only five-thirty," she groaned through the haze of sleep. "What are you doing up at this ungodly hour?"

"I thought we'd have breakfast before Paul picks us up. Our flight leaves at ten. We're meeting Martin and the others at noon, so we may not have time for lunch."

"You go," Anne moaned. "I'll settle for peanuts on the plane. If it makes you feel gallant, bring me a cup of coffee—maybe two. Once I down those, I'll *think about* getting up."

"You'll settle for peanuts and then be grouchy later because you're hungry." Arnaud pulled back the covers. "Up!"

"Must I?"

"Let's put it this way. It's either breakfast or me."

"Okay, breakfast," Anne said, grinning and suddenly sitting up.

❧

"Given the choice, I should have picked you instead of breakfast," Anne whispered as Arnaud signed the check.

"On that point, I can't argue, but why the sudden change of heart? You cleaned your plate, so it can't be the food—"

"It *is* the food. I ate so much I may not meet the plane's weight allowance, if there is such a thing."

"You'll make it, but if we don't get going, the plane may leave us both behind—though if we didn't have to be at Martin's by noon, I'd like that."

Back at the room, they packed and checked the closets and bathroom one last time before Arnaud picked up the bags. "Are you ready to go home?" he asked.

"You mean on to our next big adventure?"

At the door, Anne stopped, looked back, and mused, *And now reality sets in.*

Paul was waiting with the car. The flight was on time, and they landed at Charles de Gaulle a little after ten. "Will there be time to change before we meet Martin?" Anne asked as they left the airport parking lot.

"Sure, if we don't encounter traffic. Are we picking up the others on the way?"

"Martin's getting them. And now it's time to start praying?"

"Why, I'm sure they'll wait if we're running late."

"Not about that. Oma *needs* to find the paintings."

"Needs?"

"Absolutely. Two weeks ago we all thought she'd given up. She seemed ready to die. But after she finally shared her long-unrevealed story and then came to Paris to find her mother's paintings, everything changed. Suddenly she *wanted* to get better. She had a purpose—a reason to live."

"And you're worried if art isn't hidden in Martin's closet, she'll give up again?"

"Afraid might be a better word."

"Okay, then let's pray for the best."

Traffic was light, so it only took an hour to drive from the airport to the Île. "If you can manage your carry-on and briefcase, I'll drop you off," Arnaud said. "Before we go to Martin's I want to check my email to see if the deal I've been working on went through."

"If you need extra time, I can walk to Quai de Bethune."

"I shouldn't be long, so unless I call and tell you otherwise, I'll pick you up in forty-five minutes. Are you stopping in to see Veronique on your way up?"

"I don't think so. If I show up, she'll think she has to drive over with us. Then she'll worry about disappointing Martin. It's best if we stick with our original plan and meet her there."

Veronique, Henri, and Renee were waiting for Martin to arrive when Anne came down and entered the lobby. "How long have you been back?" Veronique asked. "You didn't come in to say hello."

"There wasn't time. Arnaud dropped me off and I went up to change."

"Arnaud's not coming with us?"

"Of course he is. He'll be here shortly. In fact here he comes now, and Martin's right behind him. It appears you have your choice of chariots, Oma."

"For the sake of family unity, we'll go with Martin," Veronique said. "And besides, if you and Arnaud are alone, he may find a way to make realize you belong here in Paris with him."

"What makes you think he hasn't already convinced me to stay?"

"I know you, my darling granddaughter. Your eyes reflect your ever-changing moods. I've always been able to tell when you're happy and when you're sad. Right now you're miserable. Why can't you face the truth? You're in love with Arnaud Lessard."

"You're absolutely right, Oma. There, I admitted my feelings, but that doesn't change anything. There's a look on your face that says you're about to offer unsolicited advice. Please don't. And don't broach the subject again, especially in front of Arnaud. I've made my decision. I'm going home."

Veronique waved to Martin and looked back at her granddaughter. Her brow furrowed, she said, "You're a stubborn woman, Anne. I hope the choice you're making now doesn't come back to haunt you later. I'm afraid when you finally figure out you've made a foolish decision it will be too late for you and Arnaud. He will have moved on." She smiled and added, "Ah, if I were fifty years younger. . ." She abruptly turned and walked away.

"Is your grandmother all right?" Arnaud asked as he opened Anne's door. "She looks upset."

"Of course she is."

"Sorry, I just—"

"Please don't apologize. My Mr. Hyde side momentarily emerged— likely because I'm nervous."

"You're sure that's it?"

"I'm sure. *So,* shall we go find out what is—or isn't—hidden in Martin's closet?"

At the entrance to the garage, Martin inserted his key in the slot, stuck his arm out the open window, and waved for Arnaud to follow him in.

"Thank you for taking my granddaughter to Geneva," Veronique said as Arnaud helped her out of the car. "You had a successful trip?"

"We did—at least in your regard. Your mother's jewels are remarkable."

"That's what Anne said. I spoke with Julien yesterday after you left the bank, and I had a safe installed in my apartment earlier this morning. The courier will deliver the contents of Mother's safe-deposit box tomorrow morning at eleven."

"You do work fast."

"When I want something, nothing stops me, young man. If you don't know that by now, you'll soon find out."

"Unfortunately we don't always get what we want." Arnaud took Veronique's arm. "Shall we bring all those paintings Denis hid so long ago from the darkness into the light where they belong?"

"I don't suppose I can put it off any longer," Veronique said tentatively. "But I'm so nervous."

"Your granddaughter is too. You both need to think positive thoughts."

∽୭

When they reached the fourth floor of Martin's house, Veronique looked back at her brother. "You should install an elevator, and soon," she said breathlessly.

"I've been thinking the same thing recently. Getting old isn't much fun, is it, Veronique?"

"Sometimes it isn't—that's for sure. So here we are. Giles thought Mother's room was at the far end of the hall overlooking the Left Bank."

Martin took his sister's arm. "If it truly was, then the room where she grew up became my son Eric's room when we came to the city. Then it was where Eric Anton stayed when he visited."

"And now your great grandson will play here," Veronique said wistfully. "Mother would love that."

"Enough reminiscing," Henri said. "Are you ready, Veronique?"

"As ready as I'll ever be."

"Then," said Martin, "shall we see if we can find the hidden closet?"

When they reached the door, he escorted Veronique inside, let go of her arm, crossed the room to a door opposite the windows, and hesitated. "Go on," Veronique urged. "As we say in America, "There's no time like the present.'"

Martin opened the closet door and gasped. When he looked back at the others the color had drained from his face.

"What?" Veronique called out from across the room. "Is something wrong?"

"This is—or rather it *was*—where Denis hid Mother's paintings—"

"Was?" Veronique approached her brother. "You just opened the door. Are you sure you're in the right closet?"

"Take a look. You'll understand what I mean. Anne correctly interpreted Mother's poem. There *is* a closet built within the closet, and it's wide open for all to see."

"Can you actually see the paintings?" Anne asked. "Are they unwrapped?"

Martin looked back at the group. "Painting without the letter's'. There is only one wrapped package in this very large space."

Veronique peered in. "Martin's right," she said, her voice quivering.

"You're kidding!" Henri said in disbelief as he and the rest of the group joined Veronique and Martin at the closet entrance. He moved inside and surveyed the empty space. "I would say the storage area is three feet wide by eight feet long. Clearly it was built to hold more than one small painting."

"And look at the toys," Arnaud said. "Is this the way you store them, Martin?"

"Never so neatly. I prefer to leave them strewn around the floor. The disarray reminds me of all the children who played in here over the years."

"Yet now they're piled neatly in the corner, probably so the hidden closet could be more easily accessed."

"Someone beat us here," Henri said, his face reddening. "Whoever it was used a cutter of sorts to get through the plaster board, and he did so recently. There's plaster dust on the floor. Clearly he knew about the space. While Martin was in Brittany, he entered the house and robbed Veronique of what Denis left in the closet so many years ago."

"But who else was privy to our plan?" Anne asked. "Several people knew we were searching for Elisabeth's paintings, but few knew we believed them to be in Martin's house." Thinking aloud, she ran through the list. "There's Giles."

"There's no way he could have managed this," Henri said.

"Nor could the others who knew about the search. There's Bertrand, Francoise, Isabelle, Isaac, Cecile, and Madame Bouffard."

"That list is laughable!"

"Who's left?" Renee asked.

"Joseph, the mason, but he was in the kitchen on the phone while we were reading Elisabeth's and Anton's letters, so he didn't know about the closeted space—that is unless you said something when you went with him to Renee's, Henri."

"Of course I didn't."

It makes no sense," Veronique said. "Could someone have gotten lucky and found the paintings?"

"After all these years? And, coincidentally, the day we were coming to look for them? Oma, did you tell anyone? What about the man who installed your safe? Maybe you casually mentioned you might need a larger safe to hold the paintings you expected to find at your brother's house?"

"Definitely not, Anne. Do you think I'm that foolish?"

"No. I'm just trying to make some sense of what's going on."

"So who could it be?" Veronique pleaded.

"Oh my God," Anne blurted out. "It's Gus!"

Veronique suddenly paled. "It can't be Gus. He returned *The Work Table*. Why would he do that and then steal the rest of Mother's paintings? Without concrete proof, I *cannot* and *will not* accept your supposition."

"I don't want to believe it either, Oma. But think about it. Gus is the only person who could have done this."

"I agree with Anne," Arnaud said. "Gus is the thief. Among everyone who knew about the hidden art, he's the only one who's capable of breaking in, cutting into the wall, and removing heavy paintings. Anne, unwrap the package that's in the closet. Let's see if we can figure out why he left one painting behind."

Tears streamed down Anne's cheeks as she struggled with crushing emotions—one minute irate; the next sad that someone she cared about could do such a thing.

"Anne," Veronique said. "Are you all right?"

"With due respect, Veronique," Henri injected. "That's a stupid question. None of us is all right."

"I know," Veronique said testily. "But—"

"What would you have me do, Oma?" Anne lashed out. "Should I yell and scream? Should I pound the walls? I show my anger differently than Henri—I cry. Yes, I'm devastated. But I'm also trying to figure out our next move, which is impossible if I'm standing here ranting and raving."

"Understood. We all react differently."

"No, *I'm* sorry. I'm just—"

"Feeling betrayed like I am."

"Something like that."

Anne picked up the twenty-four by twenty-inch package and returned to the bedroom. She removed a section of the paper and addressed the group. "Sadly, I was right! It *was* Gus who opened the wall and made off with Great-Grand'Mere Elisabeth's art."

"You have positive proof, because—"

"I do, Oma. Look at this." She stripped off the remaining paper and held up the painting for all to see.

"Okay," Henri said. "We're looking at a picture of a kitchen with blue tiles behind an old stove and a yellow farm table—"

"It's Monet's kitchen at Giverny. I didn't know he painted the inside of the house, but I *do* know Gus left this piece for me."

"Why would he?" Renee asked.

"Because the day we drove around the city looking at places Oma mentioned in her journal, I told Gus that Monet's kitchen is one of my favorite places in the world."

"I remember the painting," Veronique said. "It hung in Mother's private parlor. It must have been one of her favorites because she didn't move it around like she did the others. Oh, Anne, what else has been hidden in this closet all these years?"

"God knows! Gus knows! But I doubt we'll ever know," Henri growled.

"Don't give up yet," Arnaud urged. "The question become what are we going to do? Anne, do you know where Gus lives?"

"Only that his apartment is in Saint-Germain near rue Gît. I wrote the name of the street on the back of his card, but he never mentioned an apartment number. I programmed his phone number into my cell and put the card with my passport in my desk drawer."

"Knowing the street name may be enough. If we're lucky, Gus's car will be in front of the building."

"He's probably long gone," Veronique said, dejected.

"I'm not so sure," Arnaud said. "He still believes we're meeting Martin at three. Unless someone told him otherwise, he has no idea we moved the appointment to noon. Did *anyone* say *anything* about our change in plans?"

"I certainly didn't," Veronique said in a huff.

"Nor did I," said Henri. "Renee?"

"Definitely not!"

"Then assuming he thinks we plan to start our search for the closet within the closet at three, he would further expect it would take at least an hour to determine which one."

"Martin," Veronique said. "This may be irrelevant, especially in light of what's going on, but how could Gus break into your house in the first place? Surely you have a security system."

"Of course I do," Martin said, reddening. "But I don't know if it works."

"You don't use it?"

"Until now I've had no reason to turn it on."

"At the moment how Gus got inside isn't important," Arnaud said. "Where he took the paintings and how to stop him from leaving the country with them is the issue."

"Maybe Gus left a note. Let's take a look." Anne turned the painting to look at the back. "Just as I thought," she said. "There's an envelope taped to the frame."

"What could Gus possibly say that would justify his taking Mother's paintings?"

"We'll soon know." Anne opened the envelope and removed a letter.

"Do I need to read?" Veronique asked, this time with no smile.

"No need, Oma. Gus wrote in English. He begins,

Dear Veronique, Anne, Henri, Renee, Martin, and Arnaud,
Though I doubt you will truly understand, I must try to explain why I took Madame Boulet's paintings. I am sorry it has come to this, but all of my life I have planned for this moment—never really believing it would come. It did. I must act. Until now, life for me has been difficult. You might say fate dealt me a bad hand."

"He dares play the poor-me card," Henri snarled.

"Henri," Renee said, shooting daggers. "Stop interrupting and let Anne read. We know you're angry, and rightfully so, but we need to find Gus—and soon. Let's not prolong the process."

"Sorry," Henri said, looking contrite. "I'll try to keep my thoughts to myself—at least for the moment."

"It's okay," Anne said. "We're all upset. Let's see. Gus goes on to say, *'When I saw how well you all live, my own situation became even more apparent. Right or wrong, I want the good life. I have always struggled.'*"

"Oh my God," Henri interjected. "Sorry," he quickly added. "I can't help myself."

"Gus took the paintings because we're rich?" Veronique said, her shoulders slumped in despair. "Were we snobs? Did we make him feel unimportant? If I did, I didn't realize—"

"Absolutely not!" Renee said irately. "It has to be something else. Does Gus explain, Anne?"

"We'll soon know. He says,

I wish I could be like Damien Duplessis, but I am not so generous. Returning the paintings his father kept is his life's work. I realize his fortune was illegally attained, but right or wrong, the money gave him a life I can only imagine.

"Why the hell would Gus compare himself to Damien Duplessis?" Henri said. "He only met the man once."

"And why did he return the Bonnard?" Veronique asked, equally astounded. "Why not steal it too? It would bring a fortune. It doesn't make sense—"

"Not in light of the Gus we know. Let's see if he explains. He writes, 'I have been waiting for years. Not for you—for anyone on my list.'"

"What list?" Veronique asked. "Why would we be on a list? The first time Gus heard of me was when I contacted him to drive for you, Anne. Does he elaborate?

"Hopefully. He goes on to say,

I put out my resume years ago, hoping and praying someone would contact me to drive them or perhaps want to talk about my books or the art the Nazis commandeered during the Occupation. I never imagined it would happen. When Veronique hired me to drive Anne, my fantasy suddenly

became reality. I shamefully made you depend on me, all the time waiting
for you to find clues that would lead you to Madame Boulet's art. I actively
participated in your search. I wanted to use you. Not like you. You may be
confused—wondering why I feel so entitled. My grandfather was Didier
Dupleiss' partner.

"Oh my God!" Anne cried out. "Those six words say it all. When I first met Gus, I asked him if his grandfather's stories about the Occupation had inspired him to write. At the time, I thought his answer was odd. He said 'no,' and then quickly added, "But let's leave it at that.'"

"He didn't elaborate?"

"Not then, but now we know the reason for his reaction. Listen to this. 'It was he who forged the false papers for Veronique, Henri, and Renee. When Renee called and read the letter her father left in the Bible, her words intensified my desire to search.'"

"Gus heard?" Renee said.

"My part of the conversation. When you first called, he asked if I wanted him to step out of the car so I could talk in private. I said no. Why would it matter what he heard? At least that was my thought at the time. After we hung up, I asked if he was familiar with rue de Fleurus and told him about Didier."

"You couldn't have known he was planning to steal Elisabeth's art," Renee said.

"I agree," said Veronique. "But I still can't believe this is happening."

"Nor can I," Anne said. "Let's see if he answers our questions. He writes,

Didier was truly an evil man. He owed my grandfather compensation for
services rendered, but, to the end, he refused to pay. Instead, he used the
money he made from the sale of the paintings to purchase an expensive
home and to live the good life. Despite his initial disappointment, my grand-
father kept doing the jobs Didier assigned—ever confident that his efforts,
corrupt though they were, would further his family's station in life. I guess
we all live with some kind of hope. He certainly did. To no avail.

In early 1944, the Nazis arrested Didier for helping Jews escape occupied France. Broke, out of a job, and unable to pay the bills, my grandfather lost the family home and any hope for a bright future. One night, unable to cope any longer, he bit into a cyanide pill, leaving our family with nothing. Papa worked menial jobs—barely making enough to put food on our table and clothes on our backs. When he, too, could no deal with his miserable life, he put a gun to his head and pulled the trigger. Though I was just a child, even today, I can close my eyes and picture the bloody room. His death stirred a myriad of emotions. I was sad, angry, guilt-ridden, and resolute. I was also determined to succeed, if not for me, for him. I worked my way through college, taking seven years to graduate instead of the usual four. I drove to pay my bills and I wrote books about the Occupation. Then you came to Paris.

After Anne's telephone conversation with Renee, I contacted Damien. When we met, he talked about his goal—to return the paintings his grandfather kept for his own collection. I told him who I was, the grandson of his grandfather's partner. Then I lied. I said I was also trying to make things right. That was when he gave me the painting from Madame Boulet's collection. Greedy though I am, Veronique, I could not keep the art that purchased your new life in a free country. That is why I returned The Work Table. *Anne, if you are reading this letter, you know I left a painting for you—a depiction of Monet's kitchen at Giverny. I know how much you love* our *favorite artist's home.*

"How could Gus possibly think he'll be able to sell such valuable paintings?" Martin asked. "Does he say?"

Anne scanned the paragraph. "Actually, he does. Listen to this.

You must wonder how I plan to sell paintings by, arguably, the most well-known artists in the world. When you first came to town, I began to line up private collectors—wealthy individuals who are more interested in owning the art than reporting me to the authorities. The paintings will not be displayed in museums. The buyers' experts will verify the authenticity of each work, so provenance inquiries will not alert the authorities.

"Oh my!" Veronique removed a handkerchief from her pocketbook and dabbed her eyes. "How could Gus do this? And seemingly with so little remorse."

"It looks like he's attempting to explain in the next paragraph," Anne said.

"As if he could," Henri boomed, fire in his eyes. "Keep reading, Anne. We might as well hear his excuse."

"Clearly he feels sorry—"

"Bull. . ." Henri yelled, looking at Veronique and stopping short of finishing his declaration.

"Will you please let Anne read," Renee implored. "Tell us what Gus said, honey."

Anne sighed and said, "He writes,

In many ways my heart is breaking. I do not expect you to understand. How could you? You never wanted for anything. I never had anything. By the time you read this letter, I will have left Paris with the paintings. Will I be happy with all the things money can buy? Only time will tell. I only wish I could fulfill my dream without dashing yours.

"What are we going to do?" Veronique asked as she wiped the tears from her cheeks. "Do we have a chance to recover Mother's paintings?"

"The man's a thief," Henri hissed. "The rest of you can sit here debating while I act." He took his cell from this pocket. "I'm calling the police."

Anne reached out and put her hand on Henri's arm. "You can't," she said. "We have no choice. We have to handle this without police involvement."

"For Gus? Why the hell would we do anything for him? He screwed—."

"Please Henri," Veronique pleaded. "And you're wrong about Gus. Putting your words in more acceptable language, he didn't betray us—at least not entirely. We have two paintings—"

"True, but what about the others Denis hid? We don't even know how many there were."

"Could we stop bickering and try to figure out what to do?" Anne pleaded.

"Anne's right," Arnaud said. "We're all upset, and rightfully so. But if we're going to make rational decisions, lashing out won't help. First, we have to find Gus. My guess, he's still at his apartment. It's only twelve forty-five."

"Maybe he hasn't had time to move the paintings," Renee said.

"Unless he stole them yesterday," said Veronique.

Anne held out the letter and pointed to the heading. "Look," she said. "If Gus wrote this yesterday, why did he use today's date?"

"To fool us, of course," Henri argued. "My guess, he packed what he'd need for a trip to who-knows-where, came here to steal the paintings, loaded his car, and left Paris. Think about it! Why would he take millions of dollars' worth of art home? He'd have to move the paintings inside or leave them in the car while he packed. I doubt he'd take a chance—"

"Now wouldn't that be the ultimate irony," Arnaud said. "Gus steals Elisabeth's paintings only to have them stolen by someone else."

"I agree with Henri," Martin said. "Gus is long-gone."

Veronique shook her head. "I choose to believe he's still in Paris. But if we catch him before he leaves, then what?"

"I beat the crap out of him, and we bring your mother's art home."

"That would certainly solve everything," Renee said sarcastically.

"I agree with Henri. We need to let the police take over."

"And what exactly will we say when they arrive, Oma?"

"That Gus took Mother's paintings."

"Okay, but what specifically did he take? Could you make a list of the missing paintings? At this point, no one but Gus knows what was hidden in this closet all these years. Will you call the police and say, 'My paintings were stolen, but I can't tell you how many are missing or even who painted them?' Trust me, if we call the police, you won't get the art back. Not now! Possibly not ever."

"Why not?" Veronique asked like a protesting child ready to stomp her foot. "The paintings are mine! Mother left them to me. She said so in her letter to Martin."

"*We* all know they're yours, Oma, but if the police *do* find them, they'll open a full-scale investigation. It could take years to research the paintings' provenances."

"What the hell's a provenance?" Henri muttered.

"It's a paper-trail. A provenance tells a prospective buyer when the painting was created, who originally purchased it, either from the artist or from his or her representative, and, if it was sold again, who bought it next."

"I'm sure Mother had provenances for all her paintings."

"Probably so, Oma, but considering the pressure she was under when she asked Denis to remove the paintings from the house, she may not have thought to give him the paperwork."

"And that could cause problems?"

"Not could. Will! Without the appropriate provenances, the authorities will challenge your claim to the paintings. Let me give you an example. I couldn't just walk into the Musée d'Orsay and say, 'That Renoir over there once belonged to my great-grandmother.' I would have to *prove* it did. Otherwise the art is suspect."

"My paintings aren't suspect."

"Not to you because you know they belonged to your mother, but you can't prove your claim."

"Do you really think the government would take paintings that are rightfully mine?"

"Maybe not permanently, but they won't simply hand them over. And really, do any of us want Gus to rot in jail?"

"I do," Henri said, scowling.

"We all know how you feel, Henri," said Veronique. "I don't agree."

"Damn it! However you may personally feel about Gus, the man's a crook."

"No, Henri," Veronique continued calmly. "Like me, Gus is also an injured party. He's a victim of his grandfather's behavior and subsequent bad fortune."

"You're all a bunch of softies. Gus sure as hell doesn't deserve your pity, much less your understanding. He's a rotten son of a . . .Be thankful

I couldn't bring my gun on the plane. My Glock would do the talking for me."

"Then you'd be the one rotting in jail," Renee said, frowning at her husband.

"We've wasted enough time arguing about this," Arnaud said. "If Gus is still in Paris, we only have a few hours to find him and recover the paintings. Martin, you drive Veronique and Renee home and wait with them until you hear from us. Henri and I will take Anne by the apartment to get Gus's address. Until we know if he's still there, we can't make a plan."

"We'll leave as soon as I lock up," Martin said.

"I hope we're not too late."

"We all do, Oma." Anne squeezed her grandmother's hand. Picking up the painting of Monet's kitchen, she said again, "We all do."

CHAPTER 37

"I'll go up and get the address," Anne said as Arnaud pulled up to the mansion. "There's no need to waste time parking. I'll be right back."

While Anne went inside, the men waited. Five minutes passed. Then ten. "I wish she'd hurry," Arnaud said, glancing at his watch. "How long could it take to grab an address?"

"Maybe it wasn't where she thought she put it, and she's looking. Or maybe she's waiting for the elevator. If there were stairs to the fourth floor, I could be up and down three times before that snail traveled from the lobby to the fifth floor."

For a while longer, both men watched the door, saying nothing as they waited for Anne to emerge. Arnaud checked his watch again. "This waiting is driving me crazy," he said. "She's been gone for fifteen minutes. Where the hell is she?"

"You're asking me? I've been married over half a century, and I still can't figure out why it takes a woman so long to get ready. She's probably powdering her nose, another term I find mystifying."

"She would never stop to do something as inane as freshening her makeup. She knows we have to hurry if there's any hope of catching Gus before he leaves the country—that is if he's not already long-gone."

Three more minutes dragged by. "Okay, now *I'm* worried," Henri said. "Do you have a key to Anne's apartment?"

"No—"

"Then we have to stop at Veronique's and get the spare." He handed Arnaud a key. "This will get you from the garage to the fourth floor. I'll meet you by the elevator."

"Oh Lord," Arnaud said, the blood draining from his face as he took the key.

"What now?"

"Seeing this, I just remembered. Anne gave Gus a key to her apartment."

"Why the hell would she do that?"

"She trusted him."

"Well she made a mistake, didn't she? Pray her lapse in judgment doesn't end in—"

"Gus may be a thief, but I don't believe he'd harm Anne."

Arnaud, his heart racing and his face flushed, reached the fourth floor just as Henri exited Veronique's apartment. "Can't this damn thing go any faster," Henri groused as the elevator slowly crept upward.

When the door finally opened, Arnaud gasped.

"What," Henri yelled.

"Something's wrong! Anne's door is ajar and—"

Without waiting for Arnaud to complete the sentence, Henri shoved him aside and raced across the hall. He slammed opened Anne's door, stormed into the room, and abruptly stopped in his tracks. "What the hell—"

"Oh my God!" Arnaud shouted as he pushed by Henri and entered the room. "Anne, are you hurt?"

"I'm fine," Anne answered calmly and emphatically.

"Then what the hell are you doing on the floor?" Henri screeched, his shoulders squared—ready to do battle. "And what's Gus doing here?"

Anne pointed across the room to several brown-wrapped packages propped against the fireplace. "He returned Oma's paintings," she said, her eyes and voice warning the men to be calm. "He will explain—"

"Explain what?" Henri roared.

"Why he took the paintings and why he brought them back. Please sit—"

"Like hell I will. I'm staying right here. If Gus tries to escape—"

"That won't happen. Gus, tell Henri and Arnaud what you just told me."

"His eyes red and his face swollen, Gus looked up and, choking out the words, pleaded, "I am so sorry, I—"

"You're sorry?"

"Henri! Please! Anne said as strongly as she could without shouting. "Listen."

"Listen to what? Nothing this despicable bastard could say would *ever* justify what he did. Come on, Anne. You know what these paintings mean to your grandmother. Surely you aren't buying this crap."

"I'm not buying anything. Gus. . ."

Gus drew a deep steadying breath, let it out slowly, and began again, "When Veronique—"

"Don't you dare call Madame Ellison by her given name!"

Seemingly marshalling his thoughts, Gus once again inhaled deeply and said, "When Madame Ellison contacted me about driving Anne, I mean Madame French, suddenly my world changed—I was about to realize my life-long dream. But then when Madame French—"

"It's still Anne, Gus."

Gus smiled awkwardly and persisted. "I was on my way to Marseille when I realized I could not keep Madame Boulet's paintings."

Henri rolled his eyes in exasperation. "And now you're going to tell us what caused this abrupt change of heart. You're delusional if you think any of us will believe a word you say."

"I am sure you will think I am crazy—"

"Crazy like a fox. But please. Continue your sob story. It makes for great theater."

"For God's sake Henri, stop with the sarcasm," Anne said. "Hear Gus out. Then, if you feel you must, yell and scream to your heart's content."

"Okay, I'm listening," Henri said, his face red with ire. "But only because you asked. If anyone else—"

"Thank you," Anne said. Gus. . ."

"I was on the A6 driving toward Lyon when I suddenly realized I had to turn around. The paintings were not mine to keep. I had to bring them back—"

"And what do you think caused this come-to-Jesus moment?" Henri growled.

"I suddenly remembered the day I drove Anne to see the places Madame Ellison wrote about in her journal. As we neared Place de la Bastille, I mentioned *Liberty Leading the People,* one of my favorite paintings—"

"What the hell are you talking about?" Henri bellowed. "I've never heard anything so ludicrous in all my life, and I'm an old man. If I weren't so damn pissed I'd be rolling on the floor laughing—"

"Henri—"

"No, Anne. This time you'll hear *me* out. This son-of-a-bitch is trying to make us believe some old painting that hangs in the Louvre is the reason he miraculously repented and returned Elisabeth's art. Come on, Gus, surely you can come up with a better excuse—"

"I am not making excuses. From the moment Madame Ellison told me she was searching for her mother's paintings. I planned to steal them—that is, if you could locate them after all these years."

"Clearly you succeeded," Arnaud chided. "Yet here you are."

"I am. Though I doubt you will understand, I will explain. While we drove, Anne spoke about her grandmother—"

"Gus was showing me some of the places Oma mentioned in her journal," Anne said. "Among them was the Place de la Bastille. As we approached the square, he asked if I was familiar with the painting—"

"That's ridiculous."

"Rather, it's appropriate, Henri. The July Monument in the center of the square was erected to commemorate the Revolution of 1830, the conflict Delacroix depicts in the painting. Gus. . ."

"While Anne and I talked, I began to understand that neither she nor her grandmother was looking to recover Madame Boulet's paintings for the money they could bring at auction."

"Well at least you *finally* said something that rings true," Henri muttered. "Veronique only asked for the legacy the Nazis stole from her— the same legacy you stole again. Her search was never about money."

"I know that now. No words could adequately express my humiliation, shame, and embarrassment. As soon as I met you at the airport, you included me—made me feel appreciated. Later, when I returned *The Work Table,* you made me a part of your family."

"Bullshit!" Henri snarled, his face reddening. "You talk a good story because you were caught—"

"He wasn't caught, Henri. He came here to return the paintings."

"That's beside the point. He took them. No matter what heart-rending, half-ass explanation he's concocted to justify what he did. The man's thief. "If I had my gun—"

"You've made your opinion crystal-clear," Anne fired back. "None of us doubts how you feel. So shall we let Gus finish and move on?"

"Move on how?"

"Yet to be determined."

Looking at Arnaud, Gus said, "I am sure you called the police when you discovered the paintings were missing."

"If you knew that, why did you stay here and wait for Anne to come home?" Henri said sharply. "You could have left the paintings and gotten the hell out of France."

"I remained to explain my actions in person. I want you to understand and, hopefully, forgive me."

"I don't know about forgiveness," Arnaud said. "But you're wrong about one thing. We haven't notified the police, at least not yet."

"Call them. I deserve to be imprisoned in the Bastille, or worse, the Châtelet." Gus smiled half-heartedly.

"Definitely the Châtelet," Anne said, glad for a little humor to break the tension. "We wouldn't want you using Elisabeth's paintings to decorate the walls of your cell."

"What the hell do you mean?" Henri asked, his eyes narrowing in a squint.

"Private joke," said Anne. "Henri, go down and get Oma, Renee, and Martin." She turned to Gus "My grandmother will decide what to do next."

❧

Ten minutes later, Veronique entered the apartment with Henri and Martin following close behind. Veronique saw Gus sitting on the couch, but instead of lashing out, she walked over and sat next to him. "Henri said you returned Mother's paintings," she said. "Thank you, Gus."

"Please forgive me for betraying you, Madame Ellison," Gus said, tears welling in his eyes. "I deserve prison and—"

"Of course I'll forgive you, Gus, but only if you stop calling me Madame Ellison. As I said before, that mode of address makes me feel quite old."

"Veronique—"

"Hush, Henri. I'll handle this." She turned back to Gus. "When we were at Martin's, Anne read your letter—your justification for stealing Mother's paintings. However, for me, a letter isn't enough. I want to *hear* you explain."

"And I want to know how you got inside my house?" Martin said.

"You left a first floor window unlocked."

"And you pulled it open and climbed in. But how were you able to find the closet where Denis hid the paintings?"

"I studied the Île mansions in an architecture class at the university. Many were designed by the architect, Louis Le Vaux, so the floor plans are similar. The fourth floor was usually where the children and their nannies lived."

"And you assumed the layout of my home was similar to the other mansions before they were converted to apartments."

"It was an educated guess, but I was right. Since Madame Boulet was an only child, I further deduced hers was the large room with the best view of the Left Bank."

"So you went directly to the room where Veronique's mother grew up, cut open the wall in the closet, and stole the paintings she risked her life to hide for her daughter," Henri said, scowling.

"I did, sir. Before I broke into Monsieur Fontaine's house, I agonized—"

"Yet you went ahead. Your story's nothing but bullshit."

Veronique's eyes flew open. "Enough Henri. Instead of continuing with this interrogation that's becoming increasingly contentious, let's look at the paintings Gus returned."

"Let me help you, Oma."

Together, Anne and Veronique separated the paintings and propped them against the couch and the chairs. Veronique tore the brown wrapping off the first painting, a rendering of Monet's *Japanese Bridge*. "I remember this," she said. "It hung above the fireplace in Mother's formal parlor."

"Monet began to paint various renditions of bridge over his water lily pond around 1888," Anne said. "This appears to be an early rendition. It's a little darker than his later works, but it's a fabulous painting."

"Mother always had good taste," Veronique said, as Henri tore the wrapping from another painting.

"It's the Matisse you mentioned, Oma, but it's not the one I thought you were referencing. I assumed you meant the painting of the checker players. This scene is more intimate. See what I mean? The family is gathered together. The children are playing in front of a white fireplace covered with typical Matisse flowers. The blue vases on the mantle add color, as does the Oriental rug beneath the table containing the checkerboard. I'm pretty sure this painting, like the Monet, is from an early period in Matisse's career. He's using the familiar motifs, but they're not as bright as the colors in his later works. It's not one of the greats, but I still love it."

While Veronique stepped back to look at the Matisse from a distance, Henri unwrapped the next painting. "This is by some guy named Max Liebermann," he said. "I know about Monet, but I've never heard of this Liebermann fellow."

"I know little about his work, other than his style was similar to Manet's," Anne said. "But I do know a little something about his life."

"Why would you remember the life of a painter whose art you haven't studied?" Renee asked.

"Because the Liebermann lecture was the first time I had heard the Nazis systematically looted German art museums and seized works from privately-owned Jewish collections. It stands to reason that Elisabeth would have at least one Liebermann in her collection—possibly more."

"You're referring to the paintings she sold shortly before la rafle du Vel d'Hiv," Renee said.

"Yes. We now know the last time Auguste traveled to Geneva, he deposited monies from the sale of those last paintings. It's not unreasonable to think that some of the money was from the sale of a Liebermann."

"Why?" Veronique asked.

"Because Liebermann was a German-Jewish painter and the leading proponent of Impressionism in Germany. Elisabeth was a Jew, and she collected Impressionist works. I may not know much about the Liebermann, but I *am* familiar with that painting," Anne said as Arnaud finished opening the next package.

"So am I," said Veronique. "I believe I mentioned it to you before, Anne."

"You did. I can see why you loved the painting, Oma. It's Pissarro's *Place du Carrousel, Paris.* There's a similar work in the Ailsa Mellon Bruce Collection in Washington, though the last time I was there it wasn't on public display. This painting is from a later period in Pissarro's career. I know, because he only began to paint urban scenes after eye problems prevented him from working outdoors. This is one of twenty-eight views he painted of the Tuileries from a hotel room on rue de Rivoli. Come take a closer look."

While Veronique looked closely at the Pissarro, Henri pulled the paper off the next painting. "How about this one?" he asked.

"It's a version of one of Manet's most controversial works, *Le déjeuner sur l'herbe.* As we speak, the Met is signing contracts with the Musée d'Orsay to borrow Manet's most famous adaptation of the painting. There's another smaller version hanging in the Courtauld Gallery in London. My guess, this early rendition was painted around 1862."

"You believe this is the painting Mother referenced in the second stanza of the poem she left behind the bricks," Veronique said, moving closer.

"I do. Take a look. Do you see any rabbits running around in the scene?"

"Not at first glance, but I still think the painting looks off balance."

"I agree."

"Will you tell us about it?"

"If you'd like. When the version that now hangs in the Musée d'Orsay was exhibited at the Salon des Refuses in 1863, it stunned the French public."

"Why? Surely the French had seen plenty of nudes."

"True. It was common to see paintings of nude women. As long as the figures were romanticized and flawless, it was okay, but in this painting, a naked woman is lunching with two fully dressed men was an affront to the propriety of the time. Manet was immediately deemed incompetent and ignorant—an artist who had the audacity to disregard the concepts of decency and decorum. Ironically, the painting outraged French middle-class men who were regulars of just such women."

"Tell me more," Veronique said. "I'm surprised my seemingly-puritanical mother would own such a controversial painting."

"You're referring to the Elisabeth you thought you knew," Henri said. "I'm not so sure 'puritanical' is a term I'd use now that we know about her and my father. She hardly adhered to strict moral principles."

"That's enough, Henri," Renee said, glowering. "Tell us more about the painting, Anne."

"Manet's wife, along with his favorite model, posed for the nude woman. The two men are his brother and his future brother-in-law. They're dressed like dandies, men who were excessively concerned with looking elegant. Look at the basket of fruit, and the round loaf of bread."

"They look like still-life paintings," Veronique said.

"Very good, Oma. Now look at the perspective—"

"You may think I'm uncultured," Henri said. "Maybe I am, because I have no idea what you're talking about."

"Not understanding what I mean by perspective hardly makes you uncultured, Henri."

"Good to know," Arnaud chimed in. "I've always considered myself a cultured man, but I'm with Henri."

"What, no 'cultured' adjective by your name?" Anne teased. Before Arnaud could respond, she said, "Simply put, perspective is a technique an artist uses to create a feeling of depth and space on a flat surface. It gives the painting a three-dimensional feel to make it look real. In *Le déjeuner sur l'herbe*, Manet's perspective is off. Look here." She pointed to the woman in the background. "She is too large when compared with the figures in the foreground."

"You're raving about the painting, yet you find so many faults in it," Renee said. "Do or don't you like it?"

"It's amazing."

"But—"

"It's not the painting itself, Renee, but what it represents that makes it a significant work of art. This is not a realist painting in the social or political sense of our hashish-smoking friend Daumier, who lived here on the Île during the 1940s." She smiled at Gus. "Rather it's a statement of the artist's individual freedom."

"I'm amazed by your expertise," Veronique said, beaming with pride.

"I'm hardly an expert, Oma. As Gus says, I wore blinders when I studied here in Paris. I know about this Manet because it's a precursor to my passion—Impressionism."

"Shall we take a look at the rest of the paintings Gus stole?" Henri asked.

"And returned, Henri," Veronique said, glaring.

While Henri fumed, Arnaud opened another package. Anne walked over, tilted her head to the side, and examined the painting. "It's a work by Eugene Boudin," she said. "I'm not familiar with this one. My guess, it's one of his early seascapes. Oma, if you want to learn more, I'm sure the internet is filled with information about Boudin and his art. There may even be specifics about this particular painting."

"I'll put researching Boudin near the top of my to-do list," Veronique said as Arnaud unwrapped and held up another painting.

"This is a Courbet," Anne said. "Unfortunately I don't know too much about it either, though just last month I read a blurb about another of Courbet's works. I remember the specifics because the painting, *La Bretonnerie in the Department of Indre*, was hanging in the National Gallery until recently when it was returned to its rightful owners. The article caused me to wonder if the Met was still displaying stolen art. . ."

"What?" Veronique asked as Anne's voice trailed off.

"I was just thinking about how much has happened in so short a time. When I read about the Courbet, I never dreamed I'd soon be in Paris looking at another of his works—a painting that once belonged to my great-grandmother."

"Do you think there are still questionable paintings hanging in the Met?" Renee asked.

"I doubt it. As I said before, museums are now accountable for all the works in their collection. Oma, if you gift your mother's art to the Met or the Musée d'Orsay, they will thoroughly research the provenance of each work before it's hung."

"Because they believe Mother illegally obtained the paintings."

"They wouldn't think that, but they *would* want to be sure the art was legitimately hers. Now back to this particular painting. Courbet was one of the leaders of the Realist movement in the nineteenth-century. The Realistic School features, among others, the paintings of Gericault and Delacroix, Gus's favorite—"

"You're referring to that damn *Liberty* painting again," Henri grumbled.

"That's the one," Anne said. "You really should go to the Louvre and take another look after all these years, Henri. Maybe you'd have a better understanding of what we're discussing."

"Anne," Veronique said sternly. "Your offhanded comment was both rude and unnecessary."

"I'm sorry, Henri," Anne said, immediately retreating. "I know I sounded nasty. That was not my intent. I meant the painting is worth seeing again. I apologize for being discourteous."

"Forget it, honey," Henri said. "I've been overreacting all afternoon, but under the circumstances—"

"We're all on edge," Arnaud interjected.

"There's one more painting," Veronique said, ending the squabble. "Arnaud, please unwrap the package.

Taking care, Arnaud began to remove the paper.

"Oh my! It's another Matisse!" Veronique exclaimed when, minutes later, he held up the painting for all to see.

"You're right," said Anne. "I'm not familiar with this painting, but I'm sure 'yellow chair' is in the title."

"I realize I keep asking, but how do you know?" Renee said.

"By Matisse's use of color, especially the yellow chair and the blues and greens. This is a fabulous painting, Oma. All of your mother's paintings are priceless, and I'm not talking monetarily. Gus, you gave up your dream of a better life to return them. Thank you."

"I was returning to you what was never mine to keep." Looking directly at Veronique, he said, "I am so sorry."

"Would you fetch my pocketbook?" Veronique asked Renee.

"Of course, dear." Renee went to the table by the door where Veronique had left her purse and brought it to her.

Veronique took out her checkbook, wrote a check, and presented it to Gus. "This is for you," she said. "It's payment for the recovery of the Bonnard and an expression of my gratitude for the effort you've made on my behalf."

Gus gasped. "This is two hundred and fifty-thousand dollars. I cannot take *any* money from you, Veronique. Let alone this much. I stole your paintings. As I said before you came up, I should be in the Bastille or the Châtelet, not living the life this money would—"

"Why don't we simply say you removed the paintings from Martin's closet so I wouldn't need to waste my time transporting them across the Île? Anyway, I should be thanking you, not the other way around."

"You can't be serious—"

"Shush, Henri. It's *my* money and *my* decision. You may not approve, but I'll hear nothing more about it—unless you want to thank our friend Gus for delivering the paintings to Anne's apartment."

"But why? You should be calling the police, not paying Gus for stealing your mother's art."

"In your mind, Henri, but not in mine. In the years I have left, I intend to enjoy Mother's paintings. Yes, Gus was wrong to take them, but he brought them back."

Gus shook his head and held out the check to Veronique. "I will not take this."

"Let me explain, Gus," Veronique said sternly. "As I see it, you have two choices. You either take the check or go to jail. You and I are both victims. In your letter, you said fate dealt you a bad hand. I agree, and I think it's time you win. If Didier had paid your father the money he owed him for his work, albeit crooked, you would have had the life Damien Duplessis has always enjoyed. Instead, you were cheated out of your inheritance, as I was cheated out of mine."

"You're not comparing your situation to Gus's," Henri said, incredulous.

"I am. The Nazis ruined both of our lives. Gus was bitter and angry, and his bitterness prompted him to steal my paintings." She looked back at Gus. "In a way, I owe your family. Your grandfather helped me escape, but he was never paid for the work that saved my life. He, too, was a victim of the Holocaust."

"You're equating Gus's grandfather's difficulties to Elisabeth's?"

"Of course not. There's no comparison, but thanks to him, I'm here to enjoy my heritage. I believe, though she had no idea who was doing the work, his efforts gave Mother some measure of peace at the end."

"What do you mean?" Renee asked.

"She didn't know *who* was doing the work, but she knew *someone* was preparing papers for me, for you, Renee, and for you, Henri. So, Gus, I'm giving you what *I* believe you deserve. I have my art, and you now have a new beginning—a chance to live the life you've dreamed about."

"Oma's right, Gus."

"I'm always right," Veronique said, smirking. "Everyone in this room should know that by now."

"Oh we do," Renee said, shaking her head. "I've known since the day we met."

"I know, too," Anne said. "And I'd like to add something to what Oma said. Gus, when I realized you had taken Great-Grand'Mere Elisabeth's art, I was angry and confused, wondering how someone I trusted could do such a thing to me and, worse, to my grandmother. I was literally in shock. I couldn't wrap my mind around what was happening, and I didn't know what to do or how to respond. Henri was livid. Arnaud felt the same, though less so. Bottom line, I felt betrayed."

"And now?"

"And now, though I still have questions—"

"That can be answered later," Veronique stepped in. "Suddenly I am faced with numerous decisions, among them what happens to you, Gus. Though one thing I do know regarding your future. We won't all fit in Arnaud's car. I expect you to be here at seven-thirty to take us to dinner at Taillevent."

"Yes, Madame."

"It's Veronique, and don't come dressed as a chauffeur. You're joining us."

"But—"

"Did you hear what I just said? People don't argue with me. Be here at seven-thirty sharp."

"I will be on time."

Veronique looked around the room. "What about the rest of you? Henri? Renee?"

"It's your decision, not ours," Henri grudgingly said.

"I agree with Oma."

"So do I," said Renee.

"But can you trust me again?" Gus pleaded.

"I trust you now," Veronique said.

Martin smiled. "I trust you, too," he said. "You taught me a lesson. I am going to lock my windows and figure out how to use my alarm system."

"I will teach you how," Gus said, grinning sheepishly.

Martin shook his head and, laughing, said, "Now isn't that the ultimate irony."

"You realize we're the only ones who can know what happened here," Arnaud said. "One word about this to anyone outside this room, and the police will get involved."

"And I don't want to give up my paintings for the years it might take to track down those pesky provenances," Veronique said. "So it's decided. What was it you used to say when you were a child, Anne? Remember, when you were making me promise not to reveal one of your secrets to your mother?"

"Pinky swear." Anne went over to her grandmother and they hooked little fingers.

"So," Veronique said. "Do I have pinky swears from the rest of you? You don't have to lock your pinkies with mine, but you all must understand the seriousness of your oath."

"We do," Renee said.

"You Americans are crazy," said Arnaud.

"I'm French," Veronique said proudly. "Though, over the years, it appears I've forgotten."

"I wonder how pinky swear translates into French," said Martin.

"You work on it," Veronique said, smiling. She looked at Gus. "Now that all the important things are settled, I need to say I am rather disappointed in you, Gus."

"I know—"

"You don't know. I hoped to see the Jewish Memorials yesterday afternoon, but you weren't available. You'll have to make it up to me. How about tomorrow?"

"Tell me what time and I will be here."

"Good. Go home and relax. We'll see you tonight at seven-thirty."

Gus looked down at Veronique's check. "I don't deserve this," he said uneasily.

"It's the check or jail," said Veronique. "Make up your mind. Once you set foot outside that door, none of us will mention this episode again."

"I will be here at seven-thirty."

"I thought you might see it my way. And so you know, the Bastille and the Châtelet no longer exist."

"I do know, but for a few minutes, I pictured myself rotting in those dark, dank cells."

"I'm sure you did. So, everyone, shall we go home and meet outside number forty-five at seven-thirty?"

"I'll pick up Martin on the way," Arnaud said.

"And Sophie and Lionel?"

"They'll meet us at the restaurant."

"Excellent. I'm looking forward to a delicious dinner with my family and friends—old and new. And I don't mean age-wise."

CHAPTER 38

"It looks like you did a better job of dodging the maniacs than I did," Arnaud said as he got out of the car to greet Gus in front of Taillevent.

"Practice I guess," Gus said nervously as he opened Anne's door.

"How are you, Gus?" Martin asked, extending his hand. "We are glad to see you. I assume the others are inside?"

"They are."

While Arnaud got the ticket from the valet, Anne leaned in Gus's direction. "Relax," she whispered. "When my grandmother speaks, all listen. Keep that in mind, and you'll be fine."

"Welcome to my favorite restaurant," Veronique said when Anne, Arnaud, and Gus reached an elegantly-set table near the front of the smallish room.

"You've been here five minutes, Oma." Anne bent and kissed her grandmother on the cheek. "How could you possibly know, that, of all the restaurants in Paris, Taillevent is your favorite?"

"Let's just say if the food is half as good as the service, it will be. And you're right, darling, I'm going to have to try all the others before I make my final decision."

"I'm glad you approve," Arnaud said, kissing Veronique, then his sister before shaking hands with Lionel and Henri. I see you've met Madame Ellison, Sophie."

"Sophie and I are already good friends," Veronique said. "And I think we're going to be even better friends in the weeks and months to come."

"You've extended your stay," Anne said. "You didn't say anything last night."

"Because I didn't decide until this afternoon. Gus," she said before Anne could respond. "Come meet our new friends, Sophie and Lionel."

"How do you do." Gus shook hands with Lionel and nodded politely toward Sophie. "It is a pleasure to meet you."

"Gus," Sophie said. "Where have I heard your name?"

"I do not know, Madame."

"Oh, that's right," Sophie continued. "Now I remember. You're my brother's competition— the man with more adjectives—"

"I believe I'm slightly ahead," Arnaud said, grinning at Anne. "Didn't number three put me on top?"

"If you're number three, who's number one?" Veronique asked. "These adjectives you're always talking about have me confused."

"No one's number one, Oma, though Arnaud would like to be. Pay no attention to his absurd comments."

"Then, on your advice, I'll move on to important matters. Gus, realizing writing is now your fulltime job, Sophie has invited me to lunch at her place. Would you drive me over when we pick a date?"

"With pleasure."

"Thank you." Veronique turned to Martin, reached out her arms and said. "I'm so glad you could join us. When Henri and I came to Paris. Oh my—I can't believe we landed at Charles de Gaulle less than a week ago. So much has happened in such a short amount of time. Neither Henri nor I could have imagined we'd be dining with our brother at a *real* family dinner."

"Veronique's right," Henri said, extending his hand to Martin. Just as Martin reached out to shake hands, Henri enveloped him in a bear-hug. "Welcome, my brother," he said enthusiastically.

"Isn't it wonderful to be with family," Veronique said, looking directly at Anne.

Arnaud held out the chair for Anne to sit by her grandmother. While the others got settled, she leaned over and whispered, "I get the message, Oma. Throwing out not-so-subtle comments won't do anything to change my mind about moving to Paris. I'm going home! Period! So you can stop with the family stuff."

"Oh, I'm just beginning my campaign," Veronique whispered back. "Stubborn women like you don't respond to subtlety, so I'm initiating an all-out frontal attack."

"This is also a happy time for me," Martin was saying. "Like my sister, I am delighted to join my family for a meal and to meet new friends."

"Some of whom are already like family," Veronique said, a gleam in her eye.

"Martin, Arnaud says you grew up on Quai de Bethune," Sophie said.

"Martin owns our mother's childhood home," said Veronique. "What could be better for me in the months to come? I have a brother I never knew existed who lives within walking distance, and good friends all around." She reached across the table, took Arnaud's hand and said, "Even though Anne plans to spend most of the year in New York, I hope you'll still come to visit."

"I'll be around so much you'll order me to go home."

"I assure you, young man. That will *never* happen!"

"Oma, how long do you plan to stay in Paris?" Anne said, glowering.

"For as long as I have left."

"Seriously?"

"You heard me, darling. Less than an hour ago I realized I *must* stay."

"I don't understand. Is your health an issue? Did a doctor tell you not to make the flight home?"

"My health is fine, but I just met my new neighbors. They're wonderful people, and I'd like to know them better."

"You're staying in Paris because you like your new neighbors?"

"I am. Is that so hard to believe, Anne? Several hours ago two delightful people bought the apartment just below mine. All of you, meet my neighbors—Renee and Henri Marsolet."

"Excuse me," Anne gasped. "Henri—"

"Yup," Henri said, grinning. "Renee and I signed the intent-to-purchase documents fifteen minutes before Gus picked us up. With

Madame Labbe's expert assistance, we will soon be the proud owners of the third floor of Elisabeth's home."

"But how—"

"It turns out I have a little spare change in a Swiss bank account. When Veronique started to think about staying in Paris—"

"You really bought the third-floor apartment?" Martin interrupted.

"We did. You don't think I'm moving back to New York when my brother and sister live here in Paris. Renee and I want to be close to our family."

"Okay, help me understand," Anne said. "Henri, you and Renee purchased an apartment that, as far as I know, wasn't for sale at noon today."

"We made an offer the owners couldn't refuse. They'll be moving out in five days."

"So soon?"

"Like Veronique, at our age, we can't afford to waste time. I threw in the packers and movers and added a storage unit to the deal."

"And a furnished apartment until they find a new place to live," Renee added.

"You *are* determined."

"When I want something, I go for it."

"Now you sound like my grandmother."

"Why wouldn't I? She's been my constant teacher for seventy years."

"It seems I did an excellent job," Veronique said. Looking sideways at Anne, she added, "At least in Henri's regard."

"So you'd give up your life and all your friends in New York just to be close to Oma?" Anne said, ignoring her grandmother's look.

"That's not reason enough," Veronique said indignantly.

"That's not what I meant, Oma—"

"I know, darling, I'm joking. Henri, tell Anne the real reason you decided to stay in Paris."

"What I just said is true, at least as far as it goes. We want to live near Veronique. After all these years existing in the same house, it would be hard for all of us to separate now. But it was something Arnaud said this afternoon that put the nail in the coffin."

"The 'nail in the coffin,'" Martin said. "Did someone close to you die?"

"No." Henri laughed. "I mean what Arnaud said helped us make our final decision."

"I can't imagine—"

"Your words wouldn't be particularly memorable, Arnaud, had Renee and I not been considering this move. Remember earlier today when Veronique asked everyone to pinky swear? You said, 'You Americans are crazy.'"

"I was only joking. I didn't mean to insult—"

"We all knew your intent. It wasn't *what* you said but rather how Veronique responded to your comment. She countered, 'I'm French.' At that moment, I realized I was and always will be a Frenchman. Gertrude Stein wrote, 'America is my country, and Paris is my hometown.' Suddenly I knew I wanted to come home, and, as they say—though I often wonder who 'they' are— 'the rest is history.' Except for personal items we'll have shipped from New York, we're leaving our suite in Veronique's apartment intact. Renee and I will return to see friends from time to time."

"I'm stunned," Anne said. "My entire family is moving to Paris. How will I adjust when I get home?"

"You don't have to adjust to anything," Veronique said.

"Your grandmother's right, honey," said Renee. "Make the apartment on Île St-Louis your home. Over the last few days Henri and I have realized what we call home isn't a building. Home is where your family lives."

"I can't move to Paris, Renee. Henri said Paris is his hometown and France is his country. Clearly you feel the same way, but I don't. I'm a born-and-raised-true-blue American. Modifying what Stein said. America is my country, and *New York* is my hometown. It's that simple. But if we continue this discussion, my food will be salty from all the tears I'll soon be shedding."

"Then let's stop talking and try the cuisine in this place Arnaud calls the 'grande dame of restaurants,'" Veronique said.

"Good idea," said Anne. "But what will I do without you?"

"I'm sure you and your mother will have lots of fun," Veronique said snidely. "Maybe you could have lunch at the Carlyle once a week instead of once a month. Wouldn't you like that?"

"I don't know about the dining room at the Carlyle, but Taillevent is a lovely place." Renee said.

"Thanks," Anne mouthed.

Nodding in Anne's direction, Renee picked up a piece of Christofle flatware and held it up for all to see. "Isn't this lovely silver," she said. "I may look for a similar pattern when Henri and I start to purchase items for our new apartment. What do you think, Henri?"

"Sure," Henri said offhandedly. "But if you expect me to comb Paris for just the right plates, pots and pans, and silverware, you're out of your mind. You and Veronique can work with her decorator. Why not give the poor woman a little more money so she can buy *two* villas in Tuscany."

Everyone was laughing when their waiter, dressed in a dark gray suit and tie, put a basket of crusty rolls and a silver container filled with butter on the table. Veronique looked from person to person. "I can't tell you how I've craved glorious, salty, French butter," she said. Shooting each a warning look, she put several pats on her plate and added, "You can't find butter like this in New York."

"I agree," Sophie said. "French butter was one on the things I missed during the four years I was at Stanford."

"You studied in the States, yet you decided to return to the Île after graduation."

"I know where you're going with this, Oma, but you forget; Sophie grew up here. I was raised in New York. So, could you please stop? Let's not spend the entire evening discussing where I should or shouldn't be living."

"You already know and—"

"Please."

"Okay, darling, I'll do as you ask."

"Thank you."

"At least for now," she said so only Anne could hear.

Minutes later the sommelier arrived with a bottle of champagne. While a waiter put flutes at each place, he poured a taste for Veronique.

She took a sip, nodded her approval, and said, "Before I propose a toast to family, I have something to say. Last night when I couldn't sleep, I got up, opened the French doors, and pulled a chair onto the balcony. As I gazed out at the lights of Paris, I suddenly realized I've come full circle. After all these years, I'm finally home. I've overcome my demons, and I'm no longer afraid to face the future. Instead of running from life, I intend to embrace whatever time I have left. Thanks to all of you who helped in my quest, I have reclaimed my heritage—I have found Mother's paintings. To borrow a thought from her poem—they've been moved from darkness to the light."

"Here's to everything you just said," Henri said, raising his glass.

"Henri, I'm serious," Veronique said huffily.

"I know you are. So am I. Borrowing *your* words, Renee and have also come 'full circle.' We love America, but we finally realized we are and always have been French. Like you, Veronique, we're finally home. For the last few days, I've been thinking about our parents and what they sacrificed for us—for our freedom, for our very lives. It was their dream that we'd become friends, and later, when we found Martin, to be a family. Wouldn't they be proud if they could see us now? My father asked us to 'hold each other close.' We've certainly done that."

"Yes we have," Veronique said. "I doubt Anton could have anticipated the depth of our friendships. I hope you both know how grateful—"

"So are we," Renee interrupted. She clasped her hands in prayer. "I'll say again like I have so many times over the past seventy years—'Thank you, Anton.'"

"Amen to that," Henri said, smiling.

Gus took a deep breath and said, "I, too, have come full circle. For most of my life, I have been a bitter man. I believed stealing your paintings would give me the peace I sought. I was wrong. In the end, I could not keep what was not mine. I returned the art. With that act, I found true peace. I am a free man—in more ways than one."

"And one of the family," Veronique said, smiling.

"And speaking of families, I would like to say a few words," Martin said. "I never knew Mother and Father. When I first realized I was adopted, they were long dead. I doubted I would have an opportunity to learn about them—to know them. When I finally read Mother's letter, I was filled with joy. I had a brother and a sister. I came to the Île, hopeful that you had lived through the Occupation and we would be the family she hoped we would be. My excitement and hope quickly turned to despair. Neighbors remembered you, Veronique, but they had not seen you since the night the Nazis seized Mother. Because you didn't return to the Île, they assumed you, too, were arrested and didn't survive. Then I happened to read that Veronique Ellison had purchased two apartments at number 45 Quai de Bourbon. I waited and hoped. Imagine how I felt when Arnaud came to my door. And here I am, dining with family and new friends. As soon as Emme and the baby are able to travel, I will host a family reunion at Mother's childhood home. I am eager for you to know the rest of your family."

"Wouldn't Anton and Elisabeth love that," Henri said.

"I can't wait," said Veronique. "From now on, I intend to take Henri's advice. I will live in the present and look forward to the future. No more dwelling in the past."

"To the future," Henri said, again raising his glass.

"To happy times," Veronique added, looking at Anne.

As soon as the maître d' arrived with the menus, three waiters served tiny appetizer-size cups of gazpacho soup. "The house specialty," one of the waiters said. "Bon appetite."

With tacit approval of the others, Arnaud ordered wine for the table.

"Tell us what you chose," Veronique said. "Clearly you are a wine connoisseur."

"I'm not an expert, but leaning about fine wines is one of my hobbies."

"Arnaud has the sommelier adjective by his name," Anne said.

"I'm fascinated by your constant references to English grammar," Renee said. "But sommelier is a noun, not an adjective. I should know. I spent years learning to speak and read your mixed up language. Anne, you were saying that Arnaud is a sommelier?"

"Let's just say he knows his wine. So, Arnaud," she teased. "Tell us, do any of the wines you ordered for the table taste like pepper?"

"Why would *any* French wine taste like pepper?" Veronique asked. "I've never heard of such a thing."

"Nor have I," Arnaud said, laughing at the surprised expression on Veronique's face. "To clear my good name and ease your minds, I never told Anne the wine we chose at Calixte *tasted* like pepper. Rather I said it was peppery."

"I'm sorry you won't be able to teach Anne to appreciate peppery French wine," Veronique said, looking at her granddaughter who, again, rolled her eyes.

"What did you just order?" Henri said. "As a cultured man, I have an appreciation of fine wine."

Using yet another strange English expression, 'cultured, my foot,'" Renee said, grinning at her husband.

"For the record, Henri, I think you're extremely suave and debonair," Arnaud said. "And before the rest of you chime in with your opinions on the matter, I ordered a firmly structured chardonnay with butter and discreet fruit. I've had this wine several times. I think you'll be pleased."

"I'll take buttery wine over peppery wine any day," Henri said.

"I think we've exhausted the topic of wine *and* Henri's refinement or lack thereof," Renee joked.

While everyone laughed at Henri's pained expression, Anne leaned toward Arnaud and whispered. "I assume you saw the look on my grandmother's face when you ordered the wine. Because she's so impressed, I'm adding a gold star beside your sommelier adjective."

"I can solve the problem of word usage," Arnaud said. "Just put 'expert' under my name. That covers everything."

"Right," Anne groaned. "That one word would trump any adjective I'd give to Gus. Do you always have to be the best?"

"I don't know about *having* to be the best, but I certainly *want* the best."

Her smile turning to a frown, Anne picked up her menu.

The food was delicious. From her first course, mushroom ravioli with an infusion of chervil broth, through her scallop's meunière with butter and lemon, Anne enjoyed every bite. Veronique raved about her risotto with truffles and frogs' legs, and Sophie agreed. Though most at the table looked at Henri in amazement when he ordered pan-fried duck liver with caramelized fruits and vegetables, he said it was delicious. Both Arnaud and Lionel opted for one of the restaurant's signature dishes, a classic lobster sausage with a blend of tarragon and aniseed. And Renee, Martin, and Gus ordered lamb rubbed with the herbs and served with a sweet pepper sauce.

When the waiter brought the dessert menu, they decided to share a trio of delights including stewed Mirabelle plums in a pot, crunchy chocolate, and a sorbet of olive oil.

If the food was amazing, the conversation was even better. Veronique made it a point to include Gus who, by meal's end, seemed comfortable in his new role as friend. Anne noticed that Veronique and Sophie immediately hit it off. *Good,* she mused—though with a twinge of jealousy—as she watched them, their heads together in conversation. *Maybe Sophie will pick up the slack after I go home.*

At one point, Veronique held up her hand signaling she had an announcement to make. "I've made my decision," she said. "Mother's paintings will remain in the city she loved. I'm donating them the Musée d'Orsay. Tomorrow morning I'll call Madame Malet to tell her about my gift. I want them grouped together—at least for a while—along with a plaque that says, 'Given in Memory of Elisabeth Boulet.'"

"What about the provenances Anne keeps talking about?" Henri asked.

"As I said before, I'll deal with the issue of provenances if and when it comes up. Let Madame Malet do the research. She won't find issues with any of Mother's paintings."

"What a splendid idea to donate our mother's paintings to the Musée d'Orsay," Martin said. "I am sure the museum will be thrilled, and you and I can see them whenever we want. Though the paintings never played a direct role in my day-to-day life, I know everything I have today is the result of Mother's sacrifice. She sold her art for my future."

"And for ours," Henri said. "I'll go to the museum with you, Martin." His eyes twinkling, he added, "We Parisians can always use a little *more* culture."

"I thought we'd dropped that subject," Renee said. "But you opened the door, and I can't resist. Maybe if you hang out with Martin. . . There I go again with the American slang. I can't wait to start speaking French again."

"That will happen very soon," "Veronique said. "After Anne goes home, there won't be a need to speak English any longer." When Anne glared, she turned to Renee. "You were saying about Henri?"

"Just if he and Martin spend time together, he might learn to appreciate fine food. I'm sure there are more suitable restaurants for the cultured than the Brasserie de l'Île Saint Louis."

"But none that serve good sausage, sauerkraut, and pork knuckles," Henri argued. "Cultured though I may become, I will *never* give up the finer things in life."

"I hesitate to say, but I, too, enjoy the fine cuisine of Brasserie de l'Île Saint Louis," Martin said.

"You're both lost causes," Renee said, shaking her head from side to side.

"I'm going to miss your bantering. . ." When she saw her grandmother's smile, Anne quickly changed the subject. "But back to your announcement, Oma. No doubt after the trustees of the Musée d'Orsay see the paintings you're donating, they'll ask you to serve on the board."

"I expect to be a trustee in no time," said Veronique. "When they *do* ask, I'll immediately accept. You don't think I'm going to sit in my apartment here on the Île like I did in New York after your grandfather died."

"The thought never crossed my mind. I'm glad you're making plans."

"I have many ideas, but I haven't taken action. Arnaud, perhaps you could find time to help me invest Mother's money, not for personal profit, but to help others. I'm sure she'd wholeheartedly endorse my decision."

"I believe she would," Martin said.

"So, Arnaud, will you help me choose worthwhile charities?"

"I would be honored."

"Thank you. There are several Jewish organizations and commemorative sites I would like to support in Mother's name, beginning with the Memorial at Drancy."

"Whenever you're ready, I'll begin the process."

"We'll talk as soon as I've hired new help. I'm feeling better than I have in years, but I don't relish the thought of living alone. I need a live-in housekeeper and a valet/butler, preferably a couple. When Henri and Renee move downstairs, they can live in their suite. I've decided to retain Andre on a part-time basis. He has already agreed, and I think happily, to return to the restaurant and come in to prepare meals for me on special occasions. That is if I can find a woman who can cook."

"I know a couple who might meet your needs," Gus said. "They are in their mid-fifties. They have no family in the area, and both have domestic experience. I know firsthand; Claudine is an excellent cook."

"You'll bring Claudine and—"

"Jean-Claude."

"And Jean-Claude to meet me?"

"Whenever you're ready."

"I have plans beginning Friday and lasting through the weekend. How about Monday?"

"You have plans for the weekend?" Anne asked. "What are you doing?"

"I'll be busy with my new bff."

"Suddenly Sophie's your new bff? When did this happen?"

"Veronique and I decided when we went to the powder room."

"See what I mean," Henri said to Arnaud. "What the hell's a 'powder room? Can't the ladies say they went to the john?"

"That would seem reasonable," Arnaud said. "Or how about the toilette? That term would also be appropriate."

"Would you please let me finish what I was telling Anne," Sophie said. "When Veronique told me you're going back to New York, I volunteered to assume the bff role."

"And speaking of your imminent departure, my darling granddaughter, you know I think you're crazy, but it's your life. However, before you go would you do something for me? I don't believe what I'm asking will be a problem. Will you go with me to take Mother's paintings to the Musée d'Orsay? You know Madame Malet."

"Of course, if you think Claire will be available on such short notice."

"For hundreds of millions of euros, which I assume is what the paintings as a group would bring at auction, you can be *sure* she'll be available. You may have the painting of Monet's kitchen. When we began our quest to find Mother's paintings, I said they're my heritage—and yours. Now you have a part of your birthright. At least for now, I'll keep *The Work Table*. I'm not sure *what* to do about the Manet. Claire might not want another rendition of a painting that's already on display."

"Or she might. She could hang the two works side by side to show the progression in Manet's style. Perhaps she'll loan both paintings to the Met for the Christmas show. Wouldn't that be ironic?"

"Don't give my seat at the table," Veronique said. "I intend to fly back for the gala."

"So do we," Henri said. Grinning, he added, "Perhaps in our own private jet."

"Obviously you have everything figured out, Oma."

"Believe me, darling, I do."

⁓◌

"I'd like to talk with you," Arnaud said after they'd dropped Martin at home.

"Fine, but let's not make my leaving any harder than it already is."

Neither Anne nor Arnaud said a word as the slow-moving elevator climbed to the fifth floor. While Arnaud waited, Anne opened the front door. She had just tossed her purse on the entry table when he dropped to one knee. "Marry me," he said, taking her hand in his. "I love you."

"I love you too." Anne pulled back. "That's the problem."

"There's that infamous word again. You constantly say we have problems, but you won't look for resolutions—"

"Because there aren't any. Don't you think I've thought about marrying you? Since the night we first made love—maybe before that."

"Then what's the problem? Say yes. It's very simple."

"There's nothing simple about what you're asking me to do. Yes, I love you, but we'd end up like you and Aimee, and I can't handle another divorce."

"We're not even married and you're already talking divorce? What problem could be so great that we couldn't work them out together?'

"Well, for one, I love living in New York, and Île St-Louis is your home. And, like Aimee, I'm not happy when I don't get my way. Yes, I know, I sound like a spoiled child. Maybe I am. There, I admit it, but it's true. I've been living a dream. Now it's time to face reality."

"You want me to leave?"

"Yes! No! I don't know."

"What about tomorrow?"

"I'm going with Oma to the Musée d'Orsay."

"And after that?"

"I want to spend as much time with her as possible before I leave. She's feeling better, but at her age anything can happen. She could have a relapse—"

"If not for me, isn't that reason enough for you to stay in Paris?"

"I can fly back on a moment's notice."

"Then there's no chance you'll change your mind? Nothing I say will make your reconsider your decision?"

"No," Anne said, wiping the tears from her cheek.

"Then I guess this is goodbye. I wish—"

"So do I," Anne cried. "Thank you for a wonderful week. Maybe we can meet for lunch at Tastevin when I come to see Oma—that is if you're not too busy."

"We'll see. Good luck in New York and with your exhibition."

Before Anne could respond, he turned, and without looking back, walked out.

As soon as she heard the elevator door close, Anne picked up the phone. "May I come down, Oma," she said between sobs. "It's late, but—"

"Of course, darling. I'm still up."

"Arnaud asked me to marry him," Anne cried as soon as Veronique opened the door.

"And you said no. Come and sit. Are you sorry you refused his proposal?"

"No! Yes! I love him, but I've been living a dream. It's Paris, and it's April. Who wouldn't fall in love? But it will soon be May. Then July. Then September. Finally December will roll around. Things look different in the winter. It's time to face reality."

Veronique put her arm around Anne's shoulder and pulled her close. "You're running, Anne," she said. "And I'm speaking from experience. Like me, for some reason you can't face whatever demons are keeping you from being happy. Perhaps you're afraid. You had one bad marriage and you can't face the possibility of another. Can't you stop analyzing; stop looking to the future and what may or may not happen? Can't you trust how you feel?"

"Sometimes feelings aren't enough to make a marriage work."

"Or they are. Your grandfather and I had countless problems to overcome, and we were happy for decades."

"I know, but I'm not you."

"What do you mean you're not me? We're exactly alike. If you work hard, you can accomplish anything. I was going to say it might take you seven decades, but I thought that line might put a damper on the message I'm trying to convey. Will you at least stay here while Madeline's in town? Unless she's one of the reasons you're leaving."

Sitting up, Anne smiled through her tears. "I hadn't included Mother on my list, but now that you bring up her visit—"

"And what about the art the Nazis took from the house? Surely you want to help me search for the rest of Mother's paintings."

"Are you sure you want to pursue that angle?"

"I do. In fact I've already begun. On Tuesday I am meeting with a man who, as a boy, created displays of seized art for Rose Valland at the Jeu de Paume."

"Of course you are," Anne said. "Come to think of it, I have something that may help if you *do* persist. In all the craziness of the last few days, I forgot. Jeannine Simoneau from the Musée Marmottan had a courier deliver a package of containing declassified documents from German looting inventories. I put the envelope in my office. Until now, I never gave it another thought. I'll be sure to give it to you before I leave. I'll also provide Jeannine's contact information. You may want to call her."

"I'll do that. Perhaps Ms. Simoneau will see me. I only wish you could join me when we meet."

"I know, but I can't."

"Very well then," Veronique said. "You must know what you're giving up by going home, Anne, so there's nothing more to say. If I thought I could convince you to do what we both know is right, I'd stay up all night, but you refuse to listen to reason."

"You're sending me home?"

"I am, darling. Come down for breakfast in the morning. We'll call Claire and see if she'll see us early afternoon tomorrow. The courier will arrive with Mother's jewels around eleven. I want to be here to greet him."

"You're not the least bit sympathetic?"

"How can I be when you refuse to listen to your heart? You're bringing this pain on yourself."

"And I'm willing to live with the consequences." Anne stood and walked toward the door. "I'll be down at nine. I imagine Claire will be at work by then."

"Don't you have Met business to complete before you leave?" Veronique asked.

"I'm finished, Oma." *In more ways than one*, she mused. "The contracts are being prepared. I'm going home."

⌒〇

When eight rolled around, Anne had only slept a few hours. Throughout the night she tossed and turned, unable to settle down enough to drift off.

"You look exhausted," Veronique said when she saw her granddaughter standing in the doorway.

"I didn't sleep well."

"Which should be a clue. You know what you want—"

"Yes, I want to go home, and if you keep trying to convince me otherwise, I'll change my reservations to a flight leaving today. That's not a threat Oma. It's a promise."

"You can't leave today," Veronique said adamantly. "You're accompanying me to the Musée d'Orsay."

"Then—and I mean no disrespect—stop badgering me. Shall we see if Claire is in?"

"Good idea. If she can see us, I have a lot to do before we leave for the museum."

"Are you saying I'm to eat and leave? Anne said, equally testy. "Suddenly I know how you felt when your mother banished you to your room so she could talk in secret."

"It's not the same thing. As I said, I have a lot to do, but more importantly, you know I can't keep my opinions to myself. You're going home, and I don't want us to part on bad terms."

"Neither do I," Anne said, softening. "While you do your thing, I'll take a walk. I haven't had time to explore the Île."

"That's an excellent idea. A little fresh air and April sunshine can do a great deal to clear one's mind."

"Oma," Anne said rolling her eyes in exasperation.

"I know—I'm pushing the envelope. Shall we call Claire?"

Out of breath, Claire answered on the fourth ring. "I just got in, heard the phone, and saw your number on my caller ID," she said. "Do we have a problem I should—"

"Not that I know of," Anne replied. "This call is about the personal matter you and I discussed. If you have a moment, my grandmother Madame Ellison would like to speak with you."

"Of course," Claire said.

Anne handed the phone to Veronique, who, for the next five minutes, discussed her intent to gift the paintings to the museum.

"Madame Malet seems pleased," she said, returning the phone to the base.

"And why wouldn't she be? You've made her day—maybe her entire year."

"I'll be a trustee in no time."

"No doubt," Anne said, smiling at her grandmother's obvious delight. "Now what?"

"Now, I would like to speak with Gus. Will you call him for me?"

"Sure." Anne scrolled to Gus's number on her cell and pushed talk. "Gus, you're on speaker phone," she began. "Oma's with me. She—"

"As you know, I've decided to gift Mother's paintings to the Musée d'Orsay," Veronique interrupted. "Realizing you're no longer my official driver, would you take Anne and me to see Madame Malet?"

"With pleasure," Gus said. "What time is your appointment?"

"One o'clock."

"I shall be out front of the apartment at twelve-thirty."

"We'll let Claire know when we're ten minutes out," Anne said. "The museum guards will be waiting in front when we arrive."

"Before Anne came down, anticipating Claire's positive response to my offer, I contacted the head of the building's security company," Veronique said. "When you and I hang up, I'll call them back with the particulars. As it stands now, fifteen minutes before you arrive to pick us up, an armored truck will arrive to transport the paintings. Two cars carrying additional personnel will also join the caravan. We'll lead the way with one car behind us. The truck will follow, and the second car will bring up the rear."

"Oma thinks of everything, doesn't she?" Anne said.

"Maybe not *everything*, but I believe I have matters under control. Gus, may I amend my original plan? Could you pick me up in thirty minutes? Anne and I are having breakfast together, but we should be through by then. I just remembered I have an appointment."

"Of course," Gus said. "But at this time of day I doubt I'll find a place to park. I will call when I cross Pont de la Tournelle."

"Do you still have Anne's key?"

"I do. In all the confusion, I forgot to give it back—"

"Then I'll meet you in the garage. Keep the key. Anne won't need it." Before Anne could comment, she said, "I have to be back to meet the courier from Geneva by eleven. If you don't want to go home when you bring me back, you can wait in my apartment until we have to leave for the museum. You decide. Renee just served breakfast, so if our plans are in place, I'll see you in half-an-hour."

"What are you up to, Oma?" Anne asked as she pushed end. "You sent me home last night, and now I'm supposed to wolf down my breakfast because Gus is coming to take you on some mysterious errand?"

"Like I said, I remembered an appointment, that's all."

"Of course," Anne said, again annoyed. "You know, suddenly I'm not hungry. I'll leave you to eat breakfast without yet another argument. I'll see you back here a little after twelve."

"Fine," Veronique said, ignoring her granddaughter's irritability. "But before I forget, I intend to attend Mass this afternoon at Église Saint-Louis-en-l'Île. I want you to go with me."

"You're going to Mass?"

"I am. I want to thank God for letting me live long enough to find Mother's paintings. Is that unreasonable?"

"I guess not. What time—"

"Five-thirty."

"Okay, but now I have a favor to ask you. After we finish our museum business later today, how about we have Gus drive us around Paris? Before I go home I want to see some of the places you wrote about in your journal. I don't need to stop and get out. I just want to see them through your eyes."

"Could we do that tomorrow, darling? I imagine I'll be tired after my morning appointments and my meeting with Claire. I really should rest before Mass."

"Why don't we attend Mass tomorrow and take our excursion today?"

"No," Veronique answered immediately. "You never know. I might wake up dead in the morning. I want to be sure I've thanked God before I do."

"I certainly hope you wake up dead," Anne said, laughing.

"You know what I mean."

"I do, and, yes, we'll see Paris tomorrow. Lunch at Deux Magot?"

"An excellent idea. I know I'm not permitted to mention Arnaud—"

"Then don't."

"You won't miss him?"

"Of course I will, but we'll both get over it. If Corinne's right, every female on the Île is after him."

"But you caught him."

"Temporarily. April in Paris, remember?"

"How could I forget? How about dinner after Mass?"

"Sure. I don't have plans. I'll pack tomorrow after our tour of Paris. Maybe we can go to the memorials too."

"Gus promised to take me."

"Then I'll tag along."

"We'll see, darling."

"Excuse me?"

"I mean we'll see if there's time before you leave. I have people to interview."

"I get the picture," Anne said, irritated. "Do your thing, Oma.

CHAPTER 39

Anne left the mansion and turned right onto Quai de Bourbon. "It's still here," she said softly as she neared the small alleyway where Veronique had hidden while Henri went for her journal. She peered into the darkness, trying to picture her terrified grandmother huddling in the corner, waiting for the Nazis to find her and praying Henri would get there first.

She turned right onto rue Le Regrattier and then left onto rue St-Louis-en-l'Île. Walking slowly, she passed markets, bakeries, fromageries, upscale stores, and charming cafés. Ending up in front of Église Saint-Louis-en-l'Île, she looked up at the lacy iron spire and the delicate foundry-framed clock and thought, *I have plenty of time to kill so I might as well go inside and take a look around.*

She opened the stunning wooden door adorned with angels and stood at the back of the ornate Baroque church, remembering Gus had said the outside was nothing to look at but the inside was lovely. *He was right,* she mused as she walked into the surprisingly light, airy church with its soaring egg-shaped dome, Corinthian columns, gilded carvings, and towering altar topped by a sunburst. She paused in front of a statue to read the inscription. *In grateful memory of St. Louis in whose honor the City of St. Louis, Missouri, USA is named.* "Interesting," she whispered as she moved on, stopping to read about various religious paintings and sculptures. She was unfamiliar with most of the artists, but the paintings were impressive. After circling the entire church, she dropped ten euros in the donation box. Glad she'd be returning later in the afternoon, she left the building.

Instead of going back along rue St-Louis-en-l'Île, she walked past Square Barye toward Quai de Bethune. Pausing in front of number twenty-six, she looked up at Arnaud's wrought iron balcony. *I'll definitely miss him,* she pondered as she crossed rue des Deux Ponts. *And I'll miss* Île St-Louis.

When she reached number forty-five, Veronique was busily supervising the security guards who were loading Elisabeth's paintings into an armored truck. "Give me five minutes," Anne said. "I have to change."

"You don't have much time," said Veronique. "Gus is just crossing Pont de la Tournelle."

∽↺

"Rather ironic, don't you think," Gus whispered to Anne while Veronique gave last minute instructions to the driver of the armored truck. "I'm driving the paintings I took from your grandmother, not to Marseilles as I planned, but rather to the Musée d' Orsay."

"Don't let Oma hear you mention stolen paintings," Anne whispered back. "She might rebuild the Châtelet just for you."

"To tell the truth, for a while I was glad both the Châtelet and the Bastille no longer exist."

"I'm sure you were," Anne said, grinning.

There wasn't much traffic as the caravan made its way to the Left Bank and along the quais toward the museum. "You're awfully quiet, Oma," Anne said as they neared the turn to rue Gît "Are you okay?"

"I'm fine, darling. I was thinking about all the times I rode my bike along these quais both before and after the onset of the Occupation. For so long, I've dwelt on the last years I spent in Paris—the bad times—but starting today, I'm going to remember the happy days I shared with Mother before the Nazis came."

"That's a good thing," Anne said. "You can finally face what happened all those years ago and move on."

"But not with you."

"That's not true. I'll be back so often you'll be begging me to go home. But enough of this silly talk. We're on Rue de la Légion d'Honneur, so I'll call Claire." Anne opened her purse, took out her cell, and scrolled to Claire's private number. "Traffic permitting, we're five minutes out," she said. "The paintings are behind us in an armored car."

When the procession pulled up to the museum, Claire and six uniformed men were waiting by the curb. Anne introduced her grandmother, explaining how helpful Claire had been in their search for Elisabeth's art. "Merci, Madame," Veronique said.

"English, Oma."

"I keep saying you must brush up on your French, Anne."

"Right, because I'll be speaking French to all my friends and colleagues in New York."

"You're leaving Paris?" Claire said. "I assumed you would move to Île St-Louis to be near Madame Ellison."

"My grandmother's a Parisian, so, understandably, she wants to live here, but my home is in New York."

"You will visit the museum whenever you're in the city?"

"Of course. I'll want to see you as well as Great-Grand'Mere's paintings."

"Let me know when you are coming so I can clear my schedule." Claire turned to Veronique, "My superiors will be speaking with you regarding your involvement with the museum, Madame Ellison. Perhaps you will serve on our board."

Grinning and giving Anne an 'I-told-you-so' look, Veronique said, "I would certainly consider the offer if it comes, Madame."

"Then if you will follow me. I believe you mentioned a gift of seven or eight paintings in memory of your mother."

"That is correct. I may decide to donate *The Work Table*, but for now, I'm keeping it where it is—over the fireplace in my living room."

"Anne told me *The Work Table* is one of the paintings your mother sold—"

"To purchase my freedom."

"That is what she said. So would you like to see the space we have preliminarily chosen to display Madame Boulet's collection? Of course before we hang a new acquisition, we are required to conduct a provenance search to be sure the painting does not appear on the watch list."

"I understand. Anne has explained the difficulties museums have encountered since the war. I assure you, Madame, none of Mother's paintings are suspect."

"Nevertheless, we must follow proper protocol."

While Gus and Veronique's private security detail watched closely, the museum guards unloaded the paintings. When they were safely inside the building, Claire led Anne and Veronique to a small room near her office on the first floor. The room was empty except for a piece of paper taped to the top of the back wall. Veronique moved closer, read, turned back and tearfully said, "Thank you Madame Mallet. Just reading the words 'In Memory of Elisabeth Boulet' on an ordinary piece of paper makes me cry. I know Mother would be pleased."

"Good," Claire said. "So now will you show me your mother's collection? Since the paintings are not alarmed, the guards have placed them in a secure room down the hall."

"Of course, if one of your guards will assist. My friend Monsieur Marsolet rewrapped each one to keep it safe during the trip from my apartment to the museum."

While one guard stood outside the door of the room, two others carefully unwrapped the packages. "These are fabulous works of art," Claire said as she studied each painting, both from afar and up close. "Thank you for your generous contribution to the Musée d'Orsay, Madame Ellison." She turned to Anne. "Should I be thanking you too?"

"Donating the art to the Musée d'Orsay was my grandmother's decision. I first suggested she gift the paintings to the Met."

"It would be a logical choice since you live in New York."

"*Lived* in New York," Veronique said. "I intend to live my last years in the city where I was raised. And I want to be able to see Mother's paintings whenever I choose."

"As I said, we are thrilled with your decision."

"Before I leave, I have one final request," Veronique said. "I would like to see another of Mother's paintings."

"Here at the museum?"

"Yes. Would you show me Degas' *Dance Class at the Opera?*"

"Madame Boulet owned *La Classe de Danse*?"

"She did." For the next few minutes, Veronique told Claire about Martin and how Elisabeth sold the Degas to provide for his future. She finished, "Since Mother *sold* the painting to Didier Dupleiss—"

"You could not report it stolen and make a claim," said Claire.

"That is correct, but it gives me joy to know it is hanging here in the Musée d'Orsay."

"Perhaps we can display *La Classe* with the paintings you have donated," Claire said.

"I would like that."

"Then I will see if I can make it happen. Shall we look at your mother's Degas?"

⌒⊙

"When do you expect to open the paintings for public view?" Veronique asked Claire as she escorted them to the museum entrance.

"If there are no problems with the provenances, I would say within the next four to six months. I will be in touch each step of the way, and, of course, you will be our guest at a ceremony honoring your mother when the exhibit opens."

"Thank you," Veronique said. "You have my number."

In more ways than one, Anne mused as Claire asked, "Anne, would you fly over for the opening?"

"I wouldn't miss it for the world. In the meantime, if you need to speak with me about Madame Boulet's paintings or about business, you have my cell number and my number in New York."

"And your email address."

⌒⊙

"Shall we have a late lunch at Deux Magot?" Anne asked when they were back at the car.

"No darling. Suddenly, I'm exhausted—both physically and emotionally. You pack while I rest. Come down at five-fifteen. I don't want to be late for Mass."

"Are we walking to church?"

"I will drive you," Gus said.

"Maybe you should be Oma's permanent chauffeur,' Anne said. "I doubt she'll be happy with anyone else."

"He already is," said Veronique. "But he lives too far away. My new housekeeper and her husband will occupy Renee and Henri's suite. Gus will move into the guest room the other side of the hall. After I reconfigure the space, he'll have a bedroom, a private bath, and a room where he can write.'

"Seriously!' Anne said. "You're sure you want to do this, Gus?"

"Evidently I do," Gus said, chuckling. "At least Veronique says I should give it a try. I am keeping my apartment in case it doesn't work out."

"Oh it will," said Veronique.

"I hope it does," Anne said. "But think about it, Oma. If you use up all your guest rooms—"

"I'll have your apartment. It will be sitting empty most of the year, so why not use it for guests."

"Oma—"

"I'm not being nasty, Anne. It's a fact. After Saturday your apartment will be vacant. I'm sure you won't mind if I use the space when I entertain visitors."

❧

It was almost three when the elevator opened on the fourth floor. "Have a good nap," Anne said.

"I'll meet you out front at five-fifteen, and don't be late. You know I disapprove of Catholics who arrive after Mass starts."

"I've heard you say that more than once," Anne said, smiling. "'I'll be on time."

When Anne came down, Veronique, Henri, and Renee were waiting in the car. "You're all coming," she said as she slid in beside Renee.

"Why wouldn't I want my family with me," Veronique said testily.

"Wow, what brought that on?"

"I'm sorry, darling. I have a lot on my mind."

"Just this afternoon you talked about being positive and looking to the future."

"I know, but that doesn't mean I can instantly stop worrying."

"It seems we all have reason to worry," Anne said when Gus pulled up to the church. "Mass is letting out. Oma, did you check the time? Talk about being late—"

"We're not late. Didn't I tell you Father's saying a special Mass in Mother's memory? Let's give the congregation a few minutes to leave before we go in."

"Martin's here too?" Anne said as she got out of the car.

"Of course he is," said Veronique. "He's my brother."

Suddenly, Anne heard a familiar voice. "The Hotel du Jeu de Paume isn't the George V, but it will do. Hello dear." Madeline approached and kissed Anne on the check.

"Mother. I thought you were arriving Tuesday morning."

"I couldn't miss your wedding, though I had no idea—"

"My what?"

"Your wedding." Madeline looked at Veronique. "Oh my God, Mother! Anne doesn't know?"

"She does now, Madeline." Veronique turned to her granddaughter. "You stubbornly refuse to listen to your heart, darling, so I am forced to step in. Tom was never the right man for you. Arnaud is. You're just too blind to notice. He's the father of my great grandchildren, and I'm not letting him get away."

"Then you marry him, Oma. You can't be serious! Hasn't anyone told you it's inappropriate to throw a wedding the bride to be knows nothing about?"

"You know now. And yes, I *am* serious, Anne. If you love Arnaud as much as I believe you do, you'll work out whatever problems you've conjured up in your mind. Admit it. You like living here on the Île."

"But New York—."

"Tell me what's waiting for you there."

"My apartment."

"You have one here."

"That will soon be your guest house."

"I'll buy the second floor for guests. Now that I think about it, Gus may feel cramped living on the fourth floor with me, my cook, and my housekeeper. He can move downstairs. He'll have more room and more privacy, and he'll be close by when I need him. And besides, we should own the entire mansion."

"Of course we should," Anne said sighing. "Okay, in New York I have my work at the Met."

"And here you'd have the Musée d'Orsay. I need an art expert to supervise the hanging of Mother's paintings. If that's not enough, there are Monet's *Nymphéas* you're always bringing up—the huge canvases in the basement of the Musée de l'Orangerie."

"But I'd have *you* in New York."

"You haven't been listening, Anne. I'm staying here *permanently*. I may not return to New York more than once or twice a year." She paused and, with a twinkle in her eye, said, "Though there is something that *might* cause me to go back for a short visit. One more appointment with Doctor Richmond might be in order."

"I don't understand. . .You've been feeling so good—"

"Exactly! That's the point. The good doctor should know what delicious French butter, flaky croissants, and two glasses of French wine a day can do for a woman's health."

"You'd return to New York just to make that point."

"Of course I would. You *know* I like to win."

"But what about Mother?" Anne said, ignoring her grandmother's comment.

"I'll be fine, Anne," Madeline chimed in. "I'm—"

Before Madeline could elaborate, Anne turned to her grandmother. "And what about your apartment—"

"I'm keeping it. I've already contacted my attorney. I'm changing my will. You'll serve as trustee until my grandchild is of age—or grandchildren if you're like Sophie and Lionel and have twins."

Anne opened her mouth to protest, but Veronique shook her head. "This conversation is over!" she declared. "My decision is irrevocable. So now that the matter is settled, it's time for us to get married."

"Us?"

"Of course I mean you and Arnaud. I'm just a guest."

"A guest who's clearly in charge. I still can't believe you planned a surprise wedding—"

"Why would you be surprised? If I can have two apartments ready for occupancy in two weeks, I can plan a wedding and reception in two days."

"You've been planning for two days?"

"In truth, I've been thinking about it since I met Arnaud and saw how you feel about him. I only got to work on the details a day or so ago when I realized you were making a mistake of a lifetime. Gus has been a great help. Martin too. He spoke with Father Bernard, and with a little help from me, Catherine Labbe took care of everything else. She's here with the necessary papers to make your marriage legal. Arnaud has already signed on the dotted line— or in this case, lines."

"Maybe Arnaud doesn't want a quickie wedding," Anne protested. "You can be awfully persuasive. Oma, did you give him a *chance* to say no?"

"You can ask him when you get to the front of the church. What a nice best man he has standing up for him."

"He has a best man?"

"Doctor Victor Janne. Apparently he and Arnaud have been best friends for years. I told him I'll be giving generously to Doctors Without Borders in Mother's name."

"Really? When did you meet Doctor Janne? I haven't even met him."

"An hour ago when he came with Arnaud to pick up your wedding ring. Gus went to the jeweler's for Arnaud's ring this afternoon after we finished at the museum."

"My wedding ring?"

"The engagement ring Robert gave me and Mother's wedding band—the one with the pavé diamonds. And speaking of Mother's jewelry, here's one more gift." Veronique removed the blue velvet case from her pocketbook and hand it to Anne.

Anne opened the box. "Great-Grand'Mere's diamond pendant and bracelet—"

"And the matching earrings. I didn't have time to take them to the jeweler, so they're still clip-ons. While you're on your honeymoon, I'll have them fixed for pierced ears."

"You arranged the honeymoon too?"

"Of course not. I had to give Arnaud something to do."

"It seems I've run out of arguments," Anne said. "So, assuming I agree to your crazy plan, I can't get married looking like this. I look like a walking Picasso painting."

"Your dress is in the sacristy. I didn't have a lot of time to find a designer, but the dress will do. Your clothes for the reception are hanging with your dress."

"You also planned a reception? Where—"

"I can't claim credit for that. The reception was Gus's assignment. I must say, he did an excellent job."

"Oma, I know you mean well, but I can't marry Arnaud. I've—"

"You *can* marry the man you love, Anne. Spontaneity is good. It's the time of year when anything can happen. Aren't you one who's always talking about April in Paris?"

"Or rather trying to keep everyone else from exalting the delights of Paris in the spring."

"Either way, April is a perfect time for a wedding." Veronique took Anne's hand and said, "Shall we take a look at what Sophie accomplished?"

"Sophie?" Anne said as they entered the church. "You're in on this too?"

"Absolutely!" Sophie said excitedly. "Veronique and I planned your entire wedding during our visit to the powder room at Taillevent. Do you like the flowers?"

"They're beautiful—"

"Good. This was the first of my three assignments."

"Three?"

"Yes. Your dress was my second task, and the third is a surprise."

"Another surprise?"

"And a good one. Just wait."

"Did you ever think to tell my grandmother she was crazy to be doing this?"

"Why would I? The minute Arnaud introduced us at dinner I knew you two would eventually marry, though even I didn't expect the wedding would take place in days. Didn't we become instant bffs? My twins will need an aunt, and for that matter, a few cousins to play with."

"Do I have a chance to say no?"

"Sure," said Veronique. "That is if you want to disappoint everyone who cares about you."

"Which means I don't, but what if—"

"What if this is the best move you've ever made? I truly believe it is, Anne. I'm a pushy broad, but I would never do anything I didn't think was in your best interest."

"A pushy broad? You admit it? I never thought I'd hear you say the words—and in such an uncouth manner."

"I am what I am. Now go with Sophie and get dressed. I'm going to sit with your mother in the front row. Though I didn't recognize him, Sophie says Bertrand is on the other side of the aisle. He looks so old. Anyway, I want to say hello and meet his girlfriend. Giles is also coming, as are Jacqueline Bouffard, Cecile, Francoise, and Corinne—"

"You invited Corinne? Have you two actually met?"

"The other day when Renee and I walked to Calixte I stopped in to thank her for being so kind during your stay. And as Sophie says, if you want the entire Île to know something, you invite the main pipeline. I'll leave you to get dressed. Your mother and I will see you at the altar when we give you away."

"You mean shove me away."

"Whatever," Veronique said. Smiling, she turned and left the sacristy.

"I can't do this," Anne said when she and Sophie were alone.

"Why not? You love my brother."

"I do, but—"

"Enough said. Let's take a look at your dress. As I said, my second assignment was to find a *worthy* designer. I hope Veronique wasn't disappointed. She picked up the dress this morning. I brought it to the church while you were at the museum."

"So that's where she was going," Anne said under her breath. "I'm surprised she didn't have the dress delivered to the apartment. Picking it up herself would be beneath her."

"Well this time she did. Maybe she thought the deliveryman would show up while you were there and ruin the surprise." Sophie unzipped the dress bag and took out a simple, but elegant, off-white beaded dress.

"It's stunning," Anne said. "But how? And in so short a time?"

"Your grandmother is teaching me how to be a miracle worker. I'm a fast learner."

"Am I really doing this?" Anne asked as Sophie helped her into the gown.

"So it seems. Unless you want to race out of the church like Elaine Robinson did in *The Graduate*. But I guarantee Arnaud will catch up to you on the bus like Benjamin Braddock caught up with his great love."

Suddenly serious, Sophie said, "I have one question for you, Anne. If you answer differently than the way I believe you will, I'll personally stand at the altar and tell everyone the wedding is off—that you're returning to New York in the morning. When I asked before, I was half teasing. Now I'm sincere. Do you love my brother?"

"Yes, but—."

"No buts. Let's go." She handed Anne a lovely bouquet of white roses and orchids.

Anne put the flowers to her nose and inhaled the fragrance. "Oh Lord," she suddenly said. "What about a license—"

"You think your grandmother would forget that? Finish primping. I'll be right back."

"My grandmother's keeping you busy," Anne said as, minutes later, Sophie ushered Catherine Labbe into the room. "Now the wedding, and soon another real estate transaction. Since Henri and Renee have bought the third floor apartment, I'll bet my grandmother buys the rest of the building."

"I will soon begin to negotiate with the current owner of the second-floor apartment," Catherine said.

"Why am I not surprised?" Anne shook her head. "Okay," she conceded. "Where do I sign?"

Catherine pointed to the line beside Arnaud's signature. "You will soon be free to marry in a religious ceremony," she said. "In this matter, your grandmother exceeded my expectations."

"I don't understand."

"In France, a church wedding alone is not legal. You must first have a civil ceremony."

"How does Oma expect to accomplish that small but significant task?"

"I asked her the same question when she phoned to ask my assistance with the license. Somehow—miraculously I might add—all of the required paperwork is in order. I am in possession of your passport and your birth certificate that, by law, my secretary has translated into French. Early this morning the *marie* signed the authorization for you to marry. I picked up the papers on the way to the church."

"The mayor? I wonder what Oma had to do to make that happen so quickly."

"I didn't ask, though I must say, I was astonished. I truly believed her plans were doomed before we got started."

"She never ceases to amaze me," Anne said.

"This too is astonishing," Catherine said. "Before the religious ceremony, the *marie* himself will perform the civil ceremony—and in English. Usually this part of the marriage rite is conducted by one of the mayor's legally authorized representatives at the *mairie*, the town hall."

"Once again, my grandmother worked her magic."

"So it seems. Once the civil ceremony is completed, we will move immediately to the religious service."

"I have another question," Anne said. "Does the priest know I'm a divorced woman?"

"I am not sure, but if he does, I doubt he would object."

"My grandmother again?"

Catherine nodded. "When she invited me to attend a special Sunday Mass, she mentioned that Father Bernard will announce the installation of a new stained-glass window given by Veronique Ellison in memory of her beloved mother, Elisabeth Boulet."

"A memorial window for a Jew in a Catholic church?"

"Are you really surprised?" Sophie said. "I've only known your grandmother for a couple of days, and I wouldn't be surprised by anything she does. So, my dear sister to be, are you ready?"

Anne took a deep breath. "I guess—"

"You look gorgeous." Anne spun around. There, standing in the sacristy door and wearing a dress identical to Sophie's, was Meg.

"I can't believe it," Anne said, hugging her best friend. "How? When?"

"Last night. As you know, when Veronique speaks, we all obey."

"Amen to that," said Sophie.

"Your grandmother called after your family dinner. Within thirty minutes, I received an email confirming a first class seat on the Thursday evening Air France flight to Paris. Gus picked me up at Charles de Gaulle early this morning. I slept all day in Veronique's guest room. I was there when you came for breakfast."

"No wonder Oma wanted me out of the apartment. "Where are you staying, and for how long?"

"After you're off on your honeymoon, I'll move into your apartment. I leave Tuesday morning. Over the next couple of days, Veronique will show me *her* Paris."

"You're her weekend plans?"

"So it seems."

"And your dress. It's—"

"My third assignment," Sophie said.

"And it fits perfectly." Meg spun around. "I gave Sophie my measurements over the phone. The designer did a great job." She hugged Anne again. "I'm so happy for you, my friend. Arnaud's a hunk."

"That he is. I'm happy too—at least I think I am. This is happening so suddenly. I haven't had time to process—"

"Why process?" Sophie said. "I've always felt that excess thought unnecessarily muddles the mind."

"You sound just like my grandmother."

"I consider that the ultimate compliment."

Sophie handed Meg a bouquet. "So," she said. "Shall we help our bff get married?"

As soon as she saw Arnaud standing in front of the church, Anne knew she wasn't going to run out the back door. The mayor stood to the side of the altar. When Anne arrived, Arnaud took her hand and, in only minutes, the obviously abbreviated civil service was over. "You are now officially man and wife," the mayor said, stepping back and then entering the row of chairs behind Veronique.

"That wasn't very romantic," Arnaud whispered. "Shall we make the next ceremony more memorable?"

"I'm definitely ready," Anne said softly, as he guided her back to the altar.

The wedding was traditional. Madeline and Veronique came to the altar to give Anne away, as Sophie and Meg stood by her side.

As she said her vows, a tear fell down her cheek. Smiling, Arnaud removed a handkerchief from his pocked and wiped it away. "I love you," he whispered as he slipped Veronique's diamond engagement ring and Elisabeth's pavé diamond band on her finger.

Anne held up her hand. "They fit," she mouthed.

"Of course they do," Veronique said loudly.

When the priest pronounced them man and wife, Arnaud's kiss was soft and lingering.

"Enough for now," Veronique said, approaching the altar. She turned to face the assembled group. "I would like to introduce Monsieur and Madame Arnaud Lessard, the parents of my first great grandchild, who,

I'm hoping, will be here nine months from today. At my age, we've little time to waste."

At the back of the church, Anne and Arnaud stopped to greet their departing guests. When the church was empty except for family members, Veronique said, "Now it's time for the newlyweds to pose for the photographer, alone and then with the rest of us. When we're through and you're all putting on your jeans, I'll use the ladies' room to change into mine. Gus put them in the trunk of the car before you came down to meet me for Mass."

"You're wearing jeans?"

"I'm a modern grandmother," Veronique said, her eyes shining. "If I can work a computer, I can wear jeans." She grinned and quickly added, "Of course they're haute couture. Would you believe I ordered them online?"

Of course you did," Anne said, laughing. "What's this world coming to?"

"Gus will drive you and Arnaud to the reception," Veronique continued. "Per my orders, everyone will have gone home to change into casual clothes. We'll all be waiting for you to arrive."

Anne turned to Arnaud. "You don't know where we're going?"

Arnaud shrugged.

"I saw no need to tell him," Veronique said. "Arnaud, your jeans are in the sacristy. Try to keep your hands off each other. I won't have my great grandchild conceived in a church."

"Oma."

"Smile beautifully, my darlings."

Thirty-minutes later, the formal pictures taken, the photographer left for the reception. "The party's probably rocking by now," Veronique said. "So hurry and get ready."

"Are we going hiking," Anne called out to her grandmother who looked back, smiled, and waved as she walked toward the church door.

"So when do I wake up from my dream?" Anne said as she and Arnaud returned to the sacristy to change.

"If I have my way, you never will. "He spun her around, kissed her lightly on the lips, and then more passionately.

"Keep doing that and Oma's great grandchild *will* be conceived right here and now," Anne murmured.

"Would that be so bad?" Arnaud kissed her again.

⌒౨

Dressed in jeans and cowboy boots, Gus was waiting by the car in front of the church. "Nice boots," Anne said, grinning. "They're so you."

"I think so," Gus said, sticking his foot out and pulling up his trouser leg so Anne could see the design. "Veronique ordered them for me."

"Of course she did. And if I had a dollar—or perhaps I should say a euro—for every time I've said "of course' in the past week, well—"

"So where's the reception?" Arnaud said as he and Anne slid into the backseat.

"You'll find out soon enough."

Moments later Gus parked in front of Square Barye.

"No," Anne said. "Great idea, Gus, and how appropriate. Arnaud kissed me for the first time over on the bench by the Seine, and it's where Henri kissed my grandmother—"

"Henri kissed Veronique? Not Renee?"

"It's a long story. I'll explain some time when we're not this busy, but, so you know, when Arnaud kissed me, I suddenly understood everything you were trying to tell me about April in Paris."

"Chestnuts in blossom," Gus sang.

"I never knew the charm of spring/Never made it face to face. I never knew my heart could sing/Never missed a warm embrace."

"Wait until you hear me sing that song in the shower," Arnaud whispered.

"You're working toward your crooner adjective?"

"Or not," Arnaud said, grinning.

"Tents?" Anne said as she slid out of the backseat.

"In case of rain. Veronique wanted to be sure your reception was perfect. She hired the best caterers in Paris."

"Using my official mantra—of course she did!"

⌒⌒

The next three hours were fabulous. *How stupid I was,* Anne mused while she watched Arnaud interact with everyone she loved. She got to spend a little alone-time with Meg and met Victor Janne. She chatted for a while with Bertrand's friend Suzanne. "She's great," Anne said to a smiling Bertrand. "But I wish you'd waited for my grandmother."

"Don't quote me," Bertrand whispered. "Lovely though Veronique may be, she's a little too old for me."

It was after ten when Veronique moved to the front of the tent. Henri whistled and everyone quieted down. "Raise your glasses in a toast to my beloved granddaughter and my new grandson," she said. "May you enjoy a marriage like the one my beloved Robert and I shared."

"And here's to my beautiful bride," Arnaud said, raising his glass.

"It's my turn now," Anne said. "To Oma, who forced me to stop acting foolishly. Thank you for loving me enough to make me marry this man. If I toasted each of you separately, we would be here all night, and I'm sure, as you know, my grandmother has issued an order."

"To Veronique's great grandchild," Henri said.

"And my grandchild," Madeline chimed in. "Happiness always, darling."

"And to my husband," Anne said. "The best flower arranger, mover, cook/chef, historian, dirt disher, mighty magician, culinary genius, gardener and all around expert—"

"Don't forget number three," Arnaud said smiling.

"Ah, the mysterious number three," Sophie called out. "Care to share with everyone, sister?"

Anne sighed. "It seems I have no choice. Number three—the best kisser."

⌒⌒

"Your place or mine," Anne whispered as they were saying goodbye to their guests.

"It appears I don't have a place anymore. I'm already packed, so to Quai de Bourbon, our place, so you can pack."

"What do you mean you don't have a place?"

"My brother no longer owns the apartment on Quai de Bethune," Sophie said. "He just sold it to Lionel and me for the incredibly reasonable price of a thousand euros. He hasn't signed the papers Catherine Labbe is preparing, but I'm sure he will. We'll be neighbors."

"I'm not sure I can absorb all of this."

"Then let me give you something else to think about," Arnaud said. "Because Meg's at the apartment, you and I will spend the night at the George V."

"Not at the Hotel du Jeu de Paume?"

"With Corinne reporting our every move to all the women on the Île? Being a romantic, I thought about staying where Veronique met your grandfather but—"

"I'm glad we're not," Anne said. "You said we're spending tonight at the George V. What about tomorrow?

"We leave for Rome. I have a week to make you think Bernini's better than Monet."

"You won't succeed, but you can certainly try—that is if I let you leave the hotel."

"Before we came to the church I cancelled your plane reservations." Veronique said. "So you don't need to worry. In fact, don't worry about anything."

"You're too much, Oma."

"I know." Veronique said, grinning. "Now go give me my great grandchild."

AUTHOR'S NOTE

FULL CIRCLE is a work of fiction based on actual historical events that occurred between 1940 and 1942 during the Nazi occupation of Paris. Though the historic figures in the novel are a part of history, all of the major characters are fictitious.

The experiences described in Veronique's diary are drawn from many sources and represent actual conditions in Paris during the Occupation. Veronique, Henri, and Renee's escape from Paris to the Line of Demarcation and into Vichy France is based on recorded experiences of escapees who made the trek to freedom. The raid known as la rafle du Vel d'Hiv as well as the horrific conditions at the Velodrome d'Hiver and at Drancy are well-documented, as are the atrocities committed at Auschwitz.

For the most part, the descriptions of Île St-Louis—the streets, the restaurants, the sights and sounds— are accurate. However, for the sake of the plot, I have taken liberties. Apartments the size of those owned by the major characters are rare, and few single-family mansions, other than the famous *hotels particular*, still exist. The amount Veronique paid for the apartments in what was once her home, is an estimate based on the current price of smaller units for sale on the Île.

The paintings in Madame Boulet's collection are imagined—or perhaps not. Despite the efforts of groups like the Monuments Men, many so-called "degenerate" works of art disappeared during the Nazi Occupation—many never to be found. It's entirely possible that Monet painted his kitchen at Giverny or Manet painted yet another version of *Le dejeuner sur l'herbe*. And Pissarro, Corot, and Liebermann may have created not-so-famous renderings of their renowned works. For my purposes, I assumed they did.

The paintings Anne discusses with the fictitious curators of the Musée d'Orsay, the Musée de l'Orangerie, and the Musée Marmottan Monet, are authentic works from the museums' permanent collections. I have been privileged to see most of the paintings referenced in the novel. They are truly spectacular works of art.

"I love Paris—especially in the springtime. In FULL CIRCLE, I have described the city as it was during the Occupation—a city of darkness—and as it is now—"*La Ville-Lumière*," The City of Light.

In addition to numerous online sources, the following books have provided essential background information, especially about Paris during the Occupation and the art the Nazis plundered from museums and private collections as they overran the cities and countries of Europe. The books include:

Nazi Plunder: Great Treasure Stories of World War II—Kenneth D. Alford

The Lost Museum: the Nazi Conspiracy to Steal the World's Greatest Works of Art—Hector Feliciano

An American Heroine in the French Resistance—The Diary and Memoir of *Virginia D'Albert-Lake*— Virginia D'Albert-Lake and Judy Letoff

Nazi Paris: The History of an Occupation, 1940-1944—Allan Mitchell

Paris, a Literary Companion—Ian Littlewood

Paris Walks, Second Edition—Fiona Duncan and Leonie Glass

While writing FULL CIRCLE, I learned a great deal about World War II, about Paris, about the plight of the Jews who suffered under Nazi domination, about Drancy, about Auschwitz, and about fabulous works of art. I hope my readers, too, gain knowledge and insight as they enjoy the novel.

Made in the USA
San Bernardino, CA
02 January 2015